P9-DMJ-541

Praise for *Venus*

"With Isaac Asimov and Robert Heinlein gone, Bova, author of more than seventy books, is one of the last deans of traditional science fiction. And he hasn't lost his touch. *Venus* scorches."
—*Kansas City Star*

"An epic adventure, full of twists and turns and genuine surprises."
—*The Hartford Courant*

"As a voyage to an unknown world, it excels."
—*Publishers Weekly*

"A top-notch adventure story . . . The author's excellence at combining hard science with believable characters and an attention-grabbing plot makes him one of the genre's most accessible and entertaining storytellers."
—*Library Journal*

"Bova manages to bring the planet alive as a force of nature indifferent to the struggles, hopes, or presence of the humans who are attempting to make the first successful landing on her surface."
—*Bookpage*

TOR BOOKS BY BEN BOVA

VENUS

BEN BOVA

A TOM DOHERTY ASSOCIATES BOOK
NEW YORK

NOTE: If you purchased this book without a cover you should be aware that this book is stolen property. It was reported as "unsold and destroyed" to the publisher, and neither the author nor the publisher has received any payment for this "stripped book."

This is a work of fiction. All the characters and events portrayed in this book are either products of the author's imagination or are used fictitiously.

VENUS

Copyright © 2000 By Ben Bova

All rights reserved, including the right to reproduce this book, or portions thereof, in any form.

Edited by Patrick Nielsen Hayden

A Tor Book
Published by Tom Doherty Associates, LLC
175 Fifth Avenue
New York, NY 10010

www.tor.com

Tor® is a registered trademark of Tom Doherty Associates, LLC.

ISBN 0-812-57940-2
Library of Congress Catalog Card Number: 99-462304

First edition: April 2000
First mass market edition: May 2001

Printed in the United States of America

0 9 8 7 6 5 4 3 2 1

To D.H.G, J.L., and B.B.B.
with thanks, appreciation, and love

Heaven says nothing, and the whole earth grows rich beneath its silent rule. Men, too, are touched by heaven's virtue; yet, in their greater part, they are creatures of deceit. They are born, it seems, with an emptiness of soul, and must take their qualities wholly from things without. To be born thus empty into this modern age, this mixture of good and ill, and yet to steer through life on an honest course to the splendors of success—this is a feat reserved for paragons of our kind, a task beyond the nature of normal man.

—Ihara Saikaku

HELL CRATER

I was late and I knew it. The trouble is, you can't run on the moon.

The shuttle from the *Nueva Venezuela* space station had been delayed, some minor problem with the baggage being transferred from Earthside, so now I was hurrying along the underground corridor from the landing pad, all alone. The party had started more than an hour ago.

They had warned me not to try to run, even with the weighted boots that I had rented at the landing port. But like a fool I tried to anyway and sort of hip-hopped crazily and bumped into the corridor wall, scraping my nose rather painfully. After that I shuffled along in the manner that the tourist-guide video had shown. It felt stupid, but bouncing off the walls was worse.

Not that I really wanted to go to my father's inane party or be on the Moon at all. None of this was my idea.

Two big human-form robots guarded the door at the end of the corridor. And I mean *big,* two meters tall and almost as wide across the torso. The gleaming metal door was sealed shut, of course. You couldn't crash my father's party; he'd never stand for that.

"Your name, please," said the robot on my left. Its voice was deep and rough, my father's idea of what a bouncer should sound like, I suppose.

"Van Humphries," I said, as slowly and clearly as I could enunciate.

The robot hesitated only a fraction of a second before saying, "Voice print identification is verified. You may enter, Mr. Van Humphries."

Both robots pivoted around and the door slid open. The noise hit me like a power hammer: thumping atonal music blasting away against wildly over-amped screeching from some androgynous singer wailing the latest pop hit.

The chamber was huge, immense, and jammed wall-to-wall with partygoers, hundreds of men and women, a thousand or more, I guessed, drinking, shouting, smoking, their faces contorted with grimaces of forced raucous laughter. The noise was like a solid wall pounding against me; I had to physically force myself to step past the robots and into the mammoth chamber.

Everyone was in party attire: brazenly bright colors with plenty of spangles and glitter and electronic blinkies. And lots of bare flesh showing, of course. I felt like a missionary in my chocolate-brown velour pullover and tan micromesh slacks.

A long electronic window swept the length of the cavern's side wall, alternately proclaiming "HAPPY ONE HUN-DREDTH BIRTHDAY!" and showing clips from pornographic videos.

I might have known Father would pick a bordello as the site for his party. Hell Crater, named after the Jesuit astronomer Maximilian J. Hell. The gaming and porn industries had turned the area into the Moon's sin capital, a complete cornucopia of illicit pleasures dug below the dusty floor of the crater, some six hundred klicks south of Selene City. Poor old Father Hell must be spinning in his crypt.

"Hi there, stranger!" said a brassy, buxom redhead in an emerald-green costume so skimpy it must have been spray-painted onto her. She waggled a vial of some grayish-looking powder in my general direction, exhorting, "Join the fun!"

Fun. The place looked like Dante's Inferno. There was nowhere to sit except for a few couches along the walls, and they were already filled with writhing tangles of naked bodies. Everyone else was on their feet, packed in shoulder to shoulder, dancing or swaying and surging like the waves of some multihued, gabbling, aimless human sea.

High up near the smoothed rock ceiling a pair of acrobats in sequined harlequin costumes were walking a tightrope strung across the chamber. A set of spotlights made their costumes glitter. On Earth, performing that high up would have been dangerous; here on the Moon they could still break their necks if they fell—or more likely break the necks of the people they fell upon. The place was so tightly packed it would've been impossible for them to hit the floor.

"C'mon," the redhead urged again, pawing at the sleeve of my pullover. She giggled and said, "Don't be so twangy!"

"Where is Martin Humphries?" I had to shout to be heard over the din of the party.

She blinked her emerald-tinted eyes. "Hump? The birthday boy?" Turning uncertainly toward the crowd and waving her hand vaguely, she yelled back, "The old humper's around here someplace. It's his party, y'know."

"The old humper is my father," I told her, enjoying the sudden look of astonishment on her face as I brushed past her.

It was a real struggle to work my way through the crowd. Strangers, all of them. I didn't know anyone there, I was certain of that. None of my friends would be caught dead at a scene like this. As I pushed and elbowed my way through the jam-packed chamber, I wondered if my father knew any of these people. He probably rented them for the occasion. The redhead certainly looked the type.

He knows I can't take crowds, and yet he forced me to come here. Typical of my loving father. I tried to shut out the noise, the reek of perfume and tobacco and drugs, and the slimy sweat of too many bodies pressed too close together. It was making me weak in the knees, twisting my stomach into knots.

I can't deal with this kind of thing. It's too much. I felt as if I would collapse if there weren't so many bodies crowded around me. I was starting to get dizzy, my vision blurring.

I had to stop in the midst of the mob and squeeze my eyes shut. It was a struggle to breathe. I had taken my regular enzyme shot just before the transfer rocket had landed, yet I felt as if I needed another one, and quickly.

I opened my eyes and surveyed the jostling, noisy, sweaty throng again, searching for the nearest exit. And then I saw him. Through the tangle of weaving, gesticulating partygoers I spotted my father, sitting up on a dais at the far end of the cavern like some ancient Roman emperor surveying an orgy. He was even clad in a flowing robe of crimson, with two beautifully supple young women at his sandalled feet.

My father. One hundred years old this day. Martin Humphries didn't look any more than forty; his hair was still dark, his face firm and almost unlined. But his eyes— his eyes were hard, knowing; they glittered with corrupt pleasure at the scene being played out before him. He had used every rejuvenation therapy he could get his hands on, even illegal ones such as nanomachines. He wanted to stay young and vigorous forever. I thought he probably would. He always got what he wanted. But one look into his eyes and it was easy to believe that he was a hundred years old.

He saw me shouldering through the strident, surging crowd and for a moment those cold gray eyes of his locked onto mine. Then he turned away from me with an impatient frown clouding his handsome, artificially youthful face.

You insisted that I come to this carnival, I said to him silently. So, like it or not, here I am.

He paid no attention to me as I toiled to reach him. I was

gasping now, my lungs burning. I needed a shot of my medication but I had left it back at my hotel suite. When at last I reached the foot of his dais I slumped against the softly pliable fabric draped over the platform, struggling to catch my breath. Then I realized that the strident din of the party had dropped to a buzzing, muted whisper.

"Sound dampers," my father said, glancing down at me with his old disdainful smirk. "Don't look so stupid."

There were no steps up the platform and I felt too weak and giddy to try to haul myself up beside him.

He made a shooing motion and the two young women jumped nimbly from the platform, eagerly joining the crowd. I realized that they were just teenagers.

"Want one?" my father asked, with a leering grin. "You can have 'em both, all you have to do is ask."

I didn't bother to shake my head. I just clung to the side of his platform, trying to bring my breathing under control.

"For Christ's sake, Runt, stop that damned panting! You look like a beached flounder."

I pulled in a deep breath, then stood as straight as I could manage. "And it's lovely to see you, too, Father."

"Aren't you enjoying my party?"

"You know better."

"Then what'd you come for, Runt?"

"Your lawyer said you'd cut off my stipend if I didn't attend your party."

"Your allowance," he sneered.

"I earn that money."

"By playing at being a scientist. Now your brother, there was a *real* scientist."

Yes, but Alex is dead. It had happened three years ago, but the memory of that day still scalded me inside.

All my life my father had mocked and belittled me. Alex was his favorite, his firstborn, Father's pride and joy. Alex was being groomed to take over Humphries Space Systems, if and when Father ever decided to retire. Alex was everything that I'm not: tall, athletic, quick and handsome, brilliantly intelligent, outgoing, charming and witty. I'm on the small side, I've been sickly from birth, I'm told that I tend to be withdrawn, introspective. My mother died giving birth to me and my father never let me forget that.

I had loved Alex. I truly had. I had admired him tremendously. Ever since I could remember, Alex had protected me against Father's sneers and cutting words. "It's all right, little brother, don't cry," he would tell me. "I won't let him hurt you."

Over the years I learned from Alex a love for exploration, for seeing new vistas, new worlds. But while Alex actually went out on missions to Mars and the Jovian moons, I had to stay cocooned at home, too frail to venture outward. I flew an armchair, not a spacecraft. My excitement came from streams of computer data and virtual reality simulations. Once I walked with Alex on the red sands of Mars, linked by an interactive VR system. It was the best afternoon of my life.

Then Alex was killed on his expedition to Venus, he and all his crew. And Father hated me for being alive.

I left his house for good and bought a home on Majorca, a place all my own, far from his dismissive sarcasm. As if to mock me, Father moved to Selene City. Later I found out that he'd gone to the Moon so he could take nanotherapies to keep himself young and fit. Nanomachines were outlawed on Earth, of course.

It was clear that Father went for rejuvenation treatments because he had no intention of retiring now. With Alex dead, Father would never leave Humphries Space Systems to me. He would stay in command and keep me exiled.

So Father lived some four hundred thousand kilometers away, playing his chosen role of interplanetary tycoon, megabillionaire, hell-raising, womanizing, ruthless, corrupt giant of industry. I was perfectly content with that. I lived quietly on Majorca, comfortable with a household staff that took excellent care of me. Some of my servants were human; most were robots. Friends came to visit often enough. I could flit over to Paris or New York or wherever for theater or a concert. I spent my days studying the new data about the stars and planets that were constantly streaming back from our space explorers.

Until one of my friends repeated a rumor she had heard: My brother's spacecraft had been sabotaged. His death was not an accident; it was murder. The very next day, my father summoned me to his moronic birthday party on the Moon, under the threat of cutting off my stipend if I didn't show up.

Looking up at his youthfully taut face again, I asked my father, "Why did you insist that I come here?"

He smiled down sardonically at me. "Aren't you enjoying the party?"

"Are you?" I countered.

Father made a sound that might have been a suppressed laugh. Then he said, "I have an announcement to make. I wanted you to be on hand to hear it directly from my lips."

I felt puzzled. An announcement? Was he going to retire, after all? What of it; he would never allow me to run the corporation. Nor did I want to, actually.

He touched a stud set into the left armrest of his chair and the stupefying noise of the party blasted against my ears hard enough to crack my skull. Then he touched the other armrest. The music stopped in mid-beat. The tightrope-walking acrobats winked out like a light snapped off. A holographic image, I realized.

The crowd fell silent and still. They all turned toward the dais, like a sullen horde of party-dressed schoolchildren forced to listen to their principal.

"I'm delighted that you could come to my party," Father began, his low, modulated voice amplified and echoing across the crowded chamber. "Are we having fun yet?"

On that cue they all cheered, clapped, whistled, and yelled lustily.

Father raised both hands and they all fell silent again.

"I have an announcement to make, something that you hardworking representatives of the news media out there will find particularly worthwhile, I think."

Half a dozen camera-carrying balloons were already

hovering a few meters from the dais, like glittering Christmas ornaments floating buoyantly. Now several more drifted out of the farther reaches of the chamber to focus on my father.

"As you know," he went on, "my beloved son Alexander was killed three years ago while attempting to explore the planet Venus."

A collective sigh swept through the throng.

"Somewhere on the surface of that hellhole of a world his spacecraft lies, with his remains inside it. In that terrible heat and pressure, the corrosive atmosphere must be slowly destroying the last mortal remains of my boy."

Somewhere a woman broke into soft sobbing.

"I want to offer an inducement to someone who is bold enough, tough enough, to go to Venus and reach its surface and bring back what's left of my son to me."

They all seemed to stand up straighter, their eyes widened. An inducement?

My father hesitated for a dramatic moment, then said in a much stronger voice, "I offer a prize of ten billion international dollars to whoever can reach my dead son's body and return his remains to me."

They gasped. For several seconds no one spoke. Then the chamber filled with excited chatter. Ten billion dollars! Reach the surface of Venus! A prize of ten billion dollars to recover Alex Humphries's body!

I felt just as stunned as any of the others. More, perhaps, because I knew better than most of those costumed freeloaders what an impossible challenge my father had just offered.

Father touched the stud on his chair arm and the babble of the crowd immediately was cut down to a muted buzz again.

"Very nice," I said to him. "You'll be named Father of the Year."

He gazed disdainfully down at me. "You don't think I mean it?"

"I think you know that no one in his right mind is going

to try to reach the surface of Venus. Alex himself only planned to coast through the cloud decks."

"So you think I'm a fraud."

"I think you're making a public relations gesture, nothing more."

He shrugged as if it didn't matter.

I was seething. He was sitting up there and getting all this publicity. "You want to look like a grieving father," I shouted at him, "making the whole world think you care about Alex, offering a prize that you know no one will claim."

"Oh, someone will try for it, I'm certain." He smiled coldly down at me. "Ten billion dollars is a lot of incentive."

"I'm not so sure," I said.

"But I am. In fact, I'm going to deposit the whole sum in an escrow account where no one can touch it except the eventual prize winner."

"The entire ten billion?"

"The whole sum," he repeated. Then, leaning slightly toward me, he added, "To raise that much cash I'm going to have to cut a few corners here and there."

"Really? How much have you spent on this party?"

He waved a hand as if that didn't matter. "One of the corners I'm cutting is your allowance."

"My stipend?"

"It's finished, Runt. You'll be twenty-five years old next month. Your allowance ends on your birthday."

Just like that, I was penniless.

DATA BANK

She glows so bright and lovely in the night sky that virtually every culture on Earth has called her after their goddess of beauty and love: Aphrodite, Inanna, Ishtar, Astarte, Venus.

Sometimes she is the dazzling Evening Star, brighter than anything in the sky except the Sun and Moon. Sometimes she is the beckoning Morning Star, harbinger of the new day. Always she shines like a precious jewel.

As beautiful as Venus appears in our skies, the planet itself is the most hellish place in the solar system. The ground is hot enough to melt aluminum. The air pressure is so high it has crushed spacecraft landers as if they were flimsy cardboard cartons. The sky is perpetually covered from pole to pole with clouds of sulfuric acid. The atmosphere is a choking mixture of carbon dioxide and sulfurous gases.

Venus is the nearest planet to Earth, closer to us than Mars. At its nearest approach, it is slightly less than sixty-five million kilometers from Earth. It is closer to the Sun than Earth is; Venus is the second planet outward from the Sun, while Earth is the third. Venus has no moon.

It is almost the same size as Earth, slightly smaller, so that the gravity at its surface is about 85 percent of Earth-normal.

There the similarities end. Venus is hot, with surface temperatures well above 450 degrees Celsius (nearly 900 degrees Fahrenheit). It rotates so slowly that its "day" is longer than its "year:" the planet makes an orbit around the Sun in 225 Earth days—a Venusian year, yet it rotates around its axis in 243 Earth days—a Venusian day. And it rotates backward, clockwise as viewed from its north pole, while Earth and the other planets rotate counterclockwise.

Venus's atmosphere is so thick that atmospheric pressure at ground level is equal to the pressure of an earthly ocean more than a kilometer below the surface. That atmosphere is more than 95 percent carbon dioxide, with less than 4 percent nitrogen and only negligible traces of free oxygen.

The thick layers of clouds that perpetually cover Venus from pole to pole reflect some 75 percent of the sunlight that hits the planet and make it very bright and beautiful to look at. The clouds, though, are made of sulfuric acid and other sulfur and chlorine compounds; there is practically no water vapor in them.

There are mountains and volcanoes on Venus, and evidence of plate tectonics that have shifted vast sections of the crust. There must be Venus-quakes, as well.

Imagine trying to walk on the surface of Venus! The very ground is red-hot. The atmosphere is so thick that it warps light like a fisheye lens. The sky is perpetually clouded. Yet there is no real darkness: even during the long Venusian night there is an eerie, sullen glow from the red-hot ground.

Because Venus is moving in its orbit around the Sun while it slowly rotates on its own axis, if you stood on one spot on the surface it would take 117 Earth days from one sunrise to the next—if you could see the sunrise through those thick, all-pervading clouds. And the Sun would rise in the west, set in the east.

Looking up into the grayish-yellow clouds you might see patches of darker areas hurtling across the sky, forming and dissolving against the murky background nearly fifty kilometers overhead, scudding from horizon to horizon in about five hours. Now and then you might see a stroke of lightning flashing down, or hear the threatening rumble of a distant volcano.

No place in the inner solar system is so challenging, so dangerous. By comparison, the Moon is easy and Mars a picnic.

Could life exist on Venus, either high in the clouds (where temperatures are cooler) or deep underground? There is *something* in Venus's atmosphere that absorbs ultraviolet light; planetary scientists are not certain what it might be. Could there be bacterial forms that live underground, as there are on Earth and presumably on Mars and Jupiter's moon Europa?

If there are any creatures living on the surface, they must be capable of withstanding heat that melts aluminum and pressures that can crush spacecraft.

Formidable monsters indeed.

I t should've been you, Runt!" he howled. "It should've been you who died, not Alex."

I awoke with a start, springing up to a sitting position in the darkened hotel room, both my fists gripping the bed-sheets tightly enough to rip them. I was soaked with cold sweat and trembling from head to foot.

The dream had been too real. Too totally real. I squeezed my eyes shut, sitting there on the bed, and my father's enraged face burned before me like the wrath of some ancient god.

The party at Hell Crater. His announcement of the Venus prize. His notice that he was cutting me off without an income. It had all been too much for me. By the time I made it back to my hotel in Selene City I was near collapse, the carpeted hotel corridors swimming dizzyingly, my legs weak as tissue paper even in the low lunar gravity. I got to my room, went straight to the lavatory, and fumbled with my hyprospray syringe. At last I injected a full dose of the enzyme medication into my arm, then tottered off to bed and fell almost instantly asleep.

Only to dream. No, it wasn't actually a dream; it was a reliving of that terrible day when we learned that Alex had been killed. A nightmare. I relived every agonizing moment of it.

When we got the news that there was no possible hope left, Father had blanked his phone screen and turned to me, his face distorted with fury.

"He's dead," my father had said, his voice cold and hollow, his gray eyes like ice. "Alex is dead and you're alive. First you killed your mother and now you're still alive while Alex is dead."

I just stood there while he glared at me, grim and bitterly angry. At me. At me.

"It should've been you, Runt," he snarled, his fury mounting, his face going from white to red. "You're worthless! Nobody would miss you. But no, you're here, you're alive and breathing while Alex is dead. It should've been you, Runt!" he howled. "It should've been you who died, not Alex."

That was when I moved out of the family home in Connecticut and bought my place on Majorca, as far from Father as I could get. Or so I thought. But he went me one better, of course, and moved to Selene City.

Now I sat in a hotel bed, shaking and cold with midnight sweat, alone, totally alone.

I got up and padded barefoot to the lavatory; tottered, actually, that's how weak and wretched I felt. The light went on automatically and I fumbled with my hypospray syringe until I finally got a plastic cylinder preloaded with the proper dosage of enzyme clicked into place and pressed it against my bare arm. The faint hiss of the medication squeezing through the microneedles and into my bloodstream always reassured me. But not that night. Nothing could calm me, I thought.

I was born with a rare form of pernicious anemia, a birth defect caused by my mother's drug addiction. It could be fatal if not controlled by injections of a cocktail of enzymes that included vitamin B12 and a growth hormone that prompted my body to create new red blood cells. Without that medication I would weaken and eventually die. With it I could lead a perfectly normal life—except for the need to take the injections at least twice a day.

If anyone ever tells you that nanomachines could cure any medical condition, if only they weren't outlawed on Earth, don't believe him. The best labs at Selene City—the capital of nanotechnology research—haven't been able to program a nanobug that can build millions of red blood cells every few hours.

I went back to the bed with its tangled sweaty sheets and waited for the medication to take effect. With nothing better to do, I called out for the video news. The wall screen immediately glowed to life and showed a scene of terrible devastation: another raging hurricane had swung all the way across the Atlantic and was pounding the British Isles. Even the Thames Barrage—the high-tech dam across the river—had been overrun and large sections of London were underwater, including Westminster Abbey and the Houses of Parliament.

I leaned back against my pillows and watched, hollow-eyed, as thousands of Londoners poured into the streets in the lashing cold rain to escape the rising floodwaters. "The worst cataclysm to hit London since the Blitz of World War II, more than a century ago," the news announcer intoned in a crack-of-doom voice.

"Next channel!" I called. Death and destruction were not what I wanted to see. But most of the channels were showing London's agony, live and in full color. I could have watched it all in three dimensions if I'd called up the hologram channel. There were flotillas of boats chugging down the Strand and Fleet Street, rescuing men, women, children—even pets. Workers were struggling to protect Buckingham Palace from the encroaching waters.

Finally I found a channel that was not showing the flood. It was a panel discussion by self-proclaimed experts on the global warming that was causing such storms and flooding. One of them wore the green armband of the International Green Party, another I recognized as a friend of my father's—a sharp-tongued corporate lawyer who clearly loathed the Greens. The rest were scientists of various stripe, no two of them agreeing on anything.

I watched, glassy-eyed, hoping their quiet, mannered deliberation would lull me to sleep. As they spoke, the screen displayed animated maps that showed how the ice-caps in Greenland and Antarctica were melting and how much sea levels were expected to rise. Half the American Midwest was in danger of being turned into a huge inland sea. The Gulf Stream was going to break up, they said, freezing Britain and Europe into an extension of Siberia.

Just the perfect lullaby to soothe me to sleep. I was about to turn the wall screen off altogether when the yellow message light began blinking. Who would be calling me at this time of night? I wondered.

"Answer," I called out.

The entire wall screen turned a milky grayish white. For a moment I thought there had been some malfunction of the video.

Then a synthesized computer voice spoke to me: "Mr. Humphries, please excuse my not showing my face. It would be too dangerous for you to see me."

"Dangerous?" I asked. "For whom?"

The voice ignored my question, and I realized this was a prerecorded message. "We know you have heard the rumor that your brother's ship was sabotaged. We believe your father was responsible for his death. Your brother was murdered, sir, and your father is his murderer."

The screen went dead. I sat there in the darkened hotel bedroom, stunned, shocked, gaping wide-eyed at the faintly glowing wall screen. My father had Alex murdered? My father was responsible for his death? It was a terrible, awful accusation, made by someone too cowardly even to show his or her face.

And I believed it. That's what staggered me the most. *I believed it.*

I believed it because I remembered the night before Alex left for his ill-fated expedition to Venus. The night he revealed to me why he was really going.

Alex had told everyone that he was going to Venus to study the planet's runaway greenhouse. Which was true enough. But he had a hidden agenda as well. He told me about it that night before he left. There was a political motive behind his scientific mission. I remember Alex sitting in the cozy, quiet library of the Connecticut house, where we lived with Father, and whispering his plans to me.

Earth was just starting to feel the effects of greenhouse warming, Alex told me. Glaciers and polar caps melting. Sea levels rising. Global climate changing.

The International Green Party claimed that drastic steps must be taken before the whole American Midwest is turned back into the inland sea it once was and the permafrost in Canada melts, releasing megatons of frozen methane into the atmosphere and driving the greenhouse effect even further.

"You're one of them?" I whispered in the dark to him. "A Green?"

He chuckled in the shadows. "You'd be too, Little Brother, if you paid any attention to the real world."

I remember shaking my head and muttering, "Father would kill you if he knew."

"He knows," Alex said.

He wanted to use his mission to Venus to show the world firsthand what a runaway greenhouse can do to a planet: turn it into a dead ball of rock mantled in poisonous gases, without a drop of water or a blade of grass. It would be a powerful icon, a picture branded into the consciousness of the world's voters: This is what Earth will become unless we stop the greenhouse warming.

Powerful political forces opposed the Greens. Men such as my father had no intention of letting the IGP gain control of the international organizations that regulated environmental protection measures. The Greens wanted to triple taxes on multinational corporations, ban all fossil-fuel burning, force the evacuation of major cities, redistribute the world's wealth among the needy.

Alex's expedition to Venus, then, was actually a mission to help the Greens, to give them a powerful image to use against the entrenched political power of the Establishment, against our own father.

"Father would kill you if he knew," I had said.

And Alex had replied grimly, "He knows."

My fear of Father's reaction was merely a metaphor, kids' talk. Now I wondered if Alex had understood it that way.

I could no more sleep than I could lift Gibraltar. I prowled through my suite in the long shuffling strides that the Moon's low gravity demands, by turns angry, frightened, desperate.

Like all the lunar communities, Selene City is underground, dug into the ringwall mountains of the giant crater Alphonsus. So there is no dawn creeping through your windows, no sunrise to announce when a new day begins. The lights out in the corridors and public spaces turn up to a daytime level, bang, that's it. In my suite the lights turned on automatically as I paced, the switches activated by my body heat.

After several hours I finally realized what I would do. What I had to do. I ordered the phone computer to contact my father.

It took several minutes. No doubt his disgusting party was still going on in high gear. At last, though, his face appeared on the wall screen in my sitting room.

Father looked tired, but relaxed, smiling lazily at me. I realized he was in bed, leaning back on glistening silk-covered pillows. He was not alone, either. I heard muffled giggles from beneath his bedcovers.

"You're up early," he said pleasantly enough.

"So are you," I replied.

He huffed. "Don't look so disapproving, Runt. I offered these ladies to you, remember? It would be a shame to waste such talent."

"I'm going to take your prize money," I said.

That popped his eyes open. "What?"

"I'll go to Venus. I'll find Alex's body."

"You?" He laughed.

"He was my brother!" I said. "I loved him."

"I had to twist your arm to get you come up here to the Moon, and now you think you're going to Venus?" He seemed enormously amused by the idea.

"You don't think I could do it?"

"I *know* you can't do it, Runt. You won't even try, despite your brave talk."

"I'll show you!" I snapped. "I'll take your damned prize money!"

Smirking, he answered, "Of course you will. And elephants can fly."

"You're forcing me into it," I insisted. "That ten-billion prize is a powerful incentive to a man whose income shuts off next month."

His smirk faded and he turned thoughtful. "Yes, I suppose it would be, wouldn't it?"

"I'm going," I said firmly.

"And you assume that you'll win my prize money, eh?"

"Or die trying."

"You don't think you'll be the only one trying to grab my ten billion, do you?"

"Who else in his right mind would even think of going?"

With a sneer, Father answered, "Oh, I know someone who'll try. He'll try damned hard."

"Who?"

"Lars Fuchs. That bastard's out somewhere in the Belt right now, but as soon as the word reaches him, he'll head for Venus without blinking an eye."

"Fuchs?" I had heard my father speak of Lars Fuchs

often, and always with hatred. He was an asteroid miner, from what little I knew of him. Once he had owned his own corporation and had been a competitor of my father's, but now he was nothing more than an independent miner scratching out a living in the Asteroid Belt, a "rock rat," in my father's genteel phrasing.

"Fuchs. You'll have to wrestle my prize money away from him, Runt. I don't think you're man enough to do it."

I should have realized at that precise moment that he was manipulating me, he was *forcing* me to jump through his hoops. But to be perfectly honest, all I saw was a life of destitution unless I could take that prize money.

Well, that wasn't quite all that I was thinking about. I still saw Alex's handsome, determined face from that last night he had spent on Earth.

"Father would kill you if he knew," I had said.

"He knows," Alex had replied.

WASHINGTON, D.C.

T his is the opportunity of a lifetime," Professor Green-baum groaned like a creaking hinge, "and I'm too old to take advantage of it."

I had never actually seen an elderly person before, not close up, in the same room. I mean, poor people probably aged, but with everybody who could afford it getting telomerase treatments as soon as they reach adulthood, and rejuvenation therapy for adults who had aged before telomerase was approved for general use, no one grew old anymore.

But Daniel Haskel Greenbaum was *old*. His skin was all wrinkled and spotted. He was stooped over and looked so frail I was afraid his bones would shatter when I shook hands with him. Actually, his grip was rather firm, even though his eyes were pouchy and the skin of his face sagged and was filled with lines and creases, like a worn old arroyo eroded by centuries of weathering.

Yet he was only seventy-something.

Mickey had warned me about Greenbaum's appearance.

Michelle Cochrane had been one of his graduate students. Now a full professor herself, she still worshiped Greenbaum. She called him the greatest living planetary scientist in the solar system.

If you could call his asthmatic, arthritic, painfully slow pace of existence *living*. He had refused rejuvenation therapy, for some obscure reason. His religion, I think. Or perhaps just pure stubbornness. He was the kind who believed that aging and death were inevitable, and should not be avoided.

One of the last of that kind, I might add.

"He has the courage of his convictions," Mickey had told me years earlier. "He's not afraid of dying."

"I'm scared to death of dying," I had joked.

Mickey hadn't seen the cleverness of my *mot*. Yet I knew she had taken telomerase treatments when she finished puberty as a matter of course. Everyone did.

Greenbaum was the world's leading authority on the planet Venus, and Mickey had pleaded with me to meet with the old man. I had agreed without giving it another thought. The next thing I knew, she had arranged a meeting in Washington, D.C., not only with creaking Professor Emeritus Greenbaum, but with an angry-looking black bureaucrat from the space agency named Franklin Abdullah.

My father had immediately trumpeted to the news media that his other son—me—was going to try to recover Alex's remains on the surface of Venus. Like a proud parent, he assured the reporters that if I came back with Alex's body I would be rewarded with the ten-billion-dollar prize. I became an instant celebrity.

Fame has its advantages, I've been told, but I have yet to discover any of them. Every scientist, adventurer, fameseeker, and mentally unstable person in the Earth-Moon system sought me out, begging for a chance to go to Venus with me. Even religious fanatics had insisted it was their destiny to go to Venus and I was God's chosen method of transporting them there.

Of course, I had willingly invited a half dozen of my

closest friends to come on the voyage with me. Artists, writers, videographers, they would make valued contributions to the expedition's history and be good company as well: more so than dull scientists and wild-eyed zealots.

Then Mickey had called me from her office in California and I had agreed to meet with her and Greenbaum without even asking myself what she might be after.

At Abdullah's insistence the meeting took place in the space agency's headquarters, a musty, dreary old building in a run-down neighborhood of downtown Washington. We met in a windowless little conference room; the only furniture was a battered old metal table and four unbelievably uncomfortable stiff, hard chairs. The walls were decorated—if that's the proper word—with faded old photographs of ancient rocket launches. I mean, some of them must have gone back a century or more.

Until that afternoon, I had never seen Mickey in person. We always communicated electronically, usually through an interactive virtual reality link. We had first met—electronically—several years earlier, when I'd begun to get interested in Alex's work in planetary exploration. He had hired her to tutor me. We worked together every week in virtual reality sessions, she from her office at Caltech, I in the family home in Connecticut, at first, then later from my own place in Majorca. Together we roamed Mars, the moons of Jupiter and Saturn, the asteroids—even Venus.

Seeing her in the flesh was a bit of a shock. In our VR sessions she had apparently used a much younger, slimmer image of herself. Sitting across the conference table from me, she was a rotund little thing with mousey brownish hair that hung limply down to her earlobes. Telomerase treatments could keep you physically young, but they could not overcome years of sitting in a university office eating junk food and not getting any exercise. Mickey wore a black pullover sweater and black athletic slacks, the kind that have loops for your feet. Yet her round chubby face was so full of good humor, so sparkling with enthusiasm, that it was easy to forget her dumpy appearance.

Franklin Abdullah was something else altogether. He sat across the conference table from me, wearing an old-fashioned three-piece suit of charcoal gray, his arms folded across his chest, and scowled as if everything in his life had always gone wrong. Believe me, he didn't give the appearance of the stereotypical "faceless bureaucrat." He had an *attitude*. I didn't know why, but he actually seemed angry that I was preparing to go to Venus. A strange point of view from someone in the space agency.

"Since you asked for this meeting, Professor Cochrane," Abdullah said, "why don't you tell us what you have in mind." His voice was deep and rumbling, like the growl of a lion.

Mickey smiled at him and wiggled a little in her chair, as if trying to get comfortable on the iron-hard plastic cushion. Clasping her hands on the tabletop, she looked at me— a bit apprehensively, I thought.

"Van is putting together a mission to Venus," she said, stating the obvious. "A crewed mission."

Professor Greenbaum cleared his throat noisily, and Mickey immediately shut up.

"We are here, Mr. Humphries," the old man said, "to plead with you to bring at least one qualified planetary scientist to Venus with you."

"With a full complement of proper sensors and analytical systems," Mickey added.

Now I understood what she was after. I should have seen it coming, but I'd been too busy looking over the design and construction of my ship. And fending off all the other crazies who wanted a free ride to Venus.

I felt a little embarrassed. "Um . . . you see, this isn't a scientific mission. I'm going to Venus—"

"To win the prize money," Greenbaum interrupted, cranky and impatient. "We know that."

"To recover my brother's remains," I said firmly.

Mickey hunched forward in her chair. "But still, Van, this is an opportunity to do terrifically valuable science. You'll be beneath the clouds for days on end! Think of the observations we'll be able to make!"

"But my ship is designed strictly for the pickup mission," I explained to them. "We find the wreckage of my brother's ship and take back his remains. That's it. We won't have the space or the capacity to carry a scientist with us. The crew is at a minimum."

That wasn't exactly the truth, of course. I had already invited those friends of mine to come along on the expedition, the writers and artists who could immortalize this expedition after we returned. The engineers and designers naturally took a dim view of carrying what they considered to be nonessential personnel. I was already fighting with them over the size of the crew. I couldn't go back to them and ask them to add still another person, plus all the equipment that a scientist would want to bring along.

"But, Van," Mickey coaxed, "to go all the way to Venus without making any scientific studies of the planet . . ." She shook her head.

I turned to Abdullah, sitting at the head of the little table, his arms still folded across his vest.

"I thought that the scientific exploration of the solar system was a responsibility of the space agency's."

He nodded grimly. "It was."

I waited for more. Abdullah just sat there. So I said, "Then why doesn't the agency send an expedition to Venus?"

Abdullah slowly unfolded his arms and leaned them on the tabletop. "Mr. Humphries, you live in Connecticut, isn't that right?"

"Not anymore," I said, wondering what that had to do with anything.

"Any snow there this winter?"

"No, I don't think so. There hasn't been any snow for several winters in a row."

"Uh-huh. Did you see the cherry trees here in Washington? They're in bloom. In February. On Groundhog Day."

"Today is Groundhog Day, that's right," Greenbaum agreed.

For a moment I thought I had fallen into Alice's rabbit hole. "I don't understand what—"

"I was born in New Orleans, Mr. Humphries," said Abdullah, his deep voice like the rumble of distant thunder. "Or what's left of it, after the floods."

"But—"

"Global warming, Mr. Humphries," he growled. "Have you heard about it?"

"Of course I have. Everybody has."

"The space agency's limited resources are fully committed to studies of the Earth's environment. We have neither funding nor approval for anything else, such as exploring the planet Venus."

"But the Mars expeditions—"

"Are privately funded."

"Oh, yes, of course." I had known that; it had just never occurred to me that the government's space agency *couldn't* participate in the exploration of Mars and the other planets.

"All studies of the other bodies in the solar system are privately funded," Greenbaum pointed out.

Mickey added, "Even the deep-space work that the astronomers and cosmologists are doing has to be financed by private donors."

"Men like Trumball and Yamagata," said Greenbaum.

"Or organizations such as the Gates Foundation and Spielberg," Mickey said.

Of course I already knew that the big corporations backed the mining and manufacturing operations off-Earth. The competition for raw materials out in the Asteroid Belt was something that Father had often talked about, heatedly.

"Your father is financing this mission to Venus," Abdullah said. "We are—"

"I am raising the money for this mission," I snapped. "My father's prize money will be awarded only when and if I return safely."

Abdullah closed his eyes for a moment, as if thinking over what I'd just said. Then he corrected himself. "No matter what the ultimate source of the funding may be, we are appealing to you to allow this private venture to include a scientific component."

"For the good of the human race," Greenbaum said, his raspy voice actually quavering with emotion.

"Think of what we might discover beneath the clouds!" Mickey enthused.

I sympathized with them, but the thought of battling with those designers and engineers made me shake my head.

Greenbaum misunderstood my gesture. "Let me explain something to you, young man."

My brows must have gone up. Mickey tried to hold him back; she literally tugged at the sleeve of his pullover shirt, but he shrugged her off. Surprising vigor for a rickety old man, I thought.

"Do you know anything about plate tectonics?" he asked, almost belligerently.

"Certainly," I said. "Mickey's taught me quite a bit about it, actually. The Earth's crust is composed of big plates, the size of continents, and they slide around on top of the hotter, denser rock below the crust."

Greenbaum nodded, apparently satisfied with the state of my education.

"Venus has plate tectonics, too," I added.

"It did," Greenbaum said. "Half a billion years ago."

"Not now?"

"Venus's plates are locked," Mickey said.

"Like the San Andreas fault?"

"Much worse."

"Venus is on the verge of an upheaval," Greenbaum said, his eyes fixed on mine. "For something like five hundred million years the planet's plates have been locked together. All across the planet. She's been building up internal heat all that while. Sometime soon that heat is going to burst out and totally blow away the planet's surface."

"Sometime soon?" I heard myself squeak.

"Geologically speaking," Mickey said.

"Oh."

"For the past five hundred million years Venus's surface has been virtually unchanged," Greenbaum went on. "We know that from counting meteor impacts. Below the surface, the planet's internal heat is blocked. It can't get through the crust, can't escape."

Mickey explained, "On Earth, the planet's internal heat is vented out of volcanoes, hot springs, that sort of thing."

"Water acts as a lubricant on Earth," Greenbaum said, peering intently at me, as if to determine if I was understanding him. "On Venus there's no liquid water; it's too hot."

"No liquid water," Mickey took up, "means no lubrication for the plates. They lock in place and stay locked."

Nodding, I mumbled, "I see."

"For five hundred million years," Greenbaum said, "the heat's been building up below Venus's surface. It's got to go somewhere!"

"Sooner or later," Mickey took over, "Venus is going to erupt cataclysmically. Volcanoes everywhere. The crust will melt and sink. New crustal material will well up from below."

"It's going to be *wonderful!*" Greenbaum actually cackled with glee.

"And this might happen while I'm down on the surface?" I asked, suddenly fearful that they might be right.

"No, no, no," Mickey said, trying to soothe me. "We're talking geological time frames here, not human."

"But you said—"

Greenbaum went from cackling to gloom. "We'd never be lucky enough to have it happen while we're actually on the scene. The gods aren't that generous."

"I wouldn't call it luck," I said. "The whole surface suddenly melting and blasting out volcanoes and all that."

Mickey said, "Don't worry about it, Van. It won't happen during the few days you're below the clouds."

"Then what are you so worked up about?" I asked.

Abdullah piped up, in his bass register. "Not every scientist agrees with Professor Greenbaum."

"Most planetary scientists disagree with us," Mickey admitted.

"Damn fools," Greenbaum grumbled.

By now I was thoroughly confused. "But if it's *not* going to go through this cataclysm, then what are you so excited about?"

"Seismic measurements," Greenbaum said, staring at me again. "That's what we need."

Mickey explained, "The whole issue depends on whether Venus has a thick crust or a thin one."

It was starting to sound like a pizza contest to me, but I kept my mouth shut and kept on listening.

"If the crust is thin, then the upheaval is more likely. If it's thick, then we're wrong and the others are right."

"But can't you measure the crust with robot sensors?" I asked.

Mickey replied, "We've had some measurements over the years, but they're inconclusive."

"Then send more probes," I said. It seemed so obvious!

They both turned to Abdullah. He shook his head. "The agency is not allowed to spend a penny on studies of Venus, or anything else that isn't directly related to Earth's environmental problems."

"But private donors," I said. "Surely it wouldn't cost that much to send out a few probes."

"We've been trying to get funding," Mickey said. "But it's not easy, especially when most of the specialists in the subject think we're wrong."

"That's why your mission is a godsend," Greenbaum said, with the fervor of a missionary. "You can carry dozens of seismic sensors to Venus—hundreds! And a scientist to handle them. Plus a lot of other equipment."

"But my spacecraft won't have that capacity," I insisted. Perhaps pleaded is a more accurate term.

"It's the opportunity of a lifetime," Greenbaum said again. "I wish I were thirty years younger."

"I can't do it," I said.

"Please, Van," said Mickey. "It's really important."

I looked from her earnest face to Greenbaum's to Abdullah's and back again.

"I'd be the scientist," Mickey added. "I'd be the one going to Venus with you."

She looked so intent, so beseeching, as if her entire life depended on going to Venus with me.

What could I tell her?

I took a breath and said, "I'll talk to my people. Maybe there's a way for us to carry you along."

Mickey jumped up and down in her chair like a kid who'd just opened the biggest Christmas present in the history of the world. Greenbaum half-collapsed back in his seat, as if the effort of this meeting had drained all the strength out of him. But he was grinning from ear to ear, a lopsided, gap-toothed jack-o'-lantern grin.

Even Abdullah smiled.

GREATER LOS ANGELES

Tomas Rodriguez had been an astronaut; he'd gone to Mars four times before retiring upward to become a consultant to aerospace companies and universities doing planetary explorations.

Yet what he really wanted was to fly again.

He was a solidly built man with an olive complexion and thickly curled hair that he kept clipped very short in almost a military crew cut. He looked morose most of the time, pensive, almost unapproachable. But that was just a mask. He smiled easily, and when he did it lit up his whole face to show the truly gentle man beneath the surface.

Unfortunately, he was not smiling now.

Rodriguez and I were sitting in a small conference room, just the two of us. Between us floated a holographic image of the spacecraft that was being constructed for my flight to Venus. Hanging there in midair above the oval conference table, the ship looked more like an ironclad dirigible than anything else—which it was, almost. Of course we were using the latest ceramic-metal alloys for her exterior, rather than iron.

With a slight frown creasing his brow, Rodriguez was telling me, "Mr. Humphries, we can't hang another gondola under the gas envelope without enlarging the envelope by a third or more. Those are the numbers from the computer and there's no way around them."

"But we need the extra gondola to accommodate the crew," I said.

"The friends you want to bring along are not crew, Mr. Humphries," Rodriguez said. "The working crew can be accommodated in the single gondola, as per our original design."

"They're not just my friends," I snapped, feeling testy. "One of them is a top planetary scientist, another is a writer who'll be doing a book about this expedition . . ." My voice trailed off. Except for Mickey, the others were indeed nothing more than friends, acquaintances who wanted the thrill of flying to Venus.

Rodriguez shook his head. "We can't do it, Mr. Humphries. Not at this late date. We'd have to scrap everything that's been built and start all over again from scratch."

That would be too expensive, I was certain. Even with a ten-billion-dollar prize in the offing, the banks were already nervous about financing the construction of my ship. International lending officers I had known from childhood wrinkled their brows at me and talked about risks and the inability to get insurance coverage for their exposure. We had to design the ship as frugally as possible; adding what would actually be a separate module for nonessential passengers would be unacceptable to the money people.

The trouble was, I had already invited those people to come along with me. I couldn't disinvite them now, not without enormous embarrassment. And I had promised Mickey that she could come along, too.

Rodriguez took my silence for assent. "Then we're agreed?" he asked.

I said nothing, desperately running different schemes

through my mind. Maybe a second ship? A backup. That might work. I could present it to the bankers as a safety precaution. What did Rodriguez call that kind of thing? A redundancy, that's right. A safety redundancy.

"Okay," he said, and resumed his painstakingly detailed briefing of every single component and system of the ship. I could feel my eyes glazing over.

I had named my vessel *Hesperos,* after the ancient Greek name for Venus as the beautiful evening star. Alex's ship had been almost identical in design and he had called his *Phosphoros,* the old Greek name for Venus as the morning star, the light-bringer.

"And here," Rodriguez was droning on, "is the descent module."

A little spherical metal object appeared beneath the ship's single gondola, sort of like a bathysphere. It was attached to the gondola by a line so thin I could barely make it out.

Rodriguez must have seen my brows hike up. "That's a Buckyball cable. It'll take kilotons of tensile stress. One of 'em saved my life on Mars, during the second expedition."

I nodded and he went on and on, in infinite minutiae. Rodriguez was wearing what he jokingly referred to as his "consultant's suit:" a sky-blue collarless jacket with matching slacks and a crisp open-necked saffron shirt. The color of the shirt reminded me of the clouds on Venus, a little. Me, I dressed for comfort: salmon-pink sport shirt, authentic blue jeans, and tennis shoes.

I knew it bothered Rodriguez that we were going with virtually the identical design as Alex's ship, which had somehow failed and killed its entire crew. Rodriguez believed in caution; he claimed you didn't live long enough to be an ex-astronaut unless you knew how to be careful. But by using Alex's basic design we could save a ton of money; it would have cost a good fraction of the prize money to design a new vessel from scratch.

"That's the basic design and layout of the bird," Rodriguez said at long last. "Now I'd like to go over the modifications and improvements we're going to put in."

I felt my lips curl slightly. "You mean that some of the modifications won't be improvements?"

Rodriguez broke into a grin. "Sorry. Sometimes I slip into corporate bafflegab. Every modification will be an improvement, I promise you."

So I leaned back in my padded swivel chair and tried as hard as I could to pay attention to his earnest, plodding review. It was tedious to the point of paralysis, especially when I could see through the room's only window the wide Pacific glittering in the afternoon sun. It was so tempting to call an end to this interminable briefing and spend the rest of the day on the man-made lagoon behind the seawall.

This high up in the hills it was hard to realize that once there had been beaches and surfing and homes strung all along the oceanfront. Malibu, Santa Monica, Marina Del Rey—their beaches had all been drowned when the Antarctic icecap started melting down. Even now, on this balmy, sunny afternoon the waves were pounding the new seawall and spraying the road that ran behind it.

While Rodriguez droned on, my thoughts drifted back to that anonymous phone message I'd received in Selene City. Father had murdered Alex? It sounded too terrible to be true, even for him. And yet . . .

But if my father had anything to do with Alex's death, why had he cooked up this mission to recover his son's body? Some form of atonement? Guilt? Clever public relations to throw the suspicion off him and quiet the rumors?

Such thoughts scared me. And depressed me terribly. It was too much for me to deal with. All I really wanted out of life was to live quietly in my home on Majorca, have a few friends drop in from time to time, go visiting when the mood struck me. Not take a risk-filled flight to another world. Not listen to Rodriguez going on and on with his endless details.

I'm doing this for Alex, I told myself. But I knew that was nonsense. Alex was dead and nothing that I or anyone else could do was going to change that.

"Are you all right, Mr. Humphries?"

With an effort, I focused my attention back on Rodriguez. He looked concerned, almost worried.

I ran a hand over my face. "I'm sorry. What did you say?"

"You seemed far away," Rodriguez replied. "Are you okay?"

"Um . . . I've got to take my injection," I said, pushing my chair away from the table and the hologram floating above it.

Rodriguez got to his feet as I did. "Okay, sure. We can finish this later."

"Right," I said, and headed for the door.

I didn't really need the injection right at that moment. I even could have taken it there in the conference room; it's no big deal, just press the microneedle head of the syringe against your skin and squeeze the activator button. But I told everyone that I had to do it in my private quarters. It was a convenient fiction, a way of getting out of worrisome or boring situations, such as this dreary briefing.

So I went to the suite of rooms I was using as my private quarters in the building up atop the Malibu hills. Once it had been a research laboratory, but when the sea started rising the local government wanted to condemn the building, for fear the hills would erode so badly that it would go sliding into the ocean. Humphries Space Systems bought the complex for a pittance, then got the condemnation procedure legally stopped—with a generous application of money to the appropriate officials.

Now the former laboratory was owned by my father's corporation. More than half its space was rented to other corporations and the harried engineers and administrators of the Greater Los Angeles Seawall Project, who were working against time and the tides to keep the rising Pacific Ocean from inundating more of the city.

My quarters were on the top floor of the central wing, small but decently furnished. As I opened the door I saw that my phone screen was blinking MESSAGE WAITING in bright yellow letters.

"Play my messages," I called out, heading for the bathroom and my syringe.

The mirror above the sink flickered briefly and then my father's stern face appeared. "I warned you about Lars Fuchs, remember? Well, my people have found out that he's cobbling together some kind of ship out in the Belt. He'll try for my prize money, all right, just as I thought."

The idea that I'd have competition for the prize didn't bother me very much. Not at that moment. From the way Father described it, Fuchs wouldn't be much of a threat. Or so I thought.

Then Father delivered his bombshell. "By the way, I've picked a captain for your expedition. She'll be arriving at your quarters there in Malibu in an hour or so. Her name is Desiree Duchamp."

Father's image winked out and I was staring at my own slack-jawed reflection. "But Rodriguez is going to be my captain," I said weakly.

The door buzzer sounded.

Laying the syringe on the countertop, I went out into the sitting room and called, "Enter."

The door unlocked itself and swung open. Standing there was a tall, slim, dark-haired woman of indeterminate age, wearing a skintight jumpsuit of glittery black faux leather. Her eyes were large and luminous. She might have been beautiful if she would have smiled, but the expression on her face was hard, bitter, almost angry.

"Come in," I said, then added. "Ms. Duchamp."

"*Captain* Duchamp, thanks to you."

She marched into the room on long-legged strides. With the outfit she was wearing I expected her calf-length boots to have spike heels, but instead her heels were sensibly low. Otherwise she looked like a video portrayal of a dominating sex symbol. All she needs is a whip, I thought.

"Thanks to me?" I echoed. "This is my father's idea, not mine."

"You're the one going to Venus," she said, her voice low.

It would have been sultry if she weren't so obviously displeased.

"I have a captain already signed up," I said. "Tomas Rodriguez. He's been—"

"I know Tommy," Duchamp interrupted. "He'll be my Number One."

"He's my captain," I said, very firmly. "We've already signed a contract."

Duchamp went to the long couch on the other side of the room and sat down as if she owned the place. For a long moment I just stood by the door, staring at her.

"Close the door," she said frowning.

I called out, "Shut." The door swung and its lock clicked.

"Look, Mr. Humphries," Duchamp said more reasonably, clasping her hands together. "I don't like this any more than you do. But Hump has decided he wants me to captain your spacecraft and we're both stuck with that decision."

Her fingers were long and the nails colored fire-engine red. I walked over toward the couch and sat on the armchair facing it.

"Why did he pick you?" I asked.

She frowned again. "To get rid of me, why else?"

"Rid of you?"

"This is his idea of a kiss-off. He's tired of me; he's got a couple of new tarts to chase."

"You were his mistress?"

She actually laughed. "Christ, I haven't heard that term since I was reading novels under the blankets after lights-out at boot camp."

I shook my head. I was starting to feel giddy, a sure symptom, so I got to my feet. "Excuse me," I said, heading for the bathroom.

It took less than a minute to administer my shot, but when I returned to the sitting room she was at the desk by the window and the wallscreen displayed her biographical résumé. She was a qualified astronaut, sure enough, a veteran of eleven flights to the Asteroid Belt and three to the

Jupiter system. On four expeditions she had been mission commander.

"How long have you known my father?" I asked, keeping my eyes on the screen instead of her.

"I met him about a year ago. We were bedmates for three months. Something of a record for Hump."

"He was married to my mother for six years," I said, still studying the data on the screen.

"Yeah, but he was sleeping with a lot of other kids. She was out of it half the time with her habit—"

I whirled on her, furious. "You don't know anything about it! You might think you know, he might have told you a lot, but it's all lies. Lies! Vicious, self-serving lies!"

She jumped to her feet, as if to defend herself from assault. "Hey, don't blame me."

"That's my mother you're talking about," I snapped. "If she got hooked on narcotics it was *his* doing."

"Okay," Duchamp said placatingly. "Okay."

I took a deep, deliberate breath. Then, as calmly as I could manage, I told her, "I don't want you on my mission. Not as captain. Not in any capacity at all."

She shrugged as if it didn't matter. "You'll have to straighten that out with your father."

"It's not his decision."

"Yes it is," Duchamp countered. "Remember the golden rule—he who has the gold makes the rules."

MAJORCA

threw a sort of party of my own, a disastrous affair with just a dozen or so of my close friends. They flew in from all points of the compass obligingly enough, all dressed in the latest "in" fashion: neo-Victorian dinner clothes for the men, the women in low-cut evening gowns rich with artificial feathers and real gems.

Style is an ephemeral thing. I'm told that once, young adults such as myself and my friends dressed in grungy military fatigues and camouflage shirts. A generation later the youthful set was piercing their navels, eyebrows, even their sex organs, and wearing metal studs through their tongues and lips. Their children spent their rebellious years in plastic jackets that imitated samurai armor and tattooed their faces like Maori warriors.

The "in" style for my group was sophistication. We dressed extravagantly in vintage dinner jackets and sequined gowns. We pretended to smoke faux cigarettes of harmless organics. We glittered with jewels and bracelets and earrings of precious metals from asteroids. We spoke in the elegant tones of cultivated boredom, affecting the witty cynicism of Oscar Wilde and Bernard Shaw. Profanities and crude language were far, far beneath us.

Yet even though we dressed so elegantly and spoke so genteelly, my gathering was a fiasco. It was terribly embarrassing to have to tell them that I couldn't take them with me to Venus. I stammered through the reasons, and was surprised to see looks of relief on some of their faces.

But only on some of them.

"Do you mean to stand there and tell me that you made me fly all the way here from Boston just to tell me you're reneging on your invitation?" demanded Quenton Cleary. He looked quite splendid in a crimson Hussar's uniform, with loads of gold braid and a chestful of ribbons and medals. Something of an athlete, Quenton starred on the international volleyball team that he had organized. They had even competed on the Moon against the amateur team that Selene City had put together. And they had almost won, too, despite the totally different conditions there.

"It can't be done," I said, feeling miserable. "I even had to tell Professor Cochrane that there will be no room for her on the vessel."

When I tried to explain it all again, Quenton took the whole tray of crystal champagne flutes from the table and heaved them across my living room. They smashed against the stones of the fireplace into a thousand shards.

That was Quenton: given to physical expression. But he was no fool. No one was standing within five meters of the fireplace when he gave vent to his temper. No one was scratched. He didn't damage the Vermeer hanging over the fireplace, either.

"Really, Quenton!" said Basil Ustinov.

"Well, I had to fly all the way here from Boston, you know," Quenton said heatedly.

"And I flew here from St. Petersburg," Basil riposted. "What of it? I'm just as disappointed as you are, but if Van can't do anything about it, there's no reason to get violent over it."

They had all come from long distances, all except
Gwyneth, who was studying in Barcelona at the time. Of
course, with Clippership rockets no major transport hub on
Earth was more than an hour away from any other hub. It
took more time to drive from the airfield at New Palma to
my home up here in Majorca's hills than it did to fly from
Boston. I had often considered putting in a landing field for
copters or jumpjets, but the thought of battling the towns-
people and their dreary little community council kept me
from even proposing it.

I could see the town's point of view, I suppose. It truly
was lovely up here in the hills, away from the thundering
rockets and screeching helicopters. Not even tourist buses
could get through the town's main street, so this part of the
island stayed tranquil and relaxed.

As I sat back in the silky comfort of my favorite couch
and gazed through the sweeping windows at the Mediterranean, I realized how much I loved this home of mine. The
sea was calm, its long gentle waves touched with the pink
of approaching sunset. The hillside marched down to the
water in a series of terraces that still held vegetable gardens
and vineyards. Hannibal had seen those terraces. This land
had been under human cultivation since long before history
had begun to be written.

The rising sea level had inundated the beaches, of
course, as well as much of the old city of Palma. Even the
gentle Mediterranean was swallowing up its seacoasts.
Still, Majorca was as close to paradise as I could imagine.

And I was going to leave this all behind to live in a metal cell for months at a time so that I could risk my life and
limb trying to be the first person to set foot on the red-hot
surface of Venus. I shook my head at the absurdity of the
position I had put myself in.

But Quenton was getting pugnacious. "I don't like having promises broken," he said petulantly. "Van, you've
gone back on your word."

"There's nothing I can do about it," I said.

"I don't believe you."

My cheeks burning, I got to my feet. "Are you accusing me of lying to you?"

Quenton glared at me. "You made a promise and now you've broken it."

"Then get out of my house," I heard myself say. It surprised me, but I realized that I was suddenly quite thoroughly angry.

Francesca Ianetta huffed, "Really, Van!"

"You, too," I snapped. "All of you!" I swept the room with an outstretched hand and shouted, "You can all get out! Now! Leave me alone!"

For a moment there was nothing but shocked silence. Then Basil pulled his rotund body from the armchair he'd been sitting in. "I suppose I should get back to my work," he said.

Basil's idea of work was to smear colors across a display screen. He was a very talented artist, everyone said, but he was extremely lazy. He could afford to be; his patroness was extremely wealthy.

Nodding curtly, I said, "Yes, you should."

"I shall go back to Rome," Francesca said grandly. "I have an opera to finish."

"Good," I said. "Maybe if you put some real work into it you'd actually finish it."

"Really!" she said, appalled.

"Go on, all of you," I repeated, shooing them toward the door. "Go!"

Shocked, astonished at my outburst of poor manners, they left my house. Still hot with anger, I watched them from the window of my entertainment room, a procession of flamboyantly bright-colored automobiles, their electric engines making hardly a hum on the winding brick road that went down the hillside switchbacks and connected with the motorway.

"There they go."

I turned from the window. Gwyneth was standing next to me. She hadn't left, and I was glad of it.

The word that always popped into my mind whenever I

thought of Gwyneth was *alluring*. She had a way of looking at me, a sidelong glance through those long lashes of hers, that told me she wanted me as much as I wanted her. In earlier years she would have been called a courtesan, a kept woman, or worse. To me, she was a companion, a friend who shared her body and her mind with me. Gwyneth was serious, quiet, as steady as you'd want a companion to be. She had a wicked sense of humor, which she rarely let anyone see. She was slim, tiny, almost elfin, with long auburn hair that billowed beautifully in the breeze when we sailed together. Her face was to die for, with chiseled high cheekbones, luscious full lips, and almond-shaped eyes that were a golden, tawny brown.

"You're not angry with me, too, are you?" she asked, with a coy smile.

I felt my anger dissolve. "How could I be?"

She gave me an odd, quizzical look. "The way you told them off . . . you're starting to let the others know how strong you really are."

Surprised, I asked, "Strong? Me?"

"Real strength," Gwyneth said, her eyes studying my face. "Not the silly tantrums Quenton throws. You have real steel, Van, deep inside you."

"You think so?"

"I've known it since I first met you. But you keep it hidden, even from yourself." Then she added, in a murmur, "Especially from yourself."

Suddenly I felt uncomfortable. I turned away from her and looked out at the cars disappearing down the hillside road.

"You'd think they'd double up," Gwyneth said, coming closer to stand beside me. "Not one of them offered to ride with any of the others."

I hadn't thought about that until she mentioned it. They could have driven together if they'd wanted to; the automated cars could find their way back to the airport rental lot just as well unoccupied.

We walked together back into the broad expanse of the

living room. The robot cleaners had already swept up the shattered glassware.

"I suppose I'll never see them again," I said.

She smiled coolly. "They'll forget about your temper tantrum . . . as long as you have money."

"Don't be cruel," I said. I didn't like to think that they tolerated me only because I helped them in their chosen fields. It was true, of course, that I was a major backer for Francesca's unfinished opera, and—come to think of it— Quenton had asked me for a loan to keep his team going. That had been more than a year ago; not a word from him about paying it back.

What would they do when they realized I was broke? I hadn't found the courage to tell them that my income had been cut off. I was living on loans reluctantly advanced by banks against the ten billion prize dollars. Even though many of those bank officers were longtime friends of mine or the family's, they grew more nervous with each passing month. As if it were their own money they were playing with! I hadn't told any of the bankers about Lars Fuchs and apparently they were not as well informed about Fuchs as my father was.

Gwyneth and I walked wordlessly out onto the terrace to watch the last moments of the sunset. The sky turned flame red, flecked with purple clouds. The sea glittered crimson. From this high up the gentle waves lapping against once-dry terraces sounded like a distant sigh.

Gwyneth looked lovely in her graceful floor-length gown of gold lamé. She leaned her head against my shoulder. I slipped an arm around her waist.

"I depend on your money, too," she said, almost whispering. "Don't you forget that."

Two years ago, when I had first met Gwyneth, she had been a ballet student in London. Then she decided to major in art history at the Sorbonne. Now she was studying architecture in Barcelona. I was letting her use my apartment there. In the two years I had known her, we had never used the word *love*. Not even in bed.

"That's not important," I said.

"It is to me."

I didn't want to know what she meant. I enjoyed her company; in a way, I suppose, I needed her. Needed her common sense, her emotional support, her quiet strength.

She pulled away from me once the sun had dipped below the horizon. I gestured toward the French doors and we went back inside.

"You realize," Gwyneth said, as we sat together on the couch beneath my one and only Turner, "that most of them are glad they're not going with you."

With a nod I replied, "Yes, I thought I saw relief on their faces. Not Quenton's, though."

She smiled. "Quenton's simply better at disguising his real feelings."

"But he was so eager to go."

"At first," she said. "Over the past few weeks, though, his ardor cooled considerably. Didn't you notice?"

"No. Why do you suppose . . . ?"

Gwyneth lifted her slim shoulders slightly in a miniature shrug. "I have the feeling that the closer you got to actually taking off on your expedition, the more Quenton—and the others, too—realized that they were frightened."

"Frightened?"

"Of course."

"Were you frightened, too?"

"Of course," she repeated.

I sank back onto the cushions and thought about that for a moment. "Yet they all agreed to go. You, too."

"It sounded exciting at first. Going to Venus and all that. But it *is* dangerous, isn't it?"

I nodded. And before I realized what I was saying, I admitted, "I'm frightened, too."

"Ahh," she said.

"I don't want to go through with it. I really don't."

"Then why do it?"

"I need that prize money."

Gwyneth sighed. "It always comes down to the money, doesn't it?"

"I've made an idiot of myself."

"Not if you go through with it," she said. "When you return you'll be financially independent of your father for the rest of your life. That's worth something, don't you think?"

"I could get killed."

She gave me an odd look. "Yes, there is that."

We sat there in silence for some time as the shadows of twilight deepened and the room grew dark.

At last I said, "You know, it was Alex who turned me on to science. To planetary astronomy and all that."

"Really?"

I could barely make out her face in the shadows. "Yes. He was ten years older than I. As far back as I can remember, whatever he did, I wanted to do."

"Including scientific exploration."

Nodding, I remembered, "He started showing me where he'd been on Mars. I did virtual reality trips with him. It was fascinating! A different world. So much to see, so much to discover."

Gwyneth sat there beside me in the dark and let me babble on.

At last I said, "It's not the money! It's not. I'm going to Venus to find my brother. I'm going for Alex."

She kissed me lightly on the cheek and whispered, "Of course you are, Van."

Was it really true? Were either one of us speaking the truth? I wanted it to be true. With a pang of guilt, I recognized that I *needed* it to be true.

Then she said, "About the flat in Barcelona."

"What about it?" I asked.

She hesitated a long moment. "Well, it's only . . . you see, if you don't come back from your expedition, I have no legal right to remain there. Your father will boot me out, won't he? Or his lawyers will."

No, I thought. Father wouldn't evict you. He'd take one

good look at those promising eyes and lithe figure and take you for himself.

But I didn't tell her that. Instead, I said, "I'm having a will drawn up. The apartment will be my bequest to you. Will that be sufficient?"

She kissed me again, this time on the lips.

We never spoke about love, or gratitude either, but we understood each other perfectly well.

LIFTOFF

Rodriguez was almost pleading with me. "Look, Mr. Humphries, you've got to make a decision. Who the shit's going to be in command of this mission?"

It startled me to hear him use even a minor profanity. He's really upset about this, I realized. The expression on his face showed how distressed he felt. He looked almost desperate.

We were in my office at the launch complex on Tarawa. A Clippership was being serviced out on its pad, scheduled to lift us into orbit in an hour. Rodriguez sat across the desk from me, tension in every line of his body.

My desk chair was supposed to be stress-free. The very latest design. Soft pseudoleather padding. Adjustable headrest. Fully reclinable. Heat and massage units built in. But stress isn't merely physical, and I was feeling the muscles and tendons of my neck and shoulders tightening up like torture racks.

Rodriguez was already in his light tan flight coveralls,

ready to go. But he demanded my decision before we lifted off.

"It's her or me," he said, with real bitterness in his voice. "One of us is named captain and the other goes home. Which one will it be?"

I'd been putting off the decision for months, avoiding both Rodriguez and Duchamp as much as possible. I had the perfect excuse: I was cramming as much planetary astronomy into my brain as I could. Mickey had decided that if she couldn't come along to Venus, then I would have to be her surrogate. I would handle the seismic probes and other sensors that we would carry aboard *Hesperos* while she directed my work from California.

All through those months of preparation Desiree Duchamp had been acting as if there were no possible doubt that she was captain of *Hesperos*. She lorded it over the other crew members and treated Rodriguez as if he were her assistant. Rodriguez was entirely right. I couldn't put off this decision any longer.

Before I could say a word, though, the door from the corridor swung open and Duchamp stepped in, uninvited. She wore the same dun-colored flight coveralls as Rodriguez, but on her they looked crisper, sharper, almost like a military uniform.

"You're both here. Good," she said.

Rodriguez shot to his feet. "It's just as well you're here, Dee. We've got to—"

Duchamp pointed a long, manicured finger at him like a pistol. "Tommy, I don't mind you speaking informally to me in front of the owner, but don't you *ever* call me Dee or anything else except Captain Duchamp in front of the crew."

"Who says you're the captain?" Rodriguez snapped.

"The man who's paying for this expedition, that's who."

"I take my orders from Mr. Humphries, here."

A thin smile curved her lips. "I take my orders from Mr. Humphries, *there*." She gestured toward the ceiling. My father was still living at Selene City.

They both turned toward me. I got slowly to my feet, wondering which way to go. Decide! I railed at myself. Make a decision and stick to it.

"If you'll look at your incoming mail," Duchamp said coldly, "you'll see that he will get the banks to cut off all funding for this expedition if I'm not the captain. You'll have to go home and lose the prize money."

"My ass he will!" Rodriguez growled. Turning back to me, close enough almost to touch noses, he said earnestly, "Let your father threaten all he wants. Once we're in orbit he can't touch us. Go on to Venus, carry out the mission and you won't need his frigging money. When we get back home you'll be a hero, a celebrity! Without your old man."

Duchamp countered, "Do you think for one instant that the crew will undertake the risks of this mission knowing that their pay has been cut off?" She laughed harshly. "You'll never get off the ground!"

I felt nausea welling up in me. I was confused, torn in a dozen different directions. I clasped my hands to my head and shouted at them, "Why can't you two work something out between yourselves? Why do you have to put me in the middle of this?"

"Because you're the owner," Duchamp said.

At the same time Rodriguez said, "You're the head of the expedition."

"Whether you like it or not," Duchamp went on, "you're in charge here. It's your responsibility. You're the one who has to make the decision."

That's not true, I thought. My father's still in charge. He's making the real decisions. I'm just his puppet, dancing at the ends of his strings. He's forcing me to decide the way he wants me to.

"Well," Rodriguez demanded. "What's it going to be?"

I let my hands drop to my sides. My stomach was churning. My knees felt rubbery.

"She's right," I heard myself say. Totally miserable, I admitted, "If my father cuts off the money the crew won't even get aboard the Clippership out there."

Rodriguez began, "But I could—"

"No, no." I cut him off. I felt like sobbing, but I held myself together as best I could. "She's got to be captain. I can't risk destroying this mission. My hands are tied."

Duchamp allowed herself a smug smile. "Thank you," she said, then headed for the door. As she reached for the knob she turned halfway and said, "By the way, there's been a crew change. Nunnaly is out. I've put a biologist in her place."

She opened the door and left my office. I just stood there, relieved that the decision had finally been made, worried about how Rodriguez would react, and stunned about Duchamp adding a biologist in place of our astronomer. A biologist? What for? Nothing could possibly be living on Venus.

Rodriguez snapped me back to reality. "Okay, that's that."

His fists were clenched at his sides. He looked as if he wanted to hit somebody. Maybe me.

"Don't quit," I said. "Please take the second-in-command position. Please."

He was fuming, that was clear to see.

"I'll double your pay," I said.

He was staring grimly at the closed door, I realized.

"I'll add a bonus out of my own money. Please don't quit on me. I need you."

Slowly Rodriguez turned back toward me. "The bitch knows I couldn't turn down the chance to go to Venus. She knows I'll go no matter what rank you give me. She was counting on that."

"Then you'll go?" I asked, almost breathless. "As second-in-command?"

"I'll go," he said bitterly. "Even with *her* as captain. I can't turn my back on this. It's going to be an experience money can't buy."

I sank back gratefully into my stress-free chair. "Thanks, Tom," I said. "Thanks."

He grinned mirthlessly. "But I'll still take that doubled

pay, boss. And the bonus. I'll swallow her crap and be your second-in-command. But I want the money you promised."

I nodded, feeling weak, and he left the office.

An experience money can't buy. That's what Rodriguez had said. But he'll take the money just the same. Why not? Money is the universal lubricant. You need money to buy everything you want, every single thing. And as long as my father's money is paying for this expedition, I thought, he'll be making all the real decisions.

Meanwhile, I couldn't find any information about what Lars Fuchs was up to. Not even my father could. The man seemed to have disappeared entirely.

"He's up to something," my father warned, time and again, in his messages to me.

I asked Father's image on my screen, "But what can he do if he's all the way out there in the Belt?"

"I wouldn't be surprised if he's left the Belt and is heading for Venus," my father replied sourly. "His fellow rock rats are covering up for him, keeping silent no matter how much pressure my people put on them."

"But he'd have to register his ship with the International Astronautical Authority, wouldn't he?" I asked.

Father nodded. "Sooner or later he'll have to . . . or be declared an outlaw vessel. I'm not giving my prize money to an outlaw."

We lifted off in the Clippership with no problems. In ten minutes we were on orbit, approaching rendezvous. I started to feel queasy in zero-gravity; my stomach went hollow and I felt as if I were falling even when I could see that I was safely strapped into my seat. If I moved my head I got dizzy and nauseous, so I just sat there quietly, tying to keep myself from upchucking, while the Clippership went through its docking maneuvers.

It seemed like hours, but as soon as we were docked a

feeling of weight returned and I started to feel all right again.

My ship *Hesperos* was designed specifically for the Venus mission; she was too small and cramped for the long flight from Earth. To ferry *Hesperos* out to Venus we leased an old factory ship from the Asteroid Belt, named *Truax,* and refitted her for the task. The two vessels were connected by a Buckyball cable and rotated around their common center of gravity so there was the equivalent of a regular Earthly gravity aboard.

We didn't do that just for comfort. The gravity on Venus is only a few percent less than Earth, and if we had coasted out to Venus in zero-gee, our muscles and bones would have been deconditioned during the two-month flight. This way, with artificial gravity induced by spinning, we'd be ready for diving into Venus's clouds as soon as we parked in orbit around the planet.

Once we were cleared to unbuckle, I went straight from the Clippership to my stateroom aboard *Truax.* It had been the captain's quarters when *Truax* had plied the ore route between the Asteroid Belt and the Earth/Moon system. I saw that it was adequately furnished, although a bit shabby. Still, the foldout bed felt comfortable enough and the wall screens all worked. There was enough room to avoid the feeling of being cooped up. No windows, but the wall screens could be programmed to show any view I had in my video library.

I checked the closets and the lav. All my clothing and personal toiletries were in place. Good. The medicine cabinet was fully stocked with my enzyme supply, and three syringes were laid neatly in the drawer beside the sink. Fine.

Still, the stateroom had the faint odor of strangeness about it. The lingering residue of someone else's presence. I never got to feel completely at ease there. Certainly the built-in desk and other furnishings weren't in a style I would have picked.

That couldn't be helped now. I gave myself an injection

and then went to the desk. There was business to be attended to. Duchamp was the captain, very well. But how dare she kick our astronomer off the mission and substitute someone I hadn't even met? A biologist, no less.

I asked the intercom system to locate her. In a few seconds her lean, sharp-featured face appeared on my screen.

"I need to speak with you, Captain," I said, laying just a hint of stress on the last word.

"We're in the midst of a systems check," she said, her expression flinty. "I'll be free in one hour and . . ." Her eyes flicked away for a moment ". . . eleven minutes."

"In my quarters, then," I commanded.

She nodded and the screen went blank.

I waited in my stateroom. I could have gone out to the bridge, it was hardly ten paces down the passageway. But I decided it would be better to make her come to me. Establish the authority. She'd been named captain, she'd won that battle. But I'm the owner, I told myself, and she's not going to run roughshod over me.

I hoped.

One hour and twelve minutes later she knocked once on my door, opened it, and entered my stateroom. Her coveralls still looked crisp and fresh. If the systems checkout had strained her in any way it certainly didn't show in her appearance.

I stayed seated at my desk. With a gesture I invited her to sit in the nearest chair. She sat and crossed her legs, but for the first time since I'd met her she looked tense. Good, I thought.

"About this new crew member," I began. "It's not your place to make personnel substitutions."

"I'm aware of that," she said.

"Then what do you mean by displacing our astronomer with a biologist, of all things? You can't—"

"The fact that she's a biologist was not uppermost in my decision," she said sharply, cutting me off.

"What?" I must have blinked several times. "What do you mean?"

"Her name is Marguerite Duchamp. She's my daughter."

"Your daughter!"

"My daughter."

"That's rank nepotism! We don't need a biologist. I don't want a biologist! You can't bring your daughter on this mission!"

Duchamp merely raised an eyebrow and said, "My daughter comes with me."

"It's impossible," I said, as firmly as I could manage.

"Look," Duchamp replied, with ill-concealed impatience, "your father wants me out of his way, okay. But I'm not going to leave my daughter on the same planet with that humper. Not with him! Understood?"

I gaped at her. Beneath that icily cool surface she was burning with rage. And I understood why. My father had dumped her because he'd become more interested in her daughter. And she was furious about it.

They say that hell has no fury like a woman scorned. But what about a woman scorned because the man wants her daughter?

Then I wondered how the daughter felt about it. Was Duchamp protecting her daughter against my father's unwanted lechery? Or was she dragging her away, kicking and screaming?

Either way, it looked to me like a nest of snakes.

We left Earth orbit the following day and started on the two-month-long trajectory to Venus. We had to burn more propellant than the minimum-energy trajectory would use, but I figured that cutting the transit time in half was worth the expenditure.

I hardly felt the thrust when we broke orbit. I was standing off in one corner of the bridge doing a media interview while the working crew attended to their jobs. Off to Venus! It was a good news subject. Fine human interest: Van Humphries setting out to recover his dead brother's remains from the hellhole of the solar system. Later that evening, when I saw the network's broadcast, though, they showed more computer simulations of what Venus's surface might look like than they showed of me.

But my father kept worrying about Fuchs, bombarding me with tension-riddled messages Where was he? What was he up to? It made me worry, too.

No matter. We were on our way to Venus. That was the important thing.

DREAM

I knew I was dreaming but somehow it didn't matter. I was a mere child again, a toddler just learning to walk. There was a grown man looming in front of me, holding his arms out and calling to me.

"Come on, Van. You can do it. Walk to me."

In my dream, I couldn't make out his face. His voice sounded kind, friendly, but his face was somehow hidden from me.

"Come on, Van. Take a step. Come on."

It was enormously difficult. Much easier to hang on to whatever piece of furniture my chubby little fingers were clutching. Or just plop down and crawl on all fours. But his voice beckoned to me, half encouraging, half pleading, and I eventually let go.

I took a teetering step, then another.

"Good boy! Good boy, Van."

I saw his face. It was my brother Alex. He was only a child himself, nine or ten years old. But he was helping me, encouraging me. I tried to reach him. Step by labored, dangerous step I tried to get to his welcoming arms.

Instead, my legs buckled and I plopped onto the floor.

"You're hopeless, Runt. Absolutely hopeless." Suddenly it was my father towering over me, a disgusted look on his face.

"The ancient Greeks would have left you on a mountaintop to feed the wolves and crows."

Alex was no longer there. He was dead, I remembered. I sat there on the floor and blubbered like a baby.

IN TRANSIT

I had met the crew several times before we left Earth, of course. The crew of my ship *Hesperos,* I mean. *Truax* had its own crew—an even dozen of grizzled, experienced men and women— but I had practically nothing to do with them. Captain Duchamp handled that part of the mission. It was my crew, the crew of *Hesperos,* that I cared about.

In addition to Duchamp and Rodriguez there were only four others: three technicians, for communications, life support, and sensor systems, and the physician. The comm and sensor techs were women about my own age, rather nondescript techies who talked in jargon and kept pretty much to themselves. Same for the life support guy, except he was chubby and rather surly—the kind who always gave the impression that the least little technical problem was the end of the world.

They had to be good, though. They had been okayed by both Rodriguez and Duchamp. Naturally, all our systems were actually run by the ship's mainframe; the human techs were needed for repairs and maintenance work, mostly. For a while I had thought about using robots instead, but Rodriguez convinced me that the humans were more versatile and handier. And cheaper, too.

The one crew member I dealt with on an almost daily basis was the physician, Dr. Waller. He kept tabs on my anemia and made certain that I was in good general health. He was quite a bit older, about Duchamp's age, and claimed he had never used any rejuvenation therapy for himself. Yet he looked suspiciously young to me; the only sign of his age was his thinning hair, which he kept pulled back into a short ponytail. He was black—from Jamaica—and for some reason I usually found it hard to judge the age of black people. He always looked solemn, even grave. His eyes always seemed to be bloodshot.

"There's really not much for you to do around here, is there?" I asked him once, while he was running me through the diagnostic scanner.

His red-rimmed eyes focused on the readouts, Dr. Waller answered, "Be glad of that, Mr. Humphries."

Even though his face was somber, he constantly hummed to himself, so low I could barely hear it, a tuneless background buzzing. His voice had a sort of singing lilt to it. If I kept my eyes closed I could imagine him smiling happily instead of the dour somber face he actually wore.

"You can put your shirt on," he said as the scanner yoke lifted up and slid back into its niche in the infirmary bulkhead.

"Will I live, Doctor?" I kidded.

He nodded briefly, but said, "Your triglyceride count is rising. Too many sweets. Must I put a block on the dispensing machines?"

I laughed. "I'm the owner of this vessel, remember? I could remove any block that you code into the galley's computer."

"Then we shall have to rely on your good sense. You need more exercise and less fatty foods."

I nodded. "Right."

"Otherwise you are in excellent condition."

As I sealed the Velcro front of my shirt I asked, "With everyone in good health and no accidents to deal with, how do you fill in your time?"

His normally solemn expression brightened a little. "I am writing my Ph.D. thesis. I took this position so that I would have the time to write it. And no distractions! No interruptions. No excuses to put it off."

"What's the subject of your thesis?"

"The underlying similarities among the organisms of Mars, the Jovian moons, and Earth."

"Well," I said, "maybe we'll find some organisms on Venus to broaden your scope."

Dr. Waller actually smiled, a bright flashing smile full of white teeth. "I hardly think so, Mr. Humphries. I chose this mission specifically because I do not expect any new data to come up and cause me added complications."

During the first week of our flight I met Marguerite Duchamp exactly twice. The first time was shortly after we broke Earth orbit.

Once we were safely through the keyhole and on the proper trajectory toward Venus, Captain Duchamp left Rodriguez in charge of the bridge and asked me to come with her to the captain's cabin, as she called it. It was a compartment off the bridge, only a few paces along the passageway from my own quarters.

"I want you to meet the expedition's biologist," she said over her shoulder as she slid open the compartment door.

"Your daughter," I said as I entered the cubicle.

It was quite a small compartment, barely room enough for a bunk and a foldout table. She was at the bunk, taking clothes out of a travel bag that lay open atop it. She did not turn around when she heard the door open.

"Marguerite, I want you to meet the owner of this vessel."

She turned, looking slightly surprised. I suppose I looked surprised, too. Stunned, actually. Marguerite was a duplicate of her mother. Younger, of course, not so taut or intimidating, yet so physically alike that I thought she must be a clone. The same tall, slim figure. The same sculptured cheekbones and strong jaw. The same jet-black eyes and raven hair.

Yet where her mother was demanding and dominating, the daughter seemed troubled, uncertain of herself. The mother wore her shoulder-length hair severely pulled back; the daughter's flowed softly, and was considerably longer.

"This is Mr. Van Humphries," Duchamp said. Then, to me, "My daughter, Marguerite."

"Martin's son," she murmured, taking a step toward me. Out of the corner of my eye I saw her mother bristle.

I extended my hand. "Pleased to meet you, Ms. Duchamp."

She touched my hand briefly. Her fingers felt warm, pulsing.

"Marguerite has a doctorate in biology from Oxford," Duchamp said, flatly, as if it were a challenge, not a trace of parental pride in her voice.

Then she added, "I thought you two should meet."

"I'm happy to make your acquaintance," I said to Marguerite. Glancing at her mother, I added, "although I'm afraid there won't be much for you to do on this mission."

She did not smile back. Very seriously, she said, "Perhaps I can help with some of the other scientific observations, then." Her voice was low, soft, resigned.

The cabin seemed cold enough to start a glacier.

"We'll find something useful for you to do, don't worry," Captain Duchamp said.

"Yes, Mother. I'm sure you will."

I decided it was time to get out of there. The bitterness between mother and daughter was thick enough to cut with a chain saw.

Dr. Waller said I should exercise, so I started jogging through the warren of passageways and cargo bays of *Truax*. The old factory ship's major cargo hold, which once carried huge tonnages of asteroidal ores, was like a vast cave made of metal. Our expedition's crated supplies hardly filled one corner of it. The outgoing crew had worked hard to clean up the holds for us; they had even opened the bays to the vacuum of space for several days on end. Still the metal bulkheads were dingy with dust. I could feel it crunching on the soles of my running shoes. When I ran a hand along a bulkhead the metal felt gritty; my fingers came away stained with dust.

It made me grin, though. I was touching the dust of other worlds. Instead of sitting at home and staring at virtual reality simulations I was actually out here, touching other worlds, planetoids that had floated in the silent emptiness of space for billions of years, since the time when the solar system had been created.

Then I discovered the bay that held the old smelter, silent and unused now. Yet I could sense the heat of the big nuclear-powered ovens as they melted down the ores in the first step of the refining process. Pulverized chunks of asteroidal rock were ruthlessly liquefied here, all their minor elements driven out to be collected by the mass separators, purified into the metals and minerals that were building the human race's expanding civilization.

For the first time I got an inkling of what my father's corporations actually did. They were converting ancient leftovers from the creation of the solar system into habitats and factories and spacecraft for the men and women who were living and working in space, on the Moon and Mars, in the armored modules floating on the ice of Jupiter's major moons.

From the catwalk high above the smelter I drank in the heat that seemed to still hang in the air like a living presence. I could hear in my mind the growling roar of the rock crushers, the shuddering rumble of the conveyor belts that carried the pulverized ore into the white-hot fury of the smelter. When I closed my eyes I could see the glowing streams of man-made lava flowing into the separators in the next huge bay.

All silent now, except for the soft echo of my running shoes padding against the metal grillwork of the catwalk. All stilled, unused, because I had decided in a reckless, angry moment to take up my father's challenge.

As he knew I would! That understanding came to me as I jogged along the catwalk, hit me so hard I stopped and gripped the handrail, feeling almost dizzy. He maneuvered me into this! He knew I'd take up his challenge. Or did he merely hope that I would? Either way, I rose to his bait and snapped at it.

Why did he do it? Why did he set all that up, the party, the announcement, the prize? Just to get me off my butt and send me to Venus? To get me out of his way? To kill me, the same way Alex was killed?

Why?

COMPETITION

was walking along the passageway toward my stateroom, cooling down from my run, sweaty and smelly in my running suit, when I saw Marguerite Duchamp coming up the passageway from the other direction.

I had seen her exactly once since her mother performed that awkward, anger-edged introduction on the day we left Earth orbit. Marguerite had kept pretty much to her quarters and—to tell the truth—I kept pretty much to mine, except for my daily exercise runs. Come to think of it, she might have been poking around the big old ship or working on the bridge as much as her mother and I wouldn't have known it.

I couldn't get over how much she resembled her mother, like a younger twin or clone. The same dark hair and eyes, the same slim supple figure. She was slightly taller than me, but then almost everybody was slightly taller than me. Father called me Runt because I am small, there's no getting away from that fact.

She was wearing standard dun-colored coveralls, with

flat-heeled shipboard slippers. No matter how much she looked like her mother, though, Marguerite was obviously younger, fresher, without her mother's brittle armor of haughtiness, more—approachable.

I saw that she had sewn a bright green armband on the left sleeve of her coveralls. And as she approached me, I noticed that her thick dark hair was tied back with a green ribbon that matched the armband.

"You're one of them?" I blurted.

Her onyx eyes flashed at me. "Them?" she asked.

"The Greens."

She seemed to visibly relax. "Of course," she answered casually. "Isn't everybody?"

"I'm not." I reversed my course and fell into step beside her.

"Why aren't you?" she asked, apparently not noticing that I was sweaty and smelly and must have looked a mess.

Her question puzzled me for a moment. "I guess I've never paid that much attention to politics."

Marguerite shrugged. "With your money, I suppose you don't have to."

"My father's very involved," I said. It came out sounding defensive.

"I'm sure he is," she said scornfully. "But he's not a Green, is he?"

"No," I admitted with a little laugh. "Definitely not a Green."

She was headed for the galley, and I went along with her, smelly running suit and all.

"How well do you know my father?" I asked, realizing as the words came out of my mouth that I was being just about as tactless as a class-A boor.

She cast me a sidelong glance as we walked along the passageway. "I only met him once. With my mother."

"Only once?"

"That was enough. More than enough."

The way she said it made me wonder what had hap-

pened. Father can be quite suave and winning when he
wants to be. He can also be demanding and vicious. From
the ferocity of her mother's reaction, Father must have hit
on Marguerite very blatantly.

Although it had been refurbished along with the rest of
the ship, *Truax*'s galley looked scuffed and hard-used. No
amount of spit and polish could make the dispensers'
dulled, worn metal surfaces gleam like new again. Marguerite helped herself to a tall mug of fruit juice. No one
was sitting at the tables, so I poured a chilled mug of the
same for myself and went over to sit beside her. She didn't
seem to mind the company. And what if she does, I told
myself. I'm the owner of this vessel. This is *my* ship. I'll sit
where I damned well want to. But I was glad she didn't get
up and move away.

"So, what do people call you? Marjorie?"

"Marguerite," she said stiffly.

"Marguerite? Nothing else?"

"That's the name my mother gave me."

I suppose she realized she was being curt, almost rude.
Softening a little, she said, "I can't abide being called Marjorie or Margie. And Maggie . . ." She shuddered with dis-
taste.

I had to laugh. "All right. Marguerite, then. I'm Van."

We talked, mainly about politics. No further mention of
my father. Marguerite was an ardent, dedicated Green,
devoted to the ideals of stopping the Earth's warming by
drastically changing society. Solar energy instead of fossil
or nuclear fuels. Taxation to redistribute wealth and shrink
the gap between rich and poor. Stronger international controls on trade and information commerce.

I tried to make her see that nuclear power would help to
wean the world off fossil fuels much better than solar energy possibly could.

"Especially with helium-three for fusion generators," I
told her, with growing enthusiasm. "We could triple the
world's installed electrical power capacity and cut greenhouse emissions by seventy percent or more."

She frowned slightly. "Your father has a monopoly on helium-three, doesn't he?"

"His corporation owns a large chunk of the helium-mining operations on the Moon. I wouldn't say he has a monopoly. Besides—"

"And he controls the lunar raw materials that are needed to build solar power satellites, doesn't he?"

"He doesn't *control* them. There's also Masterson Corporation. And Astro Manufacturing."

Marguerite shook her head. "Mr. Humphries, your father is one of our most implacable enemies."

"Yes, I know. And my name is Van."

She nodded and we continued talking. I forgot about my enzyme shot, forgot about Marguerite's hard-driving mother and Rodriguez and the rest of the crew. I even forgot about Gwyneth, living in my apartment in Barcelona. I was enjoying talking with Marguerite. As we chatted on I commented on how strikingly she resembled her mother.

"Why not?" she asked, very seriously. "I'm a duplicate."

"A clone?"

With a brief dip of her chin, Marguerite said, "Mother's always said she's never met a man she'd trust to father a child with her. So she cloned herself and had the embryo implanted in herself. Eight and a half months later I was born."

I shouldn't have felt as staggered as I did. Duplicates were nothing new; people had been cloning themselves here and there for years. The procedure was outlawed in many nations and moralists railed against the supposed inhumanity of it. But here was a perfectly lovely, lively young woman who happened to be a clone of her mother.

"When did all that happen?" I asked.

Her eyes widened for a flash of a second and I felt suddenly embarrassed.

But Marguerite just laughed. "I haven't needed any rejuvenation treatments yet."

"I mean . . . I suppose I was really wondering about your mother's age. My father's past a hundred, and . . ."

I cursed myself for a fool even while my mouth blabbered on. I could easily look up their ages in the mission's dossiers.

Marguerite let it pass and our conversation drifted on, relaxed and friendly. Until we began to talk about the mission.

"Don't you think it's strange," Marguerite asked, "that no human expedition was sent to Venus until your brother went?"

"The unmanned probes scoped out the planet pretty well. There's been no need for human missions."

"Really?" Her brows hiked up. "I thought you were a planetary scientist. Aren't you curious about this planet?"

"Of course I am. I'll be running a series of seismic probes for Professor Greenbaum, you know."

"No, I didn't know."

"He has a theory about the planet's surface overturning," I explained. "He thinks the surface will get so hot it'll begin to melt."

"Fascinating," Marguerite murmured.

I waved a hand in the air. "It's not a very attractive planet."

"Attractive?" she snapped. "Are we talking about exploring a world or starting a resort hotel?"

"I mean, it's a hellhole. Hot enough to melt aluminum and all that."

"But that's just what makes it so interesting! A planet almost the same size and mass as Earth and yet with a totally different global environment. A runaway greenhouse effect. Where Earth's atmosphere cycles carbon dioxide, Venus cycles sulfur compounds. It's fascinating."

"It's a desert world," I said. "Utterly lifeless. There's nothing for a biologist to study."

"Are you certain it's dead?"

"No water," I pointed out. "Unbreathable atmosphere. It's hot and dead and dangerous."

"On the surface, I grant you. But what about up in the clouds? The temperatures are cooler there. And there's *something* in those clouds that absorbs ultraviolet energy, much the way chlorophyllic plants absorb infrared."

"None of the probes ever found living organisms or even organic material. Nothing could live in temperatures more than twice as hot as boiling water."

"Absence of proof," she said loftily, "is not proof of absence."

"Venus is dead," I insisted.

"Is it? What about all that sulfur in the atmosphere? Sulfur's an important component in the Jovian biochemistry, isn't it?" she demanded.

"Well, perhaps so . . ."

"And sulfur metabolism was present in Earth's earliest organisms. It's present today, in the hydrothermal vents at the bottom of the oceans."

"Nonsense!" I spluttered. Why is it that when you don't have any facts on your side you tend to talk louder and solidify your position into concrete?

Quite seriously, Marguerite asked, "Why do you suppose that there were more than a dozen missions to Venus before the year 2020, but since then, hardly any?"

I hadn't the foggiest notion, but I said, "The earlier probes told us what we needed to know. Oh, I admit there're lots of unknowns remaining, but the planet's so terribly uninviting that no one even thought about sending out a human team."

"Until your brother went."

"Yes," I said, my insides suddenly clenching. "Alex went."

"We have permanent research stations on Mars and the Jupiter system," she went on, relentless, "and mining operations in the Asteroid Belt. Yet nothing for Venus. Not even an orbiting observatory."

"The scientific community lost interest in Venus," I said. "It happens. With so much else to study—"

"The scientific community lost *funding* for Venus," Marguerite said firmly. "Funding that comes mainly from wealthy patrons of universities, such as your father."

"He paid for my brother's expedition," I said.

"No, he didn't. Your brother paid for his expedition out of his own funds."

I blinked with surprise. I hadn't known that. I had just assumed . . .

"And your brother died on Venus."

"Yes," I said, my guts churning. "That's right."

"Do you think the rumors are true: that your brother's craft was sabotaged?"

"I don't know." I felt perspiration beading on my brow and my upper lip. I was annoyed, irritated at the turn our conversation had taken.

"They say your father didn't want his mission to succeed. They say your brother and he had a terrible argument about it."

"I don't know," I repeated. "I wasn't there."

"Didn't your brother tell you about it?"

"Obviously not!" I snapped. I realized that, except for that last night in Connecticut, Alex had told me very little about his plans, his hopes, his fears. He'd been almost a stranger to me. My own brother. We might just as well have been born into two different families.

Silence stretched between us uncomfortably.

Then it was broken by the comm screen on the galley's bulkhead. It glowed orange and the communications computer's voice said, "Incoming message for Mr. Humphries."

"Display," I called out, glad for the interruption.

Until I saw that it was my father's face on the screen, larger than life. He was scowling with displeasure.

"I've just found out where Fuchs is," he said without preamble. "He's registered his ship and planned trajectory with the IAA, at last. He's heading for Venus, all right. The sonofabitch is on a high-gee burn that will put him in orbit around Venus days before you get there."

TRANSFER

took one last look at my stateroom. When we had boarded *Truax* the single room had seemed rather cramped and decidedly shabby to me. Over the nine weeks of our flight to Venus, though, I'd grown accustomed to having my office and living quarters all contained within the same four walls—or bulkheads, as they're called aboard ship. At least the smart wall screens had made the compartment seem larger than it actually was. I could program gloriously wide vistas, videos of almost any spot on Earth. I usually settled for the view of the Mediterranean from my hilltop home in Majorca.

Now we were ready to transfer to the much smaller *Hesperos*. At least, the crew was. I dreaded the move. If *Truax* was like a tatty old freighter, *Hesperos* would be more like a cramped, claustrophobic submarine.

To make matters worse, in order to get to the dirigible-like *Hesperos* we were going to have to perform a space walk. I was actually going to have to seal myself into a spacesuit and go outside into that yawning vacuum and trolley down the cable that linked the two vessels, with nothing between me and instant death but the monomolecular layers of my suit. I could already feel my insides fluttering with near panic.

For about the twelve thousandth time I told myself I should have insisted on a tugboat. Rodriguez had talked me out of it when we'd first started planning the mission. "A pressurized tug, just so we can make the transfer without getting into our suits?" he had jeered at me. "That's an expense we can do without. It's a waste of money."

"It would be much safer, wouldn't it?" I had persisted.

He looked disgusted. "You want safety? Use the mass and volume we'd need for the tug to carry extra water. That'll give us an edge in case the recycler breaks down."

"We have a backup recycler."

"Water's more important than a tug that we'll only use for five minutes during the whole mission. That's one piece of equipment that we definitely don't need to carry along."

So I had let Rodriguez talk me out of the tug. Now I was going to have to perform an EVA, a space walk, something that definitely gave me the shakes.

My jitters got even worse whenever I thought about Lars Fuchs.

Once my father told me that Fuchs actually was racing for the prize money, I spent long hours digging for every byte of information I could glean about him. What I found was hardly encouraging. Fuchs had a reputation for ruthlessness and achievement. According to the media biographies, he was a merciless taskmaster, a driven and hard-driving tyrant who ran roughshod over anyone who stood in his way. Except my father.

The media had barely covered Fuchs's launch into a high-velocity transit to Venus. He had built his ship in secrecy out in the Belt—adapted an existing vessel, apparently, to his needs. Unlike all the hoopla surrounding my own launch from Tarawa, there was only one brief interview with Fuchs on the nets, grainy and stiff because of the

hourlong delay between the team of questioners on Earth
and Fuchs, out there among the asteroids.

I pored over that single interview, studying the face of
my adversary on my stateroom wall screen, in part to get
my mind off the impending space walk. Fuchs was a thick-
set man, probably not much taller than I, but with a barrel
chest and powerful-looking shoulders beneath his deep
blue jacket. His face was broad, jowly, his mouth a downcast slash that seemed always to be sneering. His eyes were
small and set so deep in their sockets that I couldn't make
out what color they might be.

He made a grisly imitation of a smile to the interviewers'
opening question and replied, "Yes, I am going to Venus. It
seems only fair that I should take this very generous prize
money from Martin Humphries—the man who destroyed
my business and took my wife from me, more than thirty
years ago."

That brought a barrage of questions from the reporters. I
froze the image and delved into the hypertext records.

Fuchs had an impressive background. He had been born
poor, but built a sizable fortune for himself out in the Asteroid Belt, as a prospector. Then he started his own asteroidal
mining company and became one of the major operators in
the Belt, until Humphries Space Systems undercut his
prices so severely that Fuchs was forced into bankruptcy.
HSS then bought out the company for a fraction of its true
worth. My father had personally taken control and fired
Fuchs from the firm that the man had founded and developed over two decades.

While Fuchs stayed out in the Asteroid Belt, penniless
and furious with helpless rage, his wife left him and married Martin Humphries. She became my father's fourth and
last wife.

I gasped with sudden understanding. She was my mother! The mother I had never known. The mother who had
died giving birth to me six years afterward. The mother
whose drug addiction had saddled me with chronic anemia
from birth. I stared at her image on the screen: young, with

the flaxen hair and pale blue eyes of the icy northlands. She was very beautiful, yet she looked fragile, delicate, like a flower that blooms on a glacier for only a day and then withers.

It took an effort to erase her image and go back to the news file. Fuchs had taken off for Venus in a specially modified ship he had named *Lucifer*. The Latin name for Venus as the morning star was Lucifer. It was also the name used by the Hebrew prophet Isaiah as a synonym for Satan.

Lucifer. And Fuchs. After a high-gee flight, he was already in orbit around Venus, more than a week ahead of me. Sitting there in my stateroom, staring at Fuchs's sardonic, sneering face on the wall screen, I remembered that the time had come to transfer to *Hesperos*. There was no way to get out of it. I still wished I were home and safe, but now I knew that I had to go through with this mission no matter what the dangers.

But my thoughts went back to my mother. I had never known that she was once Fuchs's wife. My father hardly ever spoke of her, except to blame me for her death. Alex had told me that it wasn't my fault, that women didn't die in childbirth unless there was something terribly wrong. It was Alex who told me about her drug dependency; as far as my father was concerned she was faultless.

"She was the only woman I ever really loved," he said, many a time. I almost believed him. Then he would add, cold as liquid helium, "And you killed her, Runt."

A single rap on my door startled me. Before I could respond, Desiree Duchamp slid the door open and gave me a hard stare.

"Are you coming or not?" she demanded.

I drew myself up to my full height—not quite eye to eye with my captain—and forced my voice to be steady and calm as I answered, "Yes. I'm ready."

When she turned and headed down the passageway I squeezed my eyes shut and tried to conjure up a picture of my brother. I'm doing this for you, Alex, I said to myself.

I'm going to find out why you died—and who's responsible for your death.

But as I headed down the passageway after Duchamp, the image in my mind was of my mother, so young and lovely and vulnerable.

We had done simulations of the EVA procedure a dozen times, and I had suited up each time. I thought it was silly, like children playing dress-up, but Duchamp had insisted that we pull on the cumbersome suits and boots and helmets and backpacks even though we were only going to play-act in the ship's virtual reality chamber.

Now the crew was gathered at the main airlock, busily getting into their spacesuits. It looked to me like some athletic team's locker room, or a changing booth in a beachside cabana. I paid intense attention to every detail of the procedure, though. This time it would be for real. A mistake here could be fatal. Leggings first, then the thickly lined boots. Slide into the torso and wiggle your arms through the sleeves. Pull the bubble helmet over your head, seal it to the neck ring. Then work the gloves over your fingers. The gloves had a bony exoskeleton on their backs, powered by tiny servomotors that amplified one's muscle power tenfold. There were also servos built into the suit's joints: shoulders, elbows, knees.

Duchamp herself hung the life support rig on my back and connected the air hose and power lines. The backpack felt like a ton weighing on my shoulders.

I heard the suit's air fans whine into life, like distant gnats, and felt cool air flowing softly across my face. The suit was actually roomy inside, although the leggings chafed a little against my thighs.

Marguerite, Rodriguez, and the four other crew members were all fully suited. Even Dr. Waller was frowning slightly with impatience as they waited for me to finish up.

"Sorry I'm so slow," I muttered.

They nodded from inside their fishbowl helmets. Marguerite even managed a little smile.

"All right," Duchamp said at last, once she was convinced my suit was properly sealed. "Radio check." Her voice was muffled slightly by the helmet.

One by one the crew members called to the EVA controller up on the bridge. I heard each of them in my helmet earphones.

"Mr. Humphries?" the controller called.

"I hear you," I said.

"Radio check complete. Captain Duchamp, you and your crew are go for transfer."

With Duchamp directing us, they went through the airlock hatch, starting with Rodriguez. Then the doctor and, one by one, the three technicians. I followed Marguerite. Duchamp grasped my arm as I stepped carefully over the sill of the hatch into the blank metal womb of the airlock.

Once she swung the inner hatch shut I felt as if I were in a bare metal coffin. I started to breathe faster, felt my heart pumping harder. Stop it! I commanded myself. Calm down before you hyperventilate.

But when the outer hatch started to slide open I almost panicked.

There was nothing out there! They expected me to step out into total emptiness. I tried to find some stars in that black infinity, something, anything to reassure me, but through the deep tinting of my helmet I could not see any.

"Hold on." Rodriguez's familiar voice calmed me a little. But only a little. Then I saw the former astronaut—now an astronaut once again—slide into view, framed by the outline of the open hatch.

"Gimme your tether," Rodriguez said, extending a gloved hand toward me. It looked like a robot reaching for me. I couldn't see his face at all. Even though the bubble helmets gave us fine visibility from inside them, their protective sunshield tinting made them look like mirrors from the outside. All I could see in Rodriguez's helmet was the blank fishbowl reflection of my own helmet.

"C'mon, Mr. Humphries. Gimme your tether. I'll attach it to the trolley. Otherwise you'll swing away."

I remembered the drill from the simulations we had gone

through. I unclipped the end of my safety tether from its hook at the waist of my suit and handed it mutely to Rodriguez. He disappeared from my view. There was nothing beyond the airlock hatch that I could see, nothing but a gaping, all-encompassing emptiness.

"Step out now, come on," Rodriguez's voice coaxed in my earphones. "You're okay now. Your tether's connected to the trolley and I'm right here."

His spacesuited form floated into view again, like a pale white ghost hovering before me. Then I saw the others, a scattering of bodies floating in the void, each connected to the trolley by thin tethers that seemed to be stretched to their limit.

"It's really fun," Marguerite's voice called.

We were not in zero gravity. The two spacecraft were still swinging around their common center of gravity, still connected by the Buckyball cable. But there was nothing out there! Nothing but an emptiness that stretched to the ends of the universe.

Shaking inside, my heart thundering so loudly that I knew they could all hear it over my suit radio, I grasped the edge of the outer hatchway in my gloved hands and, closing my eyes, stepped off into infinity.

My stomach dropped away. I felt bile burning up into my throat. My mind raced. He missed me! Rodriguez missed me and I'm falling away from the ship. I'll fall to the Sun or go drifting out and away forever and ever.

Then something tugged at me. Hard. My eyes popped open and I saw that my tether was as taut as a steel rod, holding me securely. But the trolley seemed to me miles away. And I couldn't see any of the others even when I twisted my head to look for them.

"He's secured," Rodriguez's voice said in my earphones.

"Very well," Duchamp replied. "I'm coming out."

I was twisting around, literally at the end of my tether, trying to find the rest of us.

Then the massive bulk of Venus slid into my view. The planet was huge! Its tremendous mass curved gracefully, so bright that it was hard to look at it even through the heavy tinting of my helmet. For a dizzying moment I felt as if its enormous expanse were above me, over my head, and it was going to come down and crush me like a ponderous boulder squashing some insignificant bug.

But only for a moment. The fear passed quickly and I gasped as I stared at the overpowering awesome immensity of the planet. Tears sprang to my eyes, not from its brightness, from its beauty.

I felt someone tugging at my shoulder. "Hey, you okay, boss?" Rodriguez asked.

"Wha . . . yes. Yes, I'm all right."

"Don't freeze up on us now," the astronaut said. "We'll be ready to move soon's Duchamp gets herself connected to the trolley."

I couldn't take my eyes off Venus. She was a brilliant saffron-yellow expanse, glowing like a thing alive. Goddess of beauty, sure enough. At first I thought the cloud deck was as solid and unvarying as a sphere of solid gold. Then I saw that I could make out streamers among the clouds, slightly darker stretches, patches where the amber yellowish clouds billowed up slightly.

I was falling in love with a world.

"I'm secured. Let's get moving." Duchamp's terse order broke my hypnotic staring.

Turning my entire body slightly, I saw the seven other figures bobbing slightly around the trolley, which was nothing more than a motorized framework of metal struts that could crawl along the Buckyball cable.

I looked down the length of the cable toward *Hesperos*, which seemed to be kilometers away. Which it was: three kilometers, to be exact. At that distance the fat dirigible that was our spacecraft looked like a toy model or a holographic image of the real thing. At its nose the broad cone of the heat shield stood in place like a giant parasol, looking faintly ludicrous and totally inadequate to protect the vessel from the burning heat of entry into those thick yellow clouds.

"All right, by the numbers, check in," Duchamp commanded.

Nothing happened. Silence.

"I said, by the numbers." Duchamp repeated, her voice taking on an edge. "Mr. Humphries, as owner of this vessel, you are number one. Or have you forgotten *everything* from the simulation runs?"

I twitched with surprise. "Oh! Yes, of course. Number one, secured." As I said the prescribed words I yanked on my tether to make certain they were true. It held firmly.

Rodriguez answered next, then Marguerite. As the other crew members checked in I thought again of what a farce Marguerite's "official" title of mission scientist was. But I was glad she was with us. I could talk to her. She didn't lord it over me as her mother did; even Rodriguez made it clear, without realizing he was doing it, that he regarded me as little more than a rich kid playing at being a scientist.

"All right, then," Duchamp said. "Captain to *Truax*. We are ready for transfer."

"Copy you ready for transfer, Captain. *Hesperos* main airlock is cycled, outer hatch open and waiting for your arrival."

"Systems check on *Hesperos?*" Duchamp asked.

"All active systems in green except for APU, which is off-line."

The auxiliary power unit was off-line? My ears perked up at that. But neither Duchamp nor any of the others seemed to be worried about it.

"The main airlock is green?" Duchamp asked sharply.

"No, sir," came the immediate reply. "Main airlock is blinking red."

"That's better," she said. The airlock indicator should blink red when its outer hatch is open. I could sense Duchamp's bitter smile at catching the EVA controller in a minor slipup.

"Activate trolley," she commanded.

"Activating."

I felt a very slight tug on my tether, and then all of us

were moving toward the distant *Hesperos,* accelerating now, sliding down the long Buckyball cable like a small school of minnows flashing across a pond. *Hesperos* seemed to be coming up at us awfully fast; I thought we'd crash into her, but I kept silent. Sometimes you'd rather die than make an ass of yourself.

Sure enough, the trolley smoothly decelerated, slowly coming to a stop as the seven of us swung on our tethers like a trained team of acrobats in a silent ballet until we were facing down toward *Hesperos.* I marveled that we went through the maneuver without bumping one another, but Rodriguez later told me it was simple Newtonian mechanics at work. My respects to Sir Isaac.

The trolley stopped about ten meters from the open air-lock hatch, with us hanging by our tethers with our boots a mere meter or so from *Hesperos's* hull. As we had done in the virtual reality simulations, Duchamp unhooked her tether and dropped to the hatch, her knees bending as her boots hit the hull soundlessly.

She stepped into the airlock, disappearing into its shadowed depths for a moment. Then her bubble helmet and shoulders emerged from the hatch and she beckoned to me.

"Welcome aboard, Mr. Humphries," she said. "As owner, you should be the first to board *Hesperos.* After me, of course."

VENUS ORBIT

I've tried to contact him a dozen times, Mr. Humphries," said the communications technician. "He simply doesn't answer."

It was the longest sentence the comm tech had spoken to me since I'd first met her. Her name was Riza Kolodny. She was a plain-looking young woman with a round face and mousey brown hair that she kept short, in the chopped-up look that had been fashionable a couple of years earlier. Like the other two technicians, she was a graduate student picked by Rodriguez and okayed by Duchamp. According to her dossier she was a first-rate electronics specialist. She certainly did not look first rate in any way, not to me.

I was bending over her shoulder, staring at the hash-streaked communications screen. Riza was chewing something that smelled vaguely of cinnamon, or perhaps it was clove. She seemed apprehensive, perhaps afraid that she was displeasing me.

"I've tried all the comm freaks," she said, lapsing into jargon in her nervousness, "starting with the frequency

Captain Fuchs registered with the IAA. He just doesn't answer."

Hesperos was not built for creature comforts. The tubular gondola that hung beneath the vessel's bulbous gas envelope housed a spare and spartan set of compartments that included the bridge, galley, a single lavatory for all eight of us, work spaces, infirmary, supply lockers, and our so-called living quarters—which were nothing more than slim, coffin-sized berths partitioned off for a modicum of privacy. There was no room aboard *Hesperos* for anything but utilitarian efficiency. We all felt crowded, cramped. I had to fight off incipient claustrophobia whenever I slid into my berth; I felt like Dracula coming home for a good day's sleep.

The bridge was especially cramped. The comm center was nothing more than a console shoehorned in a bare few centimeters from the captain's command chair. I had to twist myself into a pretzel shape to get close enough to Riza's chair to see her screen. I could feel Duchamp's breath on the back of my neck; she was ignoring me, her dark eyes intently focused on the EVA displayed on the main screen before her. Rodriguez and the two other techs were outside in their spacesuits, clambering over the heat shield, checking every square centimeter of it.

"Maybe Fuchs's ship has broken down," I thought aloud. Wishful thinking, actually. "Maybe he's in trouble."

Riza shook her head, fluttering her butchered hairdo. "*Lucifer* is telemetering its systems status back to IAA headquarters on the regular data channel, same as we are. The ship's still in orbit with all systems functional."

"Then why doesn't he answer our call?" I wondered.

"He doesn't want to," said Duchamp.

I turned to face her, not exactly an easy thing to do in the jammed confines of the bridge.

"Why not?"

She gave me a frosty smile. "Ask him."

I glared at her. She was making a joke of my effort to contact Lars Fuchs. There were only the three of us on the bridge; Rodriguez's chair was empty.

"I could relay our call through IAA headquarters," Riza suggested. "He might reply to us if the request came through them."

"He won't," Duchamp said flatly. "I know Fuchs. He's not talking to us because he doesn't want to. And that's that."

Reluctantly, I accepted her assessment of the situation. Fuchs was going to remain silent. The only way we would learn of what he was doing would be to access whatever data he was sending back to the International Astronautical Authority in Geneva.

"Very well," I said, squeezing between Duchamp and the display screen she was watching. "I'm going to the observation port to do my news broadcast."

"Stay clear of the airlock," Duchamp warned. "Tommy and the others will be coming back in less than ten minutes."

"Right," I said as I ducked through the hatch. The main passageway ran the length of the gondola; it was so narrow that Rodriguez joked that a man could fall in love squeezing past someone there.

Before we left Earth the question of news coverage had come up. Should we bring a reporter along with us? Back when I thought I'd be bringing some of my friends along on the journey, I had been all in favor of the idea. I thought the nets would *love* to send a reporter to Venus, and I had several friends who could have qualified for the role. For a while I even considered asking Gwyneth to be our reporter/historian.

Live broadcasts from the mission couldn't fail to get top ratings, I figured. Unfortunately, the net executives saw it differently. They pointed out to me that newscasts from *Hesperos* would be interesting the first day or two, but they'd quickly become boring on the long voyage out to Venus. They admitted that once we got there, live reports from Venus would be a sensational story—again, for a day or two. But afterward the story would lose its glamour and become nothing but colorless, tedious routine.

"It's science stuff," one of the junior executives—a sometime friend of mine, in fact—told me. "Science stuff is boring."

They certainly were not willing to pay a reporter's expenses and insurance. It was Duchamp who suggested that I serve as the expedition's reporter, the face and voice of the *Hesperos*'s mission. "Who better?" she asked rhetorically. I liked the idea. It eliminated the need to carry an extra person along with us. I would file a personal report on the expedition's progress every day. I would become a household figure all around the Earth/Moon system. I really thought that would be terrific. Even if the nets wouldn't feature my broadcasts every day, people could access them whenever they wanted. I often wondered, as I went through my daily report, if my father ever watched me.

Duchamp was no fool. Removing the need to bring a reporter with us, she also removed any possible objections I could raise about her replacing our astronomer with a biologist. Her daughter. Fait accompli. She had manipulated me beautifully and I hardly even minded it, although we both knew we didn't need a biologist aboard. Duchamp did it for personal reasons.

Yet I didn't mind. I was actually pleased that Marguerite was with us. Except for my daily news report I had no real duties aboard *Hesperos*. Time hung heavily as we coasted out to Venus and then established orbit around the planet. Marguerite had little to do, also, as far as ship's duties were concerned, although she usually seemed busy enough when I went looking for her.

Often she was in the little cubbyhole that had been converted into her laboratory. After leaving the bridge and heading for the observation port in the nose of the gondola, I naturally passed by her lab. It was smaller than a phone booth, of course.

The accordion-fold door was slid back, so I stopped and asked her, "Are you busy?"

"Yes," said Marguerite. It was a silly question. She was

pecking at the keyboard of a laptop, one of several she had propped along the compartment's chest-high shelf. There was no room in her lab for a chair or even a stool; Marguerite worked standing up.

"Oh. I was on my way to do my news report and I thought I'd stop in the galley for a few minutes . . ." My voice trailed off; she was paying no attention to me, tapping at the keyboard of one laptop with a finger while she clicked away on a remote controller with her other hand, changing the images on one of her other screens. The images looked like photomicrographs of bacteria or something equally distasteful. Either that or really bad primitive art.

I shrugged, conceding defeat, and continued down the narrow passageway to the galley. It was nothing more than a set of food freezers and microwave ovens lining one side of the passageway, with a single stark bench on the other side, where one of the gondola's oblong windows showed the massive, curving bulk of the planet below, gleaming like a gigantic golden lamp.

I slumped down on the bench and gazed out at Venus's yellowish clouds. They shifted and changed as I watched. It was almost like staring into a fire, endlessly fascinating, hypnotic. The clouds' hue seemed to be slightly different from one orbit to another. At the moment they looked almost sickly, bilious. Maybe it's just me, I reasoned. I felt like that, sad and sick and alone.

"Mind if I join you?"

I looked up and there was Marguerite standing over me. I shot to my feet.

"Pull up a section of bench," I said brightly.

She sat next to me and I caught a scent of perfume, very delicate, but a wonderful contrast to the metallic starkness of the ship.

"I'm sorry I was short with you back there," she said. "I was running the latest UV scans of the atmosphere. Sometimes it gets pretty intense."

"Oh, sure. I understand."

Marguerite was still wrapped up in her work. "*Something* down in those clouds absorbs ultraviolet light," she said.

"You think its biological? A life-form in the clouds?"

She started to nod, then thought better of it. As if she were a long-experienced scientist, she buried her enthusiasm and answered noncommittally, "I don't know. Perhaps. We won't know for certain until we get down into the clouds and take samples."

Without thinking I argued, "What about all the sampling the unmanned probes did, years ago? They didn't find any evidence of living organisms."

Suddenly Marguerite's dark eyes snapped with annoyance. "They weren't equipped to. They all carried nephelometers to measure droplet size, but not one of them carried a single instrument that could have detected any biological activity. A Shetland pony could've flown by and those dumb-ass robots would never have noticed."

"There weren't any biological sensors on any of the probes?"

"Not one," she said. "Venus is a dead planet. That's the official word."

"But you don't believe it."

"Not yet. Not until I've looked for myself."

I felt a new respect for Marguerite. She could be just as much a tigress as her mother in matters that she cared about.

"How much longer will we stay in orbit?" she asked.

I hunched my shoulders. "We're scanning the equatorial region with radar, looking for any sign of the wreckage of my brother's ship."

"Wouldn't it be all smashed into small pieces?"

"Probably not," I answered. "The atmosphere's so thick that his ship would've gone to the bottom like a ship sinking in the ocean, back home. I mean, the pressure down at the surface is like our oceans, a kilometer or more below sea level."

She thought about that for a moment. "So it wouldn't be like a plane falling out of the sky on Earth."

"Or like a missile hitting the ground. No. More like the *Titanic* settling on the bottom of the Atlantic."

"You haven't found anything yet?"

"Not yet," I admitted. *Hesperos* was in a two-hour equatorial orbit; we had circled the planet thirty times, so far.

"How much of a chance is there that you'll spot something?"

"Well, we know where he first entered the atmosphere, the latitude and longitude. But we can only guess where he might have drifted while he was in the clouds."

"He didn't have a tracking beacon?"

"Its signal broke up a lot once he went into the cloud deck, so we've got to scan a pretty wide swath along the equator."

Marguerite looked past me, out at the clouds swirling across the face of Venus. She stared at them as if she could get them to part by sheer willpower. I watched the profile of her face. How much she looked like her mother! The same face, yet somehow softer, kinder. It made me think about how little I looked like my father. Alex resembled Father. People had often exclaimed that Alex looked like a younger replica of Martin Humphries. But I resembled my mother, they said. The mother I never knew.

Marguerite turned back to me. "Are you really a planetary scientist?"

The question surprised me. "I try to be," I said.

"Then why aren't you working at it? There's your planet, right out there, and yet you spend your time wandering around the ship like a little lost boy."

"I've got a complete set of instruments taking data," I said. It sounded weak and defensive, even to me.

"But you're not doing anything with the data. You're not analyzing it or using it to change the sensors' operating parameters. You're just letting everything chug along on their preset programs."

"The data goes back to Professor Cochrane at Caltech. If

she wants the instruments changed, she tells me and I make the changes."

"Like a graduate student," Marguerite said. "A trained chimpanzee."

That stung. "Well . . . I've got other things to do, you know."

"Like what?"

"I send in my news reports every day."

Her lips pulled down disapprovingly. "That must take all of ten minutes."

Strangely, I felt laughter bubbling up in me. I normally don't take kindly to criticism, but Marguerite had hit me fairly and squarely.

"Oh no," I answered her, chuckling. "It takes more like half an hour."

Her expression softened, but only a little. "Well, then, let's see. I'll give you eight hours for sleeping and an hour and a half for meals . . . that leaves fourteen empty hours every day! If I had fourteen hours on my hands I'd build a whole new set of biosensors for when we dip into the clouds."

"I could help you," I said.

She pretended to consider the offer. "Uh-huh. Do you have any background in cellular biology?"

"I'm afraid not."

"Spectroscopy? Can you take apart one of the mass spectrometers and realign it to be sensitive to organic molecules?"

I must have been grinning like a fool. "Um, do you have a manual for that? I can follow instruction manuals pretty well."

She was smiling now, too. "I think you'd better stick to your own specialty."

"Planetary physics."

"Yes. But get active about it! There's more to science than watching the readouts of your instruments."

"I suppose so. But so far the sensors aren't showing anything that the old probes didn't get years ago."

"Are you certain? Have you gone through the data thoroughly? You mean to tell me there's *nothing* different? No anomalies, no unexplained blips in the incoming data?"

Before I could think of an answer, Duchamp's voice came through the intercom speaker built into the overhead. "Mr. Humphries, radar scan has picked up a glint that might be wreckage. Could you come to the bridge, please?"

RECONNAISSANCE

Rodriguez was back on the bridge when we got there, and with all three chairs occupied, the bridge was simply too small for both me and Marguerite to squeeze in. I ducked halfway through the hatch and stopped there. Marguerite stayed behind me, in the passageway, and looked in over my shoulder.

The bridge felt hot, stuffy. Too much equipment jammed in there, humming away. And too many bodies radiating heat. The air seemed soggy, murky, and yet at that moment it fairly seethed with suppressed turbulence.

The main screen, in front of Duchamp's command chair, showed a frozen radar image: dark shadows and jumbled shapes of landforms with a single bright glint at its center. Rodriguez was leaning forward in his chair, studying the image, perspiration beading his brow.

"That could be it," he said, pointing to me. "It's definitely metal; the computer analysis leaves no doubt."

I stared hard at the blob of light. "Can we get better resolution? You can't tell what it is from this image."

Before Riza could reply from the comm console, Duchamp snapped, "We've magnified it as much as we can. That's the best we can get."

Rodriguez said, "It's within the footprint that your brother's craft would be expected to have, knowing what we know about when and where he went down. Nothing else metallic has shown up in the region."

"We'll have to go lower for better resolution," Duchamp said. "Get under the cloud deck and use optical sensors."

"Telescopes," I muttered.

"Yes."

"What region is that?" Marguerite asked, from behind me.

"Aphrodite," said her mother.

"It's a highland region, more than two kilometers higher than the surrounding plains," Rodriguez said.

"Then it must be cooler," I said.

Duchamp smiled humorlessly. "Cooler, yes. The ground temperature is down to a pleasant four hundred degrees Celsius."

The lowland surface temperature averages above four hundred fifty degrees, I knew.

"Are we set for atmosphere entry?" I asked.

"The heat shield's been checked out," Duchamp replied. "Propulsion is ready."

"And still no word from Fuchs?"

Riza answered from the comm console, "He entered the cloud deck two hours ago, halfway around the planet. I got his entry position from the IAA."

"Then he hasn't seen the wreckage?"

Duchamp shook her head. "If we've seen that glint, he has, too."

"The plane of his entry was almost exactly equatorial," Riza said, almost apologetically. "He'll most likely come out of the clouds in the same region as the glint."

I felt a dull throb in my jaw and realized that my teeth were clenched tight. "Very well then," I said. "We'd better get under the clouds, too."

Duchamp nodded, then touched a stud on her chair's left armrest. "Captain to crew: take your entry stations. Stand by for atmospheric entry in ten minutes." She lifted her hand and looked directly at me. "Clear the bridge of all nonessential personnel."

I took her unsubtle hint and backed out into the passageway. Marguerite was already striding away.

"Where are you going?" I called after her.

"To my lab. I want to record the entry."

"The automatic sensors—"

"They're not programmed to look for organic molecules or other exotic species. Besides, I want to get the entry process on video. It'll look good for your news report."

I started to reply, then sensed Rodriguez standing behind me.

"She threw you off the bridge, too?"

He grinned at me. "My entry station is up forward with the life support technician." He squeezed past me and started along the passageway.

The trouble was, I had no official entry station. If we went strictly by the rules I should've slid into my berth and stayed there until we jettisoned the heat shield. But I had no intention of doing that.

"Is there room for a third person up there?" I asked, trailing after Rodriguez.

"If you don't mind the body odors," he said over his shoulder.

"I showered this morning," I said, hurrying to catch up with him.

"Yeah, well, it's gonna get a little warm up there, you know. You'd be more comfortable in your berth."

I lifted my chin a notch. "You don't have to pamper me."

Rodriguez glanced over his shoulder at me. "Okay, you're the boss. You wanta be in the hot seat, come on along."

Striding down the passageway behind him, I asked, "How are you and Duchamp getting along?"

"Fine," he said, without slowing down or looking back toward me. "No problems."

Something in his voice sounded odd to me. "Are you sure?"

"We've worked things out. We're okay."

He sounded strange . . . cheerful, almost. As if he were in on a joke and I wasn't.

We passed Marguerite's tiny lab. The accordion-pleat door was folded open and I could see her standing in the cubicle, her head bent over a palm-sized video camera.

"You'll have to strap down for the entry," Rodriguez told her. "It's gonna get bumpy for a while."

"I'll help her," I said. "You go ahead and I'll catch up with you." Mr. Gallant, that's me.

Rodriguez looked uncertain for a moment, but then he nodded acceptance. "The two of you have got to be belted in for the entry. I don't care where, but you've got to be in safety harnesses. Understood?"

"Understood," I assured him. Duchamp had made us practice the entry procedures at least once a day for the past two weeks.

"ENTRY BEGINS IN EIGHT MINUTES," the countdown computer announced.

Marguerite looked up from her work. "There. The vidcam's ready."

She pushed past me and started down the passageway to the observation blister, the camera in her hand.

"Aren't you going with Tom?" she asked.

"I was," I said, "but if you don't mind I'd rather stay with you."

"I don't mind."

"Rodriguez gave me the feeling I'd just be in his way up there."

"I'm sure he didn't mean it that way."

"I know when I'm being condescended to," I insisted.

"Tom's not like that."

We reached the blister, a metal bubble that extended outward from the gondola's main body. Three small observation ports studded its side, each window made of thick tinted quartz. Four padded swivel chairs were firmly bolted to the deck.

"You won't see much through the tinting," I said.

Marguerite smiled at me, and went to a small panel beneath the port that slanted forward. Opening it, she snapped her camera into the recess. Then she shut the panel again. Three tiny lights winked on: two green, one amber. As I watched, the amber light turned red.

"What's that?" I asked, puzzled. "I thought I knew every square centimeter of this bucket."

"God is in the details," Marguerite said. "I got Tom and my mother to allow me to build this special niche here. It's like an airlock, with an inner hatch and an outer one."

"They allowed you to break the hull's integrity?" I felt shocked.

"It was all done within the standard operating procedures. Tom and Aki both checked it out."

Akira Sakamoto was our life support technician: young, chubby, introspective to the point of surliness, so quiet he was almost invisible aboard the ship.

I was still stunned. "And the camera's exposed to vacuum?"

She nodded, obviously pleased with herself. "The outer hatch opened when the inner one sealed. That's why the third light is red."

"Why didn't anybody tell me about this?" I wasn't angry, really. Just surprised that they'd do this without at least telling me.

"It was in the daily logs. Didn't you see them?" Marguerite turned the nearest swivel chair to face the port and sat in it.

I took the chair next to her. "Who reads the daily reports? They're usually nothing but boring details."

"Tom highlighted it."

"When? When was this done?"

She thought a moment. "The second week out. No, it was the beginning of the third week." With an impatient shake of her head, she said, "Whenever it was, you can look it up in the log if you want the exact date."

I stared at her. She was smiling impishly. She was enjoying this.

"I'll fry Rodriguez's butt for this," I muttered. It was a phrase I had often heard my father growl. I never thought I'd say it myself.

"Don't blame Tom!" Marguerite was suddenly distraught, concerned. "My mother okayed it. Tom was only doing what I asked and the captain approved."

"ENTRY IN SIX MINUTES," came the automated announcement.

"So you asked, your mother approved, and Rodriguez did the work without telling me."

"It's only a minor modification."

"He should have told me," I insisted. "Breaching the hull is not minor. He should have pointed it out to me specifically."

Her roguish smile returned. "Don't take it so seriously. If Tom and my mother okayed it, there's nothing to worry about."

I knew she was right. But dammit, Rodriguez should have informed me. I was the owner of this vessel. He should have made certain that I knew and approved.

Marguerite leaned over toward me and tapped a forefinger against my chin. "Lighten up, Van. Enjoy the ride."

I looked into her eyes. They were shining like polished onyx. Suddenly I leaned toward her and, reaching a hand behind the nape of her neck, I pulled her to me and kissed her firmly on the lips.

She pushed away, her eyes flashing now, startled, almost angry.

"Now wait a minute," she said.

I slid back in my chair. "I . . . you're awfully attractive, you know."

She glared at me. "Just because my mother's letting Tom sleep with her is no reason for you to think you can get me into your bed."

I felt as if someone had whacked me with a hammer. "What? What did you say?"

"You heard me."

"Rodriguez and your mother?"

The indignation in her eyes cooled a bit. "You mean you didn't know about them?"

"No!"

"They're sleeping together. I thought everyone on board knew it."

"I didn't!" My voice sounded like a little boy's squeak, even to myself.

Marguerite nodded, and I saw in her expression some of the bitterness her mother exuded constantly.

"Ever since we left Earth orbit. It's my mother's way of solving personnel problems."

"ENTRY IN FIVE MINUTES."

"We'd better strap in," Marguerite said.

"Wait," I said. "You're telling me that your mother is sleeping with Rodriguez to smooth over the fact that she's captain and he's only second-in-command?"

Marguerite did not reply. She concentrated on buckling the seat harness over her shoulders.

"Well?" I demanded. "Is that what you're saying?"

"I shouldn't have mentioned it," she said. "I've shocked you."

"I'm not shocked!"

She looked at me for a long moment, her expression unfathomable. At last she said, "No, I can see that you're not shocked."

"I'm accustomed to men and women enjoying sex together," I told her.

"Yes, of course you are."

Then a new thought struck me. "You're angry at your mother, is that it?"

"I'm not angry. I'm not shocked. I'm not even surprised. The only thing that amazes me is that you can live in this crowded little sardine can for week after week and not have the faintest inkling of what's going on."

I had to admit to myself that she was right. I'd been like a sleepwalker. Or rather, like a clown. Going through the motions of being the owner, the man in charge. All these things happening and I hadn't the slightest clue.

I sagged back in my padded chair, feeling numb and stupid. I started fumbling with my safety harness; my fingers felt thick, clumsy. I couldn't take my eyes off Marguerite, wondering, wondering.

She looked back at me, straight into my eyes. "I'm not like my mother, Van. I may be her clone, but I'm nothing like her. Don't ever forget that."

"ENTRY IN FOUR MINUTES."

ENTRY

Orbiting Venus's hot, thick atmosphere at slightly more than seven kilometers per second, *Hesperos* fired its retrorockets at precisely the millisecond called for in the entry program.

Strapped into the chair in the observation blister, I felt the ship flinch, like a speeding car when the driver taps the brake slightly.

I leaned forward as far as the safety harness would allow. Through the forward-angled port I could see the rim of the big heat shield and, beyond it, the smooth saffron clouds that completely shrouded the planet.

Except the clouds were no longer smooth. There were rifts here and there, long streamers floating above the main cloud deck, patterns of billows like waves rolling across a deep, deep sea.

Marguerite was turned toward the port also, so I could not see her full face, only a three-quarter profile. She seemed intent, her hands gripping the arms of her chair. Not white-knuckled, not frightened, but certainly not relaxed, either.

Me, I was clutching the arms of my chair so hard my nails were going to leave permanent indentations in the plastic. Was I frightened? I don't know. I was excited, taut as the Buckyball cable that had connected us to the old *Truax*. I was breathing hard, I remember, but I don't recall any snakes twisting in my gut.

Something bright flared across the rim of the heat shield and I suddenly wished I were up on the bridge, where I could see the instruments and understand what was happening. There was an empty chair up there; I should have demanded that I sit in it through the entry flight.

The ship shuddered. Not violently, but enough to notice. More than enough. The entire rim of the heat shield was glowing now and streamers of hot gas flashed past. The ride started to get bumpy.

"Approaching maximum gee forces," Duchamp's voice called out over the intercom speaker in the overhead.

"Max gee, check," Rodriguez replied, from his position up in the nose.

It was *really* bumpy now. I was being rattled back and forth in my chair, happy to have the harness holding me firmly.

"Maximum aerodynamic pressure," Duchamp said.

"Temperature in the forward section exceeding max calculated." Rodriguez's voice was calm, but his words sent a current of electricity through me.

The calculations have an enormous safety factor in them, I tried to reassure myself. It would have been easier if the ship didn't feel as if it were trying to shake itself apart.

I couldn't see a thing through the port now. Just a solid sheet of blazing hot gases, like looking into a furnace. I squeezed my eyes down to slits while the battering, rattling ride went on. My vision blurred. I closed my eyes entirely for a moment. When I opened them cautiously, I could see fairly well again, although the ship was still shuddering violently.

Marguerite hadn't moved since the entry began; she was still staring fixedly ahead. I wondered if her camera was getting anything or if the incandescent heat of our entry into the atmosphere had fried its lens.

The ride began to smooth out a bit. It was still bumpier than anything I had ever experienced before, but at least now I could lean my head back against the padded headrest and not have it bounce so hard it felt like I was being pummeled by a karate champion.

Marguerite turned slightly and smiled at me. A pale smile, I thought, but it made me smile back at her.

"Nothing to it," I said, trying to sound brave. It came out more like a whimper.

"I think the worst is over," she said.

Just then there was an enormous jolt and an explosion that would have made me leap out of my chair if I weren't strapped in. It took just a flash of a second to realize that it was the explosive bolts jettisoning the heat shield, but in that flash of a second I must have pumped my entire lifetime's supply of adrenaline into my blood. I came very close to wetting myself; my bladder felt painfully full.

"We're going into the clouds!" Marguerite said happily.

"Deceleration on the tick," Duchamp's voice rang out.

"Heat shield jettison complete," Rodriguez replied. "Now we're a blimp."

Rodriguez was inaccurate, I knew. A blimp has a soft envelope; ours was rigid cermet. It wasn't often I could catch him in a slip of the tongue. I threw a superior smile to Marguerite as I popped the latch on my safety harness. The instant I stood up, though, *Hesperos* shuddered, lurched, swung around crazily, and accelerated so hard I was slammed right back into my chair.

The superrotation.

The solid body of the planet may turn very slowly, but Venus's upper atmosphere, blast-heated by the Sun, develops winds of two hundred kilometers per hour and more that rush around the entire planet in a few days. In a way, they're like the jet streams on Earth, only bigger and more powerful.

Our lighter-than-air vessel was in the grip of those winds, zooming along like a leaf caught in a hurricane. We used the engines hanging outside the gondola only to keep us from swinging too violently, otherwise we would have depleted our fuel in a matter of hours. We couldn't fight those winds, we could only surf along on them and try to keep the ride reasonably smooth.

Truax, up in a safe, stable orbit, was supposed to keep track of our position by monitoring our telemeter beacon. This was for two reasons: to stay in constant communications contact with us and to plot the direction and speed of the superrotation wind, with *Hesperos* playing the same role as a smoke particle in a wind tunnel. But *Truax* hadn't deployed the full set of communications satellites around the planet by the time we got caught in the superrotation. Without the commsats to relay our beacon, they lost almost half our first day's data.

And if anything had gone wrong, they wouldn't know it for ten, twelve hours.

Fortunately, the only trouble we had was a few bruised shins as *Hesperos* lurched and swirled in the turbulent winds. It was like being in a racing yacht during a storm: you had to hold on to something whenever you moved from one place to another.

It was scary at first, I admit. No amount of lectures, videos, or even VR simulations can really prepare you for the genuine experience. But in a few hours I got accustomed to it. More or less.

I spent most of those hours right there in the observation blister, staring out as we darted along the cloud tops. Marguerite got up and went back to her lab; crew members passed by now and then, stumbling and staggering along the passageway, muttering curses every time the ship pitched and they banged against the bulkhead.

At one point Marguerite came back to the blister, a heavy-looking gray box of equipment in her hands.

"Shouldn't you be checking the sensors up forward?" she asked, a little testily, I thought.

"They're running fine," I said. "If there were any problems I'd get a screech on my phone." I tapped the communicator in the chest pocket of my coveralls.

"Don't you want to see the data they're taking in?"

"Later on, when the ride settles down a little," I said. It had always nonplussed me that many scientists get so torqued up about their work that they have to watch their instruments while the observation is in progress. As if their being there could make any difference in what the instruments are recording.

Marguerite left and I was alone again, watching the upper layer of the cloud deck reaching for us. Long, lazy tendrils of yellowish fog seemed to stretch out toward us, then evaporate before my eyes. The cloud tops were dynamic, bubbling like a boiling pot, heaving and breathing like a thing alive.

Don't be an anthropomorphic ass, I warned myself sternly. Leave the similes to the poets and romantics like Marguerite. You're supposed to be a scientist.

Of sorts, a sardonic inner voice scoffed. You're only playing at being a scientist. A real scientist would be watching his sensors and data readouts like a tiger stalking a deer.

And miss the view? I answered myself.

We were dipping into the clouds now, sinking down into them like a submarine sliding beneath the surface of the sea. Yellow-gray clouds slid past my view, then we were in the clear again, then more mountains of haze covered the port. Deeper and deeper we sank, into the sulfuric-acid perpetual global clouds of Venus.

The ride did indeed smooth out, but only a little. Or maybe we all became accustomed to the pitching and rolling. We got our sea legs. Our Venus legs.

It was eerie, sailing in that all-enveloping fog. For days on end I stared out of the ports and saw nothing but a gray sameness. I wanted to push ahead, to go deeper, get beneath the clouds so we could begin searching the surface with telescopes for the wreckage of my brother's vessel.

But the mission plan called for caution, and despite my eagerness I understood that the plan should be followed. We were in uncharted territory now, and we had to make certain that all of *Hesperos*'s systems were performing as designed.

The mammoth cermet envelope above us had been filled (if that's the right word) with vacuum. Its hatches had been open to vacuum all the time of our flight from Earth orbit, then sealed tight when we entered Venus's atmosphere. What better flotation medium for a lighter-than-air vessel than nothingness?

Now we were slowly filling the envelope with hydrogen gas, sucked out of the clouds' abundant sulfuric acid through our equipment that separated out the wanted hydrogen and released the unwanted sulfur and oxygen. On Earth hydrogen's flammability would have been dangerous, but Venus's atmosphere contained practically no free oxygen, so there was no danger of explosion or fire. The envelope itself was a rigid shell of cermet, a ceramic-metal composite that combined toughness and rigidity yet was lighter than any possible metal alloy.

To go deeper, we would vent hydrogen overboard and replace it with atmospheric gas: mainly carbon dioxide. When the time came to rise again, we intended to break down the carbon dioxide into its component elements of carbon and oxygen, vent the carbon overboard, and let the lighter oxygen buoy us upward. Higher up we intended to dissociate the sulfuric acid molecules of the clouds again and refill the envelope with hydrogen.

We had tested the equipment for splitting the carbon dioxide and sulfuric acid molecules before we ever took off from Earth, and now, inside the globe-girdling cloud deck of Venus, we put it to work to fill the gas envelope with hydrogen.

Eager as I was to go deeper, I was perfectly happy to see that the equipment worked in Venus's clouds. I had no desire to be stuck down at the surface with no way to come back up.

So we coasted along in the uppermost cloud deck, patiently filling the big shell above us and testing our equipment. Once in a while it seemed to me that we weren't moving at all, that we were stuck in place like a ship run aground on a reef. All we could see out the ports was that perpetual yellowish-gray sameness. But then some strong current in the atmosphere would grab us and the gondola would tilt and groan like a creaking old sailing ship and my insides would flutter just a little bit.

I was constantly worried about Fuchs, of course, but the IAA reports on his activity showed that he was also moving cautiously. He had entered the atmosphere several hours before we did, but so far had not gone much deeper than we had. Like us, he was floating in the upper reaches of the top cloud deck, pushed around the planet by the superrotation winds.

"He's no fool," Duchamp told me as we sat together in the spartan little galley. It was the only place aboard *Hesperos* where two or three people could sit together, other than the bridge.

"Lars takes risks," Duchamp said, "but only when he's certain the odds are in his favor."

"You know him?" I asked.

She made a thin smile. "Oh, yes. Lars and I are old friends."

"Friends?" I felt my brows hike up.

Her smile faded. "I first met him just after he had lost his business and his wife. He was a pretty desperate man then. Hurt and angry. Bewildered. Everything he had built up in his life had been snatched away from him." She exhaled a puff of air through her nostrils, something between a grunt and a sigh.

The expression on her face told me she knew perfectly well that the man who had destroyed his company and taken his wife was my father. She didn't have to say it; we both knew.

"But he pulled himself up again, didn't he?" I snapped. "He's done fairly well in asteroid mining, hasn't he?"

Duchamp looked at me for a long silent moment, the kind of look a university professor gives to an especially dense and hopeless student.

"Yes," she said. "Hasn't he."

IN THE CLOUDS

At least, during those first days coasting through the clouds, I had an excuse to stay close to Marguerite. I was supposed to be a planetary scientist, I kept reminding myself, and even though she was a biologist we began to work together, sampling the clouds.

Marguerite's lab was too crowded for both of us to use it at the same time, and it would have been impossible for us to work together in either her quarters or mine; each of us had nothing more than a narrow berth with a privacy screen shuttering it. We could have both fit in either berth, but no scientific research would have been done. Indeed, I found myself wondering what it would be like to have Marguerite cupped beside me in my berth. Or hers.

But she had no romantic interest in me, that was clear. Instead, we turned the observation post up in the gondola's nose into a makeshift laboratory where we took samples of the cloud droplets and analyzed them.

"There really is water in the clouds!" Marguerite exclaimed happily, after a long day of checking and rechecking the results of our spectral analyses.

"Thirty parts per million," I grumbled. "It might as well be zero for all the good—"

"No, no, you don't understand," she said. "Water means life! Where water exists, life exists."

She was really excited. I was more or less playing at being a planetary scientist but to Marguerite the search for life was as thrilling and absorbing as Michelangelo's drive to create great works of art out of rough slabs of marble.

We were sitting cross-legged on the metal decking up in the gondola's nose section because there was no room for chairs and nobody had thought to bring any cushions aboard. The transparent quartzite nose itself showed only the featureless yellowish gray of the eternal cloud deck; it might just have well been spray-painted that color for all that we could see out there. Two mass spectrometers sat to one side of us, half a dozen hand-sized computers were scattered on the deck plates, and a whole rack of equipment boxes—some gray, some black—hummed away along the bulkhead beside me.

"The presence of water," I pointed out, "does not automatically mean the presence of life. There is a good deal of water on the Moon, but no life there."

"Humans live on the Moon," she countered, with mischief in the lilt of her voice.

"I mean native lunar life, you know that."

"But the water deposits on the Moon are frozen. Wherever there's *liquid* water, like under the ice crust on Europa—"

"The water vapor in these clouds," I interrupted, jabbing a finger toward the observation port, "hardly constitute a supply of liquid water."

"They do to microscopic organisms."

I had to hold back a laugh. "Have you found any?"

Her enthusiasm didn't waver one iota. "Not yet. But we will!"

I could only shake my head in admiration for her perseverance.

"This proves that there must be at least some volcanic activity down at the surface," Marguerite said.

"I suppose so," I agreed.

The reasoning was simple enough: Any water vapor in Venus's atmosphere quickly boiled up to the top of the clouds, where the intense ultraviolet radiation from sunlight broke up the water molecules into hydrogen and oxygen, which eventually evaporated away into space. So there had to be a fresh supply of water constantly replenishing the droplets. Otherwise they would have all been dissociated and blown off the planet ages ago. The source of the water most likely came from the planet's deep interior and was vented into the atmosphere by volcanic eruptions.

On Earth volcanoes constantly blow out steam, sometimes in explosions that tear the tops off the mountains. But the water vapor they vent into the atmosphere stays in the atmosphere, on Earth. It's not lost to space because Earth's atmosphere gets cold at high altitudes and the water condenses and falls back as rain or snow. That's why Earth has oceans and Venus doesn't. Earth's upper atmosphere is a "cold trap" that prevents the water from escaping the planet. Hothouse Venus doesn't have a cold trap in its upper atmosphere: at the altitude where on Earth the temperature dips below freezing, Venus is almost four hundred degrees Celsius, four times hotter than water's boiling point. As a result Venus can't build up any appreciable water content in its atmosphere.

I wondered what this meant for Greenbaum's theory about Venus's whole surface erupting into a planet-wide upheaval. There must be *some* volcanic activity venting at least a bit of the planet's internal heat into the atmosphere.

"We'll have to go deeper to find life-forms in the clouds," Marguerite said, as much to herself as to me. "The UV absorber isn't that much further down."

I was still thinking about volcanoes. "We've been watching Venus for more than a century and no one's seen a volcanic eruption. Of all the spacecraft that we've put in orbit and landed on the surface, not one sensor's picked up a volcano in the process of erupting."

Marguerite poo-poohed me. "What do you expect? We've only sent a few dozen robot spacecraft to orbit Venus and even fewer landers. We've ignored the planet terribly."

I had to agree. "Still, if Professor Greenbaum is right and there isn't that much active vulcanism . . ."

"Maybe we'll catch an eruption," Marguerite said. "That would be a first, wouldn't it?"

She was all enthusiasm. But I thought of the ancient Chinese maxim: Be careful what you wish for; you might get it.

Fuchs still worried me. Apparently he was still sailing in the clouds, as we were. But aside from his position I could get no information about him from the IAA. For a good reason: He was giving out no information, nothing but his tracking beacon and the standard telemetering data that showed his basic systems to be operating in good order. When I tried to get details about the design of his ship or the array of sensing systems he carried, I drew a blank. *Lucifer* was his ship, his design, built out in the deep darkness of the Asteroid Belt, equipped according to his specifications and no one else's. He reported the minimum required by the IAA and kept everything else to himself.

One thing I was able to do during those first days in the clouds was to begin to build up a map of the superrotation wind pattern. By recording our position from the ship's inertial navigation system I was able to generate a three-dimensional plot of where those winds blew, a sort of weather map of Venus's jet streams. Every time a powerful gust buffeted us and made me grab for a handhold, every time a sudden upwelling bounced us or a cold spot made us drop until my stomach crawled up into my throat, I thought to myself that at least I was getting useful data.

The winds fanned outward from the subsolar point, of

course. That was where the Sun was directly overhead, blazing down on the planet's atmosphere like a blowtorch. Venus turns so slowly, once in 243 Earth days, that the subsolar spot gets blasted remorselessly. The atmosphere rushes away from there in a gigantic heat-driven flow, setting up currents and convection cells that span the girth of the planet. I measured wind speeds of nearly four hundred kilometers per hour: We were setting a Guinness speed record for lighter-than-air vessels.

Deeper down, where the atmosphere gets thicker and so much hotter, the winds die to almost nothing. At a pressure similar to that of an Earthly ocean a kilometer or so deep, there could be nothing that we would recognize as winds, only sluggish tidal motions.

At least, that's how the theory went.

My map of the superrotation winds was coming along quite nicely after a few days, and it made me proud to realize that I was making a real contribution toward understanding Venus. When I tried to extend my data down to a slightly lower altitude, though, in an effort to see how far down the winds might extend, the computer program glitched on me. Insufficient data, I thought, peering at the display screen.

I had coded the map with false colors, each color indicating a range of speeds. There they were, a network of jet streams all rushing out from the subsolar point, in shades of blue and green. With my VR goggles on, I saw it all in three-dimensional motion. But there was the damned glitch, a swath of red and a few kilometers below our present altitude. Red should have indicated even higher wind velocity than we were in now, but I knew that was wrong. The wind velocities had to get lower as we went down in altitude, not higher. Something was wrong with the program.

I mentioned it to Duchamp and Rodriguez when we met to decide on when we would start down toward the surface.

Our conference center was the observation blister, the only place in our cramped gondola where three or four people could sit comfortably. Duchamp and I sat side by side, our chairs swiveled away from the observation ports. Rodriguez sat on the floor facing us, his back against the far bulkhead.

"All systems have performed well within their design range," Duchamp said, tapping a manicured fingernail on the screen of her handheld computer. "Unless I hear otherwise, I declare this phase of the mission completed."

Rodriguez nodded. "No complaints about that. It'll be good to get out of this wind and down to a calmer altitude."

"Calmer," Duchamp said, "but hotter."

"We can handle the heat."

She smiled at him as if they had some private joke going between them.

I spoke up. "My map of the wind system keeps throwing this glitch at me." I had brought a handheld, too, and showed it to them.

"The red indicates even higher wind velocities than we're in now," I said.

"That's an extrapolation, isn't it?" Rodriguez asked. "It's not based on observational data."

"No, we haven't gone down that far, so we don't have any data from that altitude."

"A computer extrapolation," Duchamp said, like an art critic sniffing at some child's lopsided attempt to draw a tree.

"But the extrapolation is based on pretty firm meteorological data," I pointed out.

"Terrestrial meteorological data?" asked Duchamp.

I nodded. "Modified to take into account Venus's different temperature, pressure, and chemical regime."

"An abstraction of an abstraction," Duchamp said, with a *that's-that* wave of her hand.

Rodriguez was staring at the smear of red at the bottom of my map. He handed the palm-sized computer back to me and said thoughtfully, "You don't think there could be some kind of wind shear down at that altitude, do you?"

"A supersonic wind shear?" Duchamp scoffed.

"It's not supersonic at that pressure," Rodriguez pointed out.

She shook her head. "All the planetary physicists agree that the superrotation winds die out as you go deeper into the atmosphere and the pressure builds up. The winds get swamped by the increased pressure."

Rodriguez nodded thoughtfully, then said slowly, "Yeah, I know, but if there really is a wind shear it could be a killer."

Duchamp took a breath, glanced from him to me and back again, then made her decision.

"Very well," she said. "We'll rig for intense wind shear. Check out all systems. Make everything secure and tightened down, just as we did for atmospheric entry." She turned to me. "Will that satisfy you, Mr. Humphries?"

I was surprised at the venom in her reaction. I swallowed once and said, "You're the captain."

"Good." To Rodriguez she said, "Tommy, this means you'll have to go outside and manually check all the connectors and fittings."

He nodded glumly. "Yeah. Right."

Then, smiling coldly, Duchamp turned back to be. "Mr. Humphries, would you care to assist Tom?"

"Me?" I squeaked.

"We could use the extra hand," she said smoothly, "and the inspection is actually at your behest, isn't it? You and your computer program."

You bitch, I thought. Just because my computer program showed a possible problem she's blaming me for it. Now I've either got to risk my neck or show everybody that I'm a coward.

Rodriguez leaned across the narrow passageway separating us and grabbed my knee in a rough, friendly way.

"Come on, Mr. Humphries, it won't be so bad. I'll be with you every step of the way and you'll be able to tell your grandchildren about it."

If I live long enough to have grandchildren, I thought.

But I swallowed my fear and said as calmly as I could, "Sure. It ought to be exciting."

It certainly was.

Basically, our task was to check all the connectors that held the gondola to the gas envelope above us. It was a job that a plumber could do, it didn't call for any special training. But we'd be outside, in a cloud of sulfuric acid droplets that was nearly a hundred degrees Celsius, more than fifty kilometers above the ground.

Rodriguez spent two intense hours briefing me on what we had to do in the virtual reality simulator. Six main struts had to be checked out, and six secondary ones. They connected the gondola to the gas shell; if they failed under stress we would go plunging down to the red-hot surface like an iron anvil.

Akira Sakamoto, our dour life support technician, personally helped me into my spacesuit. It was the same one I had used when we transferred from *Truax*, but now its exterior had been sprayed with a special heat-resistant ceramic. The suit seemed stiffer to me than before, although Sakamoto insisted the ceramic in no way interfered with limb motion.

Without a word, without any discernible expression on his chunky broad face, he slipped the safety harness around my waist and clicked it in place, then made certain both its tethers were properly looped so they wouldn't trip me as I tried to walk.

Dr. Waller helped to check out Rodriguez, who got into his suit unassisted. But you had to have somebody go around to make certain all the seals were okay and the electrical lines and life support hoses hooked up properly from the backpack.

Marguerite came down to the airlock, too, and watched in silence as we suited up. I was trembling slightly as I wriggled into the ungainly suit, which was now sort of silvery from its new ceramic coating. But I realized with some surprise that my trembling wasn't so much fear as excitement. I knew I should have been scared out of my bleeding wits, but somehow I wasn't. I was going to *do* something, something that had to be done, and even though it was dangerous I found myself actually looking forward to it.

In the back of my mind, a jeering voice was saying, Famous last words. How many fools have looked forward to the adventure that killed them.

But with Marguerite watching me I didn't seem to care. I thought I saw a hint of admiration in her eyes. At least, I hoped it was admiration and not amusement at the foolish machismo I was exhibiting.

OUTSIDE

kay, we do it just the way we did in the sim." In my helmet earphones, Rodriguez's voice sounded harsh and tight, definitely more tense than his usual easygoing attitude.

I nodded, then realized he couldn't see me through the tinted fishbowl helmet, so I said, "Right." Just like a real astronaut, I thought.

He went into the airlock ahead of me, cycled it down, and then went outside. Once the outer airlock hatch closed again and the 'lock refilled with ship's air, the inner hatch indicator light turned green.

My spacesuit was definitely stiff. Even with the servomotors at my elbow and shoulder joints grinding away, it took a real effort to move my arms. Before I could reach the airlock control stud with my gloved hand, Sakamoto pressed it, his beefy face dour as usual. But he made a little hissing bow, the first sign of respect I had ever seen from him.

"Thanks," I said as I stepped into the airlock, hoping he could hear me through the helmet.

As the airlock cycled down and the outer hatch slid open, I had to remind myself that this was going to be different from an EVA in space. This would be more like doing steel-work at the top of a tremendously tall skyscraper. If I made a false step I wouldn't simply float away from the ship, I'd plunge screaming to the ground, fifty kilometers below.

"Take it slow and easy," Rodriguez told me. "I'm right here. Hand me your tether before you step out."

I could see his spacesuited form clinging to the hand-grips set into the gondola's outer hull, beside the hatch. Both his tethers were clipped to its rungs.

I handed him one end of my right-hand tether. He clipped it a rung beside his own.

"Okay now, just the way we did in the sim. Come on out."

The good thing was we were enveloped in the cloud, so I didn't have to worry about looking down. There was nothing to see out there except a blank yellow-gray limbo. But I could feel the ship shuddering and pitching in the currents of wind.

"Just like rock climbing," Rodriguez said, with an exaggerated heartiness. "Piece of cake."

"When did you do any rock climbing?" I asked as I planted one booted foot on a rung of the ladder.

"Me? Are you kidding? When I get up more than fifty meters I want an airplane surrounding me."

I had never gone rock climbing, either. Risking one's neck for the fun of it has always seemed the height of idiocy to me.

But this was different, I told myself. There was a job to be done. I was making a real contribution to the mission now, not just cowering in my quarters while others did the work.

Still, it was scary. I suppose Rodriguez could've done it all by himself, but long decades of experience dictated that it was far safer to have two people go out together, even if one of them was a neophyte. Besides, with me out there we could cut the time for the inspection almost in half; that in itself made the whole job a lot safer.

In a way, the pressure of the Venusian atmosphere helped us. In space, with nothing outside a spacesuit's fabric but vacuum, a spacesuit tends to balloon up and get stiff. That's why we had the miniature servomotors on the suits' joints and gloves, to assist our muscles in bending and flexing. Even at this high altitude, though, the atmospheric pressure was enough to make it almost easy to move around in the suits. Even the gloves flexed fairly easily; the servomotors of the spiny exoskeleton on the backs of the gloves hardly had to exert themselves at all.

One by one, Rodriguez and I checked the braces and struts that held the gondola to the gas envelope. All the welds seemed solid, to my eyes. Neither of us could find any sign of damage or deterioration. One of the hoses that fed hydrogen from the separator to the envelope seemed a bit looser than Rodriguez liked; he worked on it for several minutes with a wrench from the tools clipped to his harness, dangling from a support strut like a monkey in a banana tree.

As I watched Rodriguez working, I checked the thermometer on the wrist of my suit. To my surprise it read only a few degrees above freezing. Then I remembered that we were still fifty-some kilometers above the ground; on Earth we'd be high above the stratosphere, on the fringe of outer space. Here on Venus we were in the middle of a thick cloud of sulfuric acid droplets. Not too far below us, the atmosphere heated up quickly to several hundred degrees.

Dangling out there in the open reminded me of something but I couldn't put my finger on it until at last I remembered watching a video years ago, when I'd been just a child, about people hang gliding off some seaside cliffs in Hawaii. I had burned with jealousy then, watching them having so much fun while I was stuck in a house almost all the time, too frail to try such an adventure. And too scared, I've got to admit. But here I was, on another world, racing in the wind fifty klicks high!

"That's done," Rodriguez said as he returned the wrench to its place on his belt. But he fumbled it and the wrench dropped out of sight. One instant it was in his hand, then, "Oops!" and it was gone. I realized that's what would happen to me if my tethers failed.

"Is that it?" I asked. "Are we done?"

"I ought to check the envelope for any signs of ablation from the entry heat," Rodriguez said. "You can go back inside."

Without even thinking about it I replied, "No, I'll go with you."

So we clambered slowly up the rungs set into the massive curving bulk of the gas envelope, with that hot wind gushing past us. I knew the atmospheric pressure was too thin up at this altitude to really push us, yet I felt as if I were being nudged, harried, shaken by the wind.

It was slow going, climbing one rung, unclipping one tether and snapping it on a higher rung, then stepping up again and unclipping the other tether. Just like mountain climbers, we never moved a step until we had both tethers locked on safely. I could hear Rodriguez's breathing in my earphones, puffing hard with each step he took.

Duchamp was listening in on everything, of course. But I knew that if we got into trouble there was nothing she or anyone else could do about it in time. It was just Rodriguez and me out here, on our own. It was frightening and kind of exhilarating at the same time.

At last we got to the long catwalk that ran along the top of the envelope. Rodriguez knelt down and activated the switch that raised the flimsy-looking safety rail that ran the length of the metal mesh walkway. Then we fastened our tethers to the rail; it stood waist-high all the way down the catwalk, from nose to tail. A row of cleats projected up from the edge of the walkway, like the bitts on a racing yacht where you tie down the lines from the sails.

"Top of the world," Rodriguez said cheerfully.

"Yeah," I said, my voice definitely shaky.

Together we walked to the bulbous nose of the envelope, where the big heat shield had been connected. I could see the stumps of the rods that had held the shield in place, blackened from the explosive bolts that had sheared them off. Rodriguez bent over and examined the nose region, muttering to himself like a physician thumping a patient's chest during a checkup. Then we walked slowly back toward the tail, him in the lead, our tethers sliding along the safety rail.

I saw it first.

"What's that discoloration?" I asked, pointing.

Rodriguez grunted, then took several steps toward the tail. "Hmm," he mumbled. "Looks like charring, doesn't it?"

I suddenly remembered that these clouds were made of sulfuric acid.

As if he could read my mind, Rodriguez said, "Can't be the sulfuric acid, it doesn't react with the cermet."

"Are you sure?" I asked.

He chuckled. "Don't worry about it. It can't even attack the fabric of your suit."

Very reassuring, I thought. But the charred stains on the cermet skin of the gas envelope were still there.

"Could it be from the entry heat?"

I could sense him nodding inside his helmet. "Some of the heated air must've flowed over the shield and singed the butt end of the envelope a little."

"The sensors didn't record a temperature spike there," I said.

"Might've been too small to notice. If we expand the graph we'll probably see it."

"Is it a problem?"

"Probably not," he said. "But we oughtta pressurize the envelope to make certain it doesn't leak."

I felt my heart sink. "How long will that take?"

He thought before answering. "The better part of a day, I guess."

"Another day lost."

"Worried about Fuchs?" he asked.

"Yes, of course."

"Well, he's likely got problems of his—*Hey!*"

The safety rail alongside Rodriguez suddenly broke away, a whole section of it flying off into the yellowy haze, taking one of his tethers with it. He was yanked off his feet, flailing his arms and legs, the remaining tether anchoring him to the still-standing section of rail, the other one trying to pull him off the ship.

I lunged for him but he was already too far away for me to reach without taking off my own tethers.

"Pull me in!" he yelled, his voice bellowing in my earphones.

"What's happened?" Duchamp asked sharply in my earphones.

I saw him unclip the one tether from his belt. It snapped off into the clouds. I grabbed the other and began hauling him in.

But the railing itself was wobbling, shaky. It was going to tear away in another few seconds, I realized.

"Pull me in!" Rodriguez shouted again.

"What's happening out there?" Duchamp demanded.

I unclipped one of my own tethers and fastened it onto one of the cleats set into the catwalk. Then, with Duchamp jabbering in my earphones, I unclipped Rodriguez's remaining tether before the railing broke off and he went sailing into oblivion.

"What the hell are you doing?" he yelled.

His sudden weight almost tore my arms out of their sockets. Squeezing my eyes shut, I saw stars exploding against the blackness. With gritted teeth, I clumped down onto my knees and used all my strength to clamp the end of his tether to the cleat next to mine.

I saw that the broken end of the railing was fluttering now, shaking loose. And my other tether was still hooked to it. Instead of trying to reach its end I simply unsnapped it from my belt and let it flap loose, then turned back to hauling in Rodriguez's line.

He was pulling himself in as hard as he could. It seemed like an hour, the two of us panting and snorting like a couple of tug-of-war contestants, but he finally planted his boots back on the catwalk. All this time Duchamp was yelling in my earphones, "What is it? What's going on out there?"

"We're okay," Rodriguez gasped at last, down on his hands and knees on the catwalk. For an absurd instant I thought he was going to pull off his helmet and kiss the metal decking.

"You saved my life, Van."

It was the first time he'd called me anything but "Mr. Humphries." It made me feel proud.

Before I could reply, Rodriguez went on, in a slightly sheepish tone, "At first I thought you were going to leave me and go back to the airlock."

I stared at the blank fishbowl of his helmet. "I wouldn't do that, Tom."

"I know," he said, still panting from his exertion and fear. "Now," he added.

DAMAGE ASSESSMENT

Captain Duchamp and Dr. Waller were waiting for us when we came through the airlock. I could hear her demanding questions, muffled by my helmet, directed at Rodriguez.

"What happened out there? What was that about the safety rail?" And finally, "Are you all right?"

Rodriguez started to explain as I lifted my helmet off. Waller took it from my trembling hands and I saw Marguerite hurrying up the passageway toward us.

While we both worked our way out of the spacesuits, Rodriguez gave a clipped but thorough explanation of what had happened to us. Duchamp looked blazingly angry, as if somehow we had caused the trouble for ourselves. I kept glancing at Marguerite, standing behind her mother. So much alike, physically. So strikingly similar in the shape of their faces, the depth of their jet-black eyes, the same height, the same curves of their figures.

Yet where the captain was truculent and demanding, Marguerite looked troubled, distressed—and something else. Something more. I couldn't tell what it was in her eyes; I suppose I subconsciously hoped it was concern for me.

Duchamp and Rodriguez headed for the bridge. Waller went without a word back toward his cubbyhole of an infirmary, leaving Marguerite and me alone by the racks of empty spacesuits.

"Are you all right?" she asked me.

Nodding, I said, "Fine. I think." I held out my hand. "Look, I'm not even shaking anymore."

She laughed, a delightful sound. "You've earned a drink."

We went down to the galley, passing Waller's closet-sized infirmary. It was empty, making me wonder where the doctor might hide himself.

As we took cups of fruit juice and sat on the galley bench, I realized that I did indeed feel fine. Was it Churchill who said that coming through a brush with death concentrates the mind wonderfully?

Marguerite sat beside me and took a sip of juice. "You saved Tom's life," she said.

The look in her eyes wasn't adoring. Far from it. But there was a respect in them that I'd never seen before. It felt terrifically good.

Heroes are supposed to be modest, so I waggled my free hand and said merely, "I just reacted on instinct, I guess."

"Tom would have been killed if you hadn't."

"No, I don't think so. He—"

"He thinks so."

I shrugged. "He would've done the same for me."

She nodded and brought the cup to her lips, her eyes never leaving mine.

I had to say something, so I let my mouth work before my brain did. "Your mother doesn't seem to have a molecule of human kindness in her. I know she's the captain, but she was practically chewing Tom's guts out."

Marguerite almost smiled. "That's the way she reacts when she's frightened. She attacks."

"Frightened? Her? Of what?"

"Tom nearly got killed! Don't you think that scared her? She is human, you know, underneath the stainless steel."

"You mean she really cares about him?"

Her eyes flashed. "Do you think she's sleeping with him merely to keep him satisfied? She's not a whore, you know."

"I . . ." I realized that I had thought precisely that. For once in my life, I kept my mouth shut while I tried to figure out what I should say next.

The speaker in the ceiling blared, "MR. HUMPHRIES WANTED ON THE BRIDGE." Duchamp's voice.

Saved by the call of duty, I thought.

I sat scrunched down on the metal deck plate of the bridge between Duchamp's command chair and Rodriguez's. Willa Yeats, our sensors specialist, was in the chair usually occupied by Riza, the communications tech.

The four of us were staring hard at the main display screen, which showed a graph of the heat load the ship had encountered during entry into the atmosphere.

"No blip," Yeats said, with an *I told you so* tone. She was on the chubby side, moonfaced and pale-skinned, with the kind of dirty-blond hair that some people charitably call sandy.

"There was no sudden burst of heat during the entry flight," she said. "The heat shield performed as designed and the sensors show all heat loads well below maximum allowable levels."

Duchamp scowled at her. "Then what caused the charring on the envelope?"

"And weakened the safety railing?" Rodriguez added.

Yeats shrugged as if it weren't important to her. "I haven't the faintest idea. But it wasn't a pulse of heat, I can tell you that."

She had a very proprietary attitude about the ship's sensing systems. As far as she was concerned, if her sensors didn't show a problem, no problem existed.

Duchamp obviously felt otherwise. The captain looked past me toward Rodriguez. "I suppose we'll have to go out there again and see just what those charring marks are."

Rodriguez nodded glumly. "I suppose."

"I'll go with you," I said. Before either of them could object I added, with a pinch of bravado, "I'm an experienced hand at this, you know."

Duchamp did not look amused, but Rodriguez chuckled and said, "Right. My EVA lifesaver."

"You don't have to do that," Yeats said, obviously disappointed at our obtuseness. "If you simply pressurize the envelope the sensors will tell us if there's a leak."

"And what if we rip the damned envelope wide open?" Duchamp snapped. "Where are we then?"

Yeats looked abashed. She didn't have to answer. We all knew where we'd be if the envelope cracked. There was a set of emergency rockets hooked to the bathysphere; in theory it could serve as an escape pod. But none of us wanted to test that theory. The thought of all eight of us crammed into the tiny iron ball and rocketing up into orbit was far from comforting.

"Inspect the charring," Duchamp said with finality. "Then we can pressurize the envelope."

"Maybe," Rodriguez added, morbidly.

Gripping the arms of their two chairs, I pulled myself up to my feet. "Very well, then, we'd better—"

Marguerite burst into the bridge, nearly bowling me over.

"Life!" she exclaimed, her eyes wide and shining. "There are living organisms in the clouds! Microscopic but multicelled! They're alive, they live in the clouds . . ."

She was babbling so hard I thought she was close to hysteria. Her mother snapped her out of it with a single question.

"You're sure?"

Marguerite took a deep, gulping breath. "I'm positive. They're alive."

Rodriguez said, "I've gotta see this."

I took Marguerite's arm as gently as I could and maneuvered her out into the passageway. Otherwise there was no room on the bridge for Rodriguez to get up from his chair.

We trooped behind Marguerite to her cubbyhole of a lab. As we stopped there I realized Duchamp had also left the bridge to accompany us. We stared at the image from the miniaturized electron microscope displayed on the wall screen. I saw some watery-looking blobs flailing around slowly. They were obviously multicelled; I could see smaller blobs and dividing walls pulsating inside them. Most of them had cilia fringing their outer edges, microscopic oars paddling away constantly. But weakly.

"They're dying in here," Marguerite said, almost mournfully. "It must be the temperature, or maybe the combination of temperature and pressure. It's just not working!"

Straightening up from the microscope's eyepiece, I said to her, "By god, you were right."

"It's a major discovery," Rodriguez congratulated.

"Send this to the IAA at once," Duchamp commanded. "Imagery and every bit of data you have. Get priority for this."

"But I've only—"

"Do you want a Nobel Prize or not?" Duchamp snapped. "Get this data to IAA headquarters *this instant*. Don't wait for Fuchs to get in first."

Marguerite nodded with understanding. For the first time since she'd burst into the bridge she seemed to calm down, come back to reality.

"I'll get Riza to establish a direct link with Geneva," Duchamp went on. "You bang out a written statement, two or three lines will be enough to establish your priority. But do it *now*."

"Yes," Marguerite said, reaching for her laptop computer. "Right."

We left her there in her lab, bent over the computer keyboard. Duchamp headed back toward the bridge. Rodriguez and I went toward the airlock, where the spacesuits were stored.

"RIZA," we heard Duchamp's voice over the intercom

speakers, "REPORT TO THE BRIDGE AT ONCE." She didn't have to repeat the command; there was no room for doubt or delay in the tone of her voice.

"Bugs in the clouds," Rodriguez said to me, over his shoulder. "Who would've thought you could find anything living in clouds of sulfuric acid?"

"Marguerite did;" I answered. "She was certain she'd find living organisms."

"Really?"

I nodded to his back. I had just witnessed a great discovery. Duchamp was right, her daughter would get a special Nobel for this, just like the biologists who discovered the lichen on Mars.

She expected to find living organisms on Venus, I told myself again. Maybe that's the secret of making great discoveries: the stubborn insistence that there's something out there to be discovered, no matter what the others say. Chance favors the prepared mind. Who said that? Some scientist, I thought. Einstein, most likely. Or maybe Freud.

We commandeered Dr. Waller and Willa Yeats to help us into the spacesuits. With his bloodshot eyes watching me intently, Waller hummed quietly as I pulled on my leggings and boots, then wormed into the torso and pushed my arms through the sleeves. I found myself wondering how Marguerite's discovery was going to affect his thesis. I almost laughed aloud, thinking how the doctor's quiet voyage without interruptions had backfired on him.

Two meters away, Willa chattered like a runaway audio machine as she watched Rodriguez get into his suit. They checked out our life support backpacks and made certain all the lines and hoses were properly connected. Then we sealed our helmets.

Rodriguez stepped into the airlock first. I waited for the lock to cycle, my heart revving up until I thought Riza at the comm console on the bridge must be able to hear it through the suit radio. Relax! I commanded myself. You've been outside before. There's nothing to be scared of.

Right. The last time Rodriguez had nearly gotten himself

knocked off the ship. I had no desire to go plummeting fifty-some kilometers down to the rock-hard surface of Venus.

The airlock hatch slid open and Rodriguez stepped back among us.

"What's the matter?" I asked. "What's wrong?"

This close, with the ship's interior lighting shining through his bubble helmet, I could see the puzzled, troubled look on his face.

"Got a red light on my head-up." The suit's diagnostic system, which splashed its display onto the helmet's inner surface, showed something was not functioning properly.

"What is it?" I asked.

"Gimme a minute," he snapped back. Then, "Huh . . . it says there was a pressure leak in the suit. Seems okay now, though."

Dr. Waller grasped the situation before I did. "But it went red when you cycled the air out of the airlock?"

"Yeah. Right."

We spent the better part of an hour pumping up the pressure in Rodriguez's suit until it started to balloon. Sure enough, there was a leak in his left shoulder joint. The suit fabric had a resin compound that self-repaired minor leaks, but the joints were cermet covered with plastic.

"It looks frayed," Dr. Waller said, his voice brimming with curiosity. "No, more like it was singed with a flame or some source of heat."

"Damn!" Rodriguez grumbled. "Suit's supposed to be guaranteed."

I remembered the old joke about parachutes: If it doesn't work, bring it back and we'll give you a new one. It was a good thing the suit's diagnostics caught the leak in the airlock. Outside, it could have killed him.

So Rodriguez unfastened his helmet and wriggled out of his suit and put on one of the backup suits. We would have to repair his suit, I thought. We only carried four spares.

Finally he was ready and went through the airlock. No problems with the backup suit. I heard him call me in my helmet earphones, "Okay, Mr. Humphries. Come on through."

I went into the airlock and got that same old feeling of being locked into a coffin when the inner hatch slid shut. The 'lock cycled down—and a red warning light started blinking on the curving face of my helmet, flashing into my eyes like a rocket's red glare.

"Hey, I've got a problem, too," I yelled into my microphone.

The entire EVA excursion was a bust. Both our original suits were leaking and Duchamp decided to scratch the EVA until we could determine what the problem was.

I thought I knew.

BUG FOOD

don't know," Marguerite said, frowning with puzzlement. "It's too soon for me to tell."

Her voice was low, tired. The excitement of her discovery had worn off; now I was presenting her with its horrifying consequences.

We were walking down the passageway from her lab to the galley, where we could sit together in comfort. I was leading the way, for once.

"It can't be a coincidence," I said over my shoulder. "There's got to be a connection."

"That's not necessarily true," she objected.

We reached the galley and I punched the dispenser for a cold cup of juice, then handed it to her. After I got one for myself, I sat beside her on the bench.

"There are bugs out in the clouds," I said.

"Microscopic multicellular creatures, yes," she agreed.

"What do they eat?"

"I don't know! It's going to take some time to find out.

I've spent most of the day jury-rigging a cooler for them to live in!"

"What's your best guess?" I demanded.

She ran a hand through her thick dark hair. "Sulfur oxides are the most abundant compounds in the cloud droplets. They must metabolize sulfur in some way."

"Sulfur? How can anything eat sulfur?"

Marguerite jabbed a forefinger at me. "There are bacteria on Earth that metabolize sulfur. I would have thought you'd known that."

I had to grin. "You'd be surprised at how much I don't know."

She smiled back.

I pulled my handheld computer from my pocket and punched up a list showing the composition of the fibers of our spacesuits. No sulfur.

"Would they eat any of these materials?" I asked, showing her the computer's tiny display.

Marguerite shrugged wearily. "It's too soon to know, Van. On Earth, organisms metabolize a wide range of elements and compounds. Humans need trace amounts of hundreds of different minerals . . ." She took a deep, sighing breath.

"It's got to be the bugs," I said, convinced despite the lack of evidence. "Nothing else could have eaten through the suits like that."

"What about the railing? That's made of metal, isn't it?"

I tapped on the handheld. "Cermet," I saw. "A ceramic and metal composite." Another few taps. "Contains beryllium, boron, calcium, carbon . . . several other elements."

"Maybe the organisms need trace elements the way we need vitamins," Marguerite suggested.

I went back to the list of suit materials and displayed it alongside the list of the safety rail's composition. Plenty of similarities, although only the cermet had any measurable amount of sulfur in it, and not much at that.

Then I realized that both suits had leaked at joints, not

the self-repairing fabric. And the joints were made of cermet, covered with a thin sprayed-on layer of plastic.

"You've got to find out what they digest," I urged Marguerite. "It's vitally important!"

"I know," she said, rising to her feet. "I'll get on it right
away."

I thought about the charring along the tail end of the gas
envelope. "They might be chewing up the shell, too."

"I'll get on it!" she fairly shouted, then started up the
passageway back to her lab. She looked as if she were flee-
ing from me.

So I'm pushing her, I thought. But we've got to know. If
those bugs are eating our spacesuits and the ship itself
we've got to get out of here and fast.

I stood there for a dithering moment, not certain of what
I should do next. What could I do, except prod other people
to do the things that I can't do myself?

I decided to go up to the bridge, but halfway there I
bumped into Yeats, who was hurrying down the passageway in the opposite direction.

"Anything new?" I asked.

"All bad," she said as she squirmed past me. Her body
felt soft and actually pleasurable as she pressed by. I wondered how a man's gonads could assert themselves even
when his brain was telling him he's in deep trouble.

"What is it?" I called after her.

"No time," she shouted back, hurrying even faster. I'd
never before seen her move at anything more than a languid
stroll.

Shaking my head, in exasperation as much as disbelief, I
made my way to the bridge. Duchamp and Rodriguez were
both there. Good, I thought.

"We can't pressurize the gas envelope until we can determine its structural integrity," Duchamp was saying, in the
kind of stilted cadence that I knew was meant for the ship's
log. "The leak rate is small at present, but growing steadily.
If it's not stopped it will affect the ship's trim and cause an
uncontrollable loss of altitude."

She looked up at me as I stopped in the open hatchway. Jabbing a finger on the chair arm's stud that turned off the recorder, she asked impatiently, "Well?"

"We've got to get out of these clouds," I said. "The bugs out there are eating the ship."

Duchamp arched her brows. "I don't have time for theories. We've developed a leak in the gas envelope. It's minor, but it's growing."

"The shell's leaking?" My voice must have gone up two octaves.

"It's not serious," Rodriguez said quickly.

I turned to him. "We've got to get out of these clouds! You were out there, Tom. The bugs—"

"I make the decisions here," Duchamp snapped.

"Now wait a minute," I said.

Before I could go further, she said, "With all deference to your position as owner of this vessel, Mr. Humphries, I am the captain and I will make the decisions. This isn't a debating society. We're not going to take a vote on the subject."

"We've got to get out of these clouds!" I insisted.

"I totally agree," she said. "As soon as we can repair the leak in the envelope, I intend to go deeper and get below this cloud deck."

"Deeper?" I glanced at Rodriguez, but he was saying nothing.

"Have you forgotten Fuchs? The IAA just sent word that he's descending rapidly toward the clear air below the clouds."

The prize money didn't look all that enticing to me, compared to the very strong possibility that we would all be killed if the bugs chewed away enough of the ship.

Rodriguez spoke up at last. "Mr. Humphries, we can't make an effective decision until we know how badly the gas envelope's been damaged."

"It's really very minor," Duchamp said. But then she added, "At present."

"But it's getting worse," Rodriguez said.

"Slowly," she insisted.

"As long as we stay in these clouds we're going to have colonies of Venusian organisms feasting on our ship's metals and minerals," I retorted hotly.

"This is no time to panic, Mr. Humphries," she said.

I thought it over for half a second. "I could fire you and appoint Tom captain."

"That would be tantamount to mutiny," she snapped.

"Wait," Rodriguez said. "Wait, both of you. Before anybody goes off the deep end, let's repair the envelope and get back in proper condition."

"Do we have time for that?"

Duchamp said coldly, "May I point out that Fuchs is diving deeper while we fiddle around here. If your bugs are eating our ship, why aren't they eating his?"

"What makes you think they're not?"

"I know Lars," she said with a thin smile. "He's no fool. If he thought he was going into more danger by descending he wouldn't go down."

I glanced from her to Rodriguez to Riza, sitting wide-eyed at her comm console, then back to Duchamp.

"All right," I said finally. "I'm going back to the bio lab to help Marguerite determine if the bugs caused the damage to our suits. How long will it take you to repair the leak in the hull?"

"Several hours," Duchamp said.

"Yeats is suiting up now, with Akira. They're going to start the work from inside the shell," Rodriguez said. "It'll be safer that way."

"But they'll still be exposed to the bugs, won't they?" I asked. "I mean, if the outside air is leaking into the shell, the bugs are coming in with it."

Duchamp said flatly, "That's assuming you're right and it's the bugs that damaged your suits."

"You can't let them stay out too long," I insisted. "If the bugs do eat the suits—"

"The fabric is self-repairing," Duchamp said.

"The joints aren't," I pointed out.

There was one quick and dirty way to test whether the bugs were eating the suit material, Marguerite and I decided. I hacked off a small section of the cermet knee joint to my damaged suit to serve as an experimental guinea pig. It wasn't easy; the cermet was tough. I had to scrounge an electric saw from the ship's stores to do the job.

Then I brought it to Marguerite's lab, where she had set up a spare insulated cooler as an incubator for the Venusian organisms.

But when I brought the cermet sample to her, she was downcast.

"They're dying," Marguerite said, as miserable as if it was her own child expiring.

"But I thought—"

"I've tried to duplicate their natural environment as closely as I can," she said, as much to herself as to me. "I've kept the temperature inside the cooler just above freezing, right about where it was in the clouds. I've lowered the air pressure and even sprayed it with extra sulfuric acid. But it's not working! Every sample I take shows them weakening and dying."

I handed her the ragged little square of cermet I'd cut out. "Well, here, get this into the cooler with them and let's see what happens before they all die."

She had done a remarkable job of jury-rigging what had once been a spare cooler unit into a laboratory apparatus. The lid was sealed against air leaks, although there were half a dozen sensor wires and two small tubes going through the sealant into the cooler's interior.

All-in-all, it looked very much like the makeshift contraption that it was, the kind of thing that scientists call a kloodge. I once heard of such devices being named after someone named Rube Goldberg, but I never found out why.

Looking worried, Marguerite deftly sliced my cermet

sample into hair-thin slivers with a diamond saw, then inserted half of them into the cooler through one of the tubes.

"What are you doing with a diamond saw?" I asked.

That made her smile. "What are you doing without one?" she countered.

"Huh?"

"I had hoped we'd pick up samples of Venusian rock. The saw can slice thin specimens for the microscope."

"Oh, of course," I said. I knew that; I simply didn't think of it at that moment.

"I would have thought," she went on, "that a planetary scientist would have this kind of equipment with him for geological investigations."

I felt my brow furrow. "Come to think of it, I believe I do."

She laughed. "I know you do, Van. I stole this from the equipment stores that you had marked for your use."

She'd been teasing me! To hide my embarrassment, I bent over and peered into the narrow little window in the cooler's lid. All I could see inside was a grayish fog.

"That's actual Venusian air inside there?" I asked.

"Yes," she replied, frowning slightly. "I was drawing it off from the main probe we've been using for the nephelometers and mass spectrometers."

I caught her accent on the past tense. "Was?"

She made an irritated huffing sound, very much like her mother. "The probes have been shut down. Captain's orders."

"Why would she . . . ?" Then I realized, "She doesn't want to run the risk of having the bugs break loose inside the ship."

"That's right," Marguerite said. "So I've got this sample and that's all. No replacements."

"And yet she acted as if she thought I was crazy when I told her the bugs ate the suits and the railing."

Marguerite shrugged as if it weren't important to her. But it was to me.

"She's a first-class hypocrite, your mother," I said, with some heat.

"She's the ship's captain," Marguerite answered stiffly. "She might think your idea's crazy, but the safety of this ship and crew is her responsibility and she's decided not to take any unnecessary risks."

I could see the logic in that. But still ... "She's sent Yeats and Sakamoto out to repair the shell."

"That's necessary. There's no getting around it."

"Perhaps," I admitted reluctantly. "But she shouldn't let them stay out too long."

"How long is too long?"

"How long were Rodriguez and I outside? Both our suits were damaged."

Marguerite nodded. "I'm sure she's watching their readouts."

The timer on the cooler chimed, ending our conversation. Marguerite drew out a sample of the Venusian air, rich with sulfuric acid droplets and the organisms that lived in them. Quickly she prepared a microscope slide and put the display onto the screen of the laptop computer she had plugged into the electron microscope.

"They're recovering!" she said happily. "Look at how vigorously they're swimming around!"

"But where's the suit material?" I asked.

She turned from the laptop to stare at me. "It's gone. They've digested the cermet. It's food for them."

DEADLY DECISIONS

raced along the passageway to the bridge. Duchamp was in her command chair, as usual. I could hear Yeats's voice, puffing with exertion:

". . . going a lot slower than I expected. This is tough work, let me tell you."

"You've got to bring them back inside!" I said to Duchamp. "Now! Before the bugs kill them."

Rodriguez was not on the bridge. Riza Kolodny, at the comm console, looked at me and then the captain and finally turned her face resolutely to her screens, not wishing to get involved.

Before Duchamp could reply, I said, "The bugs eat cermet. It's like caviar to them, for god's sake!"

She leveled a hard stare at me. "You have proof of this?"

"Your daughter has the proof in her lab. It's true! Now get those two people back inside here!"

Duchamp looked as if she would have preferred to slice my throat, but she touched the communications stud on her chair arm and said crisply, "Yeats, Sakamoto, come back inside. Now. That's an order."

"Okay by me," Yeats said, with obvious relief. She was not accustomed to much physical exertion, clearly.

"Yes, Captain," said Sakamoto, so even and unemotional that the words might just as well have come from a computer.

Duchamp called Rodriguez back to the bridge and Marguerite came up from her lab. She and I crowded the hatchway as she displayed her experiment's results on the main screen. Within minutes, Dr. Waller, Yeats, and Sakamoto came up, making a real crowd in the passageway. I could feel them pressing me, pushing their sweaty bodies against me. My heart was racing; I felt queasy and breathless at the same time.

"I'm still checking air samples for the signature of the cermet materials," Marguerite was telling her mother, "but so far there is none. The organisms seem to have digested every molecule."

If this information rattled our steely-eyed captain, she did not show it. Turning to Rodriguez, she said, "What do you think?"

Rodriguez's brow was already deeply creased with worry. "We've got a catch-twenty-two situation here. We need to repair the shell or sink, but if we go outside the bugs will degrade our suits so badly we'll be at risk of total suit failure."

"You mean death," I said. "Someone could get killed."

He nodded, a little sheepishly, I thought.

Marguerite added, "Meanwhile the organisms are eating away at the shell. They could damage it to the point where . . . where . . ." She drew in her breath, realizing that if the shell failed, we would all go plunging into the depths of the atmosphere.

Is this what happened to Alex? I wondered. Was his ship devoured by these hungry alien bugs?

Then I realized that the organisms weren't alien at all. This was their natural environment. We were the aliens, the invaders. Maybe they were instinctively fighting against us, trying to drive us out of their world.

Nonsense! I told myself. They're just bugs. Microbes. They can't think. They can't act in an organized way.

I hoped.

Duchamp looked straight at me as she said, "This is what we're going to do. Each of us will take turns at repairing the shell. None of us will stay outside longer than Tom and Mr. Humphries did."

"But our suits were damaged," I objected.

"We will keep the excursions shorter than your EVA was," Duchamp said. "Short enough to get back inside before the bugs can damage the suits."

From behind me Yeats grumbled, "Then it's a race to see if we can plug the leaks faster than the bugs can eat through the shell."

Duchamp nodded. "In the meantime, I intend to go deeper."

"Deeper?" Riza blurted.

"There's a layer of clear air between this cloud deck and the next, about five kilometers below us," Duchamp said.

Rodriguez grinned humorlessly. "I get it. No clouds, no bugs."

I could feel Yeats start to object, but before she could the captain went on, "Willa, I want you to estimate the maximum time we can work in the atmosphere out there before we run into danger of suit damage."

"Yes, Captain," Yeats said glumly.

"Tom, you take the conn. Mr. Humphries and I will take the first shift. Everyone else will take a turn at the work," she hesitated a moment, looking past me. At her daughter, I supposed. "Everyone except Dr. Waller," she said.

I felt the doctor's gusting breath of appreciation on the back of my neck. He was in no physical condition for an EVA, true enough. But I worried about Marguerite; she had no training for this sort of thing. Or did she?

Duchamp got up from her command chair. Everyone in the passageway flattened themselves out to make room for her to pass by. I followed her, fighting down the fears that were shaking me.

In a sense, of course, none of us had any training for this sort of EVA. Virtual reality simulations were all well and good, as far as they went, but nothing could prepare you for being outside in those clouds, with the wind gusting against you and the ship shuddering and bucking like a living animal. Add to that the knowledge that the bugs were chewing away on your suit . . . it scared me down to my bladder. I felt jittery, almost light-headed.

But it had to be done, and I wasn't going to back away from my share of the responsibility.

It wasn't easy, that's for certain. Even though we worked inside the shell, grappling along its curving bulkhead, dangling from the structural support beams by our suit tethers was far more demanding than climbing mountains.

And it was dark inside the shell. Outside, even in the clouds, there was always a yellowish-gray glow, a sullen twilight that was bright enough to see by, once your eyes adjusted to it. Inside the shell we had to work by the light of our helmet lamps, which didn't go far. Their glow was swallowed up by the yellowish haze pervading the shell's interior. It reminded me of descriptions of London fogs from long ages ago, groping along in the misty gloom.

"Riza," I heard Duchamp call over the suit radio, "get Dr. Waller to put together as many lamps as he can take from stores. We need working lights in here."

"Yes, Captain," came the comm tech's reply.

Despite everything, I had to smile inside my helmet. Duchamp wasn't allowing our ship's doctor to sit idly while the rest of us worked.

We sprayed epoxy all across the shell's enormous interior. And it was huge in there; the vast curving space seemed measureless, infinite. The darkness swallowed the pitiful light from our helmet lamps. I began to think about Jonah in the belly of the whale or Fuchida exploring the endless caverns inside Olympus Mons on Mars.

There was no way to know precisely where the leaks were; the shell wasn't instrumented for that and the leaks weren't so big that you could see daylight through them. We concentrated our spraying on the aft end of the envelope, naturally, because that's where we had seen the charring.

Duchamp and I spent an exhausting half hour in the shell, then Rodriguez and Marguerite replaced us. Duchamp would have had the entire crew in there at once and gotten the job over with, except for the fact that we had only two epoxy spray guns aboard.

So, two by two, the crew worked hour after hour on sealing the leaks in the gas envelope. Exhausted as I was, I took another turn, this time with Sakamoto. Rodriguez actually went out three times. So did Yeats, grumbling every inch of the way.

When my second tour was over, I half collapsed on the deck just inside the airlock, too weary even to think about peeling off my suit. I simply lifted off my helmet and sat there, not even taking off my backpack. It wasn't only the physical exertion, although just about every muscle in my body was shrieking. It was the mental strain, the knowledge that the ship was in trouble, serious trouble, and we were all in danger.

Sakamoto, standing above me, pulled his helmet off and gave me a rare smile. "Work is the curse of the drinking man," he said, then started to get out of his suit. I couldn't have been more surprised if he had sprouted wings and flown back to Earth.

Finally it was finished. I had crawled into my berth to inject an enzyme shot into my arm when the intercom blared, a scant six centimeters from my ear, "MR. HUMPHRIES TO THE BRIDGE, PLEASE."

Bleary-eyed, I finished the injection, then slid out of the berth and padded in my stocking feet toward the bridge, not even bothering to smooth out the wrinkles in my coveralls.

Somewhere in the back of my mind I knew I was sweaty and far from sweet-smelling, but I didn't care.

Duchamp was in her command chair, as flinty as ever. Rodriguez must have been grabbing a few winks of sleep. Yeats was at the comm console.

As soon as I ducked through the hatch, Duchamp said to Yeats, "Tell him, Willa."

Looking far from jocular, Yeats said, "I have good news and bad news. Which do you want to hear first?"

"The good news," I snapped.

"We stopped the leak," she said. But her face did not show any sign of joy. "The ship is back in trim and we've broken out of the clouds into the clear air."

"We're pumping out the air we took in during the descent through the cloud deck," Duchamp added, "and replacing it with the ambient air, outside."

I nodded. "Good."

"Now the bad news," said Willa. "Every one of our suits is damaged, at least slightly. Not one of them would pass a safety inspection. They all leak."

"That means we can't go EVA?"

"Not until we repair them," Yeats said cheerlessly.

"All right," I said. "That's not as bad as it might have been."

"The question is," Duchamp said, "will there be more bugs in the deeper cloud decks?"

"It gets awfully hot down there," I said. "More than two hundred degrees Celsius. And that's thirty, forty kilometers above the surface."

"So you don't think we'll have any problems from the bugs?"

"We should ask Marguerite. She's the biologist."

Duchamp nodded. "I've already asked her. She said she doesn't know. No one knows."

I heard myself say, "There can't be anything living at such high temperatures! It gets up to four hundred degrees and more at the surface."

"I wonder," she murmured.

From being a total skeptic about the bugs, the captain had swung to suspecting them to be lurking in the next cloud deck, waiting to devour us.

Then another thought struck me. "Where's Fuchs? Has he gone down into the second cloud deck yet?"

She nodded. "No. He appears to be hovering in this clear area, just as we are, according to the latest word from the IAA."

"I wonder if he . . ." Duchamp and the bridge wavered out of focus, as if someone had twisted a camera lens the wrong way. I put out a hand to grasp the edge of the hatchway, my knees suddenly rubbery.

I heard someone ask, "What's the matter?"

Everything was spinning madly around me. "I feel kind of woozy," I heard my own voice say.

That's the last thing I remember.

COLLAPSE

I opened my eyes to see Dr. Waller, Rodriguez, and Marguerite bending over me. They all looked grim, worried.

"Do you know where you are?" Waller asked, the lilt in his voice flattened by concern.

I looked past their intent faces and saw medical monitors, green worms crawling across their screens. I heard them beeping softly and smelled antiseptic.

"The infirmary," I said. My voice was little more than a croak.

"Good!" Dr. Waller said approvingly. "Full consciousness and awareness. That's very good."

Marguerite looked relieved. I suppose Rodriguez did too.

It didn't take much mental acumen to see that I was lying on the infirmary's one bed. Located back at the tail of the gondola, the infirmary was the only place on *Hesperos* with space enough for people to stand at bedside. Our bunks were nothing more than horizontal closets.

"What happened?" I asked, still not feeling strong enough to do anything but lie there on my back.

"Your anemia came up and bit you," said Dr. Waller.

I glanced at Marguerite. I had never mentioned my condition to her, but apparently Waller had told her everything while I was unconscious. She looked concerned, but not surprised. Rodriguez had known about it, of course, but he still looked very worried, his forehead wrinkled like corduroy.

"But I've been taking my shots," I said weakly.

"And engaging in more physical exertion than you have ever done in your life, I should think," said the doctor cheerily. "The hard work caught up with you."

"A few hours . . . ?"

"It was enough. More than enough."

Talk about depressing news. Here I thought I was doing my share, working alongside Rodriguez and even Duchamp, facing the same dangers and duties as the rest of the crew. And my god-cursed anemia strikes me down, shows everybody that I'm a weakling, a useless burden to them all. Father was right: I'm the runt of the litter, in every imaginable way.

I felt like crying, but I held myself together as Waller fussed around me and Rodriguez left, half apologizing that he had to get back to the bridge.

"We're getting ready to enter the next cloud deck," he said. "We decided just to skim in and out, take some samples of the cloud droplets and see if there are any bugs in 'em."

I nodded weakly. "Good thinking."

"It was Dee's idea—Captain Duchamp's."

I turned my head slightly toward Marguerite. "It's a good thing we brought a biologist along with us," I said.

She smiled.

Rodriguez grabbed my hand and said, "You take care of yourself now, Van. Do what the doc tells you."

"Sure," I agreed. "Why not?"

He left. Marguerite remained at my bedside.

"How long will I have to stay here?" I asked Dr. Waller.

"Only a few hours, I should think," he replied, his face as

somber as ever. "I'm running diagnostics on your red cell count and oxygen transfer to your vital organs. It shouldn't take very long."

I pushed myself up to a sitting position, expecting to feel my head spin. Instead, it felt fine. Marguerite hurriedly pushed up my pillows so I could sit back against them.

"You make a good nurse," I said to her. I actually felt pretty good. My voice was coming back to its normal strength.

"You scared the wits out of everyone, collapsing like that."

"How should I have collapsed?" I joked.

"Humor!" said Dr. Waller. "That's good. A certain sign of recovery."

"There's nothing really wrong with me," I said, "except this damned anemia."

"Yes, that's true. Except for the anemia you are in fine physical condition. But as Mercutio says to Romeo, the wound may not be as deep as a well or as wide as a church door but 'tis enough, 'twill serve."

Marguerite understood. "You have to be careful, Van. Your condition could become serious if you don't take proper care of yourself."

There was a part of me that was perfectly happy to be lying on a sickbed and having her looking so concerned about me. But how long would that last? I asked myself. I've got to get up and be active. I don't want pity. I want respect.

"What you're telling me," I said sharply to the doctor, "is that if I have to do any serious physical exertion I should take extra enzyme shots."

He nodded, but pointed out glumly, "We only have a fixed amount of the enzyme supply in our medical stores. And we do *not* have the equipment or resources to make more. Your supply is more than adequate for normal usage, with a healthy additional amount in reserve. But still—you should pace yourself more carefully than you have today, Mr. Humphries."

"Yes. Of course. Now, when can I get up and back to my work?"

He glanced at the monitors lining the infirmary's wall. "In two hours, more or less."

"Two hours," I said. "Fine."

I was actually on my feet much sooner. I had to be.

Marguerite brought me a handheld computer to work with while I sat in the infirmary bed, waiting for Dr. Waller to finish his diagnostics. He left the infirmary for a while, humming to himself as usual. I checked with IAA headquarters back in Geneva and, some ten minutes later, got a reply that Fuchs had entered the second cloud deck more than an hour earlier.

He was ahead of us again. And apparently he had suffered no damage from the bugs that had attacked our gas envelope. Why not? Was his *Lucifer* made of different materials? Had he been damaged and then repaired his ship more quickly than we had been able to do?

Sitting there staring at the printed IAA report, I began to wonder what would happen if Fuchs actually did get to the surface first and recovered Alex's remains. He'd get Father's ten billion in prize money and I'd be penniless. Totally cut off. I wouldn't even be able to afford my home in Majorca, let alone the apartments I maintained here and there.

I wondered what my friends would do. Oh, they'd put up with me for a while, I supposed. After all, it would be egregiously impolite to just drop me immediately because I'd lost all my money. But sooner or later they'd turn away from me. I was under no illusions about that. They were my friends because I was their social equal or—many of them—because I had the money to support their operas and plays and dabbles at scientific research.

Penniless, I would also become friendless quite quickly. Gwyneth couldn't afford to stay with me; she needed someone to pay her bills.

What would Marguerite do? I asked myself. I couldn't see her abandoning me because I'd become poor. On the other hand, I couldn't see her supporting me, either. We didn't know each other that well, really, and besides, I doubted that she had the kind of money it would take to support me.

That's what was whirling through my mind as I sat on the infirmary's lone bed, waiting for Dr. Waller to come back from wherever he'd disappeared to and give me permission to get—

The ship lurched. I mean, *lurched*. We had bounced and shuddered when we were in the superrotation winds up higher, but once we'd sunk down to the clear region between the first and second cloud decks the air pressure had become so thick that the winds were smothered and our ride had become glassy smooth.

But now everything suddenly tilted so badly that I was nearly thrown off the bed. I clutched its edges like a child riding a coaster down a snowy hillside.

Through the closed hatch of the infirmary I could hear alarm bells blaring and the thundering slams of other hatches swinging shut automatically.

The infirmary seemed to sway. For an instant I thought I was getting dizzy again, but then I remembered that I was in the tail section of the gondola and it was the gondola itself that was swinging beneath the gas envelope. Somewhere an alarm siren started shrieking.

I jumped out of bed, glad that Waller hadn't stripped off my coveralls. The floor beneath me tilted again, this time pointing downward like an airplane starting to dive. Something behind me crashed to the floor.

"ALL HANDS STRAP IN!" the intercom blared. Great advice. I had to clutch the bed to keep from sliding down to the infirmary hatch.

The hatch swung outward and banged against the bulkhead. Dr. Waller was on the other side, his red-rimmed eyes wide with terror.

"We're sinking!" he screamed. "The gas shell has collapsed!"

SINKING

For what seemed like a century and a quarter I just hung there, clutching the bed while alarms hooted and wailed all along the gondola, staring at Waller as he held on to the hatch frame with both his hands. In the hollow of my stomach I could feel the ship dropping.

"ALL HANDS TO THE AIRLOCK," the intercom speakers blared. "GET INTO YOUR SPACESUITS. *NOW.*"

It was Duchamp's voice, sharp as a surgeon's scalpel, not panicked but certainly urgent enough to make me move.

"Come on," I said as I stumbled past Waller. He seemed frozen, mouth gaping, eyes goggling, unwilling or unable to let go of the hatch frame and start downhill toward the airlock.

I grabbed his shoulder and shook him, hard. "Come on!" I shouted at him. "You heard the captain. That means everybody!"

"But I can't breathe in my spacesuit!" he said, nearly in tears. "The one time I had to use it I nearly suffocated!"

"That doesn't matter now," I said, yanking him free. "Come with me, I'll show you how to do it."

The ship seemed to straighten out somewhat as we staggered and weaved down the passageway. We had to manually open hatches every few meters. They automatically slammed shut behind us. At least the alarms had been silenced; their wailing was enough to scare you into cardiac fibrillation.

Rodriguez was already at the airlock, helping Riza Kolodny into her suit. The other two technicians crowded behind him, getting their own suits on.

"Where's Marguerite?" I asked him.

"I don't know. Maybe up at the bridge with her mother," he said, without looking up from his work.

"These suits are all damaged," I said, holding out the sleeve of my own. The elbow joint was obviously blackened, as if singed by a flame.

"You want to go with no suit at all?" Rodriguez snapped.

Waller moaned. I thought he was going to faint, but then I saw a growing stain across the crotch of his coveralls. The doctor had wet himself.

"What's happened?" I demanded. "What are we going to do?"

Still checking Riza's backpack, Rodriguez said, "Damned shell cracked open. We're losing buoyancy. Can't keep the ship in trim."

"So what—"

"We're going to the descent module, use it in the escape pod mode. Ride it up to orbit and hope *Truax* can find us."

"Then why do we need the suits?"

"Whole front section of the gondola's leaking like a frickin' sieve," Rodriguez said, his voice edged with fear-driven tension. "If the leaks reach the bridge before we can get everybody into the pod . . ."

He didn't have to finish the sentence. I got the picture.

I helped Dr. Waller into his suit before starting to put mine on. The ship kept dipping and then rising, making my insides feel as if I were on an elevator that couldn't make up its mind. Waller seemed almost in shock, hardly able to move his arms and legs, his eyes staring blankly, his mouth sagging open and gasping like a fish. It flashed through my mind that he had the only undamaged suit on board; all the others had developed leaks, even the spares.

By the time I got my own suit on, Marguerite and her mother were still nowhere in sight. I clomped down the slanting passageway toward the bridge.

"Where're you going?" Rodriguez yelled after me. "I gotta check you out!"

"I'll be back in a few minutes," I called back, shouting so they could hear me through the helmet. "Get everybody to the escape pod. I'll catch up with you there."

Checking out the suit was nothing more than busywork at this stage of the game. They all leaked to some degree, we all knew that. But we only needed them for the few minutes it would take to clamber into the bathysphere and dog its hatch shut.

I wasn't going without Marguerite, though. What was she doing? Where was she?

Her lab was empty. The ship seemed to straighten out again; the passageway even angled upward a little, for a moment.

I pushed on to the bridge. There they were, both of them.

". . . can't stay here," Marguerite was saying, pleading really.

"Someone's got to keep the ship on as even a keel as possible," Duchamp said, her eyes fixed on the main display screen. Sitting in her command chair, she had a laptop across her knees, her fingers working the keys like a concert pianist playing a cadenza.

"But you'll—"

I broke into their argument. "Everyone's suited up and headed for the escape pod."

Duchamp looked sharply at me. Then, with a single curt nod, she turned her gaze to her daughter. "Get into your suit. Now."

"Not until you come with me," Marguerite said.

The picture is etched in my mind. The two of them, as identical as copies from a blueprint except for their ages, glaring at each other with identical stubborn intensity.

"Both of you, get your suits on," I said, trying to sound commanding. "The others are waiting for you."

The ship lurched and heaved wildly. My stomach tried to jump into my throat. I grabbed the hatch frame for support. Marguerite, standing beside her mother, staggered and fell into Rodriguez's chair with an ungainly thump.

Duchamp turned back to the main screen, banging on the laptop's keyboard again.

"We're losing the last bit of buoyancy we have," she said, not taking her eyes off the screen. I saw that it displayed a schematic of the ship's maneuvering engines.

"Then we've got to get out!" I snapped.

"Someone's got to keep the ship from diving deeper," Duchamp said. "If I don't work the engines, we'll sink like a stone."

"What about the regular trim program?" I demanded.

She barked out a single harsh "Hah!"

I said, "The computer should be able—"

"There's no way the computer can keep this bucket on a halfway even keel without manual input," Duchamp said. "No way."

"But—"

"I'm only barely managing to hold her at altitude now."

As if to prove her words, the ship dipped down again, then popped sharply upward. I thought I could hear moaning from up forward, where the rest of the crew was waiting for us.

"It's the captain's duty," Duchamp said, glancing at me. Then she smiled thinly. "I know you didn't want me for the job, but I take the position seriously."

"You'll kill yourself!" Marguerite shrieked.

"Get her off the bridge," Duchamp said to me.

Still clinging to the rim of the hatch, I thought swiftly. "I'll make you a deal."

She arched one brow at me.

"I'll get Marguerite suited up and bring your suit here to the bridge. Then you suit up and come forward to the escape pod."

She nodded.

"Come on," I said to Marguerite.

"No," she snapped. Turning to her mother, she said, "Not without you."

Duchamp gave her a look I'd never seen on her face before. Instead of her usual stern, flint-hard stare, the captain's features softened, her eyes glistened.

"Marguerite, go with him. I'll be all right. I'm really not suicidal."

Before Marguerite could reply I grasped her wrist and literally hauled her out of the chair, off the bridge, and down the slanting passageway to the airlock where the suits were stored.

"She'll kill herself," Marguerite said in a throaty whisper, as if talking to herself. Over and over, as I helped her into her spacesuit, she repeated it. "She'll kill herself."

"I won't let her," I said, with a bravado I didn't really feel. "I'll get her into her suit and up to the escape pod if I have to carry her."

I only said it to make Marguerite feel better, and I'm certain that she knew it. But she let me help her put the suit on and check out the backpack.

I took the least-used-looking of the remaining suits and we staggered back up the passageway toward the bridge again. The ship's pitching and reeling seemed to calm down somewhat. Maybe we had hit a region of calm, stable air, or we were finally in equilibrium with the air pressure outside.

We got to the bridge and I offered to run the auxiliary engines while the captain got into her suit.

She gave me a pitying smile. "If I had a few days to teach you . . ."

"Then let's get Rodriguez up here," I suggested.

"I'll go get him," Marguerite said.

Raising her hand to stop her daughter, Duchamp said, "The intercom still works, dear."

"Then call him," I commanded.

She seemed to think it over for half a second, then tapped the intercom stud on her chair arm. Before she could say anything, however, the message light on the comm console flashed on.

Duchamp called out to the computer, "Answer incoming call."

Lars Fuchs's heavy, jowly face filled the screen, glowering angrily.

"I picked up your distress call," he said flatly, with no preamble.

Hesperos's command computer was programmed to beam out a distress call when safety limits were exceeded. The instant the alarms began going off and the compartment hatches were automatically shut, the computer must have started calling for help. In ten minutes or so, I realized, we would be getting inquiries from the IAA on Earth: standard safety procedure for all spaceflights.

"We're preparing to abandon ship," Duchamp said. "Buoyancy's gone."

"Stand by," Fuchs said, the expression on his face somewhere between annoyed and exasperated. "I'm approaching you at maximum speed. You can transfer to *Lucifer*."

Strangely, Duchamp's expression softened. "You don't have to do that, Lars."

He remained irritated. "The hell I don't. IAA regulations require any craft receiving a distress signal to render all possible assistance, remember?"

"But you can't—"

"If I don't come to your aid," he snapped, "the IAA will hang me out to dry. They'd love to make an example of me. And they won't hang me by my neck, either."

I studied his face there on the bridge's main display screen, at least two times bigger than life. There was anger there, plenty of it. Bitterness deeper than I'd ever seen before. Lars Fuchs looked like a man who'd been forced to make hard decisions all his life, iron-hard decisions that had cost him all hope for ease and joy. Joyless. That was it. That was what made his face so different from anyone I had ever seen before. There was no trace of joy in him. Not even a glimmer that a moment of happiness would ever touch him. He had abandoned all hope of joy, long years ago.

It took all of two or three seconds for me to come to that conclusion. In that time Duchamp made her decision.

"We only have a few minutes before the gondola starts breaking up, Lars."

"Get into your suits. *Lucifer* will be within transfer range in . . ." his eyes shifted to some data screen out of camera range . . . "twelve minutes."

Duchamp drew in a deep breath, then nodded once. "All right. We'll be ready."

"I'll be there," Fuchs said grimly. Strangely, I thought I heard just a hint of softening in his voice.

CATASTROPHE

Rodriguez came back to the bridge and took over the conn while Duchamp struggled into her suit. She had to step out into the passageway, there was no room on the bridge to do it. Marguerite and I both checked her out. The suit had several slow leaks in it but would be good for at least an hour.

"We'll be aboard *Lucifer* by then," Duchamp said from inside her helmet. We were close enough so I could see her face through the tinted bubble. She wore the same hard-edged expression she usually showed. No trace of fear or even apprehension. If any of this frightened or worried her, it certainly did not show in her face.

"We'd better be," Marguerite said, barely loud enough for me to hear her. All our suits leaked a little, thanks to the bugs. I was grateful that we didn't have to pressurize them; Venus's atmospheric pressure at this altitude was slightly higher than Earth's.

It seemed to me that the ship's pitching and bobbing smoothed out somewhat under Rodriguez's hand, but that may have simply been my imagination—or the fact that I liked him a lot better than our hard-bitten captain.

Even so, the metal structure of the gondola began to groan and screech like a beast in pain. I stood out in the passageway and fought down the urge to scream out my own terror.

Marguerite didn't seem to be at all afraid. In fact, she knotted her brows in puzzlement. "Why are the bugs attacking just the one area of the gondola and not the entire structure?"

"What makes you think they're not?" I managed to gulp out.

"The only part being damaged so far is the section between airlock and the nose area," she said.

"How can you be sure of that?"

She jabbed a gloved thumb back toward the bridge. "Look at the life support display. That's the only section that's lost air pressure."

She was right, I saw as I peered at the life support screen. Now I furrowed my own brows. Was there any difference between that section and the rest of the gondola? I tried to remember the schematics and blueprints I had studied long months ago, when we were building *Hesperos*.

That entire section was designed around the airlock. Maybe the bugs were chewing on the plastics that we used as sealant for the outer airlock hatch?

"Is the inner airlock hatch sealed shut?" I called in to Rodriguez, who was still in the command chair.

Without stopping to think why I asked it, he flicked his eyes to the "Christmas tree" display of lights that indicated the status of the ship's various systems. Most of the lights were bright, dangerous red now.

"No," he said, shaking his head inside his helmet.

"Seal it," I said.

"It won't do any good," Marguerite said. "If the bugs have eroded the outer hatch's sealant, they'll do the same for the inner hatch."

"It might buy us a few minutes' time," I countered.

Duchamp, fully suited up now, agreed with me. "Every second counts."

She went into the bridge and repossessed her command chair. Rodriguez came out into the passageway with us. He had to squeeze a little to get through the hatch with his suit on.

"All right," Rodriguez said. "Helmets sealed. Let's go up forward with the others."

"What about her?" Marguerite asked.

Duchamp replied, "I'm needed here. I'll leave the bridge when *Lucifer* starts taking us aboard."

"I'll stay here with you, then," Marguerite said.

"No," I said. "You're coming with us."

She had to turn her entire body toward me for me to see the flat refusal in her eyes. The same rigidly adamant expression I had seen so often on her mother's face; the same stubborn set of the jaw.

"Captain," I called out, "give the order."

"He's right, *ma petite,*" Duchamp said, in a voice softer and lower than I had ever heard from her. "You've got—"

The message light began blinking again and Duchamp stopped in midsentence. "Answer incoming call."

Fuchs's bleakly somber face filled the comm screen. "I'll be maneuvering beneath your ship in four minutes. I won't be able to hold station for more than a minute or so. You'll have to be prepared to jump."

"Not below us!" Duchamp cried, startled. "We're breaking up. Debris could damage you."

Fuchs glowered. "Do your suits have maneuvering propulsion units?"

"No."

"Then if you can't fly, the only way to get from *Hesperos* to *Lucifer* is to drop." His wide slash of a mouth twitched briefly in what might have been the ghost of a smile. "Like Lucifer himself, you'll have to fall."

Jump from *Hesperos* onto *Lucifer*? The idea turned my innards to water. How could we do that? How close could Fuchs bring his ship to ours? I should have added maneuvering units to the spacesuits, I never thought of it back on Earth. We weren't planning any EVA work except for the transfer from *Truax,* and we had the cable trolley for that. Rodriguez should've known that we'd need maneuvering jets in an emergency. Somebody should've thought that far ahead.

"Three minutes, ten seconds," Fuchs said. "Be prepared to jump."

The comm screen went blank.

"Come on," Rodriguez said, nudging my shoulder to point me up the passageway.

Marguerite still hesitated.

"Go with them," Duchamp commanded. "I'll hold this bucket on course for another two minutes and then come along."

"You won't do anything foolish?" Marguerite asked, in a tiny voice.

Duchamp gave her a disgusted look. "The idea that the captain goes down with his ship was a piece of male machismo. I'm not afflicted with the curse of testosterone, believe me."

Before either of them could say anything more, I put my gloved hand on Marguerite's backpack and shoved her—gently—along the passageway.

I never found out if shutting the inner airlock hatch slowed down the bugs' destruction or not. As it turned out, it didn't matter, one way or the other.

The rest of the crew, Dr. Waller and the three technicians, were up in the nose section, already inside the descent module. As far as they knew we were still planning to use the 'sphere in its escape pod mode and rocket up into orbit, to be picked up by *Truax.*

As we hurried up the passageway toward the hatch that opened onto the airlock area, Rodriguez again ordered us to seal our helmets. "Air pressure's okay on the other side of the hatch," he said, "but there's probably a lot of Venusian air mixed in with our own. You wouldn't enjoy breathing sulfuric acid fumes."

I checked my helmet seal six times in the few steps it took us to reach the closed hatch.

Meanwhile, Rodriguez used his suit radio to tell Waller and the techs to get out of the pod and into the airlock section. They asked why, of course.

"We're going to transfer to Fuchs's ship, *Lucifer,*" he said.

"How?" I heard Riza Kolodny's adenoidal voice in my helmet earphones.

"You'll see," Rodriguez said, like a father who doesn't have the time to explain.

We got the hatch open and looked into the airlock section. It seemed safe enough. I couldn't see holes in the structure. But the metal seemed to be groaning again, and I could hear thin, high-pitched whistling noises, like air blowing through a lot of pinholes.

Rodriguez stepped through the hatch first, then Marguerite. I followed. The ship lurched again and I put out my hand to rest it on the sturdy metal frame of the airlock hatch, to steady myself.

Just then the hatch on the opposite end of the section swung back. Four spacesuited figures huddled there, anonymous in their bulky suits and reflective bubble helmets.

Duchamp's voice crackled in my earphones, "Fuchs is about a hundred meters below us and moving up closer. Connect your tethers to each other and start down to his ship."

Rodriguez said, "Right," then pointed at me. "You first, Mr. Humphries."

I had to swallow several times before I could answer him, "All right. Then Marguerite."

"Yessir," Rodriguez said.

There was no need to cycle the airlock. I just slid its inner hatch open and stepped inside, then punched the button that opened the outer hatch. Nothing happened. For a moment I just stood there like a fool, hearing the wind whistling around me, feeling trapped.

"Use the manual override!" Rodriguez said impatiently.

"Right," I answered, trying to recover some shred of dignity.

I tugged at the wheel and the outer hatch slowly, stubbornly inched open. Rodriguez handed me the first few tethers, clipped together end for end. He and Marguerite were hurriedly snapping the others onto one another.

"Attach the free end to a ladder rung," he told me.

"Right," I said again. It was the only word I could think of.

I leaned out the open airlock hatch to attach the tether and what I saw made me giddy with fright.

We were scudding along high above an endless layer of sickly yellowish clouds, billowing and undulating like a thing alive. And then the huge curving bulk of *Lucifer* slid in below us, so near that I thought we would crash together in a collision that would kill us all.

"*Lucifer* is on-station," I heard Duchamp's voice in my earphones.

Fuchs's ship seemed enormous, much bigger than ours. It was drawing nearer, slowly but noticeably closing the gap between us. Gasping for breath, I clicked the end of the tether on to the nearest ladder rung. Then I realized that Rodriguez was right behind me, feeding tether line out the hatch, past my booted feet. I watched the tether snake down toward the top of *Lucifer*'s bulbous shell, dropping like an impossibly thin line of string down, down, down and still not reaching the walkway that ran the length of the ship's gas envelope.

I suddenly realized that I hadn't taken any of my enzyme supply with me. Even if we made it to *Lucifer* I'd be without the medicine I needed to live.

Then *Hesperos* dipped drunkenly and the gondola groaned again like a man dying in agony. I happened to glance along the outer surface and saw that the metal was streaked with ugly dark smudges that ran from the nose to the airlock hatch and even beyond. I could see the thin metal skin cracking along those dark streaks.

Marguerite and Rodriguez were behind me, the four other spacesuited figures—Waller and the technicians—stood huddled on the other side of the airlock hatch. They were all waiting impatiently for me to start the descent toward *Lucifer* and safety. I stood frozen at the lip of the open hatch. Clambering down that dangling tether certainly did not look at all safe to me.

The groaning rose in pitch until it was like a screeching of fingernails on a chalkboard. I pulled my head back inside the airlock chamber, panting as if I'd run a thousand meters.

"She's breaking up!" Rodriguez yelled, so loud that I could hear him through my helmet as well as in my earphones.

Before my eyes, the front section of the gondola tore away with a horrifying grinding, ripping sound, carrying Waller and the technicians with it. They screamed, terrified high-pitched wails that shrieked in my earphones. The front end broke entirely free and flashed past my horrified eyes, tumbling end over end, spilling the spacesuited figures out into the open, empty air.

"Save me!" one of them screamed, a shriek so strained and piercing I couldn't tell which of them uttered it.

I saw a body thump down onto *Lucifer*, below us; it missed the catwalk and slid off into oblivion, howling madly all the time.

I could hardly stand up, my knees were so watery. Rodriguez, pressed in behind me in the airlock, whispered, "Jesus, Mary, and Joseph."

The screams went on and on, like red-hot ice picks jammed into my ears. Even after they stopped, my head rang with their memory.

"They're dead," Rodriguez said, his voice hollow.

"All of them," said Marguerite, quavering, fighting back tears.

"And so will we be," Duchamp's voice crackled, "if we don't get down those tethers *right now*."

The ship was bucking violently now, heaving up and down in a wild pitching motion. The wind tore at us from the gaping emptiness where the nose of the gondola had been. A ridiculous thought popped into my mind: We didn't need the airlock now; we could jump out of the ship through the jagged open end of the gondola.

I could hear Rodriguez panting hard in my earphones. At least, I assumed it was Rodriguez. Marguerite was there, too, and I thought Duchamp had to be on her way down to us by now.

"Go on!" Rodriguez yelled, as if the suit radios weren't working. "Down the tether."

If I had thought about it for half a millisecond I would have been so terrified I'd have frozen up, paralyzed with fear. But there wasn't any time for that. I grabbed the tether with both gloved hands.

"The servomotors will hold you," Rodriguez said. "Loop your boots in the line to take some of the load off your arms. Like circus acrobats."

I made a clumsy try at it, but only managed to tangle the tether around one ankle. The servomotors on the backs of the gloves clamped my fingers on the line, sure enough. All I had to worry about was making a mistake and letting go of the blasted line with both hands at the same time.

Down I went, hand over hand.

FALLING

It was hard work, clambering down that swaying, slithering line of connected tethers. Drenched in cold sweat, my heart hammering in my ears, I tried to clamp my boots around the line to take some of the strain off my arms but that was a clumsy failure. I inched down the line, my powered gloves clamping and unclamping slowly, like an arthritic old man's hands.

Lucifer seemed to be a thousand kilometers below me. I could see the end of the connected tethers dangling a good ten meters or more above the catwalk that ran the length of the ship's gas envelope. It looked like a hundred meters, to me. A thousand. When I got to the end of the line I'd have to jump for it.

If I made it to the end of the line.

And all the while I crawled down the length of tethers I kept hearing the terrified, agonized screams of the crewmen who fell to their deaths. My mind kept replaying that long, wailing, "Save meee!" over and over again. What would I scream if I missed the ship and plunged down into the fiery depths of inescapable death?

"Send the others down." It was Fuchs's heavy, harsh voice in my earphones. "Don't wait. Get started *now*."

"No," Marguerite said. I could sense her struggling, hear her breathing hard. "Wait . . ."

But Rodriguez said firmly, "No time for waiting. Now!"

I looked up and saw another figure start down the tethers. In the spacesuit it was impossible to tell who it was, but I figured it had to be Marguerite.

She was coming down the line a lot faster than I was, her boots gripping the tether expertly. Had she told me she'd done mountain climbing? I couldn't remember. Foolish thought, at that particular moment.

I tried to go faster and damned near killed myself. Let go of the line with one hand, then missed my next grab for it while my other hand was opening. There's a delay built into the servomotors that control the gloves' exoskeletons; you move your fingers and the motors resist a little, then kick in. My glove's fingers were opening, loosening my grip on the tether, when I desperately wanted them to tighten again.

There I was, one hand flailing free and the other letting go of my grip on the tether. If I hadn't been so scared I would've thrown up.

I lunged for the line with my free hand, caught it, and closed my fingers as fast and hard as I could. I thought I heard the servomotors whining furiously, although that must have been my imagination, since I'd never heard them before through the suit and helmet.

I hung there by one hand, all my weight on that arm and shoulder, for what seemed like an hour or two. Then I clasped the tether with my other hand, took the deepest breath I'd ever made in my life, and started down the tether again.

"Where's my mother?" I heard Marguerite's fear-filled voice in my earphones.

"She's on her way," Rodriguez answered.

But when I looked up I saw only their two figures clambering down the tether. *Hesperos* was a wreck, jouncing and shuddering above us, falling apart. The gas envelope was cracked like an overcooked egg. The gondola was half gone, its front end torn away, new cracks zigzagging along its length even as I watched. The bugs from the clouds must have made a home for themselves in the ship's metal structure.

Well, I thought grimly, they'll all roast to death when she loses her last bit of buoyancy and plunges into the broiling heat below.

Then I caught a vision of *Hesperos* crashing into *Lucifer,* and wondered how long Fuchs would keep his ship hovering below us.

"Hurry it up!" he called, as if he could read my thoughts.

Marguerite was sobbing openly; I could hear her over the suit radio. Rodriguez had gone silent except for his hard panting as he worked his way down the tether. They were both getting close to me.

And Duchamp was still in the ship. On the bridge, I realized, working to hold the shattered *Hesperos* in place long enough for us to make it to safety. But what about her safety?

"Captain Duchamp," I called, surprised that my voice worked at all. "Leave the bridge and come down the safety tether. That's an order."

No response.

"Mother!" Marguerite sobbed. "Mama!"

She wasn't coming. I knew it with the certainty of religious revelation. Duchamp was staying on the bridge, fighting to hold the battered wreck of *Hesperos* in place long enough for us to make it to safety. Giving her life to save us. To save her daughter, really. I doubt that she cared a rat's hiccup for the rest of us. Maybe she had some feelings for Rodriguez. Certainly not for me.

And then I was at the end of the tether line. I dangled there, swaying giddily, my boots swinging in empty air. The broad expanse of *Lucifer*'s gas envelope still seemed an awfully long way off. A long drop.

All my weight, including the weight of my spacesuit and backpack, was hanging from my hands. I could feel the bones of my upper arms being pulled slowly, agonizingly, out of my shoulder sockets, like a man on a rack. I couldn't hang on for long.

Then I saw three spacesuited figures climbing slowly up the curving flank of the massive shell. They looked like toys, like tiny dolls, and I realized just how much bigger *Lucifer* was than *Hesperos*. Enormously bigger.

Which meant that it was also much farther away than I had first guessed. It wasn't ten meters below me; it must have been more like a hundred meters. I couldn't survive a jump that long. No one could.

I looked up. Through my bubble helmet I saw Marguerite and Rodriguez coming down the line toward me, almost on top of me.

"What now?" I asked Rodriguez. "It's too far to jump."

Before he could answer, Fuchs's voice grated in my earphones. "I'm bringing *Lucifer* up close enough for you to reach. I can't keep her in position for long, so when I say jump, you either jump or be damned. Understand me?"

"Understood," Rodriguez said.

"Okay."

The broad back of *Lucifer* rose toward us, slowly moving closer. The three spacesuited figures were on the catwalk now, laying out long coils of tethers between them.

We were getting tantalizingly close, but each time I thought we were within a safe jumping distance *Hesperos* bobbed up or sideways and we were jerked away from *Lucifer.* My arms were blazing with pain. I could hear Rodriguez mumbling in Spanish, perhaps a prayer. More likely some choice curses.

I looked up again and saw that *Hesperos* was barely holding together. The gondola was cracked in a hundred places, the gas shell above it was missing pieces like an uncompleted jigsaw puzzle.

The only thing in our favor was that the air was thick enough down at this level to be relatively calm. Relatively.

Hesperos was still jouncing and fluttering like a leaf in a strong breeze.

Marguerite's sobbing seemed to have stopped. I supposed that she finally understood her mother was not coming and there was nothing she could do about it. There would be plenty of time to mourn after we had saved our own necks, I thought. When your own life is on the line, as ours were, you worry about your own skin and save your sentiment for everyone else for later.

"Now!" Fuchs's command shattered my pointless musings.

I was still dangling a tremendous distance from *Lucifer*'s catwalk; my shoulders and arms screaming in agony from the strain.

"Now, dammit!" he roared. *"Jump!"*

I let go. For a dizzying instant it felt as if I hung in midair, not moving at all. By the time I realized I was falling I thudded down onto the curving hull of *Lucifer*'s envelope with a bang that knocked the breath out of my lungs.

I had missed the catwalk and the men waiting to help me by several meters. I felt myself sliding along the curve of the shell, my arms and legs scrabbling to find a grip, a handhold, anything to stop me from sliding off into the oblivion below. Nothing. The shell's skin was smooth as polished marble.

In my earphones I heard a sort of howling noise, a strangled wail that yowled in my ears like some primitive animal's shriek. It went on and on without letup. I couldn't hear anything else, nothing except that agonized howl.

If *Lucifer* had been as small as *Hesperos* I would have slid off the shell and plunged into the thick hot clouds kilometers beneath me. I sometimes wonder if I would have been roasted to death as I fell deeper into the blistering hot atmosphere, or crushed like an eggshell by the tremendous pressure.

Instead, Fuchs's crewmen saved me. One of them jumped off the catwalk and slid on the rump of his suit to my side and grabbed me firmly. Even through the yowling noise in my earphones I could hear him grunt painfully when his tether stopped us both. Then he looped the extra tether he carried with him around my shoulders.

I was shaking so hard inside my suit that it took me three tries before I could control my legs well enough to follow Fuchs's crewman back up to the catwalk, where his companion already had his arms wrapped around Marguerite. I found out later that she had dropped neatly onto the catwalk and not even lost her balance.

. I was on my hands and knees, gasping from the efforts of the last few minutes. My shoulders felt as if someone had ripped my arms out of them. I was beyond pain; I was numb, wooden.

The catwalk seemed to shift beneath me, tossing me onto my side. I looked up and saw *Hesperos* breaking apart, big chunks of the envelope tearing away, the gondola splitting along its length.

Marguerite screamed. I saw the line of tethers flapping wildly, empty.

Raising myself painfully to my knees, I looked for Rodriguez. He was nowhere in sight.

"Where's Rodriguez?" I demanded.

No one answered.

I looked directly at Marguerite, who had disengaged herself from the crewmen who'd held her.

"Where's Tom?" I screamed.

I couldn't see her face inside the helmet, but sensed her shaking her head. "He jumped after me . . ."

"What happened to him?" I climbed to my feet shakily.

Fuchs's voice answered in my earphones. "The third person in your party jumped too late. I had to jink the ship sideways to avoid the debris falling from *Hesperos*. He missed us and fell into the clouds."

That was the long, terrified scream I heard in my ear-phones: Rodriguez falling, falling all that long way down to his death.

I stayed there on my knees until two of the crewmen yanked me up roughly by the armpits of my suit. I could hardly breathe. Every muscle and tendon in my body was in agony. And Rodriguez was dead.

Marguerite said softly, "My mother . . ." She sounded exhausted, as drained physically and emotionally as I felt.

I looked up. *Hesperos* was gone. No sign of the ship. Nothing above us but swirling sickly yellow-gray clouds. Nothing below us but more of the same. Duchamp, Rodriguez, Waller, and the three technicians—all dead. Venus had killed them. But then I realized that was not true. It was my fault. I had brought them to this hellish world. I had made them intrude into this place where humans were never meant to be. I had killed them.

And myself as well, I thought. Without my medication I'd be dead soon enough.

Tethered together like mountain climbers, we slowly, painfully, climbed down the ladder rungs set into the curving hull of *Lucifer*'s gas envelope to an airlock hatch set into its side. My heart lurched in my chest: I saw dark streaks smearing the length of the envelope, just as they had stained *Hesperos*'s shell.

The bugs were chewing on *Lucifer*'s hull, too. It was only a matter of time before this ship would break up just as *Hesperos* did. We were all going to die. There was no way around it.

"Move it!" Fuchs's voiced snarled in my earphones. "Stop your dawdling."

What difference did it make, I thought as I ducked through the airlock hatch.

My eyes widened with surprise when I saw that the inner hatch of the airlock was wide open. I hesitated a fraction of a second, only to be shoved unceremoniously by the crewman behind me through the inner hatch and into the compartment beyond it.

"I'm sealing the lock in ten seconds," Fuchs snapped. "Whoever's still outside will *stay* outside, understand me?"

As I stumbled into the compartment beyond the airlock chamber I half turned and saw, beyond the crewman's shoulder, Marguerite's spacesuited figure. The crewmen's suits were different from our own; their fabric was a dirty grayish silver, the suits looked bulkier, stiffer, and their helmets were the old-fashioned kind, mostly opaque with a faceplate visor, instead of the fishbowl bubbles that we wore.

The crewman behind Marguerite turned and pulled the airlock hatch shut.

"Stand by for emergency dive," Fuchs commanded. "Prepare to fill forward buoyancy tanks." Then he lapsed into a guttural foreign tongue; it sounded oriental to me, not Japanese but something like it. He was talking to someone on his bridge, obviously. Or perhaps to a voice-activated computer. Not to us.

One of the crewmen dogged the airlock's inner hatch

shut while the other clomped in his heavy boots to what looked like a pump. I heard it start chugging, but then its noise faded. And my spacesuit stiffened and ballooned noticeably. Finally it clicked into place. They had used this compartment as an adjunct to their airlock, so we could all get into the ship quickly rather than squeezing through the regular airlock chamber one at a time. Clever.

But as we waited for the compartment to fill with normal, breathable air, I realized that there were only two crewmen with us. I had seen three when we were descending toward *Lucifer*. Did they deliberately leave the other one outside? Even if Fuchs was ruthless enough to give such a command, what kind of men were these to obey it?

The pump's chugging grew louder again, which meant the compartment was filling to normal air pressure. At last the crewman near it checked a readout on the wrist of his suit, then bent awkwardly and shut off the pump. He and his partner raised the visors of their helmets. They were both Asians, I saw.

I unsealed my helmet and lifted it off my head. Marguerite just stood there, unmoving, so I went to her and took off her helmet. Her eyes were dry now, but they were staring, unfocused, seeing into the past, sorrowful beyond telling.

I almost told her not to regret her mother's death because we would be dead ourselves soon enough. But I didn't have the guts; actually I didn't even have the strength to open my mouth.

"Get your suits off," Fuchs's voice commanded, "and toss them out the airlock. They're contaminated. Get rid of 'em, quick."

I blinked with surprise. Apparently Fuchs was not resigned to dying.

With the crewmen helping, Marguerite and I slipped out of the backpacks and peeled off our spacesuits. The crewmen were silent, blank-faced, and quite efficient. They got rid of our suits quickly.

"Follow the crewmen up to the bridge," Fuchs said, as soon as our suits went out the airlock. I realized he must be watching us, although I couldn't see a camera anywhere in the blank-walled compartment.

One of the crewmen opened the hatch and gestured us through into a long passageway. We were still inside *Lucifer's* gas envelope, I knew. Apparently the vessel had no gondola dangling below; the living and working quarters were built inside the envelope.

The vessel was at least double the size of *Hesperos,* that was easy to see. Marguerite and I, escorted by the two silent, impassive crewmen, walked down the long passageway to a ladder. Peering up and down its well, I saw that it went two decks down and two more up.

We climbed up. One of the crewmen went before me, the other stayed behind Marguerite. I got the unpleasant feeling that they were behaving like guards escorting a pair of prisoners.

The bridge was spacious, with four crew stations and a commodious command chair. Which was empty when we arrived there. All four of the personnel present were Asians, three of them women. No one said a word.

"Can any of you speak English?" I asked.

"When they have to," came Fuchs's voice, from behind me.

I turned. He was standing in an open hatch off to one side of the bridge, framed by its metal edges.

Lars Fuchs had a thick, wide physique, built low to the ground. A barrel chest, short heavy arms and legs, but those arms looked as strong as a gorilla's. He seemed powerful, ferocious, like a black bear or some other wild animal with strong, sharp claws and a short temper. His face was set in an unpleasant, sardonic scowl, almost a sneer.

"So you're Martin Humphries's son, are you?"

I nodded as he stepped closer to me. Surprisingly, he was slightly shorter than I, only a hair or so, but definitely shorter. Yet he seemed enormous to me. He was wearing a black collarless shirt with short sleeves, and black baggy trousers

tucked into calf-length black boots that hadn't been polished in a long time.

He came up to me, looked me up and down as if I were a
specimen in a zoo, his wide thin lips turned down in an
expression of pure loathing. I tried to meet his gaze, but
what I saw in his eyes made me shudder inwardly. His eyes
were like ice, cold and Arctic blue. This man would kill me
if it suited him. Or anyone else.

He looked past me, toward Marguerite, and for just the
flash of a second his expression changed completely. I saw
surprise on his face, shock, really. His jaw dropped open,
his eyes went wide.

But only for a fraction of a second. He closed his mouth
with a click of his teeth and let out a long, snorting breath.
But his eyes remained fixed on her.

"Marguerite Duchamp, is it?"

"Yes," she said in a voice barely strong enough to be
heard.

"You look just like your mother did, twenty years ago."
Fuchs's own voice was lower, softer.

"You knew her then?" Marguerite asked, trembling.

He nodded wordlessly.

"She . . . she's dead," Marguerite said.

"I know." He turned back toward me. "This idiot killed
her."

Neither Marguerite nor I said a word of objection.

Fuchs clasped his hands behind his back. "Or rather, his
father did." He stepped closer to me again, like an inquisi-
tor examining his prisoner. "This was all your father's idea,
wasn't it?"

Anger flared through me. "You jumped at the chance to
take his prize money quickly enough," I said.

Fuchs grinned at me mirthlessly. "True enough. I certainly did."

For a long moment we stood almost touching noses
while Marguerite and the silent crew members watched us.

Fuchs pulled away. "Very well," he said, pointing a finger at Marguerite. "You'll be my guest aboard this vessel. Welcome, Ms. Duchamp."

He made a ludicrous little bow, with a smile that—on his heavy, fleshy face—was little less than grisly.

Then he turned back to me again. "And you, Mr. Humphries, can replace the man I lost rescuing you."

"Lost?" I blurted. "You lost a man?"

With a disgusted look, Fuchs explained, "My first mate was overcome by an unexpected burst of courage. When your vessel began to break up and the third man on your line started to fall away, my heroic first mate tried to reach him."

"What happened?" Marguerite asked.

"What do you think? He jumped off the catwalk and grabbed the falling man's ankles, trusting that his own tether would keep him safely anchored to my ship."

"Those tethers are supposed to be able to take tons of stress," I heard myself say.

"And so they do," Fuchs said, sarcastically. "But the railing it was clipped to doesn't. It ripped away and the two of them fell out of sight. Damned fool!"

That was Rodriguez that the first mate tried to save. The two of them plunged screaming to their deaths.

Fuchs jabbed a stubby finger at the technician sitting to the right of his command chair. She was a large, bulky woman with a round, flat face that looked to me almost like an Eskimo's.

"So you, Amarjagal, are now first mate."

He pointed again, this time at the wiry young man sitting next to her. "Nodon, you take over as propulsion engineer."

Both of them nodded. Don't they ever say anything? I wondered. Has Fuchs hired a crew of mutes?

He turned back to me. "I have a vacancy now for the position of communications technician," he said, almost politely. "You are now my comm tech, Mr. Humphries. That's an undemanding job, just right for someone with your lack of skills."

"Now just a minute, Fuchs, I'm not—"

He kicked me in my left shin, so hard that my leg exploded with pain. As I howled and bent over to clutch my leg I saw his right fist swinging at me. There was nothing I could do. He punched me in the kidney, my body spasmed upright and his left fist smashed into the side of my face. I crashed onto the deck so hard my vision went double.

Fuchs towered over me, fists on his hips, a leering smile on his jowly face. "Hurts, doesn't it?"

I couldn't speak. All I could do was writhe and groan from the pain.

"That's your first lesson in ship's discipline," he said, his voice flat and hard. "You will address me as *sir* or *Captain Fuchs*. And you will follow my orders quickly and correctly. Understand me?"

I was seeing flares of pain flashing before my eyes. I couldn't talk, couldn't even breathe.

Fuchs kicked me in the ribs. "Understand me?"

I nodded. Weakly.

He grunted, satisfied, and strode away. "Find a berth for our new comm tech," he ordered the crewmen.

I was awash with pain. But what hurt most was that Marguerite had just stood there, immobile as a statue. Even as I lay there on the deck she made no move to come to my aid.

I was losing consciousness. I could hardly breathe. As the world faded, the last thing I saw was Fuchs crooking a finger at Marguerite.

"You come with me," he said to her.

She followed him.

Everything went dark.

NIGHTMARE

I was walking in my garden outside the house on Majorca, Gwyneth at my side. She was wearing something light and so filmy that I could see her naked body beneath the sheer fabric. It billowed when the breeze blew in off the sea.

A mosquito whined past my ear. I became very annoyed. Genetic controls were supposed to have eliminated insect pests from the island. What had happened? What had gone wrong?

I turned to ask Gwyneth but it wasn't her anymore. It was Marguerite walking beside me in her spacesuit, of all things, carrying its helmet in her gloved hands. Wearing a spacesuit in my beautiful garden by the Mediterranean on a sunny springtime afternoon.

I smiled at her and she smiled back. But then I felt the sting of an insect on my bare arm and slapped at it.

"You've got to get into your suit," she said to me, and it was her mother instead of Marguerite.

"But you're dead," I said, not believing my eyes.

"So will you be if you don't get into your suit!" she replied urgently.

"But I don't have a suit," I said. "Why would I keep a suit here?"

Instead of answering she pointed a gloved hand out to the Mediterranean. The sea was boiling away, bubbling and gurgling with a mad hissing roar as immense clouds of steam rose into a sky that suddenly was no longer blue, but a grayish sort of sickly yellow. An immense glowering light was burning through the clouds, the Sun so close and huge and hot that it was like an all-devouring god come to destroy everything it touched.

"Quickly!" she yelled. I couldn't tell if it was Marguerite or her mother. She was putting on the helmet of her spacesuit.

I turned frantically, searching the garden for my suit. All I found was the beautiful flowers and vines, withering, browning, bursting into flames all around me.

And the insects were crawling all over me, biting, eating my flesh, burrowing into my skin, and chewing on my innards. I could feel them gnawing away inside me and when I tried to scream no sound came out. They had devoured even my voice.

But I heard others screaming. The long, screeching, terrified wails of men and women falling, falling through the boiling hot air, wailing, "Save me! Save meeeee!"

DEATH SENTENCE

My eyes snapped open. I lay on the bunk they had put me on, stiff and sore from the beating Fuchs had given me. My quarters consisted of a tiny section of a larger compartment, screened off from six other bunks by a thin plastic shoji-type sliding door.

How long I lay there, I don't know. I was unconscious much of the time. I could hear people moving about and talking in a low, guttural foreign language on the other side of my screen.

I felt terribly weak. Without my regular enzyme shots my red cell count would fall until I sank into a coma and died. Maybe that would be for the best, I thought as I lay there, miserable and alone. No one would care if I died. No one would mourn my death. I meant nothing to anyone. It would make utterly no difference to the world if I left it forever.

"Van?" Marguerite's voice, calling softly from the other side of the shoji screen. I could see her silhouette against the white squares of plastic sheeting.

"Van, are you awake?" she called again.

"Come in," I said, surprised at how strong my voice was. I certainly didn't feel strong, not at all.

She slid the screen back. My bunk was flush against the bulkhead, so she simply stood where she was, out in the common area of what I took to be the crew's quarters. I could see no one else in the compartment; the crew must all be on duty, I thought.

Marguerite was wearing an ill-fitting gray jumpsuit that bagged over her trim frame. She had turned the pants and sleeve cuffs up; they were far too long for her. Her eyes were red; she had been crying. But she was dry-eyed now, and her hair was neatly combed and pulled back from her beautiful face.

"How do you feel?" she asked, almost timidly.

As I looked up at her, I realized that my right eye was swollen almost shut. She bent over me and for a moment I had the inane idea that she was going to kiss me.

No such luck. I reached out to her and she took my hand tenderly in hers. But that's as far as she was willing to go.

"Are you all right?" she asked.

"What difference does it make?" I heard myself say. Whine, almost. "I'll be dead in a few days."

Her hand tightened around mine. "What do you mean? You weren't hurt that badly."

"My enzyme shots. Without them my anemia will kill me."

"Ohhh," she actually groaned. "I had forgotten about your condition."

"My medical supplies were aboard *Hesperos*," I said. "Unless there's an olympic-class biochemist aboard and a warehouse full of pharmaceutical supplies, I'm a dead man."

Marguerite looked truly distressed. "We don't even have a ship's doctor. Fuchs didn't include one in his crew."

"Then he might as well have killed me instead of just humiliating me."

"There must be something we can do!"

"You're a biologist," I said, the faintest tendril of hope flickering within me. "Could you . . . ?"

I let the question dangle between us. Marguerite stared down at me for a long, silent moment. I could see it in her eyes. There was no way she could synthesize the growth hormone I needed. I realized that I didn't know the hormone's chemical formula or even its technical name. I always had people around me like Waller to take care of those details.

God is in the details, I remembered hearing somewhere. Death is in the details, I told myself.

Marguerite broke into my thoughts. "He wants to see you," she said.

"Wants to see me?"

"The captain. Fuchs."

I actually managed to bark out a bitter laugh. "Why? Does he need more punching practice?"

"He sent me to bring you to his quarters. He said you've been resting long enough."

I growled, "So he's making medical diagnoses now. That's why he doesn't need a physician in his crew."

"Can you get up?" Marguerite asked.

"Sure," I said, propping myself on an elbow and then gripping the bunk's edge with both hands to support myself in a sitting position. My head thundered with pain.

Marguerite grasped my shoulders to steady me as I got to my feet. I wanted to slide an arm around her waist but thought better of it.

"I can stand on my own," I said, working hard to keep from moaning. Or collapsing.

Someone had taken my slippers. Marguerite checked the drawers built in under my bunk while I stood there and concentrated on standing erect. The slippers were gone.

So I headed for the hatch barefoot. The metal deck felt reasonably warm.

"See?" I said as we ducked through the hatch and out into the passageway. "Nothing to it."

In truth, I felt better than I had any right to expect. A little woozy, but that might have been nothing more than my imagination. Plenty of aches and stiffness, and my head throbbed with pain. But I made it down the passageway under my own power.

As we reached the ladder that led up to the bridge level I caught a glimpse of myself in the blank face of a display screen set into the bulkhead. My right eye was swollen and discolored, my hair a disheveled mess. I stopped and smoothed my hair into place. I had to hold on to some shred of dignity when I faced Fuchs again.

Up the ladder we went, down another passageway. Then we stopped in front of an accordion-pleated door labeled CAPTAIN.

I squared my shoulders as best as I could and rapped on the metal door frame.

"Enter," came Fuchs's muffled voice.

His quarters were a shock to me. It was only one compartment, but it was spacious enough to contain a real bed, a desk, several comfortable chairs, cabinets, and one entire bulkhead lined with shelves of books. There were even old-fashioned paper books, thick and battered from long use, alongside the cyberbook chips. The floor was carpeted with a large, colorful oriental rug.

Wearing a loose-fitting black tunic over charcoal-gray trousers, Fuchs was standing by what looked like a long picture window, gazing out at the stars. Actually, it was a wall screen, of course.

"The universe," he said, gesturing with one hand toward the panorama of stars. "I never tire of gazing at heaven."

I was gaping at the books, I suppose, because he took a couple of steps toward the shelves and said, "When your ship is your home, you bring the comforts of home along with you."

"Books?" I asked, stupidly.

"What better?" Fuchs countered. "The memory of the human race is there. All the hopes and fears, all the vice and glory, all the loves and hates."

There was one book on his desk, a leather-bound volume

that looked as if it were centuries old. I tried to make out the title on its spine, but the lettering was too cracked and faded.

"Now then," Fuchs said crisply, "I want you to spend the rest of the day familiarizing yourself with the communications gear. That's going to be your post from now on."

He spoke as if I had been a member of his crew since day one. As if the beating he had given me on the bridge had never happened.

"It's a fairly standard setup, the comm computer does all the real work," Fuchs went on, digging his hands into the pockets of his tunic. He pulled something out of his tunic pocket and popped it into his mouth. Pills of some sort. Narcotics? I wondered.

"Being comm tech won't put too much of a strain on you," he said, with a sneer. He had forgotten nothing. Neither had I.

"For as long as I live," I said.

His eyes narrowed. "What does that mean?"

"He's ill, Captain," Marguerite said.

"Ill?"

"I have a pernicious anemia that was being controlled by enzyme injections that generated red-cell proliferation," I said, all in a rush. Then I added, "Captain."

Fuchs glanced from me to Marguerite, then back again.

"My pharmaceutical supplies went down with *Hesperos*," I went on. "Unless we return to orbit and rendezvous with *Truax* I'll be dead in a few days."

He huffed. "Really."

"Really," Marguerite said.

Fuchs looked at me intently, chewing on his pills, then paced over to his desk.

"How do I know this isn't some crackbrain fraud that you've cooked up to keep me from winning your father's prize money?"

I almost laughed at him. "Wait a few days and watch me die."

With a shrug, Fuchs said, "Okay. That's what I'll do, then. In the meantime, you'll work the comm console."

"You can't!" Marguerite blurted.

Fuchs leveled a stubby finger at her. "Don't presume that my feelings for your mother will allow you to behave disrespectfully to me. I'm the captain of this vessel and you will *not* tell me what I can and cannot do."

Marguerite drew herself up to her full height, several centimeters taller than either Fuchs or I. Her eyes blazed.

"If you allow Mr. Humphries to die, Captain, I will bring charges of willful murder against you as soon as we reach Earth."

Strangely, he grinned at her. A mirthless, sardonic grin, almost a grimace. "You've got your mother's spirit, sure enough," he said.

Then his normal scowl returned and he said to me, "Report to the comm console. Now!"

Marguerite started to object. "But you—"

Fuchs silenced her with a wave of his hand. "You bring up all the charges you want. We're a long way from Earth, and as long as we're on this vessel my word is the law. Understand me?"

"But he'll die!" Marguerite wailed.

"What of it?" Fuchs said.

Neither Marguerite nor I had an answer for him.

COMM TECH

So I dutifully followed Fuchs to the bridge and sat at the horseshoe-shaped communications console. What choice did I have? I ruefully wondered which hurt more, my bruised face or my bruised ego.

Marguerite came to the bridge also, and just stood near the hatch staring at Fuchs unwaveringly. If she made the man uncomfortable, he gave no outward sign of it. I called up the operations manual for the comm system and concentrated on studying it.

There were two others on the bridge, both silent, stocky, dour-faced Asians. Fuchs had apparently recruited his crew exclusively from the Orient. I started to wonder why. Are they more loyal? Less likely to resent or resist his tyrannical ways? Perhaps they're willing to work for less pay. Or, more likely, they're simply more docile and obedient. I was totally wrong in each of my surmises, but I didn't know it then.

Fuchs had been right about the communications system. If the operations manual was to be believed, the system was

quite simple and logically set up. Its own internal computer
did most of the work, and it interfaced with the ship's central computer very easily.

I saw on one of the console's screens that there were
dozens of messages from *Truax* that had gone unanswered.
The communications technicians up there in orbit kept trying to get some answer out of Fuchs, but he refused to
speak to them. The messages became demanding, even *Truax*'s captain angrily complaining about Fuchs's silence.

The screen began to blur slightly. I squeezed my eyes
shut and when I opened them everything seemed normal
again. But I knew that symptom well enough. It was the
first sign that I had missed an enzyme injection. Soon there
would be others.

Then I heard Fuchs say, "You're not needed here on the
bridge. Go to your quarters."

I looked up from my screen and saw that he was speaking to Marguerite, who was still standing by the hatch.

"You have to do something about Mr. Humphries," she
said, without taking her eyes off him.

Fuchs glanced at me, his frown deeper than usual.
"There's nothing that can be done," he said.

"What about a blood transfusion?"

"Transfusion?"

"If we can't produce the hormone that promotes his red-
cell production, then perhaps transfusions of whole blood
will keep him alive."

They were discussing me as if I weren't there, as if I
were some experimental animal or a specimen in a laboratory. I felt my face burning, and I knew my cheeks must be
flame red.

But neither of them was looking at me.

Fuchs barked out a rough laugh. "Do you seriously think
any of my crew has a compatible blood type?"

"Perhaps I do," Marguerite said. "Or you."

To my shame, I didn't dare turn around to look at him. I
was afraid of him, pure and simple. I expected him to laugh
Marguerite's idea to scorn. Or to get angry. Instead, I heard

nothing but silence. Neither of the other two crew members raised a murmur. For long moments the only sounds on the bridge were the inescapable background hum of electrical power and the faint beeps from some of the sensor systems.

Marguerite broke the lengthening silence. "I can call *Truax* for his medical records."

"No!" Fuchs snapped. "There will be no communications with *Truax* or anybody else."

"But why?" she asked. "You're beaming your telemetering signal back to the IAA on Earth. Why not—"

"Every vessel is *required* to report its status to Geneva," Fuchs interrupted. "But I'm not required to communicate with anyone else and I'm not going to do it. Nobody's going to get any claim on my prize money. Understand me? Nobody!"

"You can't be serious," Marguerite protested.

Fuchs replied, "The ship's computer has complete medical dossiers on all the crew. There's a medical diagnosis system in the sick bay; it may not be state-of-the-art, but it'll do. When Humphries is finished his watch here on the bridge you can run him through the medical scanners and determine his blood type, then see if anyone aboard matches it."

Marguerite said, "Thank you, Captain," in a tone that was far softer than her previous words.

"Now get off the bridge," Fuchs snapped, as if to make up for the small concession he'd just granted her.

As I returned my full attention to the screens before me, I realized that Fuchs had made his concession to Marguerite, not to me. He actually didn't care if I lived or died, but he had a much different attitude toward her.

A full watch on the bridge was eight hours long, under Fuchs's command. On *Hesperos,* watches had been the more normal four hours, and Duchamp had been lenient about even that, since the ship was so heavily automated.

Lucifer carried a crew of fourteen, I eventually found

out. All of them Asians, two-thirds of them men. Only Fuchs's iron discipline kept order among the crew. They did their jobs with a silent efficiency that was almost eerie. There must have been some sexual relationships among them, but I never caught a hint of any. Of course, they were wary about me. I was definitely an outsider among them.

I tried to work the full eight-hour shift at the comm console, tried as earnestly as I could. It wasn't just that I was afraid of Fuchs, although I certainly was terrified of his brutality and strength. But there was something more: my own pride. I hated being considered a weakling, a Runt. I was determined to show Fuchs and all the rest of those silent, watchful Asians that I could do a man's work.

But my body betrayed me. Hardly a full hour into my watch, my vision began to blur again and no amount of blinking or knuckling my eyes could help. It's all right, I told myself. You can still do your job. Stick with it. Hang tough. Futile words. After another little while I grew lightheaded, dizzy. The screen before my blurry eyes began to spin around and around. No matter how I commanded my body to behave, things just got worse. I felt weak and nauseous. I knew that I couldn't get up from my chair if I wanted to.

I couldn't breathe. My chest felt as if someone had clamped a vise around it and I couldn't lift my ribs to get air into my lungs. I gasped like a hooked fish.

I swiveled the chair around a little, my vision going gray. The last thing I remember was saying, "Captain, I'm not . . ." Then I slumped out of the chair and sprawled on the deck. Darkness overwhelmed me.

I heard voices from a long, long distance away. They echoed hollowly, as if coming through a tunnel.

And I felt a sudden, sharp, stinging pain on my face. Again. And again.

My eyes cracked open slightly.

"See? He's coming out of it."

It was Fuchs leaning over me, slapping me. Quite methodically he slapped my face, first one cheek, then the other.

"Stop it! Stop it!" someone was yelling. Not me. The only sounds I could make were faint groans.

I tried to raise my arms to protect myself but couldn't. Either I was too weak or my arms were strapped down. I couldn't tell which.

"I'm not hurting him," Fuchs said.

"He needs a transfusion right away." It was Marguerite's voice, concerned, determined.

"You're certain he's not faking?" Fuchs asked. I was trying to open my eyes all the way but the effort was too much for me. I let my head turn and tried to see Marguerite but she wasn't within the range of my vision.

"Look at the monitors!" she said sharply. "He's dying."

Fuchs exhaled a long, sighing breath from deep in his barrel chest, almost like the warning growl a dog makes just before it attacks.

"All right," he said at last. "Let's get it over with."

They were going to let me die, I thought. They were going to stand over my prostrate body and watch me die.

I realized at that moment that no matter how much I philosophized or tried to justify the end of my existence, I did not want to die. Maybe I deserved death. Certainly no one would miss me or grieve over me. Not my father. Not Gwyneth or any of my so-called friends. No one.

But I did not want to die. With every atom of my being I wanted to survive, to be strong, to get up and live.

Instead, my eyes closed again and darkness returned to envelope me totally.

I must have dreamed. A weird, mixed-up dream it was. Alex was in it. But sometimes he was Rodriguez. Both of them were dead, killed on Venus.

"Don't give up," Alex told me, with his carefree grin. He tousled my hair. "Don't ever give up."

But I was falling, plummeting like a stone through dark

roiling clouds that flashed lightning like the strobe lights at a concert. Rodriguez was beside me in his spacesuit, screaming that last primal scream that I had heard when he died.

"Don't give up!" Alex called to me from afar.

"He's already given up," my father's disdainful voice answered. "He's got nothing to live for."

"Yes he does," Alex insisted. "He's got me. And he's got himself. Find me, Van. Find yourself."

I woke up.

I guessed that I was in the sick bay. I was on a thin mattress atop what seemed more like a narrow table than a bed. Medical monitors beeped and clicked all around me. The metal overhead curved low above my eyes.

I felt strong and clear. No blurred vision. No dizziness. I took a deep breath.

"You're awake."

Turning my head, I saw Marguerite standing beside my table. She looked fresh, newly scrubbed. She was wearing a crisp jumpsuit of deep blue that fitted her much better than the shapeless bag she'd been wearing before.

"I'm alive," I said. My throat was dry, but otherwise my voice was almost normal.

"Do you think you can sit up?"

I started to nod, but instead I pulled myself up to a sitting position, no hands.

"How's that?" I asked, marveling that I felt no giddiness at all.

"Fine," said Marguerite. She touched the foot of the table with one finger and the mattress inflated behind me to form a pillow that I could sit back against.

"Would you like something to eat?"

I realized that I felt hungry. Starving, in fact. "Yes, thank you," I said.

Her smile beamed at me. "I'll fix you a tray."

She ducked through the hatch behind her. When I flexed

my arms I saw that a plastic bandage had been sprayed onto my left inner elbow. She must have done a blood transfusion.

I looked around. The sick bay was the size of a small closet, crammed with medical sensors. There was no room for a desk or even a chair, only this table I was sitting on. I touched my right cheek. The swelling was down. In the glassy reflection of the nearest display screen, my face looked almost normal.

Marguerite came back with a tray of cold cereal and fruit juice.

"You did a blood transfusion," I said, rather than asked.

Standing beside me, she nodded.

"Who gave the blood?"

"Captain Fuchs did," Marguerite said. The expression on her face was unfathomable: quite serious, like a judge about to sentence a felon to a very long term. But there were other things in her eyes as well.

She looked away from me. "He's the only person on board who has a blood type similar enough to yours."

I chewed on a mouthful of cereal, then swallowed. It tasted bland, pointless. "Maybe it'll give me some of his personality," I muttered.

Marguerite did not smile. "No," she said, "I wouldn't want to see that happen."

Before she could say anything more, Fuchs himself pushed through the hatch. Suddenly the sick bay was overcrowded. I felt distinctly uncomfortable.

But I lifted my chin a notch and said, "Thank you, Captain, for saving my life."

He sneered at me. "I couldn't afford to lose another crewman." Then, gesturing toward Marguerite, he added, "Besides, it wouldn't do to have Ms. Duchamp here accuse me of murder while I'm claiming your father's prize money. It would be just like your father to renege on the prize because I let his son die."

I shook my head. "You don't know my father."

"Don't I?"

"He wouldn't care about my death."

"I didn't say he would," Fuchs corrected. "I said he'd use your death to renege on giving me the prize."

He stressed the word *me* ever so slightly, but enough for us both to hear it. I glanced at Marguerite. She wouldn't meet my eyes.

"How soon can you resume your duties on the bridge?" Fuchs asked gruffly.

Before I could reply, Marguerite said, "He should rest and—"

"I'm ready now," I said, pushing my tray aside.

Fuchs made a sardonic little smile. "My blood must be doing you some good." He looked at his wristwatch. "Jagal's on the comm console at the moment. You can relieve her in two hours."

Before either of us could say anything, Fuchs turned to Marguerite and asked with mock beneficence, "Will that be enough rest and recuperation time for your patient? Never mind answering. It'll have to do."

Looking back at me, he said, "Two hours."

Then he grasped Marguerite's wrist and led her out of the sick bay. He held her possessively, like a man who felt he owned her. Marguerite glanced back over her shoulder at me, but she went with Fuchs without a word of resistance, without a moment of hesitation.

Leaving me sitting there, hot anger welling up in my gut.

WAVERIDER

I served my eight-hour watch on the bridge under Fuchs's sardonic eye. No sign of Marguerite. I should have eaten a bigger meal; I was ravenously hungry, but I gave no outward sign of it—except for an occasional growl from my hollow stomach.

One of the burly, blank-faced Asians relieved me at the end of my stint. I got up and headed for the passageway, determined to find the ship's galley.

But instead Fuchs called to me. "Wait right there, Humphries."

I froze in place.

He shouldered past me and through the hatch. "Follow me," he said, without turning back.

He led me to his quarters, the compartment stuffed with books and comfortable furniture. The bed was neatly made. I wondered where Marguerite was.

"How do you feel?" he asked.

"Hungry," I said.

He nodded, went to his desk, and spoke into the intercom in that Asian language that might have been Japanese.

"Sit down," he said, gesturing to one of the leather-and-chrome chairs in front of the desk. He himself took the creaking swivel chair behind it.

"I've ordered dinner for us. It should be here in a few moments."

"Thank you."

"I wouldn't want you to starve to death on my ship," he said, with just the hint of a malicious smile.

"Where's Marguerite?" I asked.

The hint of a smile disappeared. "Where's Marguerite, *sir*," he corrected.

"Sir."

"That's better. She's in her quarters, resting."

I began to ask where her quarters were, but before I could get the first words out he jabbed a thumb over his shoulder. "Her quarters are next to mine. It's the most comfortable compartment on the ship, except for this one. And it allows me to keep a close watch on her. Several of the crew members are very attracted to the young lady—not all of them male, either."

"So you're protecting her."

"That's right. None of them will dare try anything as long as they know she's mine."

"Yours? What do you mean?" I saw his face cloud again and quickly added, "Sir."

Before he could reply the door slid open and one of the crewmen carried in a large tray filled with steaming bowls. He parceled out the food between us, putting Fuchs's dinner on his desk and dropping legs from underneath the tray to turn it into a table for me.

I shook my head inwardly at the contradictions I was seeing. Fuchs ran a tightly disciplined ship, yet there were touches of . . . well, luxury was the only word I could think of. He liked his creature comforts, obviously, although he didn't care to extend the same level of amenities to the rest of the crew.

I looked around at the books that filled his shelves: philosophy, history, poetry, fiction by old masters such as Cervantes, Kipling, London, and Steinbeck. Many of the volumes were in languages I did not know.

"Do you approve?" he asked, with a pugnacious air.

I nodded, but heard myself answer, "I prefer more modern writers, Captain."

He snorted with disdain. "I suppose we can dispense with the formalities while we're alone in here. No need to address me as 'captain' or 'sir'—unless someone else is in the room."

"Thank you," I said.

He grunted, almost as if embarrassed by his small concession. Then he pulled a small vial from one of the desk drawers, shook a few tiny yellow pills into his hand, and tossed them into his mouth. Again I wondered if he was a narcotics addict.

I tried to make out the lettering on the spine of the old book on his desk. Its leather cover was cracked and peeling.

"*Paradise Lost*," he told me. "John Milton."

"I never read it," I confessed.

"Very few have."

That made me feel rather uncomfortable. Fishing around in my memory, I came up with, "Isn't there a line in it that goes, 'Better to reign in Hell than serve in Heaven'?"

Fuchs grimaced. "Everybody knows that one. I prefer:

> Infernal world! And thou, profoundest Hell,
> Receive thy new possessor—one who brings
> A mind not to be changed by place or time.
> The mind is its own place, and in itself
> Can make a Heaven of Hell, a Hell of Heaven."

He spoke with such fervor, such a dark deep-rooted passion, that I was totally taken aback. I didn't know what to say.

"You may borrow it if you wish."

"What?"

"The book. You may borrow it if you'd like to."

My brows must have hiked up to my scalp. Fuchs laughed harshly, "You're surprised at a show of generosity? You're surprised that I'm pleased to have someone aboard with whom I can talk about philosophy or poetry?"

"Frankly, I am surprised, Captain. I had thought that you'd want nothing to do with Martin Humphries's son."

"Ah, but you forget, you have *my* blood in you now. That's an improvement. A vast improvement."

I had no reply for that. Instead, I began, "About Marguerite—"

"Never mind her," he snapped. "Don't you want to know about my *Lucifer?* Aren't you curious about why my ship survived and yours broke apart? Aren't you wondering about where we are and how close we are to your father's prize money?"

"Is that all that interests you, the money?"

"Yes! What else is there? Your father took everything else from me: my career, the company I founded, my reputation, even the woman I loved."

I could see we were moving into dangerous territory, so I tried to change the subject to a safer ground.

"Very well," I said, "tell me about your ship."

He stared at me for a long, wordless moment, gazing blankly, those cold, ice-blue eyes of his seemingly looking through me into another dimension. What was going through his mind I have no way of knowing. His face went as blank as a catatonic's. He must have been revisiting the past, reminding himself of what he had lost, how he had reached this point in space and time. At last his broad, heavy-jowled face regained life; he shook his head slightly, as if clearing it of painful memories.

"Overdesign," he said at last. "That's what you learn when you stake your life on a vessel that's got to carry you across interplanetary distances. Overdesign. That's the lesson I learned out in the Asteroid Belt. Bigger is better. Thick skin is better than thin."

"But the weight penalty—"

He snorted again. "Your problem is that you had that astronaut guiding your hand."

"Rodriguez," I said.

"Yes. He spent his life on scientific excursions to Mars, didn't he? Rode out there on elegant, state-of-the-art spacecraft designed to be as efficient as possible, slimmed down to the least possible gram, worried about every cent of cost and every newton of rocket thrust."

"That's the way spacecraft have to be designed, isn't it?"

"Oh, certainly," Fuchs answered sarcastically. "If you're working with academics and engineers who've never moved their own carcasses farther than the vacation centers on the Moon. They produce highly refined designs, so highly refined that they use the very latest materials, the most sophisticated new systems and equipment they can conceive."

"What's wrong with that?" I asked.

"Nothing, if you're designing the craft for someone else to use. If you're worried about spending the boss's money. If your design philosophy is to give your master a vessel that has the very latest of everything *and* is built at the lowest possible cost. An impossible contradiction, don't you see?"

"Yes, but—"

"But if you're prospecting out among the asteroids," Fuchs went on, overriding my objection, "then you learn pretty quickly that your ship has got to be strong, powerful, with as many redundant systems as you can pack onto it. You're a billion kilometers from anywhere out in the Belt; you're on your own. You can't expect somebody to come out and repair you or bring you a fresh pot of coffee when you run out."

He was enjoying this lecture, I could see. He was smiling with unfeigned pleasure.

"So here we are, you and me, both determined to get to the surface of Venus. You allow your astronaut to design as dainty a vessel as he can, sleek and slick and pared down to a hairsbreadth in every detail. Why? Because that's the way he's always operated. Because his attitude, his training, his whole life has been spent in demanding the most elegant designs the engineers can create."

And we failed, I admitted silently. *Hesperos* broke up and crashed. And *Phosphoros* before her, I finally realized.

"Now me," Fuchs tapped his chest with two fingers of his right hand, "I'm not elegant. I'm a prospector from the Asteroid Belt. A rock rat. I was out there with Gunn and the other pioneers, before your father even dreamed about sticking his grubby fingers into asteroidal mining.

"I saw that the ships that succeeded were the overdesigned, overbuilt, overequipped clunkers that could take a beating and still bring their crews back alive. Now which type of vessel do you think would do better against the . . . uh, *rigors* of the Venusian environment?"

I asked, "Did you suspect that there would be metal-eating organisms in the upper clouds?"

"No. Not for a minute. But I knew that my ship had to have a skin thick enough to take whatever Venus could dish out. Not a cockleshell like yours."

"The bugs are eating away at your hull, too, aren't they?"

He waved a hand. "Not anymore. We're so deep into the second cloud deck that the outside temperature is rising to well over a hundred degrees Celsius: the boiling point of water." He made a sardonic smile. "The bugs are roasting nicely."

"And there aren't any other organisms at this level?"

"I've assigned Marguerite to sample the clouds. So far, no signs of bugs. I suspect that the hotter it gets out there, the less likely that anything could live in it."

I nodded agreement. He spoke on and on about the superior design of *Lucifer* and how well the ship was holding up to the constantly increasing pressure and high temperature of the atmosphere outside the hull.

"In another ten or twelve hours we'll break out below the clouds into clear air. Then we can begin the search for what's left of *Phosphoros*."

"And my brother's body," I mumbled.

"Yes," he said. "I'm looking forward to seeing your father's face when he has to hand me that ten billion. That should be something worth waiting for!" He chortled with unalloyed glee.

His laughter was cut short. The ship lurched as if some giant hand had slapped it sideways. My dinner bowls clattered off the tray-table and onto the carpeted floor. I nearly slid off my chair. An alarm started hooting.

Fuchs gripped the arms of his swivel chair, his face turning into blind rage. He pounded a fist on the phone keyboard and roared something in that Asian language the crew used. I could not understand the words but easily recognized the tone: "What the hell's happening?"

A high-pitched, frightened voice replied in a rapid staccato over the keening of the alarm.

Fuchs jumped out of his chair. The deck was slanting noticeably as he came around the desk. "Come with me," he said grimly.

We staggered along the passageway, walking uphill the few steps it took to reach the bridge. The alarm's wail cut off, but the deck beneath our feet continued to buck and toss.

Fuchs went straight to his command chair. The other crew stations were occupied, so I stood by the hatch, holding on to its rim. Marguerite came up behind me, and I slid an arm around her waist to steady her without thinking about it.

The bridge's main screen showed a bewilderingly rapid flow of graphs, sharply curving lines in many different colors laid out over a gridwork of lines.

Fuchs spat out an order and the screen cleared momentarily. Then a computer-enhanced image came up that made no sense to me. It showed a circle with a dot off to one side and pulsing rings of light flowing outward from it, like the ripples made in a pond when you throw a stone into the water.

"Subsolar point," Fuchs muttered. "Even down at this level."

I understood what he meant. Venus turns so slowly on its axis that the spot on the planet directly beneath the Sun stays at "high noon" for more than seven hours at a time. The atmosphere beneath that subsolar point heats up tremendously, as if a blowtorch were blazing away at it hour after hour.

That terrible heating is what drives the superrotation winds, high up in the Venusian atmosphere, where the air is thin enough for winds of four hundred kilometers per hour to race around the planet. Lower down, where the atmosphere is much thicker, such winds are damped down.

But not completely, we were finding. Like sluggish ripples in a thick, soupy pond, there were waves flowing out from the subsolar point even at the depth to which *Lucifer* had already penetrated.

We were being tossed along that wave front, like a surfer caught on a gigantic curl, driven across the planet like a very tiny leaf caught in a very large, deliberate, slow but inexorable wave.

While I stood there, gripping the hatch frame with one hand and Marguerite with the other, Fuchs battled to right the ship and break it free of the wave that was blowing us halfway around Venus.

The crew, for once, were not impassive. As Fuchs rattled out orders, their faces showed grim intent, even the wide eyes and gaping mouths of fear.

Fuchs took his eyes off the screens for a moment and saw Marguerite and me standing there, hanging on while *Lucifer* bobbed and pitched in the grip of the massive wave.

"The engines are useless," he said to us. "Like trying to stop a tsunami with a blowgun."

The two technicians glanced at him when they heard *tsunami*, but one glare from Fuchs and they got back to their work of trying to hold the ship in trim.

"The only thing we can do is ride it out until we get to the night side again," Fuchs murmured, thinking aloud. "It ought to damp out over there."

Yes, I thought. It ought to. But we had believed that the

subsolar wave would be no problem at this depth into the atmosphere. Venus believed otherwise.

Now we were in the grip of a mammoth wave of energy that pushed us along at gale-force velocity, flinging the ship headlong across the planet like a frail dandelion tuft at the mercy of the inexorable tidal wave.

"Deeper," Fuchs muttered. "We've got to go deeper."

MUTTERINGS

stayed at the hatch, clinging to Marguerite, for what seemed like hours. The ship kept bucking and shuddering, riding the massive wave that was driving us halfway across the planet.

But although my body was still, my mind was working furiously. This subsolar wave was like a moving wall that pushed us away from the daylit side of Venus. If the wreckage of *Phosphoros* and Alex's body were on that side of the planet it was going to be next to impossible to reach them, unless the wave truly did peter out at lower altitude. If it didn't, we would have to wait a month or more for the planet's ponderously slow rotation to swing the Aphrodite region to the nightside.

I doubted that Fuchs had supplies enough for us to dawdle down here for several weeks. I know that *Hesperos* certainly hadn't. I wondered if *Lucifer,* overdesigned though it was, could physically survive in Venus's thick, hot atmosphere for a month.

We must have stood there at the hatch for hours. It wasn't until the next watch showed up and pushed past us that Fuchs looked sternly at me and said, "Get back to your quarters, Humphries. You too, Marguerite."

The ship's motion had smoothed out considerably, although *Lucifer* was still pitching up and down enough to make my stomach uneasy.

"You heard me!" Fuchs snapped. "When I give an order I want it obeyed! Move!"

"Yes, sir," I said, and led Marguerite down the passageway toward her compartment.

She slid her door open, then hesitated. Turning to me, she asked, "How are you feeling?"

"Fine," I said. Beyond her I could see the compartment Fuchs had given her. It was spare, utilitarian, probably the quarters for the first mate who had been killed trying to save Rodriguez. It was next to Fuchs's more luxurious quarters, but there was no connecting door, I saw.

"No problems with the anemia?" she asked.

"We have more immediate problems to worry about," I said. As if to emphasize my point, the deck lurched, throwing her against me. I held her with both arms.

She disengaged herself, gently, perhaps even reluctantly, I thought. But she did pull away from me.

Yet she seemed genuinely concerned about me. "We have no way of knowing how long the transfusion will help you. . . ."

"Never mind that," I said. "What's he doing to you?"

Her back stiffened. "What do you mean?"

"Fuchs. What's he doing to you?"

"That's not your concern," Marguerite said.

"Isn't it?"

"No, it isn't."

"You're trying to protect me, aren't you?"

"By sleeping with him, you mean?"

"Yes."

For an instant I thought I was looking at her mother; her expression went cold, hard as steel.

"Don't flatter yourself," she said.

I felt anger flaring through me. "Then you're sleeping with him to protect yourself."

"Is that what you think?"

Exasperated, I shot back, "What else can I think?"

Icily, Marguerite said, "I am not responsible for what goes on in your mind, Van. And what is happening between Captain Fuchs and me is our business, not yours."

"You don't understand," I said, "I—"

"No, *you* don't understand," she said, her voice venomously low. "You think that I'll flop into bed automatically with the highest-ranking male aboard, don't you?"

"That's what your mother did, isn't it?" I spat.

For a moment I thought she was going to slap me. She drew back a bit, and I must have inadvertently flinched.

Instead, she hit harder with her words. "You're jealous, aren't you? My mother picked Rodriguez over you and now you're jealous that Fuchs is the top dog in this pack."

"I don't want you to be hurt," I said.

"Worry about yourself, Van. I can take care of myself."

With that she turned on her heel, stepped into her compartment, and slid the folding door shut. She didn't slam it, but it banged into place quite firmly.

"I thought I told you to go to your quarters."

I whirled and saw Fuchs standing just outside the hatch to the bridge, no more than ten meters away. How long he'd been standing there, I had no way of knowing.

"Now!" he snapped.

Right at that moment I wanted to leap at his throat and strangle him. Instead I slunk away toward the crew's quarters, docile as the defenseless Runt that I was.

Even through the self-absorbed funk that I was in, I could sense the tension in the crew's quarters. None of the burly Asians paid the slightest attention to me as I crawled into my bunk and slid the shoji screen shut. They were all huddled around the long table in the middle of the compartment, bending their heads together and muttering to one another in their Asian tongue.

I could hear their tone through the flimsy screen: heavy, dark, foreboding. It didn't sound at all like the jabbering I had heard earlier. I tried to tell myself it was nothing more than my imagination at work, yet I couldn't overcome the feeling that the crew was definitely unhappy. Something was bothering them, and they were talking about it with grim intensity.

At least, while I lay there trying to get some sleep, the ship's plunging and lurching smoothed out. We must be on the nightside, I told myself, or deep enough into the atmosphere for the subsolar wave to have damped out.

I fell asleep at last, with the crew's guttural mutterings serving as a rough sort of lullaby.

I dreamed, but my memory of it is hazy. Something about being weak and sick, and then somehow overcoming it. I think I was sitting up on a dais, like my father did at his birthday party. Marguerite was in the dream, I'm pretty sure, although sometimes she was someone else—maybe her mother.

Whatever, when I woke I trudged out to the galley and put together a meal from the selections in the freezer. Then I showered and pulled on a fresh set of coveralls from the storage drawers built in beneath my bunk. Strangely, my old slippers had reappeared. There they were, in the drawer with the underwear.

There was precious little privacy in the crew's quarters. I pulled my screen shut when I dressed, but that meant bending and twisting like a contortionist in the narrow space between my bunk and the shoji screen.

I thought I'd have several hours to myself before going back on duty, but the ship's intercom speakers put an end to that idea.

"MR. HUMPHRIES, REPORT TO THE CAPTAIN'S QUARTERS IMMEDIATELY."

It was Fuchs's voice. He said it only once; he expected me to hear it and obey. Which is precisely what I did.

Marguerite was there, sitting in one of the chairs in front of his desk. Fuchs was on his feet, hands clasped behind his back, pacing slowly the length of the compartment, chewing on something; those pills of his, I thought.

"Have a seat," he said to me.

I took the chair next to Marguerite.

"We've lost the better part of a day because of the subsolar wave," he said, without preamble. "I propose to make it up by diving below the last cloud deck and making best speed back to the Aphrodite region."

I glanced at Marguerite. She seemed aloof, distant, as if none of this had anything to do with her. Fuchs's bed was still neatly made up, I saw, but I knew that didn't mean much.

"The crew seems unhappy with my decision," he said.

I wasn't surprised that he had sensed the crew's tension. "Do you have the entire ship bugged?" I asked.

He whirled on me, fists clenched. I quickly added, "Captain."

Fuchs relaxed, but only a little. He went to his desk and touched a key on the phone console. A large section of the bare metal bulkhead turned into a display screen. I saw the crew's quarters from a vantage point up in the ceiling. Several of them still sat huddled around the central table, muttering.

"They're speaking in a Mongol tribal dialect," he said, with a disgusted smirk. "They think I can't understand what they're saying."

"Can you?" Marguerite asked,

"I can't, but the language program can."

He jabbed a stubby finger on the keyboard again, and the mumbling, guttural voices were overlain by a computer's flat, emotionless translation:

". . . he is determined to get down to the surface, at all costs."

"He will kill us all."

"He wants the prize money. Ten billion dollars is an enormous incentive."

"Not if we all are killed."

"What can we do?"

"Take the ship and get the hell out of here."

I looked from the screen to Fuchs, still standing with his hands clasped behind his back. His face was as unemotional as the computer's translation.

"But how? He is the captain."

"We are twelve, he is one."

"There are the other two."

"No problem. One woman and one weakling."

I felt my face redden.

"The captain is no weakling."

"And Amarjagal will not go along with us, now that she is first mate."

"Who else would be against us?"

"Sanja, perhaps."

"I can convince Sanja to stand with us."

"But if we take the ship and head back to Earth, we won't get the prize money."

"To hell with the prize money. My life is more important. You can't spend money when you are dead."

Fuchs clicked off the display and the computer's translation.

"Don't you want to hear more?" Marguerite asked. "The details of what they're planning?"

"It's all being recorded," he said.

"What are you going to do about this, sir?" I asked.

"Nothing."

"Nothing?"

"Not a thing. Not yet. So far, they're just griping. Our little joyride on the wave shook them. If things settle down, if we don't encounter any more scares, they'll forget about it. Their share of the ten billion overrides a lot of complaints."

Marguerite said slowly, "But if we run into more trouble . . ."

Fuchs snorted. "They'll try to kill us all. After raping you, of course."

BELOW THE CLOUDS

Whatever possessed you to hire such a gang of cutthroats?" I demanded.

Fuchs gave me a humorless grin. "They're a good enough crew. All of 'em learned their trade out in the Belt. They're rough and unpolished, but they know how to run this ship—and survive."

I said, "And should we run into any more difficulties—"

"Which we will," Marguerite interjected.

"They're going to take over this ship and kill us all," I finished.

Fuchs nodded somberly. He sat heavily in his desk chair and let out a gust of air that would have been a sigh, had anyone else breathed it. From him, it sounded more like an animal's growl.

"I suppose a little demonstration is in order," he said at last.

"A demonstration, sir?" I asked.

He eyed me disdainfully. "Yes. A calculated show of

force. Something to make them more afraid of their captain than they are of Venus."

"What are you going to do?" Marguerite asked, genuine fear in her voice.

Fuchs made a grisly smile for her. "Something aggressive, I imagine. They'll understand that. They'll get my message."

"What do you mean?"

"You'll see." Then, as if he'd made his decision and didn't have to worry about it anymore, he pressed his hands flat on the desktop and pushed himself up out of the chair. "I should be on the bridge. You two, attend to your duties."

"I'm off watch, sir," I said.

"Yes, but you're the closest thing we have to a planetary scientist here. We'll be poking out below the clouds soon. Get to the observation station up in the nose and make certain all the sensors are recording properly."

The first thing that flashed through my mind was that I had done my eight-hour stint on the bridge. He had no right to ask me to pull double duty. Almost instantly, I remembered that he was the captain and there was no court of appeals here.

"Yes, sir," I said, getting to my feet.

Marguerite got up, too. "I'll go with you," she said. "I wouldn't miss this moment for the world."

The view through the observation port up forward was still nothing but blank yellowish-gray clouds. Fuchs's so-called observation center was little more than a jumble of sensing instruments packed in around a bank of thick viewing ports. The ports themselves had been shuttered when Marguerite and I first got there. Heat shields, of course. It had taken me several minutes to figure out how to raise them.

"It 's warm up here," Marguerite said. Her face glistened with a sheen of perspiration.

"Not only here," I replied. "The deeper we go, the hotter it gets."

She touched the thick port with her extended fingertips, then jerked them back quickly.

"Hot, eh?" I asked needlessly. "You can't run coolant through the ports, it would ruin their transparency."

I pulled up the schematic of the ship's cooling system on the computer terminal built into the bulkhead below the ports. Coolant was piped through the entire hull and carried back to the heat exchangers for recycling. The heat exchangers dumped the accumulated high-temperature fluid into the engines that controlled our flight. The heat of the Venusian atmosphere was helping to drive *Lucifer*'s steering engines. We had built the same type of system into *Hesperos*, naturally. It not only cooled the ship, it helped run the engines.

Still, it was getting hotter. I felt sweat trickling along my ribs, felt my coveralls sticking to my damp skin.

Marguerite made a nervous little laugh. "At least it's a dry heat. The humidity outside must be zero."

I glanced at the sensor displays. The air temperature on the other side of our ports was climbing far past a hundred degrees Celsius. And we were still more than thirty kilometers above the surface. Sure enough, there wasn't enough water vapor in the atmosphere to measure. For all practical purposes the humidity out there was zero.

"He said we'd be breaking out of the clouds," Marguerite murmured, staring out into the endless yellow-gray haze.

"Yes, but there's no way of knowing how—"

"Did you see that?" Marguerite cried.

For just the flash of an instant the clouds had thinned enough to see what appeared to be solid ground, far, far below us. But then the mist had closed in again.

"We must be close," I said.

Then the clouds broke and we were beneath them. Marguerite and I stared down at the distant landscape of barren rock. It was utter desolation, nothing but bare hard stony ground as far as the eye could see, naked rock in shades of gray and darker gray, with faint streaks here and there of lighter stuff, almost like talc or pumice.

"We're the first people ever to see the surface of Venus," Marguerite said, her voice low, breathless.

"There've been radar pictures," I said. "And photos from probes . . ."

"But we're the first to *see* it, with our own eyes," she said.

I had to agree. "Yes, you're right."

"Are all the instruments working?" she asked.

I swiftly scanned their displays. "All recording."

She stared down at the scene of bleak devastation as if unable to pull her eyes away. The ground down there looked hot, baked for aeons, blasted by temperatures hotter than any oven.

"We'll be passing into the nightside soon," Marguerite said, more to herself than me.

I was starting to recognize geological formations on the surface. I saw a series of domes, and the wrinkles of a pressure-deformed region. There seemed to be mountains out near the horizon, although that might have been a distortion caused by the density of the thick atmosphere, like trying to judge shapes deep underwater.

"Look!" I pointed. "A crater."

"It must be fifty kilometers across," Marguerite said.

"It looks new," I said.

"Do you think it is? Pull up the map program and check it."

I did, and the display screen on the bulkhead showed the same crater on the radar map.

"There's not much erosion going on down there," I remembered. "That crater will still look new a hundred million years from now."

Marguerite looked dubious. "In all that heat and that corrosive atmosphere?"

"There's chemical weathering of the rock, but it goes very slowly," I told her. "And the heat is steady, constant. There's no hot-then-cold cycle to make the rocks expand and contract. That's what erodes rock on Earth, that and water. It just doesn't happen on Venus."

Nodding, she asked, "Are the telescopes recording all this?"

For the tenth time I checked the instruments and the computer that monitored the sensors. They were all toiling away faithfully, recording every bit and byte of data: optical, infrared, gravimetric, even the neutron scattering spectrometer was running, although we were much too high above the ground for it to capture anything.

We stayed there for hours, watching the landscape unfold beneath our straining eyes. When *Lucifer* drifted across the terminator and into the night-shadowed side of Venus, we could still see the ground perfectly well. It glowed, red-hot.

"It's like looking down into hell," I muttered.

Marguerite said softly, "But there aren't any doomed souls to see."

"Yes there are," I heard myself answer. "We're the doomed souls. We'll be lucky to get out of here. It might take a miracle to save us."

We stayed in the observation center for almost exactly eight hours. As the time drew to a close, the ship's intercom blared in its computer-generated voice: "ALL THIRD WATCH PERSONNEL REPORT TO YOUR DUTY STATIONS IN FIFTEEN MINUTES."

I realized that I was ravenously hungry. Still, Marguerite and I left those viewing ports reluctantly, as if we were afraid to miss something that might show up, despite the fact that we knew there was nothing to see down there but more heat-blasted bare rock.

Except for the wreckage of a spacecraft.

We were too high to see the wreckage of *Phosphoros* with our naked eyes, but I was hoping the telescopes and their electronic boosters would pick it up. Then I realized that we might also find what was left of *Hesperos*. Maybe even Rodriguez's spacesuited body was waiting for us somewhere down among those glowering rocks.

We stopped at the galley for a quick snack, then I headed up toward the bridge and dropped Marguerite off at her quarters.

"I'm still hoping to find something biologically interesting down at this altitude," she told me, "although I doubt that anything could live in such heat."

I had to grin at her. "Your last biological discovery nearly killed us."

She didn't see it as funny. Her face fell, and I mentally kicked myself for reminding her of her mother's death.

Fuchs was not on the bridge when I reported for duty, but he showed up shortly afterward, looking grim. I wondered what he was planning as his "calculated show of force." I remembered how he had punched me and wondered if the violence he had spoken of would be something of the same.

All through my eight-hour stint the bridge was quiet and tense. *Lucifer* was cruising lower and lower as we sailed around the nightside of the planet, scanning the surface below with all our sensors, including the radars. We knew Alex's last reported position; he was drifting along the equator when his beacon stopped transmitting. The last word he had transmitted was that his ship was breaking up and the crew was getting into their escape pod. We calculated that he must have gone down somewhere near the equator, or close enough to it so that our sensors could spot his wreckage as we sailed purposively around Venus's middle.

The man at the life support console was one of the leaders we had seen conspiring in the crew's quarters, a sizable Asian named Bahadur. He was a full head taller than I, with broad shoulders and long, well-muscled arms. He kept his head shaved, but a thick dark beard covered his jaw. His skin was sallow, almost sickly looking, and his eyes gave the impression that he was thinking secret thoughts.

Fuchs spoke hardly a word to any of us during the watch. But when we were replaced by the next shift, he stepped out into the passageway after us.

"Humphries," he called out, "follow me." Almost as an afterthought he added, "You too, Bahadur."

He marched us to the sick bay and told Bahadur to stand by the table. There wasn't enough room in the bay's narrow confines for the three of us, so I stayed out in the passageway by the open hatch.

"Bahadur, you look unhappy," Fuchs said, in English.

"I, Captain?" The man's voice was low and deep, almost a basso. I was surprised that he could speak English, but then I remembered that English was the standard language among space crews.

"Yes, you. Any complaints? Any problems you want to speak to me about?"

Bahadur blinked several times. He was obviously thinking as fast as he could. At last he said, "I do not understand, Captain."

Fuchs planted his fists on his hips, then switched to the Asian language he used on the bridge. He must have repeated his question.

Bahadur swung his head slowly from side to side. "No, sir," he said in English. "I have no problems to speak to you."

Fuchs considered his response for a few silent moments. Then he said, "Good. I'm glad."

"May I go now, Captain?" With Fuchs standing a hand's breadth in front of him, Bahadur was pinned against the sick-bay table.

"Are you certain everything is okay?" Fuchs asked, his tone openly mocking now. "I don't want any member of my crew to be unhappy."

Bahadur's brows knitted. Then he replied, "I am happy, Captain."

"That's fine. And the rest of the crew? Are they all happy, too?"

"Yes, Captain. Happy."

"Good. Then you can tell them for me that I would be very unhappy to see them frightened like a bunch of cowardly rabbits."

Bahadur jerked back as if he'd been slapped in the face.

"Remind them that I explained to each and every one of

you that this would be a dangerous mission. Do you remember that?"

"Yes, Captain," Bahadur said slowly. "You said there would be dangers."

"And a great reward at the end. Do you remember that, also?"

"A great reward. Yes, Captain."

"Good!" Fuchs said, with conspicuously false cheer. "Remind the rest of the crew. Danger, but a great reward afterward."

"I will do so, Captain."

"Yes." Fuchs's expression became iron-hard. "And tell them that I don't want my crew to be weeping and wailing like a pack of old women. Tell them that."

Bahadur's shaved head was bobbing up and down now like a puppet's. Fuchs stood aside and the man scuttled past him, through the hatch, and rushed by me like a schoolboy running from the wrath of the headmaster.

I turned from the crewman's retreating back to Fuchs, still standing there with his fists planted on his hips. So this was the captain's "calculated show of force." He had cowed the man completely.

"Surprised?" Fuchs asked, sneering at the awe that must have been clearly written on my face. "What did you expect me to do? Beat him to a pulp?"

SPYING

I have to confess that that was exactly what I had expected Fuchs to do: unleash the same kind of furious violence on the crewman Bahadur that he had vented on me the first time we met face-to-face.

But he was far cleverer than that. He had cowed the big Mongol with moral superiority and a caustic, withering tongue. Would it be enough, I wondered as I started back to the crew's quarters. Would the big technician stay cowed?

"I wouldn't go back there just now," Fuchs said to me as I started down the passageway.

I turned back toward him. "Sir?"

With a sardonic little smirk he explained, "They probably think you're spying on them."

My eyes nearly popped out of my head. "Me? Spying?"

"How else would I know about their grumbling?"

"Don't they realize you have cameras watching them?" I asked. "Microphones listening? Computers to translate their language?"

Fuchs actually laughed, a harsh, bitter barking. "They're

tearing their quarters apart right now, searching for my bugs. They won't find any."

"Why not?"

"Because they've crawled away on their built-in wheels, down along the air shaft and into my compartment." He looked smugly pleased with himself. "Want to see 'em?"

Without waiting for my reply he headed down the passageway. He didn't bother to look back. I followed, as he knew I would.

"I'm sure they're doing an especially good job of ripping your bunk apart," he said as we reached the door to his quarters. "When they find nothing, they'll be certain that you're the spy in their midst."

"That's why you had me come with you when you braced Bahadur!" I realized.

Fuchs's only reply was a sly grin.

We entered his compartment. He went to his desk and pulled a slim flat black object from the top drawer. He pressed a thumb against it and several tiny lights winked green on across its top.

"Remote controller," he explained. "Set to operate only when it's activated by my thumbprint. Otherwise, it runs the wall screen."

The wall screen stayed blank, though. Fuchs aimed the remote at the ventilation grid in the overhead. The lights blinked briefly, and then a pair of miniature metallic objects crawled through the grid and along the metal overhead toward him.

No bigger than my thumb, they looked like minuscule metal caterpillars. Midget-sized wheels lined their lengths. Looking closer, I saw that they were actually ball bearings.

"Magnets hold them against the overhead," Fuchs said, almost as if speaking to himself. "Nanomotors provide propulsion."

"But nanotechnology is outlawed," I said.

"On Earth."

"But—"

"This is the real world, Humphries. My world."

"Your world," I repeated.

"The world your father exiled me to, more than thirty years ago."

"My father exiled you?"

Fuchs turned off the remote and sat heavily in his desk chair. The two bugs clung to the overhead, inert.

"Oh, the old humper didn't have me officially driven out. I still have the legal right to return to Earth. But I could never build my own company there. Your father saw to it that I'd never be able to raise a penny of capital. None of the major corporations would even take me on as an employee."

"Then how did you survive?" I asked, taking one of the chairs in front of the desk.

"It's different off-Earth. Out on the frontier you're worth what you can accomplish. I could work. I could control other workers, supervise them. I could take risks that nobody else would even think of taking. What did I care? Your father had stolen my life, what difference did it make?"

"You built your fortune off-Earth."

"What fortune?" he snorted. "I'm just a derelict, a man who's captained ore ships and run prospecting probes out in the Belt. One of thousands. A rock rat. A drifter."

My eyes turned to the battered book on his desk. "'Better to reign in Hell than serve in Heaven,'" I quoted softly.

He laughed bitterly. "Yes. The original sour-grapes line."

"But you'll be a very wealthy man when you come back from Venus."

He stared at me a moment, then said, "Satan sums it up neatly:

> All is not lost—the unconquerable will,
> And study of revenge, immortal hate,
> And courage never to submit or yield."

I had to admire him. Almost. "That's how you feel?" I asked.

"That is precisely how I feel," he said, with fervor.

"All these years you've nursed a hatred against my father because he beat you in business."

"He *stole* my company! And stole the woman I loved. She loved me, too."

"Then why did she—"

"He killed her, you know."

I should have felt startled, I suppose, but somehow I had almost expected that from him.

Seeing my disgust, Fuchs leaned forward intently. "He did! She tried to be a good wife to him but she still loved me. All that time, she still loved me! When he finally understood that, he murdered her."

"My father's no murderer," I said.

"Isn't he? He killed your brother, didn't he?"

"No, I can't believe that."

"And now he's killing you, as well."

I shot to my feet. "I may not be on very good terms with my father, but I won't listen to you making such accusations."

Fuchs started to frown, but it turned into a sneering, maddening chuckle.

"Go right ahead, Humphries. March off in righteous dudgeon." He waved a hand in the general direction of the door. "They ought to be finished tearing your bunk apart by now. Be careful what you say to them. They're convinced you're spying on them for me, you know."

The atmosphere in the crew's quarters was as thick and venomous as the Venusian air outside the ship. They all stared at me in sullen silence.

My bunk was torn to shreds. They had ripped apart my sheets, my pillow, even the mattress. The drawers beneath the bunk were pulled out, thoroughly rifled. Even my shoji screen had been slashed, every single pane.

I stood beside my bunk for a long moment, my heart

pounding in my ears. It felt hot in the crowded compartment, oppressively hot and sticky. Hard to breathe.

I turned to face eight hostile Asian faces staring at me, eight pairs of hooded brown eyes focused accusingly upon me.

I licked my lips, felt sweat trickling along my ribs. Their overalls looked stained with sweat, too. They must have been working very hard to find the captain's bugs.

I looked directly at the tall and broad-shouldered Bahadur, his shaved head rising above all the others.

"Bahadur, you understand English," I said.

"We all do," he told me, "but most of us do not speak it well."

"I am not the captain's spy," I said firmly.

They did not reply.

"He has planted electronic bugs in the air shaft. He uses the computer to translate your language."

"We searched the air shaft," Bahadur said.

"His bugs are mobile. He takes them away when you search for them."

One of the women pointed at me and spoke in a rapid, flowing tongue.

"She says you are the bug," Bahadur translated. "You spy on us."

I shook my head. "Not so."

"The captain likes you. He shares meals with you. You are the same race as he."

"The captain hates me and my father," I said. "He is watching this scene now and choking with laughter."

"The punishment for spying is death," said one of the men.

"Go ahead and kill me, then," I heard myself say. "The captain will enjoy watching you do it." I had no idea where such foolish courage came from.

Bahadur raised a hand. "We will not kill you. Not where it can be seen."

Whatever shred of courage I had in me evaporated with

those words. It took a real effort of will to stand there facing them all. My knees wanted to collapse. And a voice in my mind was screaming at me, *Get away! Run!*

Before I could say anything aloud, though, the captain's voice blared through the loudspeaker, "EMERGENCY! ALL HANDS TO EMERGENCY STATIONS! THE PRIME HEAT EXCHANGER HAS FAILED. THE SHIP IS DANGEROUSLY OVERHEATING. ALL HANDS TO EMERGENCY STATIONS!"

OVERHEATING

They all raced past me and out the hatch, leaving me standing suddenly alone in the crew's quarters. My bunk was a mess and the others had just threatened my life. But I found myself ridiculously worried over the fact that I hadn't the faintest idea where my emergency station was.

The captain would know, of course. So I trotted down the passageway to the bridge. All the stations were occupied, I saw.

Fuchs looked up from the display screens. "Mr. Humphries. So pleased you decided to join us."

His sarcasm was like acid. I simply stood at the hatch, not knowing what I should be doing.

"Take over the comm console, Humphries," he snapped. Then he spat out a harsh command to the woman already seated there.

She got up and quickly left the bridge. I took over the comm console. I saw that, despite the emergency, the communications systems were running quite normally. Our automated telemetering beacon was functioning as it should. Intercom channels within the ship were filled with jabbering voices that I couldn't understand.

"Should I send out a distress call, sir?" I asked.

"To whom?" he snapped.

"IAA headquarters in Geneva, Captain. At least, we should let them know what's happening to us."

"The telemetering data will give them the full picture. We will maintain silence otherwise."

I knew that a distress call wouldn't help us one iota. We were ninety million kilometers from any possible rescue. Not even *Truax*, up in orbit above us, could enter the atmosphere and come to our aid.

We sat in tense silence on the bridge for hours. I was sweating, and not merely from the rising heat. I was frightened, truly frightened. A nasty voice in my mind told me with biting irony that if the crew was able to repair the heat exchanger and save the ship, their next action would be to murder me. Maybe it would be better if we all went down, I thought.

It had been madness, every millimeter of the way, this insane expedition to Venus. What had ever made me do it? I racked my brain, seeking answers for my own foolish behavior. It wasn't the money, I told myself. It wasn't even my feeble hope of earning some respect from my father. It was Alex. All my life, Alex had been the one person I could rely on. He had protected me, encouraged me, taught me by his example how a boy should grow into manhood. He had been all that a big brother should be, and more.

I'm doing this for you, Alex, I said silently as I watched the communications screens. I could see the faint reflection of my own face in the main screen in front of me. I didn't look at all like Alex. No two brothers could look less alike.

But Alex had loved me. And I was ready to give my own life to be worthy of that love, that trust. It was a vain, self-serving excuse, I told myself. But it was also true.

"Let me see the heat exchanger bay," Fuchs commanded. I roused myself from my thoughts and punched up the

ship's inboard schematic, then tapped the area marked HEAT
EXCHANGER BAY. The screen filled with an image of four
crew members stripped to their waists, sloshing in sweat, as
they labored over the malfunctioning exchanger. Bahadur
seemed to be their chief. With something of a jolt I realized
that two of the bare-chested crew were women. Their com-
rades paid no attention to their nudity.

Fuchs began to speak to Bahadur in his own language,
growling and snarling at him. I slipped a phone plug into
my right ear and activated the translation program.

I might as well have listened to their native tongue. They
were using such heavy tech-talk jargon that I barely understood anything. Apparently there was a blockage in one of
the main tubes that resulted in a growing hot spot that
threatened to erode the high-temperature ceramic that coated the inner walls of the tubing. Fuchs spoke sarcastically
of "hardening of the arteries" to the laboring crew.

"We must take the main exchanger off-line to make the
necessary repairs," Bahadur said. I got that much clearly.

"For how long?" Fuchs asked.

"Two hours. Maybe more."

Fuchs tapped swiftly on the keyboard built into his armrest, then stared hard at his main display screen. It showed a
graph that was meaningless to me, except that it shaded from
light blue through a bilious pink to a blaring fire-engine red.
A single curve arched across the gridwork, with a blinking
white dot hovering on the edge of the blue-shaded region.

"All right," Fuchs said. "Take it off-line. You've got two
hours, no more."

"Yes, sir," said Bahadur.

It took more than two hours, of course.

Fuchs gave orders to lift the ship to a higher altitude,
where it was slightly cooler. I realized that we were dealing
with a few tens of degrees now, desperately hoping that we
could tolerate two hundred degrees Celsius for a bit longer
than two hundred and fifty.

The ship rose slowly. Our altitude readings inched higher, but the temperature outside the hull did not fall more

than a few degrees. And it was growing constantly hotter inside.

We sat at our stations on the bridge, literally sweating out the repairs to the heat exchanger. The temperature rose steadily. I watched that blinking white cursor travel along the graph's curve from the blue into the pink, heading inexorably toward the red area that marked danger.

Marguerite called from the sick bay. "I have a man here suffering from heat prostration, according to the diagnostic program."

I could see past her worried face one of the crewmen lying flat on the table, eyes closed, his face bathed in sweat, his coveralls soaked.

"Baldansanja," Fuchs muttered. "I need him at the pumps. We have to climb out of this soup, get up to a cooler altitude."

"He's totally exhausted."

"Give him a couple of salt tablets and get him back to the pumps," Fuchs commanded.

"But the diagnostic program says he needs rest!" Marguerite pleaded.

"He can rest after we've repaired the heat exchanger," Fuchs snapped. "I need every joule of work those pumps can give us, and Sanja's the man who knows those pumps better than anyone else. Get him on his feet! Now!"

Marguerite hesitated. "But he—"

"Inject saline into him, give him a handful of uppers, do whatever you have to do to get him back at those pumps," Fuchs demanded. It was the first time I had seen him appear to be worried.

The man on the table stirred and opened his eyes. "Captain," he pleaded in English, "please forgive this weakness."

"On your feet, Sanja," Fuchs said, in a more conciliatory tone. "The ship needs you."

"Yes, sir. I understand, sir."

Fuchs punched off the channel from the sick bay before Marguerite could say anything more. In a few minutes Baldansanja reported from the pump station, back at the aft end of the ship. He sounded weak, but Fuchs seemed satisfied to have him on duty again.

After nearly three hours Bahadur called in. In English he reported, "The heat exchanger is back on-line, Captain."

The man looked happy: grimy, his bald head glistening with perspiration and rivulets of sweat trickling into his beard, but a big toothy grin spreading almost from one dangling gold earring to the other. I had seen that kind of expression on people's faces before. It was the exhausted yet triumphant smile of an athlete who has just broken a world record.

I looked from his image to the graph. The white cursor was blinking on the edge of the red zone.

Fuchs gave no congratulations. "How long will it stay on-line?"

"Indefinitely, Captain! For as long as we need it!"

"Really?"

"If we step up the maintenance routine," Bahadur amended. "Inspect and clean one tube at a time, every twenty-four hours, sir."

Rubbing a hand across his broad jaw, Fuchs replied, "Yes, I think that's in order."

He pointed at me. "Get me the pump station, Humphries."

"Yes, sir," I said.

Baldansanja was back there, sitting grimly in front of a maze of dials. His face was dry, his eyes wide, pupils dilated. I wondered what medication Marguerite had given him.

"Sanja," said Fuchs, "we're going down again. The emergency is over. Report to sick bay."

"I will monitor the pumps, Captain," he said doggedly.

"Report to the sick bay. Don't make me repeat my order again."

The man's eyes went still wider. "Yes, Captain. I will go."

It took a while for the bridge to cool down to a relatively comfortable level. Fuchs called off the emergency, but by then it was time for my normal watch so I stayed at the comm console. Fuchs gave me a ten-minute break to get something to eat and relieve myself. I was back on duty in nine minutes and thirty seconds.

"Have you ever heard of Murphy's Law, Humphries?" he asked from his command chair.

"If anything can go wrong, it will," I replied, then hastily added, "Sir."

"Do you know the reason behind Murphy's Law?"

"The reason behind it, sir?"

He gave me a disdainful huff. "You think of yourself as something of a scientist, don't you? Then you ought to be interested in the reasons behind phenomena. Root causes."

"Yes, sir," I said.

"Why does the air-conditioning system break down during the hottest weather of the year? Why did our heat exchanger fail when we needed it most?"

I saw where he was heading. "Because that's when the maximum strain is put on it."

"Exactly," he said, leaning back in his chair. "Now tell me, what else is going to fail? Where will Murphy strike next?"

I had to think about that. We needed the heat exchanger to keep us from cooking to death as we descended deeper into Venus's atmosphere. We also needed the life support systems, but no more so now than we did the day the crew came aboard, back in Earth orbit.

"Well?" Fuchs goaded.

"The pumps," I guessed. "The pumps keep the gas envelope filled with outside air so we keep descending."

"And stay in trim," he added.

"And when we're ready to go up again," I reasoned aloud, "we'll be dependent on the pumps to drive the air out of the envelope and lighten us."

"Very good, Humphries," Fuchs applauded mockingly. "Very astute. As soon as you end your watch, I want you to go to Sanja and start learning how to run the pumps."

"Me?"

"You, Mr. Humphries. Your talents are wasted here at the communications console. That's much too simple a task for a man of your brilliance."

He was jabbing at me; why, I had no idea. The two other technicians on the bridge were as blank-faced as usual, although I thought I saw their eyes meet briefly.

"Yes, Humphries," Fuchs went on, "it's time you got those lily-white hands of yours dirtied a little. A bit of honest work will make a man of you, mark my words."

I definitely saw the glimmerings of a smile on the navigation technician's lips before she could mask it. I was the butt of Fuchs's scornful humor. But why?

Fuchs left the bridge shortly afterward, and Amarjagal, the first mate, took the conn. She gave me a sour look, but said nothing.

When I finished my watch, I left the bridge, intending to find Baldansanja and start learning about the pumps. But I only got as far as the open door to the captain's quarters.

"Take a look at this, Humphries," he called to me.

That was an order, not a request, I knew. I stepped through the doorway and saw that his big wall screen showed the ground below us, glowing hot in the darkness of the Venusian night.

"Like Milton's lake of fire," he said, staring grimly at the bleak barren rock.

He touched a control on his desk and the overhead lights went out. There was no illumination in his compartment except the eerie hellish glow from those red-hot rocks more than thirty kilometers below us. Their fiery light made his face look evil, satanic—and yet exultant.

"A dungeon horrible," he quoted,

"on all sides round
As one great furnace flamed; yet from those flames
No light, but rather darkness visible . . ."

He turned to me, still smiling devilishly. "Have you ever seen anything like it?"

I stared at him.

"No, of course not," he answered his own question. "How could you? How could anyone? Look at it. Just look at it! Terrible and magnificent. Awesome and beautiful in its own ghastly way. This is what hell must have looked like before Lucifer and his fallen angels were condemned to it."

I was speechless. Not so much with the view of the ground, but with Fuchs's obvious fascination.

"A whole world to explore," he said, still staring at the screen. "An entire planet, so much like our own in size yet so utterly, confoundedly different from Earth. How did it get this way? What made Earth into paradise and Venus into hell?"

Despite myself I stepped closer to the screen. It truly was awesome, beckoning in a terrifying, grotesque way, like the old horror tales of vampires luring their prey to them: a vast plain of bare rock glowering sullenly, so hot that it glowed. There's never darkness on Venus, I realized. Despite the clouds it is never dark down there.

That's where we were going. That's where we had to go, down there, into that infernal red-hot hell. Alex was down there; what remained of him, at least.

And Fuchs was fascinated by it. Absolutely enthralled. He stared wordlessly at the searing-hot rocky landscape below us, his lips pulled back in an expression that might have been a smile on any other human face. On him it looked more like a snarl, a look of defiance, the face of a man staring at his archenemy, his nemesis, a foe so powerful there is no hope of overcoming it.

Yet he dared to face this enemy, face him and battle against him with all his might.

How long we stood there staring at the blistering scorched landscape I can't tell, but at last Fuchs tore his gaze away and turned on the overhead lights. It took a real effort of will for me to turn away from the screen and look at him.

For once, Fuchs was silent. He dropped down into his desk chair, his face somber, thoughtful.

"I could have been a scientist," he said, looking back at the scorched surface of Venus again. "My schooling wasn't so good, though; I never had the grades to make it into a university. Or the encouragement. I went to a technical college, instead. Got a job before I was twenty. Earned my living instead of earning a PhD."

I had no reply for him. There was nothing I could say.

His eyes finally met mine. "Well, once I've got your father's money in my fist, then I can take all the schooling I want. I'll come back to Venus with a proper scientific mission. I'll explore this world the way it deserves to be explored."

He's entranced by Venus, I finally understood. I pretend to be a planetary scientist, but he's truly enthralled by this horrible world. In a strange and bizarre way, he's in love with Venus.

Yet this was the man who had casually set me up for the crew's suspicions, who had cruelly badgered me on the bridge less than half an hour earlier.

"I don't understand you," I murmured.

He cocked a brow at me. "Because I'm fascinated by this alien world? Me, a rock rat, an asteroid bum, excited by the mysteries and dangers we're facing? You think that only certified scientists with the proper degrees in their dossiers are allowed to become enraptured by the new and unknown?"

"Not that," I said, shaking my head. "It's the contradictions in you. You're obviously a man of intelligence, yet you behave like a barroom tough most of the time."

He laughed. "What would you know about barroom toughs?"

"Just a little while ago you were ridiculing me in front of the crew."

"Ah! That hurt your feelings, did it?"

"I just don't understand how you can do that and still invite me to share your feelings about exploring this planet."

He clicked off the display, frowning. "We're not here to explore. We're here to find your brother's remains and go back to claim your father's prize money."

I must have blinked with surprise a half dozen times before I could find my voice again. "But just now, only a few minutes ago, you said—"

"Don't mistake dreams for reality," he snapped. Then he seemed to relent slightly. "Someday, maybe," he murmured. "Maybe someday I'll come back. But we've got to live through this mission first."

I shook my head. There was much more to this man than I had realized.

"As for my ragging you on the bridge," he said, "all I was doing was trying to save your life."

"Save my life?"

"The crew thinks you're my spy among them."

"Thanks to you!"

He whisked a hand through the air, as if brushing away an insect. "Now they might have some doubts. I'll probably have to kick your butt a few more times to convince them."

Wonderful, I thought.

"And I shouldn't invite you into my quarters, of course. That makes them really suspicious. So don't expect this kind of treatment anymore."

"I understand . . . I guess."

"Yes. I shouldn't have asked you in right now, but I just couldn't sit here alone watching the planet unfolding below us. I had to share it with somebody, and Marguerite's sleeping right now."

It wasn't until I was halfway up the passageway to the crew's quarters that I wondered how Fuchs knew Marguerite was asleep.

MUTINY

That session with Fuchs brought home something important to me. I was supposed to be a planetary scientist, yet I had done precious little to live up to the claim.

The instruments that I had put on board *Hesperos* to satisfy Professor Greenbaum and Mickey Cochrane had done their work automatically. I hardly needed to look at them, much less do actual scientific work. And now even they were gone and I was little more than a captive among Fuchs's crew.

I mean, Alex came to Venus to find out how the planet had turned into a greenhouse hell. He wanted to determine what had happened on Venus to make it so different from Earth, and whether our own world might take the same disastrous turn. Sure, there was plenty of politics involved. The Greens trumpeted Alex's mission and were all set to use his findings to bolster their own pro-environment, anti-business programs.

But beyond all that Alex was genuinely interested in learning about Venus simply for the sake of knowledge. He truly was a scientist at heart. I know my brother, and I know that he was using the Greens—accepting their money for his mission to Venus—as much as they were using him.

And me? I had sworn to follow in Alex's footsteps, but I had done precious little about it. Here was Fuchs, of all people, embarrassing me with his passion about exploring the planet while I stood there like a tongue-tied dolt, a dilettante who's merely pretending to play at being a real scientist.

No more, I swore to myself as I cleaned up the mess the crew had made of my bunk. I said not a word to them, and they watched me in silent hostility. As I tacked a ripped sheet onto the torn shoji screen, I told myself that I was going to find out as much about Venus as I could and everyone and everything else could be damned, as far as I was concerned.

The trouble was that I didn't have any of the equipment we had carried aboard *Hesperos*. Still, *Lucifer* bore its own battery of sensors. I resolved to tap their data and begin a comprehensive investigation of the atmosphere. After all, we had an excellent profile from the sampling we had done. Marguerite had her airborne, metal-eating bacteria to study; I was going to learn everything I could about the Venusian atmosphere.

And, in a few days, when we finally reached the surface, I was determined to collect samples of those scorching-hot rocks and bring them back to Earth.

A fine and noble intention. But then my damned anemia began to gnaw at me again.

I ignored the symptoms, at first. Tiredness, shortness of breath, occasional dizzy spells. Forget them, I told myself. Concentrate on your work.

I tried to convince myself that I was merely working harder than normal, between my new duties learning about the pumping systems and my studies of the data Fuchs had accumulated on the Venusian atmosphere. But at heart I knew that my red-cell count was sagging; hour by hour I was growing worse.

Marguerite noticed it. She had turned the sick bay into something of a biology lab, where she pored over the data she had amassed on the Venusian aerobacteria. She had not been able to bring any samples aboard when we had jumped the failing *Hesperos,* and Fuchs would not have allowed samples on his ship anyway, I knew.

"I'm trying to figure out what kind of container we could use to hold them," Marguerite told me, "so we can collect samples on our way back up and bring them to Earth."

The little display screen on the sick bay partition showed a chemical analysis of the aerobacteria's protoplasm, a senseless hash of chemical symbols and numbers as far as I was concerned.

She was biting her lower lip as she studied the screen. "If only I'd had the time to do a DNA workup," she murmured.

"Assuming they have DNA," I said. I was sitting on the table, legs dangling. The bay felt slightly chilly to me, but considering the hot atmosphere just on the other side of the hull, I felt no urge to complain.

"The Martian bacteria have helical structures in their nuclei. So do the lichen."

"And if the Venusian bacteria do too, does that prove that helical structures are a basic form for all living organisms, or does it show that life on all three planets must have come from the same origin?"

Marguerite looked at me with a respect in her eyes that I had never seen before.

"That's a very deep question," she said.

I tossed it off nonchalantly. "I'm a very deep fellow."

Her gaze became more intent. "You're also a very pale fellow. How have you been feeling?"

I started to put up a brave front, but instead heard myself say, "It's coming back."

"The anemia?"

"Yes."

"The transfusion didn't work, then."

"It worked fine, for the past few days," I said. "But getting a transfusion of whole blood doesn't cure my anemia.

My DNA doesn't make enough red blood cells to keep me alive."

She looked terribly concerned. "You'll need another transfusion, then."

"How often can he give blood?" I wondered aloud.

Marguerite cleared her display screen with the jab of a finger and called up a medical reference. "No one can donate a half-liter of blood every few days, Van. We'd merely be killing the donor."

"He won't be that generous, believe me," I said.

She looked up sharply at me. "How do you know?"

I answered, "Fuchs has a much more active sense of self-preservation than that."

"Then why did he give you his own blood in the first place?"

"Because you said you'd accuse him of murder if he didn't, remember?"

"That's right, I did, didn't I?" she said, with the hint of a rueful smile touching her lips. "I had forgotten that."

"I don't think it would work again."

"It won't be necessary," she said.

"Why not?"

"He'll donate his blood voluntarily."

"Really?"

"Really," she said, with great certainty.

"How can you be so sure?" I asked.

She looked away from me. "I know him better now. He's not the monster you think him to be."

"You know him better," I echoed.

"Yes, I do," she said defiantly.

"He's sleeping with you, isn't he?" I demanded.

Marguerite said nothing.

"Isn't he?"

"That's none of your business, Van."

"Isn't it? When you're going to bed with him to keep me alive? When you're doing this for my sake?"

She looked truly stunned. "For your sake? You still think I'd pop into bed with him for your sake?"

"Isn't that . . . I mean . . ."

Marguerite's dark eyes held me like a vise. "Van, don't you realize that what I do, what he does, even what you yourself do, is strictly for our own individual benefits? We're all trying to stay alive here, trying to make the best of what we've got to deal with."

Now I was completely confused. "But . . . you and Fuchs," I stammered. "I thought . . ."

"Whatever you thought is wrong," Marguerite said firmly. "If I were you I'd stick to the real problem: how to get enough blood transfusions from the captain to keep you alive without killing him."

I glared at her, feeling as hotly angry inside as the fiery red-glowing ground below us.

"You don't have to worry about him," I growled. "He won't risk his neck for me, and he knows you can't accuse him of murder if giving me more transfusions will kill him."

Before she could reply, I pushed past her, out of the sick bay, and up the passageway toward the observation center in the ship's nose.

I never got that far.

As I passed the open hatch of the crew's quarters, Sanja called out to me, "Mr. Humphries, come in here, please."

He was the one crew member who had shown something more than suspicious hostility toward me, the man in charge of the ship's pumping systems, my direct superior.

I stepped through the hatch and saw that Bahadur and two others—including one of the women—were standing along the bulkhead on either side of the hatch.

Sanja looked distinctly uneasy. He was slightly built, almost birdlike, with darker skin than the others, sort of a cocoa brown.

The other three eyed me in grim silence. Bahadur especially seemed to be glowering menacingly.

"Mr. Humphries, we must go to the secondary pump station," Sanja told me.

"Now?" I asked, looking around at the others. They seemed like a death squad to me.

With an unhappy nod, Sanja said, "Now. Yes."

My pulse was thundering in my ears as we trooped down the passageway, past the bridge, heading for the aft end of the ship. Fuchs was not in the command chair when we passed the bridge, I saw; Amarjagal had the conn. The doors to both the captain's quarters and Marguerite's were tightly closed as we went by.

Fine, I thought. They're in bed together while the crew murders me. Bahadur has timed his move perfectly.

I didn't know what to do. My knees started to shake as we approached the secondary pump station. My palms felt sweaty. Neither Bahadur nor any of the others had spoken a word to me, except for Sanja. For a ridiculous instant I remembered old Western videos that I had watched as a child. This certainly looked like a lynching party to me.

With each step we took Bahadur seemed to grow larger. He was a big man, taller than anyone else aboard, broad in the shoulder and narrow in the hips. His shaved head and bushy beard gave him an appearance of savagery. Baldansanja looked slim and weak next to him, a harmless man driven by the stronger Bahadur. The other man and the woman were both solidly built, a bit taller than I and much more thickly muscled.

The secondary pumping station was two ladder-flights down, at the tail end of the passageway, nothing more than a pie-slice-shaped chamber with a pair of backup pumps housed in hemispherical metal covers.

"Sit there," Bahadur said, pointing to one of the hemispheres.

"I know you think I'm a spy for the captain," I started to say, "but that's entirely wrong. I'm not—"

"Be quiet," Bahadur said.

But I couldn't keep my mouth shut. Fear loosens the bowels in some men. In me, apparently, it loosened the tongue. I babbled. I couldn't stop talking. I gave them chapter and verse of how Fuchs hated my father and me and would congratulate them for murdering me, how they

couldn't get away with it, how the IAA and the other
authorities would find out about this when they returned to
Earth and investigate my death and—

The woman slapped me hard across my face. I tasted
blood in my mouth.

"Be silent, Mr. Humphries!" hissed Bahadur. "We have
no intention of harming you unless you force us to."

I blinked, the whole side of my face stinging as I swallowed salty hot blood. The woman glared at me and muttered something in her native tongue. I understood the tone:
"Shut your mouth, foolish man."

I sat there in silence. But I couldn't help fidgeting. My
hands refused to stay still. My fingers drummed along the
thighs of my coveralls. Every nerve in my body was jan-
gling, quivering.

The others took flat little black boxes from their pockets
and scanned the bulkheads, overhead, and deck. Looking
for bugs, I figured. The woman grunted and pointed to a
plate in the metal overhead. While Sanja stood beside me,
looking downcast, they unscrewed the plate and removed a
tiny piece of plastic. It looked like nothing more than a
speck of dust to me, but Bahadur frowned at it, threw it to
the deck, and ground it beneath the heel of his boot.

I looked up at Sanja. "What's this all about? What are
they going to do?"

He shushed me with a finger to his lips.

So I sat there in terrified silence for what seemed like
hours. Sanja stood irresolutely beside me, obviously miserable, while the others arrayed themselves on either side of
the compartment's hatch and occasionally peered up the
passageway that ran along the keel of the ship.

At last the woman hissed something that sounded like a
warning and they flattened themselves out against the bulkhead. Sanja seemed to be trembling just as hard as I was,
but he whispered to me, "Be absolutely silent, Mr.
Humphries. Your life depends on it."

Sitting there on the pump housing, a prisoner in a

makeshift cell, I leaned over slightly so I could see up along the passageway. Fuchs was striding toward us, his face a thundercloud, his hands balled into fists.

Bahadur pulled a knife from his coveralls. I recognized it as a steak knife from the galley. The other two drew the same weapons.

I glanced up at Sanja. He seemed paralyzed with fear, biting his lip, staring up the passageway at the approaching captain. I could hear Fuchs's footsteps now, treading along the metal decking swiftly, firmly.

They meant to kill him, I finally understood. I was nothing more than the bait. This trap had been set for him.

So they kill him, I thought. And we pull out of Venus and go home. If I keep my mouth shut I can survive this. I can back up their story. I can convince them that if they kill me too the authorities will know they'd committed murder, but if they let me live I'll corroborate whatever story they concoct about Fuchs and we'll all get out of this alive. After all, Venus is so damnably dangerous almost any story they invent would be believable.

We can live through this! I won't get Alex's remains, but I can always come back. What we've learned on this mission will allow me to build a better, safer vessel for the return trip.

Fuchs was a few strides from the hatch. Bahadur and the two others stood on either side of the hatch, out of his sight, knives drawn.

If our positions were reversed Fuchs would let them kill me, I told myself. He set me up for this in the first place, making the crew think I was spying for him.

They could hear his footsteps too, I realized. They were waiting, poised to strike. Sanja stood frozen beside me, unwilling or unable to utter a peep.

I leaped off the pump housing and dove out the hatch, screaming, "It's a trap!" at the top of my lungs.

I barreled into Fuchs, who simply pushed me aside. As I climbed to my feet, Bahadur and the two others pushed through the hatch, roaring with frustrated rage.

Bahadur reached Fuchs first, and the captain leveled him with a single powerful punch. The other crewman staggered back as Bahadur slumped to the deck. Fuchs kicked Bahadur in the head, then stood waiting in a semi-crouch, his lips pulled back in a ferocious grin.

The crewman slashed with the knife but Fuchs ducked under it and punched up into the man's midsection so hard it lifted him off his feet. I heard the air gush out of his lungs and he dropped to his knees. Fuchs smashed a rabbit punch to the back of his neck and he fell atop the prostrate Bahadur.

All this happened in the time it took me to get to my feet. The woman stood in the hatch, amazed and confused, knife in hand, glancing from Fuchs to the inert bodies of her fellow conspirators.

Fuchs was still grinning terribly. The woman hesitated, wavered. Sanja hit her from behind with a karate chop that knocked her senseless.

It was over. Fuchs bent down and took the knives from them. Bahadur was moaning, his legs twitching slightly, the other crewman still on top of him, still unconscious.

Turning to me, the three knives in one hand, Fuchs said, "Well, that's over."

"Captain," Sanja said, his voice shaking as he stepped over the women he'd knocked out, "I was forced by them . . . I would not betray you, I was—"

"Quiet, Sanja," said Fuchs.

The man closed his mouth so quickly I could hear his teeth click.

"That took some nerve, warning me," Fuchs said to me.

I was panting, my legs felt weak, my bladder full.

"I knew what was going on, of course," he went on. "Clever of them to use you as bait. They would have slit your throat afterward, of course."

"Of course," I managed to choke out.

"Still, it took some guts to bolt out like that and try to warn me." His face was almost devoid of expression; neither pain nor pleasure showed; not relief; certainly not gratitude.

"It made it easier to take them, bringing the fight out here to the passageway," he went on, almost musing, reviewing the brawl like a general going over the after-action reports from a battle.

"They would have killed you." I heard my own voice quavering.

"They would have tried," Fuchs said. "It would have been a tougher fight inside the pump station, I admit."

I was starting to feel almost angry. He was acting as if nothing much out of the ordinary had happened.

Bahadur moaned again and tried to sit up. Fuchs watched him struggle to get out from under the other crewman. He leaned his back against the bulkhead and held his head in both hands, eyes still closed.

"Hurts, doesn't it?" Fuchs taunted, leaning slightly toward him. "Not as much as a knife in the ribs would hurt, but still I imagine your head's pretty painful right now."

Bahadur opened his eyes. There was no defiance in them, no hatred, not even anger. He was whipped and he knew it.

"Sanja," the captain commanded, "you and Humphries take these three mutineers back to the crew's quarters. They are confined to their bunks until further orders."

"Mutineers?" I asked.

Fuchs nodded. "Attempting to kill the ship's captain is mutiny, Humphries. The penalty for mutiny is summary execution."

"You're not going to kill them!"

Fuchs gave a disdainful snort. "Why not? They were going to kill me, weren't they?"

"But . . ."

"You want to give them a fair trial first, don't you? All right, I'll be the prosecutor, you can be the defense attorney, and Sanja will be the judge."

"Here and now?"

Ignoring my question, he leaned down and slapped Bahadur smartly on the cheek. "Were you going to kill me?"

Sullenly, Bahadur nodded.

"Speak up," Fuchs said. "For the record. Did you intend to murder me?"

"Yes."

"Why?" I asked.

"To get away. To leave this place before all of us are killed."

Fuchs straightened up and shrugged at me. "There you are. What need have we for further witnesses? Sanja, how do you find?"

"Guilty, Captain."

"There," Fuchs said. "Neat and legal. Put them in their bunks. I'll deal with then later."

DEATH

Sanja and I led a trio of very cowed would-be mutineers back to the crew's quarters. None of them spoke a word as they shambled along the passageway. In the crew's quarters, the other off-watch personnel stared silently as Bahadur and the other two slumped onto their bunks. No one said anything; it wasn't necessary. They all had known what Bahadur was planning, I thought. They all were content to stand back and let it happen.

I couldn't stay in the crew's quarters, not anymore. I saw to it that the three mutineers were in their own bunks, stiff and sore from the beating they had taken, then I headed back toward Fuchs's compartment.

Marguerite was in his quarters, spraying a bandage around his left biceps.

"Come in, Humphries," Fuchs called from the chair where he was sitting with his sleeve rolled up to the shoulder.

"You're injured," I said, surprised.

"Bahadur sliced me with his first move," Fuchs answered easily. "My vest didn't protect my arms."

He gestured with his free hand to a mesh vest that was draped over one of the other chairs. I went to it and fingered the mesh: cermet, light but tough enough to stop a kitchen knife.

"You didn't go into the fight unprepared, did you?" I said.

"Only a fool would," he replied.

Marguerite finished the bandaging and stepped back. "You could have been killed," she said.

But Fuchs shook his head. "Sometimes the captain has to bring things to a boil. Let the crew simmer in their complaints and fears for too long and they might cook up something you can't handle. I saw this coming from the moment we were blown off course by the subsolar wave."

"You knew this was going to happen?" she asked.

"Something like it, yes."

"And you used me to set it up for you," I said.

"You played your part."

"They might have killed me!"

He shook his head. "Not until they'd got to me first. You were perfectly safe as long as I was still alive."

"That's your opinion," I said.

He gave me a tolerant grin. "That's the fact of the matter."

Before I could reply, Marguerite changed the subject. "Van is going to need another transfusion."

Fuchs's brows rose. "Already?"

"Already," she said.

"Too bad we cleaned up the blood from my wound," he muttered.

"I'm worried about this," Marguerite said. "If Van's going to need a transfusion every few days—"

"We'll only be here a few days more," Fuchs interrupted. "Either we find the wreckage or we pack it in and leave."

"Still . . ."

He silenced her with a wave of his hand. "I'm good for another liter or two."

"No, you're not. You can't—"

"Don't tell me what I can and can't do," Fuchs said, his voice ominously low, threatening.

"If I could call back to Earth," Marguerite said, "and tap into Van's medical records, perhaps—"

"No."

"It's for your own good," she said, her voice almost pleading.

He glared at her.

"I might be able to synthesize the enzyme Van needs from your blood. Then you wouldn't have to give any more transfusions."

"I said no."

"Why not?"

"There will be no communication between this ship and Earth until we've recovered Alex Humphries's remains," Fuchs said, with steel in his voice. "I will not give Martin Humphries any excuse to renege on his prize money."

"Even if it kills Van?"

He glanced at me, then turned back to Marguerite. "I'm good for another liter or two of blood, over the next few days."

I spoke up. "*Truax* has my complete medical records in its computer files. You could get the full description of the enzyme from them."

Fuchs started to shake his head, but hesitated. "*Truax,* eh?"

"In orbit around this planet," I pointed out. "Nowhere near Earth."

He mulled it over as he rolled his sleeve down and closed the Velcro seal at its wrist. "Okay," he said at last. "Access *Truax*'s medical computer. But that's all! You're not to speak to anyone. Not a word, do you understand?"

"Yes, I understand," Marguerite said. "Thank you."

Then she looked over at me. It took me a moment to realize what she expected.

"Thank you, Captain," I mumbled.

He brushed it off. "You're still going to need a transfusion, though, aren't you?"

"Until I can synthesize the enzyme," Marguerite said.

"Assuming you can," Fuchs pointed out. "*Lucifer* isn't equipped with a biomedical laboratory, you know."

"I'll do what I can," Marguerite said.

"Okay." Fuchs got to his feet. "Let's get down to the sick bay and get this damned transfusion over with."

Marguerite made me lay on the table and had Fuchs sit on a chair that she wedged into the sick bay's cramped space. He seemed perfectly relaxed, chewing on a mouthful of those pills of his. I couldn't stand to watch the needle go into my arm or Fuchs's; I had to close my eyes.

As I lay there, I remembered my other problem.

"I can't go back to the crew's quarters," I said.

"Why not?" Fuchs asked calmly.

I opened my eyes and saw that damnable tube sticking in his arm, filled with bright red blood. Suppressing a shudder, I focused on Marguerite, standing over us with a concerned expression on her beautiful face.

"After what happened with Bahadur and those others," I began to explain.

"You've nothing to be afraid of," Fuchs said.

"I'm not afraid," I answered. And it was true. It surprised me, but I really wasn't afraid of them.

"Then what?" Fuchs demanded.

"I just can't sleep in the same room with people who would've murdered me."

"Oh," Fuchs said condescendingly, "you're uncomfortable with ruffians as your bunk mates."

Marguerite chided, "It's not a joking matter."

"I'm not joking," Fuchs said. "Tell me, Humphries, just where do you think you can bunk, if not in the crew's quarters?"

I hadn't given that any thought at all.

"There's no place else aboard," Fuchs said, "unless you want to sleep on the deck someplace."

"Anywhere—"

"And then you'd be sleeping alone," he went on. "Unprotected. At least, in the crew's quarters there are some loyal souls nearby: Sanja, or Amarjagal, for example. Nobody will try to slit your throat while one of them is around to witness it."

"How can I sleep when people in the other bunks want to slit my throat?" I demanded.

Fuchs chuckled. "Don't worry, you'll be perfectly safe. They've shot their bolt."

"I can't sleep there."

His voice hardened. "This isn't a cruise ship, Humphries. You'll follow my orders just like all the others. You go back to your bunk. Put some iron in your spine! At least you can pretend you're not afraid of 'em."

"But you don't understand—"

Fuchs laughed bitterly. "No, *you* don't understand. You're returning to the crew's quarters. End of discussion."

He has my life in his hands, I told myself. There's nothing I can do. So I shut my mouth and squeezed my eyes shut when Marguerite slid the transfusion tube out of my arm.

"Let my blood circulate through you for a few minutes," Fuchs said, amused. "That ought to give you enough courage to crawl into your bunk and go to sleep."

I was furious with him. But I said nothing.

Not even when he draped his beefy arm on Marguerite's shoulders as the two of them left the sick bay for their quarters.

No one said a word to me when I returned to the crew's quarters. They wouldn't even look in my direction. Not even Sanja, who was off duty when I got there.

Amarjagal, the first mate, must have been up on the bridge. Fuchs was in his quarters. With Marguerite, I knew.

The two of them, together. I tried to shut the images out of my mind.

Despite everything, I fell asleep. Perhaps Marguerite had slipped a sedative or tranquilizer into my veins along with the transfusion. I slept deeply, without dreams. When I woke up I actually felt refreshed, strong.

I swung out of my bunk and padded barefoot to the lavatory. Two crewmen were washing up. When I entered they hastily rinsed themselves off and left.

A pariah. They were treating me as an outcast. Very well, I shrugged to myself. At least I get the exclusive use of the toilets and showers.

I always wrapped a towel around my middle when I went back to my bunk from the lav. Most of the others were not so modest. Even the women apparently thought little of nudity, although I must say that none of them stirred my interest at all. It wasn't racism; some of the most exciting, erotic women I've ever known were Asians. But the women aboard *Lucifer* were either dour and chunky or dour and so gaunt you could count their ribs from across the compartment. Not my type at all.

At any rate, as I went back to my bunk with my hair still wet from the shower and a towel modestly knotted around my waist, I saw that several crew members were clustered around one of the other bunks. They didn't seem to be doing anything, just standing there with their backs to me.

I thought little of it as I slid my sheet-covered shoji screen shut and pulled on a fresh set of coveralls. It was the last clean pair in the drawer beneath my bunk. I'd have to either find more in the supply locker or find out if the ship had a laundry unit aboard.

The crowd was still standing in the same spot as a few minutes before, their backs still to me. I recognized Bahadur's tall form and shaved head.

I was curious, but they obviously didn't want to have anything to do with me. It seemed to me, though, that they were clustered around Sanja's bunk. At least, I thought that's where his bunk was.

What was going on? I wondered. But I decided it would cause trouble if I asked or tried to push in among them to see what was going on.

I didn't have to. They melted away from the bunk, each of them seemingly going in a different direction. Bahadur walked slowly toward the intercom unit set into the bulkhead by the hatch, shaking his head and muttering in his beard.

I could see Sanja's bunk now. The privacy screen was open. He was lying on his back, eyes staring blankly upward. His throat was ripped open, caked with blood.

I threw up.

PUNISHMENT

Fuchs stared down at Sanja's dead body. No one had touched it. Bahadur had called the captain. One of the women had handed me a tissue to clean my face. Another handed me a wetvac to clean the floor of my vomit.

Fuchs prodded the corpse, flexed Sanja's wrists and ankles.

"He's been dead several hours," he muttered, more to himself than the rest of us.

Turning, he spotted me trying to mop up my mess. He gestured bruskly and rattled off some commands in the Asian dialect that the crew spoke. One of the men grabbed the buzzing wetvac out of my hands, his face surly.

"Come here, Humphries," Fuchs called.

Reluctantly I stepped closer to the bunk. My stomach heaved and I tasted burning bile in my throat.

"Control yourself!" Fuchs snapped. "What happened here?"

"I . . . I was asleep."

Fuchs seemed more irritated with me than concerned

about Sanja's murder. I was convinced it was murder.

He looked across the compartment. The other crew members were sitting on their bunks, or huddled around the table in the open area in the center. A few were standing near the hatch, clustered around Bahadur.

Fuchs gestured to the tall, bearded Bahadur. He walked slowly, with as much dignity as a man can muster when he's sporting a blackened, swollen eye.

"Well?" Fuchs demanded.

Bahadur answered in English. "He committed suicide."

"Did he?"

Bahadur pointed to the knife resting on the bunk at San-ja's side.

Fuchs asked more questions in their Asian language. Bahadur gave answers. From their tone I gathered that Bahadur was offering no information at all.

At last Fuchs heaved a heavy, deep sigh. "So Sanja slit his own throat because he was ashamed of betraying your mutiny," he summarized.

"Yes, Captain. That is the truth."

Fuchs eyed him with utter disgust. "And who's going to commit suicide next? Amarjagal? Or maybe Humphries, here?"

I nearly threw up again.

"I cannot say, Captain," replied Bahadur. "Perhaps no one."

"Oh?"

"If we lift ship and leave this evil place, then no one will need to die."

"Maybe you're right," Fuchs said, his ice-blue eyes colder than ever. "Maybe you're right. Come with me."

He started for the hatch, Bahadur following him. "You too," he said, crooking a finger at the man with the wet-vac. He'd been one of the mutineers back at the pump station. "And you," he added to the woman who'd been there also.

The three mutineers glanced at one another. The rest of

the crew hung back from them, as if afraid to be contaminated by their presence.

"And you, Humphries," Fuchs said. "Come with me."

He paraded the four of us up the passageway, toward the
nose of the ship, and then down a ladder to a hatch set into
the lower deck.

"Open it up," he commanded Bahadur.

I watched, puzzled, as the man tapped out the standard
code on the electronic control box set into the heavy metal
hatch. It sighed open a crack and Bahadur pulled with both
hands to swing it open all the way. It must have been heavy;
he grunted with the effort.

"There's one of *Lucifer*'s three escape pods," Fuchs said
in English, pointing downward with a blunt finger. "Plenty
of room for the three of you and several others. You can
ride it up to orbit and make rendezvous with *Truax* up
there."

Bahadur's eyes widened. "But, Captain—"

"No buts," Fuchs snapped. "You want off this ship,
there's your ticket back to orbit. Get in."

Eyeing his two companions uneasily, Bahadur protested,
"None of us knows how to navigate, sir."

"It's all preset," Fuchs said, iron-hard. "I'll handle the
launch sequence from the bridge. The pod is programmed
to boost above the atmosphere and establish itself in orbit.
I'll tell *Truax* to pick you up. When they go back to Earth
you'll go with them."

The woman said something in swift, rasping tones.

Fuchs laughed harshly. "That's entirely correct. I'll tell
Truax that you are mutineers and murderers and you're to
be kept in custody for trial."

The three of them chattered among themselves for a few
moments, more frightened than angry.

"It's up to you," Fuchs said. "You can get up to *Truax*
right now or you can stay and obey my orders."

Bahadur asked meekly, "If we stay and obey orders,
there will be no trial later?"

Fuchs looked up into his pleading eyes. "I suppose I could forget your pathetic little attempt at mutiny. And we can log Sanja's death as suicide."

"Captain!" I objected.

He ignored me and kept his eyes locked on Bahadur. "Well?" he demanded of the crewman. "What's it going to be?"

Bahadur glanced swiftly at his two companions. I wondered how much English they knew, how well they were following this exchange.

Drawing himself up to his full height, Bahadur at last decided. "We will stay, Captain."

"Will you?"

"Yes, Captain."

"And you'll follow all my orders?"

"Yes, sir."

"With no grumbling? No complaints?"

"Yes, Captain."

"All three of you?" Fuchs waved a finger to include the two others. "There'll be no more . . . suicides?"

"We are agreed, Captain, sir," said Bahadur. The other two nodded glumly.

Fuchs smiled broadly at them. But there was no humor in it. "Good! Excellent! I'm glad we're all agreed."

They started to smile back. I wanted to say something, to object to his simply forgetting about Sanja's murder. But before I could form the words, Fuchs's smile evaporated.

"I'm afraid I'm going to have to give you three some very difficult tasks, you know," Fuchs went on. "Each of you will have to take double watches now, to make up for Sanja's death."

Their faces fell.

"And all the EVA work we'll have to do in preparation for reaching the ground, that'll be your job, too."

The two others looked toward Bahadur. His eyes had gone so wide I could see white all the way around the pupils.

"And of course, once we get down to the surface I'll need

a volunteer to test the excursion craft. You'll be that volunteer, Bahadur."

The man backed away several steps. "No, Captain. Please. I cannot—"

Fuchs stalked toward him. "You said you would follow my orders, didn't you? All my orders? You agreed to that just a minute ago."

"But I am not . . . that is, I don't know how—"

"You either follow my orders or get off my ship," Fuchs said, his voice as cold and sharp as an ice pick. "Or would you rather we had a trial here and now for Sanja's murder?"

"Captain, please!"

It was uncanny. This big, broad-shouldered man was holding out his hands pitifully, begging for mercy from the short, snarling captain who confronted him like a pugnacious badger spitting defiance at a confused, frightened hunting dog.

"What's it going to be, Bahadur?" Fuchs demanded.

He looked at his two companions. They seemed just as frightened and confused as he was.

"I'm going to make your life into an unending hell, Bahadur," Fuchs promised. "You'll pay for Sanja a hundred times a day, you can count on that."

"No," Bahadur whimpered. "No."

"Then get off my ship!" Fuchs snarled, jabbing a hand toward the open hatch. "And take your two accomplices with you."

Bahadur just stood there, totally whipped. I thought he was about to break into tears.

"Now!" Fuchs snapped. "Obey or leave. Make up your mind now."

It was the woman who decided. Silently she went to the hatch and started climbing down into the escape pod. The other crewman followed her. Bahadur watched them, then shambled past the captain and disappeared down the shaft that connected to the escape pod.

Fuchs went over to the hatch and kicked it hard. It swung over and clanged shut.

"Seal it," he ordered me. "Before the sniveling little shits change their minds."

Shaking inside, I touched the key that sealed the hatch. Fuchs had orchestrated this to the last detail. He wanted Bahadur and his two fellow mutineers off his ship and he maneuvered them into going.

Wordlessly he tramped back to the bridge, with me trotting along behind him. He seemed to radiate fury, now that he no longer had to pretend to be conciliatory with Bahadur.

He relieved Amarjagal of the conn and took the command chair. "Humphries, take the communications console."

My first impulse was to say it wasn't yet time for my watch, but I swallowed that idea immediately. The captain was in no mood for contradictions, not even delays. I went to the comm console; the crewman already sitting there got up, looking slightly puzzled, and left the bridge.

"Give me the escape pod," he said flatly.

There were three pods on the ship, I saw from the display screen. Before I could ask, Fuchs told me, "They're in number one."

I opened the channel. Fuchs spoke to them briefly in their own language, then called out, "I'm initiating the separation sequence in five seconds."

I tapped the timer. It clicked down swiftly.

"Separated," said the other technician on the bridge, in English.

Before I could ask any questions, the technician reported, "Ignition. They're heading into orbit."

"Put them on the main screen, Humphries," Fuchs commanded.

It took me a few seconds to figure it out, and then I saw Bahadur's tense, sweaty face on the screen. He was pressed back into his chair by the acceleration of the pod's rockets. The two others were sitting slightly behind him. There were four empty chairs in view, as well.

"You're on course for orbit," Fuchs said to them.

"I understand, Captain," Bahadur answered.

Fuchs nodded and turned off his image.

I asked, "Should I notify *Truax* that—"

"No!" he snapped. "We will make no contact with *Truax*. It's bad enough Marguerite is querying their medical files. No contact!"

"But, sir, how will they know that the escape pod is in orbit? How will they make rendezvous?"

"That's Bahadur's problem. The pod has communications equipment. He'll call *Truax* soon enough, never fear."

"Are you sure? Sir?"

He gave me a sour look. "What difference does it make?"

I turned my attention back to my duties. In a few moments, though, Fuchs said, "Give me their course and position."

The graphic showed their trajectory curving up from our altitude, through the sulfuric acid clouds and levelling off above the cloud deck into a slightly elliptical orbit around the planet. I punched up *Truax*'s position. They were orbiting on the other side of Venus, out of direct contact.

Puzzled, I punched up the extended orbital positions for the pod and *Truax*. They would be on opposite sides of the planet for a dozen orbits before the pod would inch close enough to *Truax* for rendezvous maneuvers to be started.

I told Fuchs about the problem.

He shrugged. "They have enough air to last," he said.

"What about electricity?" I asked.

He frowned at me. "If Bahadur has the wits to unfold the pod's solar panels and align them properly, they'll have all the power they need. Otherwise they'll have to go on the pod's internal batteries."

"Will that last long enough, Captain?"

"That's not my problem."

"In all fairness, sir, we should notify *Truax*—"

"If we do, I'll have to report that those three people are mutineers and murderers."

"That's better than letting them die in orbit! Sir."

"They won't die in orbit," Fuchs said calmly. "They won't even make it to orbit."

"What do you mean?"

He pointed a finger toward the screen on my console that displayed their trajectory. "Put that plot on the main screen."

I did, and Fuchs leaned forward in his chair slightly, studying the graph. "I don't think they'll get through the clouds fast enough to avoid being chewed up by the bugs," he muttered.

"They'll only be in the clouds for twenty minutes or so," I said.

"Yes," he said slowly. "That pod has a pretty thin skin, though. It ought to be interesting."

I watched in fascinated horror as the blinking cursor that represented their pod crawled slowly, ever so slowly, along the curve that represented their trajectory. They were solidly in the clouds now. I remembered how *Hesperos* had been eaten away by the aerobacteria. But that had taken days; the escape pod would be in the clouds only for minutes, less than half an hour.

It would have been better to fire it straight up and get out and above the clouds as quickly as possible, I thought as I stared at the screen. But to establish orbit the pod had to be moving parallel to the planet's surface. The only way to do that was to follow a curving course, up and over, like the lob of a ball that's being thrown completely around the world.

No, I told myself. You could fire straight up, and once at a high-enough altitude, make a course change that moves you into a parallel with the ground. But that would take much more rocket propellant than the pod could carry. They had to get through the clouds more slowly. I only hoped that it was fast enough.

I glance over at Fuchs. He was staring at the screen, too, but grinning slightly. He reminded me of a Roman emperor watching gladiators battle to the death in the arena. Which one will die? Will those three poor miserable people in the escape pod make it to orbit, to safety?

I wondered why I cared. They had killed Sanja. They would have killed Fuchs, too. And me. They were mutineers and murderers. Yet I was worried about them, hoping that they would get through their ordeal alive.

Fuchs had no such conflicts. He had known they'd have to get through the clouds; he had remembered the bugs. He hadn't forgiven them for their crimes. This was his kind of justice.

The yellow message light started blinking at me. I clamped on the headset and pulled the microphone close to my lips. Then I touched the key that put the message on the small screen on the right side of my console.

Bahadur's face was frantic. "We are losing pressure!" his voice wailed in my ear. "The bugs are destroying the seal around our main hatch!"

"Put that on my screen," Fuchs commanded before I could turn to inform him.

I did. Bahadur's chest was heaving, his hands waving up and down. "The bugs! They are eating away at us!"

Fuchs said nothing.

"We must do something!" Bahadur screeched. "Pressure is falling!"

Behind him the other crewman and the woman were sitting tensely, safety harnesses crisscrossed over their chests, their faces grim and accusing.

"There's nothing to be done," Fuchs said, his voice cold and hard. "Just hang on and hope that you get through the clouds before the seal fails."

The woman burst out in a long string of sibilant words.

Fuchs shook his head. "I can't save you. Nobody can."

"But you must!" Bahadur was on the verge of hysteria, his eyes popping, chest heaving, hands windmilling in the air. If he hadn't been strapped into his seat, I thought, he would have been running around the pod's cramped little compartment like a madman. "You must!" he kept repeating.

"Turn off the sound," Fuchs said to me.

I reached for the keyboard, hesitated.

"Turn it off!" he snarled.

I tapped the key. Bahadur's frantic pleading cut off, but

we could still see his face and the panic in his eyes.

There was no telemeter link between the pod and *Lucifer*. We had no way of monitoring the conditions inside their compartment. But I watched the terror on their faces as their pod flew through the bug-laden clouds. I was holding my breath, I realized, staring alternately at them and the graph showing their progress through the clouds.

The blinking white cursor inched toward the upper edge of the cloud deck slowly; seconds seemed to stretch into hours. All the while Bahadur and his two companions were goggle-eyed and stiff with horror, their mouths screaming silently, their hands windmilling with frustration and panic.

Then they broke through the clouds. The cursor climbed above the top of the cloud deck, into clear space.

"They've made it!" I shouted.

Fuchs replied sardonically, "Have they?"

"They're establishing orbit," I said.

"Good," said Fuchs.

Bahadur was still wide-eyed, I saw, his chest heaving. But in a few moments he'll realize that he's safe, I thought.

Instead, his face turned blood-red. His eyes bulged and then—exploded. Blood burst from every pore in his skin. The two others, as well.

"Explosive decompression," Fuchs said flatly. "The bugs must have chewed through enough of their hatch seal to weaken it too far to hold the air inside their pod."

With a strangled cry, I snapped off the video imagery.

"Turn off the graph, as well," Fuchs said calmly. "It doesn't matter where their pod is now."

I couldn't move my hands. I squeezed my eyes shut, but still the picture of those three people bursting into showers of blood filled my mind.

"Turn it off!" Fuchs growled. "Now!"

I did. The screen went blank.

Fuchs took a deep breath, ran a hand across his broad jaw. "They had a chance. Not much of one, I admit, but they had a chance."

"Yes, they certainly did," I heard myself say.

He glared at me.

"You knew it all along. You knew they couldn't make it through the clouds. You sent them to their deaths."

He shot to his feet. I saw his fists clench and for a moment I thought he was going to haul me out of my chair and beat me senseless. I felt myself cringing inwardly and tried my best not to let it show.

Instead, Fuchs stood there for a few undecided moments, then turned and stalked out of the bridge. Before I could say or even think anything else, one of the other crewmen came in and took the conn.

CONFLICT

I finished my watch, went off duty, and stood another watch, all without seeing a trace of Fuchs. He was in his quarters the entire time as the ship spiraled lower and lower, deeper into Venus's hot, dense atmosphere.

Between watches I checked on the ship's pumps, which were now manned by the propulsion engineer who had doubled as Sanja's assistant, the Mongol named Nodon. Strong and agile as a young chimpanzee, he was wiry, all bone and tendon, with a wispy black moustache and ornamental spiral scars on both his cheeks that were meant to make him look fierce. But Nodon was at heart a gentle person. It was impossible for me to guess his age; even though he had probably never been able to afford rejuvenation therapy, he could have been anywhere from thirty to fifty, I thought. Unlike the other crewmen, he spoke English rather well and didn't hesitate to converse with me.

He had been born in the Asteroid Belt, the son of miners who had fled their home in Mongolia when the Gobi desert engulfed the grasslands on which the tribes had lived since time immemorial. He had never been to Earth, never set foot on the Mother World.

We were in the main pump station, one level below the bridge and captain's quarters. Kneeling on the metal mesh deck plates, I could feel the throb of the engines, separated from the pump bay by nothing more than a thin partition. Nodon was explaining how the pumps could be powered by hot sulfur dioxide from the heat exchangers.

"It saves electrical power for those systems that cannot run on heat," Nodon was saying, patting the round metal pump housing as if it were a faithful hound.

"But the nuclear generator provides plenty of electricity, doesn't it?" I asked.

He nodded and smiled cheerfully. "Yes, true. But when the world outside gives us so much free energy, why not accept the gift? After all, we are guests in this world. We should be grateful for anything it offers to us."

A different attitude, I thought. I began to ask him more about the pumps when a shadow fell over Nodon's face. Literally. His smile vanished. I turned and saw the captain standing behind us.

"Learning the pumps, eh? Good."

I couldn't say that he looked cheerful; Fuchs never seemed to show good humor. But he wasn't glaring or angry. My little outburst up on the bridge the day before had apparently been forgotten. Or more likely, I thought, tucked away in memory for later retrieval.

Nodon and I both scrambled to our feet.

Fuchs clasped his hands behind his back and said to me, "When you're finished here, Humphries, report to the observation center. We have several radar images to check on."

"Yes, sir," I said.

"Teach him well, Nodon," he said to the youth. "Once he learns the pumps, I can bring you up to the bridge."

"Yes, sir, Captain!" Nodon said, beaming.

I grew weary of Nodon's explanations long before he did. He seemed truly to be in love with the pumps, their importance to the ship's performance, their intricacies, their nuances, every weld and part and vibration of them.

I thought I could learn just as much from the computer's files on the pumps, but I patiently endured Nodon's smiling, eager dissertation for seemingly endless hours.

At last I excused myself and went up the ladder to the main deck. The observation center was up in the nose, but there was something else that I wanted to do first.

I went down the passageway to the sick bay. It was empty, so I walked down to Marguerite's door and tapped at it. No reply. I rapped harder.

"Who is it?" came her muffled voice.

"Van."

No response for several moments. Then the door cracked open. "I was sleeping," she said.

"May I come in? Just for a couple of seconds?"

She slid the accordion-fold door all the way and I stepped into her quarters. The bed was rumpled, but otherwise the compartment looked neat and orderly. Marguerite had pulled on a pair of wrinkled, faded coveralls. I realized that my own were not all that clean and sweet.

"What do you want, Van?" she asked tightly.

It was the first time we'd been alone in a while. She looked tired, hair tousled, her eyes puffy from sleep, but still very beautiful. The lines of her cheek and jaw would have inspired any sculptor, I thought.

"Well?"

"I'm sorry I disturbed you," I began.

"That's all right," she said, a little more lightly. "I had to get up anyway; someone was pounding at my door."

My brows knit with confusion. "But I was . . . oh, I see! It's a joke."

"Yes," she said, smiling a little. "A joke."

"I wanted to ask if you were able to get my medical records from *Truax*."

She nodded and gestured toward the laptop computer sitting open on the compartment's desk. "Yes, no problem."

"And?"

"And what?"

"Can you synthesize the enzyme for me?"

Marguerite sighed wearily. "Not yet. Probably not at all."

"Why not?" I demanded.

Frowning, she asked, "How much biochemistry do you understand?"

With a shrug I admitted, "Very little."

"I thought as much." She sighed again. Or perhaps it was a stifled yawn. "I have the formula for your enzyme. The computer file gave me the complete breakdown for it: all the amino acids and the order in which they need to be put together."

"So what's the problem?" I asked.

"Two problems, Van. One is getting the proper constituents; most of the factors have to come from someone's blood."

"Well, you can get Fuchs's blood, can't you?"

"The second problem," she went on, ignoring my comment, "is the equipment. We simply do not have the necessary equipment for this kind of biochemical synthesis."

"Can't you rig something together?"

She scowled at me. "What do you think I've been trying to do for the past day and a half? Why do you think I've been pushing myself so hard I started to fall asleep in the sick bay an hour ago and came back here for a nap?"

"Oh. I didn't realize . . ."

She focused her jet-black eyes on mine. "I'm trying, Van. I'm working as hard as I can on it."

"I appreciate that," I said.

"Do you?"

"I don't want to have to keep getting transfusions from Fuchs. I don't want to be obligated to him for my life."

"But you are."

"I am what?"

"Obligated to him for your life."

"Because of a couple of transfusions?"

Marguerite shook her head. "That, and much more."

"What do you mean by that?"

She looked as if she was on the verge of answering me, but then she said, "Nothing. Forget it."

"No, tell me."

Marguerite shook her head.

"I don't owe Fuchs anything," I said, feeling anger welling up in me. "The man's a monster."

"Is he?"

"I had to sit on the bridge and watch him kill three of the crew," I snapped.

"He executed three murderers."

"He toyed with them the way a cat plays with a mouse. He tortured them."

"He saved your life, didn't he?"

"All he's done is what you forced him to do."

"No one forced him to rescue us from your ship," Marguerite answered hotly.

"No. He was trying to save your mother, not me."

"He loved her!"

"And now he's loving you," I yelled.

Marguerite slapped me. It stung.

"Get out of my quarters," she said. "Get out!"

I scowled at her, feeling the heat of her fingers against my cheek.

Pointing to her mussed-up bed, I growled, "At least it's good to see that you sleep by yourself once in a while."

Then I left quickly, before she slapped me again.

SEARCHING

I t's about time you got here," Fuchs said to me when I
arrived at the observation center, up in the ship's nose.

"Sorry to be late, sir," I apologized. "I had to stop at—"

"When I give an order I expect it to be obeyed at once,
Humphries, without any delays. Understand me?"

"Yes, sir."

It was just as cramped as ever in the observation center,
with all the sensors crammed into the compartment. With
Fuchs in there it seemed crowded to the point of bursting.
Lucifer's nose tapered to a rounded point, glassed in with
thick quartz ports that could be shuttered when necessary.
They were unshielded now and I could see the seething barren surface of Venus, far below us.

Fuchs stood in the midst of all the instruments and computers like a heavy dark thundercloud, hands clasped
behind his back, eyes taking in the unending panorama of
devastation below.

"She looks so beautiful from a distance," he muttered,

"and so desolate up close. Like quite a few women I've known."

From Fuchs, that was an unexpected burst of humor.

"You knew Marguerite's mother, didn't you?" I asked.

He looked at me and huffed. "A gentleman doesn't discuss his women, Humphries."

That ended *that* line of conversation.

Gesturing to the bleak rocky landscape below, Fuchs said, "Radar's picked up several returns that are apparently metallic. We've got to decide which one is your brother's wreckage."

There were no chairs in the observation center; no room for them. The sensors were mounted in the bulkhead and decking; their computers lined a shelf that stood at shoulder height. So we remained standing as we reviewed the computer files of the various radar images. Most of them were little more than glints, either random artifacts in the programming or natural projections of rock that gave sharp radar reflections similar to bare metal.

But wherever there were mountains I saw strong radar reflections indicating metal, starting at roughly nine thousand meters. It reminded me of snowcaps on the mountains of Earth: below that nine-thousand-meter line was bare rock, above it, the Venusian equivalent of snow, bare metal.

"The atmosphere's cooler up at the altitude by about ten degrees or so," Fuchs told me. "There must be some kind of chemical change in the rock at that temperature and pressure."

"But what could it be?" I wondered.

He shrugged. "That's for Venus to know, and us to find out—someday."

Out of curiosity I called up the computer's file of radar reflectivities. The metallic returns from the upper slopes of the mountains might have been any of several metals, including iron sulfide: pyrite, "fool's gold."

I stared hard at the distant peaks as we cruised through the hot, turgid air. Mountains coated with fool's gold?

Then a new worry hit me. "If *Phosphoros*'s wreckage

is on a mountainside above the 'snow line,'" I mused aloud, "its radar return will be lost in the reflection from the metal."

Fuchs nodded somberly. "Pray that they hit the ground below nine thousand meters."

As we drifted across the baking hot landscape of bare rocks and metal-coated mountains, I saw a sharp spike on the graph the computer screen was displaying.

"What's that?" I said, sudden excitement quickening my pulse.

"It's nothing," Fuchs answered, with barely a glance at the screen.

"That can't be a glitch in the system," I insisted.

"I agree," Fuchs said, looking up at the graph, "but it's too small to be the wreckage of *Phosphoros*."

"Too small? The return's peak is like a signal beacon."

He tapped the screen with a knuckle. "The intensity is high, granted. But the extent of the return across the ground is too small to be a ship."

"Maybe it's part of the wreckage," I insisted. "The ship probably broke up into several chunks."

But Fuchs was already speaking into the computer's input mike, "Correlate the displayed radar return with known artifacts on the surface."

VENERA 9 appeared on the bottom of the screen in blocky white alphanumerics.

"The first spacecraft to return photographic images from Venus's surface," Fuchs said.

"Heaven and hell," I breathed, awestruck. "That thing has been sitting down there for a hundred years!"

Fuchs nodded. "I'm surprised there's anything left of it."

"If we could recover it," I heard myself thinking aloud, "it would be worth a fortune back on Earth."

Fuchs focused the ship's full battery of telescopes onto the remains of the old Russian spacecraft, while ordering me to make certain the electronic image enhancers were up and running.

It took almost half an hour to get a decent image on our

computer screen, but fortunately *Lucifer* was drifting slowly in the sluggish lower atmosphere. The slant range between us and Venera 9 actually decreased slightly while we brought the optics into play.

"There she is," Fuchs said, almost admiringly.

It looked very unimpressive to me. Not much more than a small round disc that had sagged and half collapsed on one side to reveal the crumpled remains of a dull metal ball beneath it, sitting on those baking, red-hot rocks. It reminded me of an old-fashioned can of soda pop that had been crushed by some powerful hand.

"You're looking at history, Humphries," Fuchs said.

"It's so small," I said. "So primitive."

He gave a snorting laugh. "It was the height of technology a century ago. A marvel of human ingenuity. Now it's a museum piece."

"If we could get it to a museum . . ."

"It would probably crumble to dust if anybody touched it."

I wondered about that. In that hot, high-pressure atmosphere of almost pure carbon dioxide, the metal of the ancient spacecraft had held up astoundingly well. That told me that the atmosphere down there wasn't as corrosive as we'd expected. Perhaps the sulfuric acid and chlorine compounds we had found in the clouds did not exist down near the surface; at least, not in such high concentrations.

All to the good, I thought. That meant that the wreckage of Alex's *Phosphoros* should be easier to spot. And maybe his body was still fairly intact, after all.

Fuchs was already scanning through the computer's files for other radar returns. We were close enough only to one of them to use the telescopes. When their electronically enhanced images appeared on the display screen my heart jumped.

"That's wreckage!" I shouted. "Look . . . it's strewn along the ground."

"Yes," he agreed, then muttered into the computer's input microphone.

NO CORRELATION, the screen showed.

"But that's got to be *Phosphoros!*" I said excitedly. "Look, you can see—"

"*Phosphoros* went down a thousand kilometers farther west," Fuchs said, "near Aphrodite Terra."

"Then what . . ." I stopped myself. I realized what we were looking at. The wreckage of *Hesperos*. My ship. We had been blown far off course by the subsolar wave and now we were just about back where we had been when *Hesperos* broke up.

Fuchs was manually typing in something, and sure enough, the screen displayed HESPEROS with the date when she went down.

I stared at the wreckage. Rodriguez was down there. And Duchamp and Dr. Waller and the technicians. Looking over at Fuchs I saw that he was deep in thought, too, as he gazed at the screen. He was brooding about Duchamp, I guessed. Had he loved her? Was he capable of loving anyone?

He seemed to shake himself and pull his attention away from the screen. "Unfortunately, *Phosphoros*'s wreckage is now over on the night side of the planet. The optics aren't going to be much use to us."

"We could wait until it swings back into the daylit side," I suggested.

He sneered at me. "You want to wait three or four months? We don't have supplies to last another two weeks down here."

I had forgotten that the Venusian day is longer than its year.

"No," Fuchs said, with obvious reluctance, "we're going to have to find your brother's wreckage in the dark."

Great, I thought. Just simply great.

So we sailed slowly through that hot, turgid atmosphere, sinking lower all the time, closer to the baked rocks of the surface.

It was difficult for me to keep track of time. Except for

the regular rounds of my watches on the bridge and with Nodon at the pumps, there were no outward cues of day and night. The ship's lighting remained the same hour after hour. The views outside, when I went to the observation center, seemed unchanged.

I ate, I slept, I worked. My relationship with Marguerite, such as it had been, was in a shambles. Except for Nodon, who was hell-bent on teaching me everything I had to know about the pumps so that he could be promoted to the bridge, the rest of the crew regarded me as a pariah or worse, a spy for the captain.

Strangely, Fuchs was my only companion, yet even he grew distant, distracted. For long periods of time, whole watches in fact, he was absent from the bridge. And when he did take the command chair he seemed distracted, his attention focused somewhere else, his mind wandering. Often I saw that he was chewing on those pills of his. I began to wonder if his drug habit was getting the better of him.

Finally I couldn't stand it any longer. Taking my courage—or perhaps my self-esteem—in my hands, I went to the sick bay and faced Marguerite.

"I'm worried about the captain," I said, without preamble.

She looked up from the microscope she'd been bending over. "So am I," she replied.

"I think he's addicted to those pills he takes."

Her eyes flashed, but she shook her head and said, "No, you're wrong. It's not that."

"How do you know?" I demanded.

"I know him much better than you do, Van."

I suppressed the angry retort that immediately sprang to mind and said merely, "Well then, is he sick?"

With another shake of her head, she said, "I don't know. He won't let me examine him."

"Something's definitely wrong," I said.

"It might be the transfusions," said Marguerite. "He can't give so much blood and not feel the effects."

"Have you made any progress on synthesizing the enzyme?"

"I've gone as far as I can," she said. "Which isn't far enough."

"You can't do it?"

Her chin went up a notch. "It can't be done. Not with the equipment we have here."

I saw the flare of irritation in her eyes. "I didn't mean to suggest that you were at fault."

Her expression softened. "I know. I shouldn't have bristled. I suppose I've been working too hard at this."

"I appreciate your trying."

"It's just that . . . I know what to do, I even know how to do it—in theory, at least. But we don't have the equipment. This is a sick bay, not a pharmaceutical laboratory."

"Then, if we don't get back to *Truax* quickly . . ." I let the words fade away. I didn't want to admit where they were leading.

But Marguerite said it for me. "If we don't get back to *Truax* in forty-eight hours you'll need another transfusion."

"And if I don't get it?"

"You'll die within a few days."

I nodded. There it was, out in the open.

"But if the captain does give you a transfusion," Marguerite went on, "he could die."

"Not him," I snapped. "He's too hateful to die."

"Is he? Is that what you think?"

I had touched on a sensitive nerve again. "What I mean is that he won't allow himself to die just to keep me alive."

"Is that what you think?" she repeated, more softly.

"Certainly," I said. "It wouldn't make any sense. I surely wouldn't kill myself over him."

"No," Marguerite said, almost in a whisper, "you wouldn't, would you?"

"Why should I?" I growled.

"You're jealous of him."

"Jealous? Of him?"

"Yes."

Before I had time to think it over I answered, "Yes, I'm jealous of him. He has you, and that makes me angry. Furious."

"Would it change your attitude if I told you he doesn't have me?"

"I wouldn't believe you," I said.

"He doesn't."

"You're lying."

"Why should I lie?"

I had to think a few moments about that. "I don't know," I replied at last. "You tell me."

"I'm not sleeping with him," Marguerite said. "I've never slept with him. He's never asked me to sleep with him."

"But . . ."

"He may have been attracted to my mother once, many years ago. I remind him of her, of course. But he's a different man now. Your father changed him."

"He was in love with my mother, too," I snapped. "Or so he said."

"He told me that your father killed her."

"He's a liar!"

"No," said Marguerite. "He might be wrong, but he's not lying. He's convinced that your father killed your mother."

"I don't want to hear that."

"He believes your father had your mother murdered," Marguerite said, her voice edged in steel.

I couldn't stand it. I turned on my heel and fled from the sick bay.

But even as I ran, her words echoed in my mind: *I'm not sleeping with him. I've never slept with him. He's never asked me to sleep with him.*

FANTASY

knew it was a dream even while I was dreaming it.

Marguerite and I were making love, slowly, languidly, on the beach of some undiscovered island beneath a big gibbous tropical Moon. I could feel the warm sighing breeze coming in off the ocean, hear the soft thrumming of the surf along the coral reef that ringed the lagoon.

There was no one else on the island, no one else in the world as far as we were concerned. Only the two of us, only this timeless place, this haven of tenderness and passion.

Far, far away, though, I heard a distant voice calling my name. It was barely a whisper at first, but it grew more urgent, stronger, more demanding. I realized at last that it was Marguerite whispering in my ear, her breath warm and alive against my bare skin.

"He killed her," she whispered, so softly I could hardly make out her words. "He killed your mother. He murdered her."

"But why?" I begged her to answer me. "How could he kill her? Why would he do it?"

"You know what it's like to feel jealousy. You've felt the rage that boils inside."

"Yes," I admitted. "I know. I've felt it."

"He has the power to give vent to his fury. He has the power to destroy people."

And there was Fuchs standing over us, snarling, "I'll kill you! Just as I killed Bahadur and all the others!"

Marguerite had vanished. Our tropical island had disappeared. We were standing on the hellish surface of Venus, standing in nothing more than our coveralls on those searing hot rocks, breathing that poisonous air, ready to fight to the death.

NODON'S STORY

I awoke with a start and sat up on my bunk like a jack-in-the-box popping up. I was soaked with sweat, my coveralls a soggy, smelly mess.

The digital clock set into the partition at the foot of the bunk told me it was time to start another watch at the pumps. Sliding my battered shoji screen back, I saw that the other crew members were getting ready for duty, too. They quite conspicuously ignored me, turning their backs to me as I stepped out of my compartment.

Only Nodon, smiling broadly, paid any attention to me. He seemed very pleased with my understanding of the pumping system. He was looking forward to leaving the pumps to me and being promoted to the bridge.

"You will handle everything by yourself this watch," he told me, with a crooked little grin, as we headed for the main pumping station. "I will observe only."

I nodded and focused my attention on the dials and gauges that monitored the pumping system. It seemed odd, when I thought about it, but Nodon did almost all the talk-

ing between us. Where he was concerned, I was the taci-
turn, dour one, hardly ever speaking. An ancient scrap of
wisdom drifted through my memory, something to the
effect that when it comes to learning, it's best to keep one's
mouth shut and ears open.

The pumps chugged along smoothly enough, although I
saw that one of them was beginning to overheat. I had to
take it off-line and bring the backup into action.

Then I had to disassemble the ailing pump to find the
cause of its overheating. A gas bearing had clogged slightly, causing enough friction to send the pump's temperature
rising. With Nodon watching over my shoulder, I pulled the
bearing out and began the laborious task of cleaning it
while Nodon watched me intently.

"The captain," I said to him as I worked. "How long have
you known him?"

"All my life," he replied. "He was a great friend to my
father even before I was born."

I shook my head. "I have a difficult time imagining him
as a friend to anyone."

Nodon nodded somberly. "But you did not know him
when he was a happy man. He was very different then. The
war changed him."

"War?" I looked up from the pump-bearing parts scattered on the deck.

Nodon told me about the Asteroid War. I had read about it
in history classes, of course, and seen all the videos: the
struggle between competing corporations to gain major
shares of the asteroid mining business. The histories told of
the economic competition, and how major corporations
inevitably bought out most of the small, independent miners and prospectors.

But Nodon was there, and he saw a savagely different
kind of conflict. The term "war" was not a metaphor; the
corporations hired mercenary troops to hunt down the independents and kill them. Out there in the eternal darkness of

deep space battles were fought between spacecraft armed with lasers originally designed to bore through nickel-iron asteroids. Men in spacesuits were shredded with rapid-firing flechette guns. Women, too. Neither side made any distinctions. It was a war of annihilation.

Lars Fuchs was a leader of the independents, a strong and brave young man who had built up a small but highly successful company of his own. He was smart, as well: too wily to be captured by the mercenary troops who combed the Belt to find him. He led the counterattack, raiding the corporate facilities on Ceres and Vesta, battling the mercenaries ceaselessly, driving up the corporations' costs and the mercenaries' body counts, driving men such as my father to rage and desperation.

Fuchs was on the verge of winning the Asteroid War when my father—Nodon told me—crushed him. Not with troops, not with death-dealing weapons, but with a single slender woman. Fuchs's wife. My father's corporate security forces captured her and threatened to kill her. Fuchs surrendered, even though he knew they would murder him as soon as he handed himself over. Instead, though, his wife made a deal with my lecherous father—who had quickly become enamored of her beauty. She offered to marry my father if he let Fuchs live.

That is how my mother returned to Earth to become Martin Humphries's fourth and final wife. And Lars Fuchs remained in the Asteroid Belt, a broken man, robbed of his company, his leadership, and of the woman he had loved. The Asteroid War ended then with the corporations' victory. Independent miners ceased to exist, although a few prospectors still roamed through the vast reaches of the Belt, under contract to the corporations. Fuchs became a rock rat, one of the prospectors who lived at the sufferance of the almighty corporations, a bitter man, hard and burning with inner rage.

"Then he heard of this prize being offered to recover the remains of your brother," Nodon said, his voice soft and faraway with old memories. "He jumped at the chance! It was a cosmic irony to him. That is how he described it: a cosmic irony."

By now I had cleaned the bearing and was putting the pump back together.

"How did he build this ship, then?" I asked. "If he had no money, no resources."

Nodon smiled gently. "He had friends. Friends from the old days, survivors of the war, men and women who knew him and still respected him. Together, they built this ship, out there in the Belt. In secret. I helped, you know. It was our way to get back at the corporations, our pitiful way to gain just a little bit of revenge against men like your father."

I closed the pump covering and started it up. It thrummed to life immediately. Nodon and I both beamed with satisfaction as the gauges showed it working in its normal range.

"And this crew?" I asked. "They all came from the Belt, too?"

His pleased smile evaporated. "Yes, from the Belt. But most of them are scum. Very few people were brave enough to join his crew."

"Venus is a very dangerous place," I said.

"Yes, that is true. But what they were afraid of was to be seen helping Captain Fuchs. It was one thing to help build his ship, deep in the Belt, unseen by prying eyes. But to openly join his crew? Very few had the courage to do that. He had to hire cutthroats like Bahadur."

The memory of poor Sanja dead in his bunk flashed through my mind. And of Bahadur, exploding into a shower of blood.

"Do not think badly of the captain," Nodon told me. "He is a man who has suffered much."

At the hands of my father, I added silently.

MAKING HEADWAY

We were sinking lower and lower as we drifted slowly toward the planet's nightside. It was a planned decrease in altitude that Fuchs calculated would bring us above the eastern highlands of Aphrodite Terra, where *Phosphoros* most probably lay. I only hoped Alex's ship had come to rest low enough so that we could spot it against the bright radar reflections of the mountain's upper slopes.

I felt the need for a shower after my shift at the pumps but didn't have the time. Instead I merely pulled on a clean set of coveralls, popped my pile of ripe-smelling ones into the automated laundry unit, and then hurried up to the bridge.

Fuchs frowned at me as I took over the comm console, but said nothing. I couldn't help staring at him. If I had been in his place, if I had gone through what he'd gone through, how would I feel about having Martin Humphries's son aboard my ship? Why didn't he just let me die? What was going on in that angry, bitter mind of his?

Toward the end of the watch, a call came through from the heat-exchange station. I slipped the receiver plug into my ear and tapped into the translator program.

"Captain, sir, it will be necessary to shut down the central unit for maintenance now," the technician was saying. The computer's flat unemotional translation took all the expression out of the message, but I could hear the technician's guttural, growling dialect in the background.

I swiveled my chair slightly so I could see Fuchs's face reflected in one of my empty screens. He frowned sourly.

"It is necessary, Captain, sir, if we are to avoid a failure of the main heat exchanger," the technician went on.

"I understand," Fuchs said. "Proceed."

"Should I alert the crew—"

"You do your maintenance job," Fuchs snapped. "I'll handle the crew."

"Yes, sir."

To me, Fuchs called, "Humphries, put me on the ship's intercom."

"Yes, sir," I said, with a crispness I did not really feel.

"This is the captain speaking," Fuchs said. "We're going to get a little warmer for a few hours while one section of the main heat exchanger is down for maintenance."

He thought it over for a moment, then said, "That is all."

As I closed the intercom circuit, he ordered me, "Get Dr. Duchamp onscreen, Humphries."

I got no answer from her quarters. She was in the sick bay.

"You heard my warning about the heat?" Fuchs said to her image on his main screen.

"Yes, Captain," she said. "I'm in the sick bay, preparing for heat-related complaints."

"Good," he said. "Don't let anyone go off duty unless they've collapsed with heat prostration. Understand me?"

Marguerite's lips curved slightly. "You don't want me to . . . what's the word? Mollycoddle?"

Fuchs grunted.

"You don't want me to mollycoddle the crew," Marguerite finished.

"That's right," he said. "No pampering."

"Yes, Captain."

It was probably my imagination but it seemed to get hotter in the bridge almost immediately. Or could it be my anemia? I wondered. No, fever had never been a symptom I'd experienced, I told myself. The temperature in here is rising. And fast.

We were down to within ten kilometers of "sea level," the arbitrary altitude the planetary scientists had picked as a baseline for measuring the heights of Venus's uplands and the depths of her craters. The Aphrodite Terra region rose a bit more than three klicks from its surrounding plains, so we had plenty of leeway in altitude. Aphrodite Terra was the size of Africa, and most of it looked fairly rugged on our radar maps. Finding the wreckage of one lost spacecraft was not going to be easy.

For the first time, my mind began to picture what we looked like: a minuscule metal pumpkinseed floating in the dark, still, thick atmosphere of Venus; a tiny artifact from a distant world bearing fragile creatures who needed liquid water for their existence, drifting slowly through a murky soup hot enough to boil water three or four times over, groping our way across this strange, barren, alien landscape, seeking the remains of others of our own kind who had perished in this harsh, inhospitable place.

It was madness, pure and simple. No one but a madman would come here and try this. No one but a maniac such as Fuchs could look out at that blasted, scorched landscape where the rocks were hot enough to melt aluminum and find a fierce kind of *beauty* there. I should have been home, in my house by the gentle sea, where I can walk out in the open green hills and breathe the cool, wine-sharp air, brisk and free and safe.

Instead, here I was, locked in a metal womb with a tyrant who was by any unbiased judgement as insane as Nero or

Hitler, comparing himself to Satan incarnate, defying man and nature alike and telling himself it was better to be supreme *here,* in this hell, than to serve some other master back on Earth or out in the Belt.

And I was just as crazy, undoubtedly. Because in my own foolish, haphazard way I had worked just as hard to be in this place and—I shook my head with the realization of it—I was just as determined to play this game until the last, bitter moment.

That moment would end in death, I knew. Either for me or for Fuchs. For the first time in my life, I resolved that I would not be the one to die. I would not be the passive little Runt. I would not let others steer my life, not my father, not my frailties, not even my illness. I was going to survive, no matter what I had to do. I swore it to myself.

Which was easy enough to do, within my own mind. Making it work in the real world was another matter entirely.

But I was determined, for once, to make it work, to make something of myself, to be equal to the love and trust that Alex had shown me.

Suddenly the yellow message light beneath my main screen began blinking urgently. I tapped the keyboard and the display screen spelled out: INCOMING MESSAGE FROM *TRUAX.*

Swiveling in my chair, I called out, "Captain, we have—"

"So I see," he said. "Put it on my main screen, but under no circumstances are you to acknowledge receiving it. Understand me?"

"Understood, sir."

One of *Truax*'s technicians appeared on the screen; she looked puzzled, intent.

"*Truax* to *Lucifer.* Our sensors have just detected a seismic disturbance of some kind in the Aphrodite region. It might be a volcanic eruption. Please acknowledge."

Volcanic eruption? I immediately remembered Professor Greenbaum and Mickey, their theory about Venus's surface overturning.

The technician's face was replaced by a radar display of the western end of Aphrodite. A blinking red dot marked the site of the disturbance.

"That's nearly a thousand kilometers from our position," Fuchs grumbled. "No problem for us."

I started to say, "But it might be—"

"Maintain course and speed," Fuchs said, ignoring me and clicking off the display.

"Should I tell *Truax* we received their message, sir?" I asked.

"No. No contact."

"Sir," I tried again, "that eruption might be the beginning of a major tectonic upheaval."

He scowled at me. "Then we'd better get to the *Phosphoros* pretty damned quick, hadn't we?"

NIGHTSIDE

On Earth, nights are usually cooler than days because the Sun is not beaming its heat down onto the ground. On Venus this is not so. It makes no difference if the Sun is overhead or not, the thick sluggish cloud-topped Venusian atmosphere carries the Sun's heat all the way around the planet, while Venus's slow, ponderous rotation gives that soupy hot atmosphere plenty of time to spread its heat all across the world from pole to pole.

So we sweated and grew ever more irritable in the heat as we slowly groped toward the upland of Aphrodite Terra. The heat exchanger came back on line, but still it grew hotter inside the ship. We were floating through an atmosphere as dense as an earthly ocean thousands of meters below the surface. The temperature outside our hull went past two hundred degrees Celsius, then past three hundred.

Still we descended into the murk. My life became a monotonous routine of watches on the bridge, watches at the pumps, and a few hours to eat, wash, and sleep. Nodon was indeed promoted to the bridge, but Fuchs did not free me from my shifts at the comm console. I still was pulling double duty.

I began to feel the first faint tendrils of my old weakness. A slightly dizzy feeling if I moved my head too suddenly. A trembling in the legs, as if they were threatening to fold under me when I walked. I wished I could feel the chill that once accompanied my anemia; a chill would have felt good in the mounting heat.

I fought off the symptoms as much as I could. Mind over matter, I told myself. Sure. But even the mind is based in matter, and when the blood supplying that matter lacks red cells, the mind itself will soon enough collapse.

Marguerite must have been concerned, because Fuchs ordered me to take a medical checkup and I was certain he wouldn't have thought of that without her prodding him.

"Your red cell count is sinking fast," she said unhappily. "You're going to need another transfusion right away."

"Not yet," I said, trying to sound brave. "Give him a chance to recover from the last one."

"Don't you think—"

"I don't want to kill him," I snapped, trying to sound as coldly callous as the captain himself. "I need him alive."

Marguerite shook her head, but said nothing.

During my watches on the bridge I tapped into the comm console's translation program and eavesdropped on the crew in their various workstations. Plenty of griping about the heat. Several men reported to the sick bay, complaining of dizziness or exhaustion. The women seemed to take the growing heat better than the men, or perhaps they were merely more stoic.

It was getting *hot*.

I wondered if Fuchs still was bugging the ship, or if he felt that his punishment of Bahadur had cowed the rest of the crew sufficiently to eliminate the possibility of mutiny.

He seemed moody, distracted, his mind focused on other things rather than the immediate problems of steering this submersible dirigible toward its ten-billion-dollar destination. It appeared to me that Fuchs was concentrating his attention on something in the future—or perhaps something from his past. And he was chewing those damned pills of his constantly.

Lucifer ran well enough. Except for the mounting heat inside the ship, all systems were performing within expected limits. The crew worked fairly smoothly despite their grumbling; after all, they knew that their lives depended on their doing things right. Literally.

I began to study the radar imagery as we groped along the planet's nightside. There was little else for me to do, except log incoming messages from *Truax* that were never answered or even acknowledged. The volcanic eruption had subsided, they told us. The Aphrodite region was seismically quiet once more, like the rest of the planet. I felt decidedly relieved at that.

We were creeping pretty much along the equator, making slow headway in the massively turgid atmosphere by using our engines to force us through the soup. There was no wind to speak of, just a slow, steady current flowing outward from the subsolar region, barely five kilometers per hour. Our engines easily compensated for that.

The elegance of the engines pleased me in a cerebrally aesthetic way. We were using the heat of the planet's own atmosphere to drive the turbines that ran the big paddle-bladed propellers that pushed us through the thick, hot air.

But each meter of altitude we lost meant the air was thicker and hotter. Heat rejection was becoming a problem. The crew nursed our heat exchangers along, mumbling worriedly over them more and more.

Fuchs paid almost no attention to their fears. His thoughts were obviously elsewhere. I kept searching the radar scans, looking for signs of wreckage down on the surface. I found three strong glints, but they were all far too small to be *Phosphoros*. Only one of them matched the known landing sites of earlier spacecraft probes, though. I wondered what the other two were, and found myself wishing we had enough daylight to use the telescopes.

I became fascinated with that strange, stark, utterly hostile landscape drifting below us. Even off-duty I made my way to the observation center up in the ship's prow to stare for hours on end at the radar imagery unfolding before my eyes. I began to understand Fuchs's fascination with this alien scenery, glowing red-hot in the darkness of night. It really was like looking down at the surface of hell, a barren, blasted, wretched expanse of total devastation, without a drop of water or a blade of grass, without hope or pity or help for pain.

"It's incredible, isn't it?"

I nearly hopped out of my skin. I'd been staring so intently at the radar images and the dull, stygian, sullen glow coming through the observation ports that I hadn't heard Marguerite come up behind me.

She didn't notice how startled I was; all her attention was on the views through the ports. The ruddy light from the surface made her face seem mysterious, exotic.

"It's terrifying and fascinating, both at the same time," she said in a near whisper. "Horrible and beautiful in its own deadly way."

I said, "More horrible than beautiful."

"What's that?" She pointed to the screen that displayed the radar imagery.

It showed a set of circular fractures, as if something gigantic had smashed the rocky surface like an enormous hammer.

"That's called a corona," I said. "An asteroid hit there; a big one. And look here, see these pancake features? Volcanoes, set off by the heat when the asteroid struck."

"As if it weren't hot enough down there already," Marguerite murmured.

"I wonder how old that corona is?" I asked myself more than her. "I mean, we don't know very much about how fast erosion works down on the surface. Did that asteroid hit recently or was the impact a hundred million years ago?"

"There's a lot to learn, isn't there?" she said.

"Not on this trip. We won't be able to do much science. We're here for the money this time around."

Marguerite gave me a strange look. "Do you expect to come back?"

I almost shuddered. But I heard my mouth blabbing, "Maybe. There really is a lot to learn. Greenbaum believes the whole surface of the planet is going to boil over, sooner or later. Maybe I can use some of the prize money to endow—" And then I stopped short, realizing that it was going to be Fuchs who got the prize money, not me.

Marguerite took a step closer to me, close enough to touch my shoulder with her hand. "Van, you have to start thinking about how much of . . . I mean, what condition your brother's body will be in."

"Condition?"

"There might not be much left to recover," she said, very gently.

"There's no oxygen down there to decompose his body," I mused aloud. "No bacteria or other scavengers."

"He was in the ship's escape pod, wasn't he? Sealed in?"

"Yes, that's the last word he sent out."

"Then he was in an oxygen atmosphere when he went down."

"But still . . ." I wanted to think that Alex's body would be preserved, somehow, waiting for me to carry it back home.

Marguerite had no such illusions. "There's the heat," she said. "And the pressure. Under those conditions even carbon dioxide becomes corrosive."

I hadn't considered that before. "You think he'd be . . . totally decomposed?"

"Temperatures that high destroy the chemical bonds that hold proteins together," she said.

"But he'd be in a spacesuit," I speculated. "In the escape pod. If he had time enough . . . he knew the ship was going down. . . ."

"Even so," Marguerite said.

"Do you think there might not be anything? Nothing at all?"

"It's a possibility. As you said, we simply don't know enough about the conditions on the surface, how they affect protein-based tissues."

If there had been a chair or even a stool in the observation port I would have slumped onto it. My legs felt rubbery, my insides a jumble.

"Nothing at all," I muttered.

Marguerite fell silent.

I gazed out onto that hellish landscape, then turned back to her. "To come all this way and find . . . nothing."

"There'd be artifacts, of course," she said. "Parts of the ship. Wreckage. I mean, you could certainly prove that you'd reached his ship, what remains of it."

"You mean Fuchs could prove it."

"Either way."

I almost wanted to laugh. "I can just see my father refusing to pay Fuchs because he failed to bring back my brother's remains."

"You don't think he'd do that, do you?"

"Don't I? It would be the final joke in this whole ridiculous farce."

"It's not really funny, is it?" she said.

But the more I thought about it, the more poetically absurd it all seemed. "Fuchs would tear my father's head off."

"I don't think so," Marguerite countered.

"Oh no? Him with his violent temper?"

"He doesn't have a violent temper," she said.

"The hell he doesn't!"

"He uses violence very deliberately. It's part of his way for getting what he wants. He's perfectly cool about it. Ice cold, in fact."

I didn't believe a word of it. "That's crazy," I said.

"No, it's the truth."

I stared at her for several long moments, watching the

glow of Venus's searing heat playing across the planes of her cheeks, the curve of her jaw, striking sparks in her jet-black eyes.

"All right," I said. "I'm not going to argue with you about it. You know him better than I do."

"Yes," Marguerite replied. "I do."

I took a deep breath and turned away from her. Marguerite seemed willing to call an armistice, as well.

"Are those cliffs?" she asked, pointing to the screen that displayed the forward-looking radar imagery.

It took me an effort to shift mental gears. I studied the screen for a few moments, gathering my wits.

"Yes," I said, finally recognizing what the radar was showing. "Those cliffs mark the edge of Aphrodite Terra. That's where the *Phosphoros* went down, most likely."

CONTACT

I slept like a dead man, thankfully without dreams. But when I awoke I felt just as tired as I had when I'd crawled into my bunk. Exhausted. Drained.

The crew's quarters werc hot. The entire ship was uncomfortably hot, soggy, pungent with human sweat and the enervating inescapable heat that was seeping in from the torrid blanketing atmosphere outside our hull. The bulkheads felt warm to the touch, despite the ship's cooling system. The deck felt slippery, slimy to my bare feet.

At first I thought my exhaustion might have been the symptoms of my anemia coming back. But as I showered and shaved, with a trembling hand, I realized that it was emotional exhaustion as much as the anemia or the heat. My emotions were being whipsawed; it was more than I could deal with.

Marguerite claimed she was not sleeping with Fuchs, yet she seemed tied to him more strongly each time I spoke with her.

There might not be anything left of Alex for us to recover, and even if there were it would be Fuchs claiming the prize money when we got back, if we got back, not me.

I needed Fuchs's blood to stay alive, yet the transfusions were endangering his health. He was obviously not his old powerful, self-confident self. Something was gnawing at him. Were the transfusions sapping that much of his strength? Or was he feeling some form of guilt over the deaths of Bahadur and the two other mutineers?

I couldn't imagine Fuchs feeling guilt over anything, nor allowing himself to slowly die by giving his blood to me—especially to the son of Martin Humphries, the man he hated more than anyone else.

But Fuchs was weakening, whether it was physically or emotionally or a combination of the two. And that frightened me more than anything else. I realized that I would have preferred to see him at his old tyrannical, demanding self than to watch him sinking into moody, listless malaise. I needed him, we all needed him, to run *Lucifer*. Without Fuchs, the crew would up-ship and leave Venus for good.

Without a strong and vigorous captain, I'd be defenseless against the crew. If I tried to keep them from leaving they would slit my throat just as they'd murdered Sanja.

And without Fuchs to protect her, what would happen to Marguerite?

No wonder I felt overwhelmed and exhausted. And helpless.

I was in the galley, trying to get some breakfast down my throat while the sour body smells of my crewmates were making me gag, when the intercom blared, "MR. HUMPHRIES REPORT TO THE CAPTAIN'S QUARTERS AT ONCE."

The others sitting around the crowded galley table glared at me. I gladly dumped my meal into the recycler and hurried down the passageway to Fuchs's compartment.

It seemed slightly cooler in his quarters, but that was probably because there were only the two of us in the compartment. He was sitting on his rumpled bed, tugging on his boots.

"How are you feeling?" he asked as soon as I closed the sliding door behind me.

"All right," I said warily.

"Marguerite tells me you need another transfusion."

"Not just yet, sir."

He got to his feet and went to the desk. His face wore a sheen of perspiration.

"I thought you'd like to see the latest radar pictures," he said, pecking at his desktop keyboard.

The wall screen lit up. I saw the rugged mountains of Aphrodite and, down in the narrow sinuous cleft, the bright scintillations of a strong radar return.

My heart leaped, "The *Phosphoros?*"

Fuchs nodded, his face somber. "Looks like it. Has the right profile."

I stared at the screen. The wreckage of my brother's ship. Whatever was left of Alex was down there, waiting for me to recover it.

"He could have picked a worse spot," Fuchs muttered, his eyes also fixed on the screen, "but not by much."

"That's a pretty narrow valley," I said.

Nodding, Fuchs muttered, "On Earth there would be devilish air currents threading through that valley. Here, well . . . we just don't know."

The mountains looked raw, new, even in the radar image: sharp and jagged, as if they had been thrown up only recently. Those mountains couldn't be new, I thought. Not if Greenbaum and Cochrane were right, and Venus's plate tectonics had been locked up solid for the past half billion years. Vulcanism was also a puzzle. There were plenty of volcanoes to see, but none of them appeared to be active. Yet *something* had to be pumping sulfur compounds into the clouds, and volcanic eruptions seemed the only reasonable source for the sulfur. But in the century or so that probes had been observing Venus, none had ever seen a volcano erupt. Except for the eruption that *Truax* reported, and that scared me to the marrow with visions of Greenbaum's theory erupting in our faces.

I knew that a mere hundred years is less than an eyeblink when it comes to geological processes such as plate tectonics and vulcanism, but still—Earth and Venus are almost exactly the same size. Earth's interior is still bubbling hot; given such a similar mass and size, Venus's interior must be just as hot. Hardly a year goes by on Earth without some of that interior heat forcing its way to the surface in a major volcanic eruption. If there were no volcanoes blasting out boiling lava and steam for a whole century on Earth, the geologists would go insane.

Yet for the hundred or so years that spacecraft had been observing Venus there had been no recorded volcanic eruptions, until now. Why? Was Greenbaum right? Was Venus's crust getting hotter and hotter, edging toward the moment when all the surface rocks actually begin to boil into molten lava? Was it all going to blast right into our faces?

"Come with me," Fuchs said, snapping me out of my terrifying thoughts.

Turning away from the wall screen, I saw that he was already at the door and already scowling at me in his old impatient way. I almost felt glad.

He led me aft along the central passageway, then down a ladder into a small, bare compartment. A heavy hatch was set into its deck. Fuchs worked the control panel on the bulkhead, and I realized the hatch opened onto an airlock. He clambered down into it, then after a moment or so, popped his head up above the level of the deck again.

"It's all right, Humphries. There's pressure on the other side. Come down here."

I stepped to the lip of the hatch and saw that he had opened the airlock's bottom hatch and was starting to crawl through it. I climbed down the rungs set into the circular wall of the airlock. The metal was shining, new, hardly used. There was a ladder extended below the bottom hatch and I went down, one rung at a time, and planted both my feet on the deck.

Turning around, I saw that we were in a small chamber, something like a hangar or a narrow boathouse.

And sitting there, filling most of the chamber's space, was a sleek, arrow-shaped craft of gleaming white cermet. Its pointed nose was transparent. Its flared back end was studded with a trio of jet nozzles.

"What do you think of it?" Fuchs asked, actually grinning at the sight of the vehicle.

"Rather small," I said.

"One man, that's all it'll hold."

I nodded. Walking slowly around her, I could see several manipulator arms folded tightly against the vehicle's sides. I also saw the name that Fuchs had stencilled on the side of the ship: *Hecate*.

He saw the questioning look on my face. "A goddess of the underworld, associated with witchcraft and such."

"Oh."

"This ship will take me to the surface of hell, Humphries. You see the allusion?"

"It's a little rough," I said.

He huffed. "I'm only an amateur poet. Go easy on your criticism."

"This ship will maneuver on its own?" I asked. "It won't be tethered to *Lucifer*?"

"That's right. No tethers. *Hecate* will move independently."

"But—"

"Oh, I know you had a regular bathysphere on your ship. It wouldn't have worked."

That nettled me. "The best designers in the world built that bathysphere for me!"

"Yes, of course," Fuchs sneered. "And you were going to hover your *Hesperos* over the wreckage and lower your armored bathysphere to the surface."

"Right. And the tether connecting us would also be an umbilical that carried my air and electrical power and coolant."

"So I gathered. Did you think anyone—Duchamp or Rodriguez or God and his angels—could keep your mother ship hovering in place over the wreckage for more than ten

minutes at a time? You'd be swinging back and forth in that
stupid 'sphere like a pendulum."

"No!" I snapped, with some heat. "We did simulations
that showed we could pinpoint the ship's position. The air's
so dense down there that hovering is no problem."

"Maybe in a nice open plain with plenty of elbow room,
but could you hover precisely in that snaky valley where
the wreckage is?" Fuchs scoffed. "What did your precious
simulations show you about that?"

I glared at him, but I had to admit, "We didn't do a simulation of those conditions."

"But those are the conditions we actually face, aren't
they?" he gloated.

"Do you really expect this vehicle of yours to get you
safely down to the surface and back?"

With a confident sweep of his hand, Fuchs answered,
"*Hecate* was designed after the submersibles that oceanog-
raphers use back on Earth. They get to the bottom of the
deepest Pacific trenches, ten kilometers and more below the
surface. The pressure down there is six times worse than
the pressure here on the surface of Venus."

"But the heat!"

"That's the big problem, right enough," he said easily.
"*Hecate* doesn't have enough room for heat exchangers and
the cooling equipment we're using on *Lucifer*."

"Then how—"

"*Hecate*'s hull is honeycombed with piping that carries
heat-absorbing fluid. Even the observation ports are thread-
ed with microducts."

"But what good does that do?" I demanded. "Just moving the heat from one area of the ship to another doesn't
help much. You've got to be able to get rid of the heat, get it
off-ship."

He broke into a wide, wolfish grin. "Ahh, that's the elegant part of it."

"So?"

"Most of *Hecate*'s mass is ballast: ingots of a lead-based
alloy. A very special alloy, one we developed out in the Belt

just for this purpose. Quite dense. Melts at almost precisely four hundred degrees Celsius."

"What's that got to do with anything?"

"It's simple," Fuchs said, spreading his hands. "So simple that your brilliant designers didn't think of it."

He looked at me expectantly, like a teacher I remember from prep school who always thought I was better prepared for the day's lesson than I actually was. I turned away from Fuchs, feeling my face twisting into a frown of concentration. A metal alloy. What was the point of carrying ingots of metal for ballast when you're going down to the surface—

"It's hot enough down there to melt lead," I heard myself say.

"Right!" Fuchs clapped his hands in mock applause.

"But I don't see . . ." Then I caught on. "The alloy ingots absorb the heat inside the ship."

"Precisely! And I vent the molten metal off-ship, thereby getting rid of the heat they've soaked up."

"But that will only work for as long as you still have ingots on board."

"Yes. The calculations show I can spend one hour on the surface. Maybe I can stretch it to seventy, seventy-five minutes. But not longer."

"It's . . ." I searched for a word . . . "ingenious."

"It's ingenious if it works," he said gruffly. "If it fails then it was a crazy idea."

I had to laugh at that.

But he was looking past me, past *Hecate* and this tight little chamber.

"I'm going down there, Humphries, down into the pit of hell. I'll be the first man to reach the surface of Venus. Live or die, no one will ever be able to take that away from me. The first man in hell."

My jaw fell open. He was looking forward to it, relishing the idea. Nothing else mattered to him. He was totally focused on it, eyes burning, lips pulled back in an expression that might have been a display of ecstacy or a snarl of defiance. And he was not chewing any pills, either.

"Ironic, isn't it?" he went on, glowing with expectation. "We finally reach a peak of knowledge where we've virtually eliminated aging, banished death. We can live and stay young as long as we like! And what do we do? We fight our damnedest to reach the surface of hell. We risk our foolish necks on escapades that only a madman would undertake! There's human nature for you."

I was speechless. There were no words in me to equal his fierce, maniacal intensity.

At last he shook his head, pulled himself together. "Okay, come along. I don't have more time to waste on this." He jabbed a thumb toward the ladder that led up into the airlock.

As we made our way back to his quarters I wondered why he had bothered showing me *Hecate* at all. Was it pride? Did he want me to admire the little ship, and the thinking that had gone into it? His thinking, of course.

Yes, I thought as we neared the bridge, he wanted to show off to somebody. To me.

And he certainly seemed to be his old, strong self again. Not a shred of uncertainty or infirmity in his appearance. He was looking forward to piloting *Hecate* down to the surface of Venus.

Then it struck me. He brought me down there not merely to show off his ship. He wanted to gloat over it, to show me how much smarter and stronger he was than I, to rub my nose in the fact that he was going to go down to the surface and claim the prize money while I sat up here in *Lucifer* like a hapless, helpless dimwit.

My hatred for him boiled up again. And to tell the truth, I enjoyed the emotion.

I served my watch on the bridge and then made my way back to the main pumping station. Fuchs had the ship circling above the wreckage now, some five thousand meters above the jutting peaks that surrounded whatever was left of my brother and his ship.

I had been fighting off the growing alarm signals that my body was sending to my brain. All through my watch at the pumps I felt the tingling and weakness in my legs slowly spreading to my arms. My vision went slightly blurry, no matter how hard or often I rubbed at my eyes. It took a conscious effort to lift my rib cage and breathe. I even began to feel chilled, fluttery inside.

I stuck it out for the duration of my watch, but I knew I couldn't last much longer without help. Like a drunk trying to prove he's still in command of his faculties I walked stiffly up the passageway, past the bridge, past Fuchs's quarters and then Marguerite's, heading for the sick bay.

She wasn't there. The sick bay was empty. I felt so wiped out that I wanted to crawl up onto the table and close my eyes. But maybe I'd never open them again, I thought.

She had to be somewhere. If my brain had been functioning right I would have used the intercom system to track her down. But I wasn't reasoning very well. She had to be somewhere, that much I knew. Perhaps in her quarters.

I forced myself back down the passageway and rapped on her door. It rattled, but there was no answer. She *ought* to be here, I said to myself, nettled. I slid the door open; it was unlocked. Her quarters were empty.

Where in the seven golden cities of Cibola could she be? I raged to myself.

Fuchs's quarters! That's where she is. She claims she's not sleeping with him but she's in his quarters, just the two of them by themselves together.

It was only three or four steps to Fuchs's door. I didn't bother to knock. I yanked on the door and it slid open easily.

He was on the bed, half naked. And she was bending over him.

Marguerite must have heard me as I stepped into Fuchs's compartment. She turned her head. The expression on her face was awful.

"He's had a stroke," she said.

I realized that she was fully dressed. Tears were running down her face.

"He came off the bridge and called me here," she said, all in a rush. "The instant I came in he collapsed. I think he's dying."

The first thing that flashed through my mind, I'm ashamed to say, was that I needed Fuchs alive for another transfusion. The second, even worse, was that if he died I could drain all his blood and use it; that would be enough to keep me going until we got back to *Truax*. I felt like a vampire, but those were my thoughts.

Fuchs opened his eyes. "Not dying," he growled. "Just need . . . medication." His speech was slurred, as if he were drunk.

"Medication?" I asked.

Fuchs raised his left hand slightly and pointed shakily toward his lavatory. His right arm lay inertly by his side.

Marguerite got up from the bed and rushed to the lavatory.

"Kit . . ." Fuchs called weakly after her. "Under . . . the sink . . ."

I wasn't feeling all that strong myself, so I dragged up a chair and plopped into it, facing Fuchs on the bed.

The right side of his face was pulled down slightly, the eye almost closed. It might have been my imagination, but that side of his face seemed gray, washed out, almost as if it had been frozen.

"You don't . . . look so good," he said, weakly.

"Neither do you."

He made a sardonic rictus of a half smile and murmured, "Two of a kind."

Marguerite came back with a small black plastic case. She already had it open and was reading from the printout on the display screen set into the back of its lid.

"I'm going to inject you with TPA," she said, her eyes on the screen.

Fuchs closed both eyes. "Yeah . . ."

"TPA?" I asked stupidly.

Fuchs tried to answer. "Tissue plasmino . . ." He ran out of strength.

"Tissue plasminogen activator," Marguerite finished for him as she slapped a preloaded cylinder into the metal syringe from the medical kit. "It will dissolve the clot that's blocking the blood vessel."

"How can you be sure—"

"Clot buster," Fuchs said, his words blurred as if his tongue wasn't working right. "Works . . . every time."

I saw in the open medical kit that Marguerite had dropped on the bed beside him that several loops where cylinders had once been stored were now empty.

"How many times has this happened to you?" I blurted.

He glowered at me.

"He's had several mini-strokes," Marguerite said as she pressed the microneedle head of the syringe against Fuchs's bare biceps. Its hiss was barely audible. "This one's the worst yet, though."

"But what's causing it?" I asked.

"Acute hypertension," Marguerite said. Fuchs turned his glower on her.

I was stunned. "What? High blood pressure? Is that all?"

"All?" Marguerite snapped, her eyes suddenly blazing. "It's causing these strokes! It's killing him!"

"But blood pressure can be controlled with medication," I said. "Nobody dies of high blood pressure."

Fuchs laughed bitterly. "Very reassuring . . . *Doctor* Humphries. Feel better . . . already."

"But . . ." I was confused. Hypertension was something you treated with pills, I knew. That was the pills he'd been chewing! If he had the medication he needed, though, why was he having strokes?

"The medication controls the blood pressure only up to a point," Marguerite said, a little more calmly. "But it doesn't do anything about the root causes."

"Does that mean I'm going to come down with it, too?" I asked. After all, I was getting his blood; did his disease come along with it?

Fuchs's expression turned to contempt, or perhaps it was disgust. He started to shake his head.

"Not from the transfusions," Marguerite said. "It's not carried by the blood."

"But doesn't his medication help?" I asked.

"It helps, but not enough not counteract the stress he's under."

"Stress?"

"Do you think captaining this ship isn't stressful?" she demanded. "Do you think dealing with this crew has been easy?"

"Not the stress," Fuchs mumbled. "The rage. How do

you stop . . . the rage? Inside me . . . every minute . . .
every day . . ."

"Rage," I echoed.

"Medication . . . can't control it," he said weakly. "The
fury inside . . . the hate . . . even my dreams . . . nothing
can control it. Nothing."

The rage. That boiling anger within him was what drove
Fuchs. His hatred of my father. His blazing frustrated fury
seethed within him like those red-hot rocks of hell below
us, burning, boiling, waiting to burst loose in a torrent of
all-consuming vengeance.

Every minute, he'd said. Every hour of every day. All
those years with that hot relentless rage burning inside him,
eating away at him, twisting his life, his being, his every
moment waking or sleeping, into a brutally merciless tor-
ment of hate and implacable fury.

It was killing him, driving his hypertension relentlessly,
pushing his blood pressure to the point where the microscopic capillaries in his brain were bursting. He always
seemed in complete control of everything and everyone
around him. But he couldn't control himself. He could keep
the rage hidden, bottled up within him, but now I saw what
a merciless toll it was taking on him.

"It's a vicious circle," Marguerite went on, as she pulled
out one cylinder from the syringe and pressed in another.
"The medication loses effectiveness so he increases the
dosage. But the cause of his hypertension is still there! The
stresses are getting worse, and so are the strokes."

He was suffering strokes. This tough, hard-handed captain was suffering from blockages in the blood supply to his
brain. I stared at him with newfound awe. A normal person
would be hospitalized for at least a few days, even with the
mildest kind of stroke. I wondered what it felt like, how I
would react.

I didn't want to find out.

"What are you doing now?" I asked.

She nodded toward the little display screen as she prepared the syringe. "VEGF to stimulate blood vessel growth and then an injection of neuronal stem cells to rebuild the damaged nerve tissue."

I had asked enough dumb questions, I thought. Later on I checked and found that vascular endothelial growth factor made the body build bypass blood vessels to reroute the circulation around the vessel damaged by the clot. Stem cells, of course, had the potential to build any kind of cells the body required: brain neurons, in this case, to replace those damaged by the stroke.

"If we had proper medical facilities we could treat him and get his pressure down to normal," Marguerite was muttering as she pressed the microneedle syringe home. "But here aboard ship—"

"Stop talking about me in the third person," Fuchs grumbled.

We sat and watched him for long, silent minutes. Vaguely I recalled reading that hypertension makes the blood vessels thicken and stiffen, which raises the blood pressure even more, and so on and so on. It can lead to strokes, I remembered, and even heart failure, all kinds of ailments. Fortunately, if you catch a minor stroke quickly enough, you can prevent most of the long-term damage to the brain. Or so I seemed to remember.

At last Fuchs struggled up to a sitting position. Marguerite tried to make him lie back down, but he pushed her hands away.

"It's all right," he said, his speech stronger, surer. His face was back to its usual color. "The clot buster worked. See?" He lifted his right arm and wiggled his fingers. "Almost back to normal."

"You need rest," Marguerite said.

Ignoring her, Fuchs pointed a thick finger at me. "The crew isn't to know about this. Not a hint of it! Understand me?"

"Of course," I said.

"Are you going to tell him the rest?" Marguerite asked.

His eyes went wide. I had never seen Fuchs look startled before, not even when he was flat on his back from the stroke, but he did at that instant.

"The rest of what?" I asked.

"You're going to make the flight down to the surface," Fuchs said.

"Me?"

"Yes, you. You're relieved of your duties on the bridge. Spend the time in the simulator, learning how to pilot *Hecate*."

My jaw must have dropped open.

"You're a qualified pilot," he said. "I read that in your résumé."

"I can fly a plane, yes," I said, then added, "on Earth." It never occurred to me to ask when and how he saw my résumé.

"Don't think you can claim the prize money because you actually go to the surface," Fuchs added. "I'm still the captain of this ship, and that prize is mine. Understand me? Mine!"

"I don't care about the prize money," I said. My voice sounded hollow, far away.

"Oh no?"

I shook my head. "I want to find my brother."

Fuchs looked away, glanced up at Marguerite, then back at me.

"Very noble," he mumbled.

But Marguerite said, "That's not what I meant."

He said nothing. I sat there like a sack of wet laundry, feeling physically exhausted, emotionally coiled tight, my mind jumping and jittering. How can I pilot *Hecate* with only a few hours of simulator time as training? No matter, I'll do it. I'll get down to what's left of *Phosphoros* and Alex. I'll do it. I will.

"You need another transfusion, don't you?" Fuchs asked gruffly.

"You can't!" Marguerite cried.

"Don't you?" Fuchs repeated sternly to me.

"Yes," I answered, "but in your condition . . ."

He made a dismissive gesture with one hand. "In my condition another transfusion will be helpful. It'll lower my blood pressure, won't it, Maggie?"

Her eyes flashed sudden anger, but then she half-smiled and nodded. "Temporarily," she said.

"You see?" Fuchs said, with mock geniality. "It's a win-win situation. We both gain something."

"That still isn't what I meant," Marguerite said to him, so softly I barely heard her.

Fuchs said nothing.

"It would be better if he heard it from you," she said.

He shook his head.

"If you don't tell him, I will."

"He won't believe you," he said sourly. "He won't believe me, either, so forget about it."

I spoke up. "I don't like being talked about in the third person any more than you do, you know."

"He's your father," Marguerite said.

I blinked. I couldn't have heard her correctly. She couldn't have said what I thought she had. My ears must be playing tricks on me.

But the look on her face was utterly somber, completely serious. I turned my eyes to Fuchs. His features seemed frozen in ice, hard and cold and immobile.

"It's the truth," Marguerite said. "He's your father, not Martin Humphries."

I wanted to laugh at her.

"I was born six years after my mother left him and married my father," I said. "If you're implying that she had an affair while she was married to my father . . ." I couldn't finish the sentence, the very thought of it made me so furious.

"No," Fuchs said heavily. "Your mother wasn't that kind of woman."

"That's right," I snapped.

He glanced at Marguerite, then said to me, "We were really in love, you know." His voice was gentler than I had ever heard it before. Or perhaps he was simply exhausted from the ordeal he'd just gone through.

"Then why did she leave you?" I demanded, even though Nodon had told me why.

"To save my life," he said, without an instant's hesitation. "She agreed to marry your father as the price for his letting me live."

"That's . . . unbelievable," I said.

"You don't believe that your father's had people killed? You never heard of the Asteroid War, the battles the corporations fought to drive out the independent prospectors?"

"In school . . ."

"Yes, I'm sure they told you all about it in your fancy schools. They taught you the official, sanitized version, nice and clean, no blood, no atrocities."

"You're getting off the subject," Marguerite said.

"If my mother hadn't seen you for six years before I was born, how can you claim to be my father?" I challenged him.

He let out a deep, painful sigh. "Because when we were living together we had some of her ova fertilized with my sperm and then frozen."

"Frozen?"

"We were going to have a family," Fuchs said, his voice low, his eyes looking into the past. "As soon as I got my mining company up and running, we were going to have children."

"But why freeze the embryos?" I demanded.

"Zygotes," he corrected. "They weren't embryos yet, merely fertilized eggs that hadn't begun to divide."

"Why go to all the trouble—"

"Because I had to spend so much time in space," he explained. "We wanted to avoid the risk of radiation damage to my DNA."

"But then she married my father."

"To save me."

"She married him."

"But she never had a child by him," Fuchs said. "I don't

know why. Maybe he'd gone sterile. Maybe she wouldn't sleep with him once she found out that instead of killing me he destroyed me financially."

Marguerite said, "She had herself implanted with a fertilized egg and you were the baby she bore." Nodding toward Fuchs, she added, "His son."

"How did you know I'm your son?" I insisted.

"I didn't. Not until Marguerite started looking for a way to produce the enzymes you need. She ran DNA scans on both of us."

"I don't believe it," I said.

Marguerite glared at me. "Do you want me to show you the DNA scans? Why do you think his blood type is compatible with yours?"

"But—she waited six years?"

"I don't know why she did it or why she waited," Fuchs said. "She was heavily into drugs by then, I know that much. Living with your father turned her into an addict."

I had no reply to that.

With another groaning sigh, he went on, "Anyway, she got one of the fertilized ova and had herself implanted. He must have realized it wasn't his child as soon as he found out that she was pregnant. . . ."

"And he killed her," I said.

"She died in childbirth, didn't she?" Marguerite asked.

"He probably tried to kill you both," Fuchs said.

"He's always hated me," I said, in a whisper.

Marguerite added, "Your anemia came from her blood, while she was carrying you."

"He's always hated me," I repeated, feeling empty inside, hollow. "Now I know why."

"Now you know it all," Fuchs said.

I looked at him as if seeing him for the first time. I was about his height, although my build was much lighter, much slimmer than his. My face was nothing like his, probably much more like my mother's. But his ice-blue eyes were not far from the shade of my own.

My father. My biological sire. Martin Humphries was

not my begetter, he was only my caretaker, the man who
had wanted me dead, the man who belittled and scorned me
all my life.

"Do you really think he killed my brother?" I wondered
aloud.

Fuchs sank back down on the bed, as if all this had suddenly become too much for him to bear.

"Do you think he killed Alex?" I repeated, raising my
voice.

"You'll find out when you're down on the surface, going
through his ship's wreckage," Fuchs said. "You'll either get
your answer there, or you'll never know."

SIMULATIONS

I left Fuchs's quarters like a sleepwalker and stumbled down to the virtual reality chamber, to start my hurried training for piloting *Hecate*.

My mind was spinning. Fuchs was my biological father? My mother had loved him so much that she bore his baby even though she was married to Martin Humphries? Yes, I realized, that would be entirely possible. Probable, even. She didn't want a child by Martin Humphries, that was clear. For six years she lived with him, allowed him to shame her with his womanizing, make a mockery of their marriage. Talk about trophy wives! My mother was his prize, the living symbol of his victory over Lars Fuchs. Her life must have been a pit of hell.

And here was Fuchs, my biological father, dying of the stresses that drove him. Obviously he wanted his revenge on my foster father, and just as obviously for all the years of my life he knew there was no way he could touch Martin Humphries, no way he could make Humphries suffer as he himself had suffered, no way he could make Martin

Humphries pay for the death of my mother, the woman he loved, the woman who sacrificed her life to save his.

Until this idiotic Venus prize. Once Fuchs heard that Martin Humphries was offering that ten-billion-dollar prize he recognized his chance to score at least a little of the vengeance he had nursed for more than a quarter of a century.

As I slowly pulled on the protective suit that I was to wear in *Hecate,* I went over and over what little I knew about my own origins, wondering who and what I could believe.

Why did she do it? Why did my mother flaunt her love for Fuchs after six years of marriage to my . . . to Martin Humphries? She must have known how it would enrage him. Perhaps that was why she did it; to hurt him, to strike back at him, to humiliate him in the only way she could.

And he killed her. Did she know he'd go that far? Did she care? She must have protected me, somehow. Must have seen to it that I was safe from his malice, from his hatred.

Yes, she made certain I was physically safe even though she couldn't protect her own life. Or perhaps she didn't care about herself. Perhaps his killing her was a release for her, an end to the pain that had filled her life.

Yet Martin Humphries did not kill me. I was probably cared for by people my mother had chosen. Or, more ironic still, probably it was my terrible physical condition that saved my life. For my first few months I was maintained in a special medical facility while my various birth ailments kept me hovering on the brink of death. Perhaps Martin Humphries figured that I would die of my own accord; he wouldn't have to bother with me, after all.

But I survived. I lived. How that must have tormented him! Me, the constant reminder that no matter how wealthy he was, no matter whom he could buy or sell, whom he could destroy financially or murder outright, I had survived. Me, the weakling, the Runt, the child sired by the one man in the solar system that he hated the most, I lived under his own roof.

He made my life as hellish as he dared. Did Alex know the entire story? Was Alex standing between me and my foster father's murderous wrath? When Alex had his shouting match with his father, just before he left for Venus, was the fight about politics—or about me?

There was only one way for me to find out; only one person in the entire solar system knew what had really happened. Martin Humphries. I had to face him, confront him, get the truth out of him. And to do that, I had to survive this journey to the surface of Venus. I had to go through hell to get back to learn the facts of my own existence.

"Are you asleep down there?" Fuchs's acrimonious voice snarled in my earphones.

That snapped my attention to the job at hand. He must be back on the bridge, I told myself, back in command. Until his next stroke.

"I'm suited up and entering the VR chamber," I said into my helmet mike.

"Okay," he replied. "The *Hecate* simulation is ready whenever you are."

"Good," I muttered as I clomped to the hatch that opened into the virtual reality chamber.

The special protective suit included most of the features of a regular spacesuit, of course, although to me it looked more like the cumbersome rigs worn by deep-sea divers in those ancient days before the invention of scuba gear. Heavy metal helmet with a tiny faceplate, bulky armored torso, arms and legs of thick cermet, boots that felt as if they weighed a ton apiece. The entire suit was honeycombed with tubing that circulated coolant, of course. Actually the tubes carried a true refrigerant and the backpack that I would have to wear included a miniaturized version of the type of cryostat used in physics labs to liquify gases such as hydrogen and helium.

So I shambled through the hatch like some old video monster, the servomotors on the suit whining and wheezing away with every plodding step I took. Without the servos

I'd never have had the muscular strength to move my arms and legs.

The VR chamber was a blank-walled compartment. One of the crew had put in a bunk, which would serve as a crude simulation for the couch in *Hecate's* cockpit. The virtual reality stereo goggles were resting on the bunk, together with a set of data gloves and slippers. It took me several minutes to open the faceplate of my helmet and hook the goggles over the bridge of my nose, even longer to worm on the gloves and work the slippers over my clumsy boots. Fuchs grumbled impatiently every moment of the time.

"The way you're going at it, it'd be easier on my blood pressure for me to pilot *Hecate* myself," he complained.

That was the first time I'd ever heard him mention his blood pressure in front of the crew. He must have been truly disturbed by my slowness.

"I'm getting onto the couch now," I said, once I had closed the faceplate again.

"About time," he muttered.

Once I was stretched out prone on the couch my vision suddenly began to swirl giddily, flashes of color flicking on and off. For an instant I thought this was some new symptom of my anemia, but then the flashing ended as abruptly as it had started and I was looking at *Hecate's* control panel. The virtual reality simulation had kicked in; my goggles were showing what I'd see when I actually was piloting the little ship.

Above the panel I saw the strewn wreckage of *Phosphoros,* torn and twisted sections of the ship's metallic hull. A computer-graphics illusion, I knew, generated for the VR program. But it looked very real to me, fully three-dimensional.

My imaginary *Hecate* was hovering three kilometers above the illusory wreckage of *Phosphoros,* so my virtual instruments told me. I could see nothing inside the wreck, because we had no idea of what to expect in there. My task was to learn how to bring *Hecate* smoothly down to the wreckage, search its interior for any sign of Alex's remains, and then get safely back to *Lucifer* again.

The ship's controls were simple enough. The computer did most of the work. I merely ran my gloved fingertips over the touchpads in the control panel and the ship responded almost instantly. Whoever had designed the control system had done an admirable job; it all worked intuitively. Right hand controlled pitch and yaw, left hand controlled roll. When you wanted to go left you moved your right index finger leftward along the touchpad. When you wanted to pitch the nose down, you slid your forefinger down the pad. The right foot pedal controlled the thrusters at the ship's tail; the left pedal worked her fins, which pivoted like the diving planes of a submarine.

Simple. But not easy.

I won't tell you how poorly I did, at first. My clumsy attempts at piloting had Fuchs swearing and me sweating.

"You're overcorrecting," he would shout into my earphones.

Or, "Too steep! You're coming in too steep!"

It took more than a dozen tries before he was satisfied enough to let me descend down to the wreckage. Then I practiced working the waldoes, the glovelike implements that controlled the manipulator hands outside the hull. Again, it was simplicity itself in principle. Whatever motions your fingers made were reproduced faithfully by the mechanical hands outside. Again, it was devilishly difficult in practice to get the feel of those manipulators, to learn how to work them deftly enough to pick up a scrap of twisted metal or a piece of shattered equipment.

By the time Fuchs finally agreed to end the VR session I was soaked with perspiration and gasping for breath.

"Meet me in the sick bay," he said as I wearily picked myself up from the bunk that had served as the virtual *Hecate*'s couch.

Nodon came to the VR chamber to help me out of the heat suit. A good thing, too. I don't think I could have done much more than lift the heavy metal helmet off my head.

"How long was I in there?" I asked, panting, as he tugged the suit's heavy torso up and over my head.

"One full watch, almost," he said.

Nearly eight hours. No wonder I was exhausted.

A sly grin cracked his thin, almost fleshless face. "Captain said you did very well," he confided.

"He did?"

"Oh yes. He said you didn't wreck the ship once. Almost! But no wreck."

Faint praise from Fuchs was like a Nobel Prize from anyone else, I thought.

"He also said not to tell you," Nodon added, his smile turning into a boyish grin.

Marguerite was in the sick bay with Fuchs when I got there.

"I don't think we should go through with this transfusion," she said. "You've just suffered a serious stroke and—"

"And he's not going out in *Hecate* with his damned anemia gnawing at him," Fuchs snapped. He was sitting on the narrow examination table, Marguerite standing beside him.

"But your condition . . ." Marguerite objected.

He made a grisly smile for her. "Your ministrations have worked wonders. I'm fine."

She could be just as stubborn as her mother, though. Marguerite insisted on doing a scan of Fuchs's brain before proceeding with the transfusion. I stood in the hatch of the crowded sick bay, feeling tired and weaker every second, while she made him lie down, fixed the scanner to his head, and ran off a reading.

Watching him lying there, his eyes closed while the scanner buzzed softly, I realized anew that this man was my father. It was hard to accept that, even though I knew it was true. I mean, it's one thing to know something is true intellectually, up in the front of your brain. But to *feel* it, to accept it down in your guts, that's something else entirely.

He's my father, I said silently to myself over and over

again. This man who can be so brutal at one moment and then quote poetry a moment later, this bundle of contradictions, this wounded snarling animal is my father. I'm made from his genes.

I believed it, but still I had no real feeling for Fuchs—except a grudging respect and a healthy amount of outright fear.

The scanner stopped its buzzing. Marguerite removed it from Fuchs's head while the main display screen on the bulkhead began building up a three-dimensional view of his brain. We all peered at the image intently, even though I really didn't know what I was supposed to be looking for.

"See?" Fuchs said, sitting up again as he pointed to the false-color image of his own brain. "No permanent damage."

The image looked like a normal brain to me; all of it tinged a sort of bluish gray. No alarming areas of red, which I presumed was the color that would be used to show damage.

"New blood vessels are developing," Marguerite said, cautiously. "But the area where the blockage occurred isn't fully repaired yet."

With an impatient shake of his head, Fuchs said, "It's too small to matter. I feel fine. Take a liter of my blood and my pressure will go down to normal."

"A liter!" Marguerite's eyes flashed wide. "Not even half that much."

Fuchs chuckled. He had been joking, I realized. He had a strange sense of humor, dealing with people's lives, including his own.

Rolling up his sleeve and lying back down on the table, he growled, "Come on, get it over with."

I sat in the chair Marguerite had jammed in next to the table and closed my eyes. I couldn't stand to watch anyone get a needle jabbed into his flesh, especially me.

I went back to my bunk in the crew's quarters and slept very soundly. If I dreamed, I don't remember it. When I awoke, I felt strong, refreshed.

Then I realized that in a few hours I would be donning that heavy heat suit again and crawling into the real cockpit of the actual *Hecate*.

I would be going down to the surface of Venus, the first live human being to do so. Me! Alone down there where the rocks are red-hot and the air is so thick it can crush a spacecraft into crumpled wreckage.

To my surprise, I wasn't terrified. Oh, there were butterflies in my stomach, true enough. I didn't feel like one of those ultracool adventurers you see on video. I fully realized that there was a fine chance that I'd die out there, beside my brother.

But most of those butterflies inside me were from anticipation. To my utter surprise, I was looking forward to this! I told myself I was a fool, but it didn't matter; I *wanted* to go, *wanted* to be the first living human being to reach the hellhole surface of Venus, *wanted* to get down there and search for Alex's remains.

I forced myself to picture my home in Majorca and the cool, lovely blue sky and sea. And Gwyneth. My friends. My life before this mission to Venus had shattered everything. It all seemed pale and senseless now. Pointless. Mere existence, not living.

Even as I began to pull on the heat suit, with Nodon and bulky, sulky Amarjagal helping me, I couldn't help thinking, I'm alive! I'm doing something real, something that's never been done before, something that matters in the ongoing development of the human race.

A voice in my head warned sardonically, What you are doing is very likely to kill you.

And the other side of my mind quoted Shakespeare: We owe God a death . . . he that gives it this year is quits for the next.

In other words, I had gone slightly crazy.

HECATE

hings started going wrong right from the start.

Hecate's actual cockpit was different from the VR simulation's. The differences were subtle, but significant.

For one thing, the foot pedals that controlled the thrusters and diving planes were a couple of centimeters too far away for my boots to reach comfortably. I had to stretch my legs and point my toes to get a solid contact with the pedals. In those Frankenstein boots I had to wear, that was a guaranteed method of developing leg cramps. Or foot cramps. Or both.

The layout of the controls was the same, thank goodness, but *Hecate* didn't respond to the controls in the same smooth, clean fashion as the virtual reality sim. As I went through the checklist, lying there prone in the heat suit and sweating bullets even before the ship was released from *Lucifer*'s hold, it seemed to me that there was a slight lag between my touching a control and the response from the ship's systems. It was only a tiny hesitation, but it was noticeable—and annoying.

I was wondering if there was some way to speed up the ship's response even while we went through the checklist and started the separation countdown.

In my helmet earphones I heard Fuchs ask perfunctorily, "T minus two minutes and counting. Any problems?"

"Uh, no," I said, quite unprofessionally. "Everything's pretty good here."

He caught the doubt in my voice. "Pretty good? What does that mean?"

The countdown would go into automatic mode at T minus one minute, we both knew. This was no time to try to fiddle with the control responses.

"Nothing, forget it. Ready for separation sequence."

Silence from the bridge, until the computer's synthesized voice came on, "T minus one minute. Separation sequence engaged."

"Right," I said.

"T minus fifty seconds. Internal power on."

I heard pumps start chugging. The instrument panel flickered for an eyeblink, then its lights steadied. I knew my suit's cooling system was working, I could hear the tiny fan in my helmet buzzing. Yet I was already drenched with cold sweat. Nerves. Nothing but nerves.

"T minus thirty seconds. Bay hatch opening."

Through *Hecate*'s thick hull and my own suit's heavy insulation I heard the low rumble of the hatch swinging back slowly. From my position, flat on my belly in *Hecate*'s pointed nose, I looked down at the thick quartz panel set into the floor of the cockpit just below the instrument board. All I saw was the inside of my stupid helmet! I had to twist my head and crane my neck to see the window through the tiny faceplate of my helmet.

And there it was, the sullen, incandescent surface of Venus, glowing like a sea of molten lava. I could *feel* that heat boiling up at me, clutching for me. I knew it was my imagination; we were still several kilometers above the surface, yet I felt the hot breath of the planet smothering me.

I stared at those red-hot rocks as the countdown ticked away.

"Three . . . two . . . one . . . release," said the computer's impassive voice.

With a heart-stopping bang the latches that held *Hecate* firmly in their grip suddenly released and I was falling through the thick, still air of Venus toward its distant hard surface. I was frozen with terror, paralyzed as I felt my stomach surging up into my throat. It was like dropping down the longest elevator shaft in the universe toward a blazing hot furnace. But slowly, slowly as in a nightmare.

Fuchs's voice crackled in my earphones:

> "Hurled headlong flaming from th' etheral sky,
> With hideous ruin and combustion, down
> To bottomless perdition . . ."

And he laughed. Laughed!

That broke my terrified paralysis. I kicked at the pedals, ran my fingers across the controllers, struggled to get *Hecate* leveled off and gliding properly.

"Pull her nose up," Fuchs commanded. "Don't dive her! Get your speed right and she'll sink at her natural rate."

"Right," I said, kicking the pedals and working the touchpad controls as furiously as I could.

"You're overcontrolling her!" he shouted so loud in my earphones it made me wince.

I was desperately trying to get the feel of the controls. They didn't respond the way the VR sim did. I got a flash of memory from the first time I tried to ride a horse and realized that this substitute for an automobile had a mind of its own; it did not respond mechanically to my steering.

"I should've gone down myself," Fuchs was grumbling.

Slowly I was getting the feel of the controls, but a glance at the course profile indicator on the panel showed me I was far off my intended speed and angle of descent. The dive-plane control felt especially stiff; the pedal barely budged even when I tried to kick it.

The flight plan was for me to spiral down toward the *Phosphoros*'s wreckage, while Fuchs kept *Lucifer* circling overhead some three kilometers up. I was scanning the wreckage with every instrument aboard *Hecate,* which wasn't really all that much: radar, infrared, and optical sensors. The infrared was practically useless, swamped by the enormous heat flow from the surface.

Greenbaum's theory of planetary upheaval popped into the front of my mind. What if Venus decided to overturn its surface right now, at this precise time? A volcano had erupted less than a thousand kilometers from here. What if everything down there suddenly began to melt and all the stored heat that's been trapped deep below ground suddenly comes bursting out? Murphy's Law on a planetary scale. After five hundred million years of waiting, the planet decides to blow off its surface while I'm there. I'd be roasted in a minute; not even *Lucifer* could escape the catastrophe.

That's not going to happen, I told myself sternly. Put it out of your mind. I remembered the gloomy look on Greenbaum's face when he admitted that there was practically no chance that the cataclysm would happen while we were there to observe it—or be incinerated by it, more likely.

"Stay on the profile!" Fuchs snapped.

I was struggling to do just that, but I wasn't succeeding fast enough to avoid stirring his wrath. Gritting my teeth, I traced my fingertips across the touchpads, feeling more like a child playing with a magnetic sketching toy than an intrepid astronaut making the first controlled descent to the surface of Venus.

"Where's your imagery?" Fuchs demanded.

I saw from the control panel that I hadn't switched on the channel that telemetered the pictures that *Hecate*'s sensors were getting.

"On its way," I said, imitating the clipped tone of astronauts I remembered from old videos.

I put the optical camera view on my own screen, right in front of my face. Now I could see why Fuchs was complaining; it showed nothing but bare hot rocks. It should have been focused on the wreckage.

Gradually I smoothed out *Hecate*'s flight, got the ship on course. I wasn't using the thrusters, they weren't needed until I had to lift from the surface, so I put both my booted feet on the pedal that controlled the diving planes. It was a little easier to work them that way. Sure enough, my calf muscles started cramping, hard enough to make me want to scream from the pain. But I kept at it, grimly determined to get down to the wreckage and find what was left of my brother's body.

In a way it really was like riding a horse. *Hecate* had a will of her own, and I had to learn to deal with it. The controls were terribly stiff and slow to respond, but little by little I got the feel of them, and focused the sensors on the wreckage below. It wasn't anything like flying; Venus's atmosphere was so thick that my descent was more like a submarine groping for the bottom of the ocean.

There wasn't much to see, at first. *Phosphoros*'s gas envelope had collapsed atop most of the ship's gondola. I could only see one end of the gondola sticking out from beneath the warped, twisted metal. Huge sections were missing, eaten away, it looked like. They must have spent even more time in the bug-laden clouds than we had in *Hesperos,* with disastrous results.

As I edged lower, I began to see the characteristic charring-like streaks along what little of the gondola was visible beneath the crumpled gas envelope. The envelope itself was smudged and streaked with the dark char stains from the bugs in the clouds. *Phosphoros* wasn't sabotaged, I realized. It didn't have to be. Those aerobacteria destroyed my brother's ship just as they destroyed my own.

Then I noticed something strange. Curving lines were criss-crossed over the wreckage, a dozen or more thin lines almost like twine or string looped around a package. I wondered what they were. Nothing I remembered from the design drawings or pictures of *Phosphoros* showed strapping or any other kind of structural supports strung across the gas envelope.

Curious.

"Spiral in tighter," Fuchs commanded. "Stay focused on the wreckage."

"That's what I'm trying to do," I said, feeling testy.

"Don't *try*," he sneered. "Do!"

I snapped, "You come and do it if you don't like the way I'm handling it!"

He went silent.

I could see the wreckage in more detail as I descended cautiously through the thick air. It was clear enough; no haze or dust in the air. But the pressure was so high that it was like peering through seawater. Things were distorted, twisted.

At first I couldn't tell which end of the gondola was sticking out from beneath the collapsed envelope, but as I got closer I recognized it was the forward section. It had split open like an overcooked sausage, ripped right down the middle. I saw plenty of charring streaks that the aerobacteria had left on the outer surface of the hull. The insides looked strangely bare and empty.

With a sudden gasp of hope I saw that the compartment where the escape pod had been housed was empty. Had Alex gotten away? Had he used the pod to ride up into orbit?

Then I realized that it made no difference if he had; it was more than three years since *Phosphoros* went down. He couldn't be alive even if his pod had made it to orbit. Besides, there had been absolutely no radio messages from the escape pod, not even an automated beacon.

Then, to seal the question, I saw the pod. It had rolled a few dozen meters from the rest of the wreckage, coming to rest against a big, hot, glowing rock the size of a suburban house.

And several of those strange dark lines went across the bare rock to the escape pod. They were too straight to be cracks in the surface, and they came from too many different angles to be the track of the pod's rolling across the rocky surface.

"What are those lines?" Fuchs asked.

"That's what I'd like to know," I said.

"They seem to radiate outward from the escape pod."

"Or to come together at the spot where the pod came to rest," I corrected.

"Impact cracks?" he mused.

"There's more of them crisscrossed over the gas envelope," I said.

"Can't be cracks, then."

"Right," I answered. "But what are they?"

"Go find out."

"Right."

"We're using up a lot of fuel, keeping station above you," he said. That was Fuchs's way of telling me to hurry up.

"I'll be on the surface in a few minutes," I said. Inwardly, I was trying to decide if I should put *Hecate* down alongside the pod or next to the wreckage of the ship's main body.

"Check out the pod first," Fuchs said, as if he could read my mind. "Then you can lift and shift over to the gondola."

"Right," I said again. I realized it had been some time since he'd insisted on my addressing him as "sir" or "captain." Did he respect me now as an equal? Or was it the father-son relationship? That was tricky. It was just as wrenching for him to find that I was his son as it was for me to learn he was my father. Neither one of us was prepared to handle that load of emotional freight.

Something flickered in the corner of my eye.

"What was that?" Fuchs snapped.

"What?"

"That light."

I scanned the control panel, looked through the observation port in the deck. Everything seemed to be functioning properly.

"What light?"

"On the horizon," he said, his voice hesitant, uncertain. "In the east."

Trying to remember which way was east, I looked through the forward port. Far off on the horizon there was a glow lighting the grayish-yellow clouds. It pulsed, brightened.

"Sunrise?" I guessed.

"Too soon," said Fuchs. "Besides, the sun rises in the west."

That's right, I said to myself. Then what was the light in the east?

"Wait," Fuchs said. "We're getting a message from *Truax*."

What would *Truax* be sending? I wondered. A warning, the other side of my mind answered. Yes, but a warning about what?

It only took a few moments to get the answer.

Fuchs's voice came back into my earphones. "It's another volcanic eruption."

"Another eruption?"

"Nothing to worry about. It's four hundred kilometers away."

I swallowed hard and tried not to think about Greenbaum. But in my imagination I could see the glee on his face. This might well be only the second Venusian volcano blast in half a billion years. And he'd be getting data from us on it!

Unless we got killed first.

ERUPTION

I stared too long at that sullen pinkish glow on the horizon, thinking about volcanoes and Greenbaum and the whole surface of the planet below me opening up and frying me with the stored heat of half a billion years suddenly released into my face.

Two volcanoes within days of each other meant either that Greenbaum was wrong or that Venus was beginning to boil over.

"You're spraying the wreckage!" Fuchs shouted in my earphones.

"What?"

"The exhaust!" he yelled, exasperated. "You're letting it spray over the wreckage."

The molten metal from *Hecate's* heat sink, I realized. The ship was spitting the melted alloy out from its rear, carrying the built-up heat away from me. Venusian guano, I thought wryly. It was settling over the wreckage.

"Point her nose properly!" Fuchs demanded. "You're covering up the whole blasted wreck!"

He was excited, up there. Hovering high above me in *Lucifer,* Fuchs must have felt completely frustrated at having to sit on his bridge and watch my clumsy efforts to do what he thought he could perform flawlessly.

I wondered what that was doing to his blood pressure as I fought to orient *Hecate* so that I spiraled ever closer to the wreckage without burying it under the ship's excretion of molten alloy.

Could that be the strange lines crisscrossing the wreckage? I wondered. But a quick look at the scene below me showed it was not. Those lines were thin and mostly quite straight, although some of them curved here and there—rather gracefully, actually. *Hecate*'s hot droppings clearly splashed when they hit the ground, forming bright new-looking puddles of liquified metal.

Some of the droppings had spattered one end of the crushed gas envelope. Nothing important had been covered by the alloy, I saw. Fuchs was getting worked up over very little, it seemed to me.

I blinked sweat from my eyes as I worked *Hecate* lower and lower. And then I saw something that made my eyes pop wide.

One of those lines moved. No, more than one. Several of them whipped across the oven-hot rocks to converge on the splashes of alloy that had dropped from *Hecate.*

"You only have fifty-five minutes left on the heat sink," Fuchs's voice warned, a bit more calmly now.

"Did you see that?" I yelled, excited, more puzzled than afraid. "Those lines moved!"

"Moved?"

"Yes! Didn't you see them?"

"No."

"They went to the alloy puddles," I said, almost shouting, trying to convince him.

Fuchs was silent for a few moments, then he replied, "I don't see any movement."

"But I saw them move! And fast, too! Like lightning."

"You can attend to that later," he said, his voice betraying his doubts about my powers of observation. "Get to the escape pod. The clock keeps ticking."

The plan was to use the manipulator arms to open up the escape pod and see if Alex had made it inside successfully. But if he had retreated into it as his ship went down, wouldn't it be better to leave it sealed and bring it up in its entirety? That way, if he really was inside, his body would remain protected from the Venusian atmosphere; at least, as much protection as the pod could give.

"Can *Hecate* lift the whole pod, intact?" I asked into my helmet mike.

No response for a few moments. Then Fuchs asked, "How much does it weigh?"

"I have no idea," I admitted. "A ton or so, I guess."

"Very precise," he said acidly.

"How much can *Hecate* carry?"

Another pause. I imagined him hurriedly scanning the computer files. It was getting hot in the cockpit, despite the heat sink and the ship's cooling system. Really hot. My suit was sloshing with sweat. I felt as if I were lying facedown on a big, soaking-wet sponge.

"*Hecate* can lift four tons," Fuchs replied at last, "once the ballast is off-loaded."

"That should be more than enough to take the pod," I said.

"Right," he agreed. "Should be enough space in the cargo bay to hold it, too."

"All right, then. I'm going to inspect the gondola first and then bring up the pod intact."

Marguerite's voice came through. "Even if your brother was in the pod, Van, there's practically no chance that any organic matter could survive this long."

I was almost close enough to the ground to touch it. The heat was getting ferocious.

"You mean there won't be any physical remains of his body," I said to Marguerite.

"Yes, I'm afraid that's what you've got to expect," she said. "Even if he got into the pod."

Nodding inside my helmet, blinking stinging sweat out of my eyes, I replied, "I'm still going to go for returning the whole pod. Is that all right with you, Captain?"

Fuchs immediately answered, "Okay. Proceed."

Edging *Hecate* toward the burning hot rocks, feeling the glare of the heat on my face even through the ship's thick ports and my helmet, I worked carefully, slowly to keep the ship's tail end pointing away from the wreckage.

"We read ten meters," Fuchs said tensely.

"Ten meters, right."

I had the radar altimeter displayed on the observation port, so I could see the ground inching up toward me and the altitude numbers at the same time.

"Five meters . . . three . . ."

I felt a short of crunching, grinding sensation as the landing skids beneath little *Hecate*'s hull grated across the bare rocks. Very little noise. Then the ship lurched to a stop.

"I'm on the ground," I said. I should have been exultant, I suppose, but instead I was almost exhausted from tension and the searing, overpowering heat.

"Word is being telemetered back to Earth," Fuchs said. "You've touched down on the surface of Venus."

A moment of triumph. All I felt was hot, sopping with sweat, and anxious to get the job done and get out of this hellish furnace.

"I'm activating the manipulators," I said, touching the stud on the control panel that powered up the remote grippers and the outside flood lamps.

Then all the lights went out. The control panel blacked out completely and the steady background hum of electrical equipment died away.

I damned near wet myself. For a breathless moment I was completely in the dark, except for the angry glow of Venus's red-hot rocks, just on the other side of my observation port. I could hear my pulse thudding in my ears.

And then a really scary noise: a kind of a thump, light but definite, as if someone had dropped a cable across the top of the ship.

Before I could say anything, the auxiliary power came
up. The control panel glowed faintly. The pumps gurgled
somewhere in the back of the ship. Fans whined to life
again.

"Power's out," I said, surprised at how steady my voice
sounded.

Fuchs sounded worried. "Must be an overload from the
manipulator motors."

"And the floodlights," I added.

"Shut them down and try to restart the main batteries."

I did that and, sure enough, the ship powered itself up
nicely. I blew out a breath of relief.

Then I realized that if I couldn't use the manipulators
there was no point being down here by the wreckage.

A very powerful urge to light off the thrusters and get up
and away almost overcame me. I actually had both boots on
the thruster pedal before I realized it.

But I stopped and fought back the itch to flee. Think,
dammit, think! I raged at myself. There's got to be a way to
fix this.

"We're scanning your telemetry," Fuchs said, his voice
sounding edgy in my earphones. "Looks like the servo
motors in the manipulators are drawing almost twice as
much power as they were designed to do. Might be from
the heat."

"Listen," I said, my mind racing, "what if I put the
manipulators and lamps on the backup power system? The
auxiliaries can power the arms and lights while the main
batteries run everything else."

After a moment's hesitation, Fuchs replied, "Then you'd
be without backup power if the main goes out again."

"It's a risk," I admitted. "But we've got to do *something*.
There's no sense being down here without the manipulators
working."

"You could get trapped down there!" Marguerite
chimed in.

"I want to try it," I said. "Tell me how to reset the
manipulators."

"You're sure you want to do this?"

"Yes! Now stop wasting time and tell me how to get the manipulators on the auxiliary system. And the lamps."

It seemed to take hours, but actually within less than ten minutes I had the manipulators powered up from the backup electrical system while the rest of the ship ran as normal on the main batteries. The floodlights seemed dimmer than they had been in the VR simulation, but still bright enough to light the area that the arms would be working in.

"All right," I said at last. "I'm going to poke into the gondola now."

"Okay," said Fuchs.

That's when I found out that my hands wouldn't fit into the waldoes while I had my gloves on.

I could have screamed. I wanted to pound the control panel with my fists. They had fit all right in the virtual reality simulator, but here aboard the real *Hecate* the cursed-me-to-hell-and-back waldo fittings were too tight for me to get my hands into them while I was wearing the heat suit's gloves.

It was the servomotors on the gloves' backs, I saw. Those spiny exoskeletons that powered the gloves and boosted my fingers' natural strength jutted out from the backs of the gloves about two centimeters or so, just enough to prevent me from sliding my hands into the waldoes that controlled the manipulator arms and grippers.

The clock was ticking. I was running out of alloy ballast to keep the ship barely livable, running out of time.

"What's going on down there?" Fuchs demanded. "What's the holdup?"

"Wait a second," I mumbled. No sense telling him what the problem was; neither he nor anyone aboard *Lucifer* could do a cursed thing about it.

I hesitated only a moment longer, then started to pull off the gloves. The air inside the cockpit was at Earth-normal pressure, there was no danger of decompression, as there would be if I'd been in space. It was hellishly hot, though.

And if *Hecate*'s hull got punctured, I'd be dead meat with out my suit fully sealed up.

So be it. I yanked both gloves off and stuck my hands into the waldoes.

"Ow!" I yelled involuntarily. The metal was *hot*.

"What's the matter?" Fuchs and Marguerite asked simultaneously.

"Bumped my hand," I lied. The metal of the waldoes was hot, all right, but I could stand it. At least, it would take a while before the skin of my hands started to blister.

It was like pushing my fingers into boiling water, but I gritted my teeth and began to work the manipulators. The arms reacted sluggishly, not at all the way they did in the simulator, but I got them extended and gripped the torn edge of the gondola in their metal pincers.

"I'm opening up the gondola. Looking inside," I reported.

"Get the camera lined up with the manipulators," Fuchs snapped.

I pulled my left hand out of its waldo and blew on it, then worked the camera control, slaving it to the manipulators. Wishing I had the time to rip the servomotors off my gloves, knowing I didn't, I stuck my hand back into the waldo. It was like having your face wrapped in a steaming hot towel, except that the waldo didn't cool off. If anything, it was getting hotter.

The remote arms peeled back the thin metal of the gondola. Actually, the metal broke away, snapping like brittle panes of glass. Inside I saw two spacesuits still hanging limply in their open lockers. The helmets were on the deck, though, rather than on the shelves above the suits. The inner airlock hatch was ajar. Another suit was draped over the bench in front of the lockers, a pair of boots sitting precisely where a person's feet would be while he or she began putting on the suit.

But there were no human remains to be seen. Nothing but a whitish powder sprinkled here and there.

And a strange, pencil-thin wire or cable of some sort running up and over the broken side of the hull and down along the center of the deck. It disappeared into the darkness beyond the pool of light from *Hecate*'s floodlamps.

That's when I heard it. A dull, low growling noise, like the rumble of distant thunder, but longer, more insistent, growing louder and stronger until I could see the ground beneath *Hecate*'s skids shaking.

Earthquake? It couldn't be! It was *Hecate* itself that was shaking, rattling, skidding across the oven-hot rocks with a brittle piece of *Phosphoros*'s hull clamped in its manipulator pincers. I could see the wreckage skittering away from me as I banged around inside *Hecate*'s cockpit, rolling and sloshing on my belly while the ship skidded across the ground as if some giant hand were shoving it along.

"Full power!" I heard Fuchs yelling, whether to me or his own crew I couldn't tell. "Maintain trim!"

Then with a smashing impact that nearly tore my insides apart *Hecate* hit something and tilted dangerously up on one skid.

And everything went black.

TIDAL WAVE

I must have been unconscious for only a few moments. My head had slammed against the inside of my helmet when *Hecate* banged against whatever it was that stopped our skidding across the landscape.

That low-pitched thundering was still shaking the ship, but except for a throbbing pain in my head there seemed to be no major damage. The panel was lit, no indications of hull puncture. I almost laughed to myself; if the hull had been punctured I wouldn't be alive to read the panel, not with my gloves off.

". . . the volcanic eruption," Marguerite was saying in my earphones, her voice tight with fear. "It's blown us away from your position."

"I got pushed around, too," I said, surprised at how calm my voice sounded.

"Are you all right?"

"I think so . . ." I was scanning the control panel. No red lights, although several were in the amber. I raised my head to look through the forward port. *Phosphoros*'s wreckage was several hundred meters away now.

"What the hell happened?" I snarled.

"That volcano eruption," she explained. "The glow we saw off on the horizon."

"You mean it's pouring out lava?"

Marguerite's voice was a little softer now, less tense, but only a little. "It's too far away to threaten you, Van. That's no worry."

No worry for them, I thought, up in the air.

"But the explosion sent a pressure wave through the atmosphere," she went on, "like an underwater tidal wave. It blew *Lucifer* almost upside down and pushed us at least a dozen kilometers away from you. The captain's struggling to get the ship trimmed again and back into position above you."

"I've been pushed along the ground like a dead leaf in a gale-force wind," I said.

Fuchs's voice came on. "We're heading back toward you, but it's taking all the power the engines can give to push against this pressure wave. Get set to lift as soon as I give the command."

"I have to get the escape pod."

"If you can," he said. "When I give the order to lift you pull out of there, whether you have the pod or not."

"Yes, sir," I said. But to myself I added, As soon as I have the pod in my grip.

Marguerite's voice returned. "He's got his hands full piloting the ship. It's like riding against a hurricane up here."

I nodded, checking over the control panel again. Everything seemed all right. But was it?

"This is the first time any human has eye-witnessed a volcanic eruption on Venus," Marguerite said. She sounded pleased.

I remembered Greenbaum and felt a tremor of near-hysteria quivering inside me. Are these eruptions the beginning of the cataclysm that Greenbaum had predicted? Was the ground beneath me going to open up and swallow me in boiling magma?

Get away! a voice in my aching head screamed. Get the fuck out of here and back to safety!

"Not without the pod," I muttered grimly.

"What?" Marguerite asked instantly. "What did you say?"

"Nothing," I snapped. "I'm going to be too busy to talk with you for a while."

"Yes. I understand. I'll monitor your frequency, in case you need anything."

Like what? I asked silently. Prayers? Last rites?

I nudged the thruster pedal, to lift off the ground enough so I could make my way back to the wreckage. Nothing happened. I pushed against the bar harder. The ship still wouldn't move. I could hear the thrusters whining, but no motion.

Taking a deep breath, I considered what choices I had. I punched the ballast release, and felt a clunk rattle through the ship as a block of the heat-absorbing alloy was ejected from its bay. That lightened the ship, but it cut down on the time I could stay on the surface without burning to a crisp.

I tried the thrusters again. The ship quivered but did not rise off the ground. Is something holding me down? I wondered.

Something slithered over the ship's hull. I could hear it, sliding, scratching across the metal skin above me. The sound made me shudder with fright.

This was no time for half measures. Either I got away from here or I fried, and pretty soon, too. So I tromped on the thruster pedal with both boots, really kicked it hard. The thrusters suddenly howled and *Hecate* lurched up off the ground and wobbled into the air a good hundred meters.

I fought madly to get control of her. For a moment I thought she would flip over onto her back and nosedive into the ground. But *Hecate* came through. My fingers played across her control pads madly and she responded, straightened out, and pointed her nose toward the wreckage once again.

When we settled down on the rocks I saw that *Hecate* tilted badly over on her left, as if the landing skid on that side had been crushed or ripped away. No matter, I thought, as long as the hull is still intact.

I had put her down alongside Alex's escape pod. Now I had to slide my blistered fingers back into those damnable waldoes and get the manipulators working again.

I did it, although the pain forced tears from my eyes. I made the metal pincers firmly grip the handholds on the escape pod's surface, locked them on, and then gratefully withdrew my fingers from the waldoes. For a few moments I simply lay there, awash in perspiration, my fingers sizzling with pain. I pictured myself swimming in the Arctic ocean, playing among ice floes. My hands still hurt.

I should have pulled my gloves back on, that would have been the smart thing to do. The cautious, safety-minded thing to do. But my scorched hands burned too much even to consider it.

"I've got the pod," I reported, "and I'm ready to lift."

For a heart-stopping moment there was no reply. Then Marguerite's voice came through. "The captain estimates we'll be in place above you in ten minutes."

I let out an inadvertent whistle. They must have been blown a long way off position.

"I'm lifting now," I said. "I'll hover at two kilometers' altitude until you give the order for rendezvous."

A much longer delay before she answered. I had no desire to stay down on the surface a nanosecond longer than I had to.

Fuchs's voice came on. "Okay, but keep below two klicks. The *last* thing we want is a midair collision."

"Agreed," I said. But I thought, No, the last thing I want is to be stuck down here in this oven.

Trying to use my fingernails on the control pads, to avoid touching them with my seared skin, I began to set up the ship's controls for liftoff.

Then my eye caught something strange. As if anything in this landscape of hell wasn't strange.

But some of those lines that had crisscrossed the wreckage had moved again. I was certain of it. In fact, as I stared, goggle-eyed, one of them rose up off the wreckage and wavered in the air like an impossibly thin arm beckoning for help.

And then another. And another.

"They're alive!" I screeched.

"What?"

"Look!" I babbled. "Look at them! Arms, tentacles, feelers—whatever they are, they're alive!"

Marguerite said, "We're barely close enough to see you and the wreck. What are you talking about?"

"Look at the camera imagery, dammit!"

"It's grainy . . . the picture's breaking up too much . . ."

I tried to calm down and describe what I was seeing. The arms—if that's what they were—were all up and waving slowly back and forth in the sluggish current of thick, hot air.

"There can't be anything alive down there," Marguerite insisted. "The heat—"

"Put your telescope on them!" I yelled. "All your sensors! They're alive, dammit! Probably the main body lives deep underground, but it sends feelers, antennas, *something* up to the surface."

"It's hotter underground than it is on the surface," Fuchs growled.

"I see them!" Marguerite's voice jumped an octave higher. "I can see them!"

"What are they doing?" I wondered aloud. "Why are they waving around like that?"

"They weren't doing that before the tidal wave passed through?" Marguerite asked.

"No, they were lying on the ground. Most of 'em were draped over the wreckage."

"And now they've raised themselves . . ." Her voice trailed off.

I had forgotten about raising the ship, staring out the port and watching something that should have been impossible. Was there some other explanation? Could they be something that isn't living?

"Feeding tubes," Marguerite said at last. "Perhaps they're taking in nutrients carried in the air from the volcanic eruption."

"But why here? Why haven't we seen them anywhere else on the planet?" I asked.

"We haven't looked this closely at any other area on the surface," she replied.

I recalled, "They were draped across the wreckage."

"The bugs up in the clouds ate metal ions," said Marguerite.

"Like vitamins. You said they needed the metal ions the way we need vitamins."

"And maybe this underground organism also needs metallic ions," she said.

"It sensed the wreckage!" We were jumping to conclusions, I knew in the back of my mind. But they seemed to fit what we were seeing.

"Is the pod marked in any way?" she asked, her voice rising again with excitement. "Any scars where the feeding tubes might have been eating on the metal?"

Before I could look, Fuchs's voice came through, dry and cold. "You have exactly seven minutes' worth of alloy left. Play at being a biologist once you're back up here, Humphries."

That was like a douse of cold water. "Right," I said. "I'm starting liftoff procedure *now*."

After all, I had the pod in my grip and Marguerite must have every sensor aboard *Lucifer* focused on those feeding arms, or whatever they were. Time to get back to safety.

I quickly scanned the control panel one more time, then pushed on the thruster pedal. The engines whined to life, the ship shuddered—but didn't budge one centimeter off the ground.

CAPTURED

"I'm stuck!" Inside the helmet, my voice sounded like a terrified shriek.

"What do you mean, stuck?" Fuchs demanded.

"Stuck!" I hollered. "The goddamned ship isn't moving!"

"Wait . . . the telemetry shows everything functioning okay," he said. "Thrusters on full."

"But I'm not moving!"

Silence from *Lucifer*. I pressed both boots against that damnable thruster bar. I really kicked it hard, again and again. The thrusters growled and *Hecate* shuddered, but I didn't budge off the ground. How many minutes were left for the heat rejection system? When the alloy ran out the heat inside the cockpit would build up and cook me within minutes.

"All your telemetry checks out," Fuchs said, an edge in his voice.

"Fine," I retorted. "Then why doesn't the ship move?"

"We're trying to get the telescopes on you. It's not easy,

that damned tidal wave is still making the air turbulent up at this level."

For a mad instant I thought I might crawl out of *Hecate* and get into the escape pod that was still lodged in the manipulator arms and use its escape rockets to blast off into orbit.

Great plan, I said to myself. *If* your suit would keep you alive outside the ship, which it can't, and *if* you could get into the pod before you roast to death, which you couldn't, and *if* the pod's escape rockets would work, which they probably wouldn't.

"Well?" I shouted. "What are you doing up there?"

Marguerite replied, "We have you on-screen now." Her voice was shaky; she sounded as if she were on the verge of tears.

"And?" I demanded.

Fuchs said, "Four of those feeding arms are wrapped around *Hecate.* They must be holding you down."

I don't know what I said. It must have been atrocious because Fuchs snapped, "Calm down! Hysteria won't help."

"Calm down?" I screeched. "I'm trapped here! They're *feeding* on the ship!"

"You've tried full power?" Fuchs asked.

"What do you think I'm doing down here?" I raged. "Of course I've applied full power!"

"They're holding you down!" Marguerite stated the obvious.

"What do I do?" I demanded. "What do I do?"

"They're strong enough to hold the ship down even when the thrusters are firing at full power," Fuchs said, also stating the obvious. Or perhaps he was thinking out loud.

"They must all be connected underground," Marguerite said. "It must all be one gigantic organism."

Wonderful. I'm about to be killed and she's spinning biological theories.

I heard that slithering noise again. It was the feeding tubes, the arms that were holding me down. They were eating the ship's hull! They were going to break into the cockpit and eat me! I wanted to scream. I should have screamed. But my throat was frozen with terror. Nothing but a thin squeak came out of my mouth.

"We can't get down to him," Fuchs was saying. "We don't have the time to attach a tow line and pull him loose."

"We don't know if we could pull him loose even if we could attach a line," Marguerite said.

They were talking about me in the third person. As if I weren't able to hear them. As if I were already dead. They thought they were running through possible ways of saving me, but to me it sounded as if they were making excuses for letting me die alone down on the rocks.

My mind was churning, working harder than I had ever worked before. Awash with sweat, lying prone in *Hecate*'s cramped cockpit, trapped and alone on the surface of hell, I realized that only one person in the universe could help me, and that was me myself.

How did those feeder arms find me so fast? They were draped over the old wreckage, including the escape pod. But they wrapped themselves around me within minutes.

"Marguerite!" I yelled into my helmet microphone. "The arms that were on *Phosphoros*'s wreckage? Are they still there? Are they still waving in the air?"

A moment's hesitation, then she answered, "No. They've extended from the wreckage to your ship."

"How many of them are on me?"

"Four . . . no, there's five of them now."

Great. I'm attracting them like flies to garbage. They left the old wreckage for the new meat. But why? Why leave the food they've been grazing on for more than three years now?

Think! I screamed silently at myself. The only advantage you might possibly have over this Venusian monster is your brain. Use it!

Why leave the wreckage for me? What sensory organs did they have that told them fresh meat had arrived?

They sensed the metal ions that surged through the air on the volcano's tidal wave, I remembered. They can sense metal ions even at very low concentrations, they way a human being can sense the nutrients he needs in food: it tastes good.

"Marguerite!" I called again. "Are the arms laid out straight across the ground? Straight from the old wreckage to *Hecate*?"

"No," she said. "They curl and twist . . . it looks as if they followed the trail of the alloy you pumped out. Yes! They run along the splashes of alloy on the ground and follow it to your ship."

That's what interested them: the alloy I'd been excreting.

"I've got to eject the ballast," I shouted with the realization of it. "All of it! Now!"

"You can't eject all the ballast," Fuchs said testily. "It's your heat sink."

I yelled, "It's their picnic food! It's what's attracting them to me!"

"But your cooling system will overload!" Marguerite cried.

"I've only got a couple of minutes before they break the hull apart! I've got nothing to lose!"

Fuchs's voice, tight with tension, said, "Lower left screen on your main panel. Touch the ballast icon."

"I know. I know."

I jabbed at the panel, suppressing a yelp of pain. Even the panel was so hot it burned to touch it. A short menu appeared. Thank god the electronics still worked, despite the heat. But how long would they work once I had tossed the heat sink alloy overboard?

No matter. I was going to fry down here anyway unless I could move those feeder arms off the ship.

My fingertips were scorched, so I used a knuckle to touch the ballast-eject command. I heard the ejector springs bang, rattling the ship.

"Tell me what they're doing," I said, fighting to keep my voice level.

Fuchs said heavily, "The ingots fell just a meter or so from the tail of your ship."

"Are the arms moving?"

"No."

A new fear cut through me. How much damage had the arms already done to the ship's hull? They'd been eating on the metal for only a few minutes, I knew, but was that long enough to weaken the hull's integrity? If I actually could shake loose of them, would *Hecate* fall apart when I applied the thrusters again?

"Any motion?" I asked.

The temperature in the cockpit was soaring. My suit gave me some measure of protection, but still I felt as if I were being roasted alive. The control panel seemed to waver before my eyes. The plastic was starting to melt.

"Anything?"

Marguerite said, "One of them is moving . . . I think."

I could hear the pumps in my suit gurgling madly, trying to carry away the heat that was swiftly building up. But there was no place to carry the heat. It was everywhere, all encompassing, smothering me, boiling me in my own juices.

"Definitely moving!" Marguerite said breathlessly.

"How many . . . ?"

"Two of them. Now a third—my god! They move so fast!"

"Fire the thrusters," Fuchs commanded.

Everything was swimming, melting. I felt dizzy.

"Fire the thrusters!" he roared. *"Now!"*

I wedged my burned hands against the melting plastic of the control panel and pressed both boots against the thruster bar as hard as I could. The thrusters growled, rumbled. The ship shook.

I realized it wouldn't be enough. I was still pinned down, helpless, unable to move.

Then she broke loose! *Hecate* lurched forward, shuddered, then shot up from the ground so hard I was pushed back painfully inside my suit.

Fuchs was yelling commands in my earphones. I saw the ground whipping past and then receding. It should feel cooler, I thought stupidly. It ought to feel cooler.

But it didn't. It was still so hot I was suffocating, boiling inside the protective suit. I wanted to rip it off and be free of it. I think I might actually have started to unfasten the helmet.

Then the ground beneath me opened up. A gigantic crack pulled the solid rock apart with a grinding, terrifying roar that sounded like the howling of all the demons of hell baying at me. Frozen into immobility, stupefied, I stared down into the blinding glare of white-hot magma that blasted a wave of heat up through the thick turgid atmosphere.

Hecate shot up like a dandelion puff caught in the searing blast of a rocket's fiery exhaust. Bouncing and shuddering in the blazing breath from the planet's deep interior, I stared down petrified into the mouth of hell.

What was left of poor old *Phosphoros* tumbled into the widening pit. I saw it melting as it fell deeper into the infernal heat. But the thought that welled up in my mind was, That tentacled monster must be tumbling down into hell, too. Good! Die, you bastard. Go to hell, where you belong.

RETRIEVED

The thrusters' throttle bar jammed in the wide-open position while *Hecate* soared up and away from the white-hot fissure yawning below me. Fortunately they ran out of fuel within a few seconds. Otherwise the ship would have risen up like a rocket-driven artillery shell and arced halfway around Venus, then fallen back to splatter on the surface. As it was, little *Hecate* shot up from the surface like a scalded cat, her nose pointed toward the clouds thirty-some kilometers above.

The temperature cooled off to a "mere" four hundred degrees as *Hecate* soared upward. I was groggy, exhausted. All I wanted to do was close my eyes and sleep. But Fuchs wouldn't allow that. He bellowed in my earphones, screaming and roaring at me. His bawling, blaring voice became more insistent, penetrating into my mind, shaking me out of my heat-induced daze.

"Answer me!" he snarled. "Don't you die on me, don't you take the easy way out. Wake up! Snap out of it!"

It took me several moments to realize that he wasn't raging at me. He was pleading. He was begging me to stay awake and alert, to save myself, not to die.

My eyes were still staring with fascinated horror at the mammoth fissure burning below me. The pit of hell, I thought. I'm looking into the pit of hell. And I understood what Fuchs's mind was like, inside. The burning rage. The fury that he had pent up within him. It was enough to kill any ordinary man. It was a wonder it hadn't killed him already.

"Answer me, damn you," Fuchs was demanding, urging, cajoling. "I can save you, but you've got to give me some help, dammit."

It was still burning hot inside *Hecate* and I felt as weak and limp as an overcooked strand of spaghetti.

"I'm . . . here . . ." I said. My voice was little more than a rasping exhausted whisper.

"Good!" he snapped. "Now listen to me. You're coasting about fifteen klicks above the ground. You're out of fuel and gliding like a soarplane. I'm coming up after you, but *Lucifer* can't reach you fast enough unless you help."

Fast enough for what? Then I realized, fast enough to get me before I died.

I looked out the forward port and saw that *Phosphoros*'s escape pod was still in the manipulator arms' grip.

"I've got . . . the pod," I said. "You'll win the prize . . . no matter what happens . . . to me."

"Idiot!" Marguerite's voice screeched. "He's trying to save your life!"

That popped my eyes open.

"Pay attention," Fuchs said, almost soothingly. "You've got to do some flying. Your control surfaces should still be working."

"Yes . . ."

He started giving me instructions, his voice calm but imperative, trying to get me to swing around in a great descending arc so that he could bring *Lucifer* up close enough to take me aboard.

I'm not that good a flier, I told myself tiredly as I tried to understand his commands and respond to them. I'm no jet-jockey. What does he expect of me? Why doesn't he leave me alone? Why is he doing this?

The memory of Marguerite's shrill voice answered my question: *"He's trying to save your life!"*

"You're overcorrecting," Fuchs said sharply. "Pull the nose up or you'll dive back into the ground."

"I'm trying . . ."

It was a good thing that all I had to do was slide my fingers across the control pads. It wasn't easy, though; my fingers were burned and blistering so badly that I used my knuckles against the pads. The controls were much livelier than they'd been down close to the surface. Up at this altitude the air was about ten times thicker than Earth's at sea level. *Hecate* was operating in a regime somewhere between a submersible and a soarplane.

The ship was trembling, shaking almost like a living creature swimming through the thick, oven-hot air. I realized that holding the spherical pod up in front of her was not helping her aerodynamics. I could fly more easily if I released the pod. But I shook my head inside the helmet. Whatever's left of Alex is inside that pod, I was certain of it. We're going through this together, big brother, I said to him silently. We live or die together, Alex.

Suddenly Fuchs yelled, "No, no, no! Level off! Use the horizon as your guide. Keep your nose on the horizon."

That wasn't as easy to do as he thought. The air was still thick enough to distort long-distance vision. The horizon wasn't flat. It curved upward conspicuously, like a bowl, like the meniscus of a thick liquid in a narrow glass.

"The body of your ship will provide lift if you maintain the proper attitude," Fuchs said, more calmly. Then he added, "And speed. You've got to maintain speed, too."

Hecate was soaring along now; still shaking, vibrating, but gliding on a more or less even keel. I felt giddy from the heat, my mouth dry, every muscle in my body screaming with pain.

"Attitude and speed determine altitude," Fuchs was saying, almost as if he were reciting an ancient formula. "You're doing well, Van."

"Thanks," I mumbled.

"Stay with it."

"I don't know . . . if I can stay . . . conscious much longer," I stammered.

"You've got to!" he snapped. "There's no alternative. You've got to keep awake and pilot your ship, Otherwise we won't be able to make rendezvous."

"I'm trying."

"Then try harder! Stay awake."

"It's hot—"

"Just a few minutes more," Fuchs said, suddenly coaxing, almost pleading. "Just a few minutes more."

I blinked my eyes. Far off against that baking-hot horizon I saw a dark spot moving. We were still on the nightside of Venus, but the glow from the ground was bright enough for me to make out a dot against the sullen yellowgray clouds above me. It couldn't be anything else except *Lucifer*.

Or eyestrain, that sardonic voice in my head sneered. Or even a hallucination.

Fuchs's voice crackled in my earphones again. "I can't see you visually yet but we've got you on radar. Maintain your current speed and attitude, but turn left ten degrees."

"Ten degrees?" I blinked at the control panel. It seemed blurred, baffling.

"Turn left. I'll tell you when to stop."

I slid my knuckles across the control pads, slowly, carefully, my failing eyes on that dark spot off along the curving horizon.

"Too far! Hold it there! Hold it. I'll adjust our course to match yours."

All I wanted to do was sleep. Collapse. Die. It didn't matter anymore. I didn't care. But then I remembered why I was here, what I had promised myself that I'd do. Very well, I said to whatever gods were watching over me, if I die it won't be because I gave up.

Just at the moment, as if in answer to an unvoiced prayer, *Lucifer* lit up like a Christmas ornament. Running lights came to life all along her teardrop-shaped body and began blinking on and off, like a welcoming beacon.

Whatever reserves of adrenaline or moral fiber or just plain stubbornness that remained in me rose up. I still ached from scalp to toes, still felt as weak as a newborn kitten, my suit was still sloshing with perspiration and the heat was suffocating me. But I kept my eyes open and my burned hands on the control pads despite the heat, trying my best to hold the speed and attitude that Fuchs wanted.

Then he said, "Now comes the hard part." And my heart sank.

"You've got to lose a little altitude and a lot of speed, so you can pass beneath us where we can grab you."

I remembered that rendezvous was such a tricky maneuver in the simulations that I had botched it more often than not, and that had been with *Hecate* flying on her own power. I was piloting a glider now; I had used up all the thrusters' fuel trying to break free of those arms that were holding me down on the surface.

"You'll only get one shot at this," Fuchs warned, "so you've got to do it right the first time."

"Understood," I said, my voice a dry, harsh cough.

"I'd do this with the automatic controls from here in *Lucifer*," he added, "but your systems aren't responding to my signals."

"Must be damaged," I said.

Fuchs said, "Maybe the heat." But I remembered *Hecate* slamming into a boulder or something when the tidal wave first struck. Most likely the antennas for the remote-control receivers were damaged then.

"Okay now," Fuchs said. I could hear him taking a deep breath, like a man about to start an impossibly difficult task. "Diving planes down five degrees."

I knew where the diving plane control was. I had to stretch my leg to get the toe of my boot on the left pedal. My foot cramped horribly, but I think the pain actually helped to keep me awake. The digital display read minus one, minus two . . .

Abruptly I heard a tearing, grinding noise and *Hecate* flipped over onto her back so hard I was banged against the overhead in the narrow cockpit.

I must have screamed, or at least yelled out something. Fuchs was bellowing in my earphones but I couldn't understand his words. The ship was spinning madly, slamming me around inside the cockpit like the ball in a jai-alai game bouncing off the walls. My head rattled inside the heavy metal helmet; despite the padding I saw stars and tasted blood in my mouth.

One thought came screeching through my pain, one lesson I had learned in the simulations. The stabilizing jets. *Hecate* had a set of small cold-jet units placed at her nose, tails, and along the sides of the hull. I started to reach for the bright yellow pad that would fire them, then realized that all this had started when I'd moved the diving planes. I'd have to bring them back to neutral before the jets could stabilize the ship's spin.

I saw a glaring red light blinking at me from the control panel. One of the diving planes had not responded to my command. That's what flipped *Hecate* into this spin. It must have been damaged down on the surface, bent or broken against that boulder.

Fuchs was still roaring at me, but I concentrated every gram of my will on the control panel. Bracing myself against the constant slamming around caused by the ship's spin, I brought the diving plane back to its neutral position and then fired the stabilizing jets.

For a moment I thought *Hecate* would tear herself apart. But the spinning slowed and then stopped. The ship was under my control again.

And diving straight for the ground.

"Pull up! Pull up!" Fuchs was bellowing. "Get her nose *up!*" His voice was hoarse, scratchy.

"Trying," I croaked.

The smaller control surfaces seemed to work all right.

Hecate swooped up in a zoom that dropped my stomach far behind me.

Following Fuchs's painfully rasping commands I made *Hecate* climb back up almost to his altitude, then slowly coasted toward *Lucifer*. Staying away from the diving planes, I jinked and jerked my ship raggedly closer and closer. My strength was fading fast. It was so damnably hot, and whatever reserves of adrenaline I had been riding on were totally spent now.

Looking up through the forward port I saw *Lucifer* looming bigger and bigger, its lights still winking and blinking insanely. Its cargo bay doors swung open and the grappling arms extended down toward me. I lowered my manipulators slightly so I could get a better view of the grapples.

"Velocity looks good," Fuchs was saying, almost crooning like a father lulling his baby to sleep. It would be good to sleep, I thought. Then I realized again that he was my father. Did he have any paternal feelings for me? Until a day or so ago he despised me as the son of his deadliest enemy. Now he was guiding me back to safety.

"Hold it there," he said softly.

I couldn't hold it. *Hecate* wasn't an inanimate object but a ship alive in the sluggish winds and currents of Venus's thick hot air. She had a soul of her own, and I was not her master, only an exhausted, terrified mortal trying to get this willful creature to go along with me for just a few moments more.

"Nose up."

Automatically I moved my scorched hands against the control pads.

"Little more . . . little more . . ."

Hecate began to shake again, more violently this time, bucking like a stubborn bronco that didn't like the way she was being handled.

"Don't let her stall!" Fuchs shouted. "Drop the nose a bit!"

Lucifer's cargo bay loomed before me, with the grappling arms dangling, reaching. It looked to me as if I was going to crash into them.

"Another few meters," Fuchs coaxed.

"I . . . can't. . . ." Everything was fading, melting, running together like watercolors in the rain. It would be wonderful to feel the rain, I thought, to stand in the cool gentle rain of Earth and feel blessed water splashing on my face, running across my burned and aching body.

I heard the clang of metal against metal at precisely the moment I blacked out.

THE ESCAPE POD

H e's coming out of it."

Those were the first words I heard: Marguerite's voice, brimming with expectation.

I opened my eyes and saw that I was back in *Lucifer*'s sick bay, flat on my back, looking up at the curving metal overhead. I felt too weak to turn my head, too exhausted even to speak.

Then Marguerite came into my view, leaning over me, smiling slightly.

"Hello," she said.

I tried to say hello to her but nothing came out except a moaning croak.

"Don't try to speak," she said. "It'll take a while before the fluids rehydrate you properly."

I managed to blink my eyes, too weak to nod. I could see several intravenous tubes on either side of the table on which I lay. The thought of having needles puncturing my skin normally made my flesh crawl, but the fluids in those tubes looked like nectar and ambrosia to me.

"Your hands will be fine in a few hours," Marguerite told me. "The ship's medical supplies included enough artificial skin to hold you until we get back aboard *Truax* and regenerate your own skin tissue."

"Good," I whispered.

She moved to one of the IV drips and stabbed a finger at its control box. "I'm taking you off the analgesics now, but let me know if you're in pain."

"Only . . . when I breathe," I joked feebly.

It took her a moment to realize I was joking. Then she broke into a grin. "Humor is a good sign, I think."

I nodded weakly.

"Are you hungry?"

"No," I said, then I realized it wasn't so. "Yes. A little." In truth I was too tired to eat, but my stomach did feel empty.

"I'll get you something easy to digest."

When she came back, carrying a small tray, I asked, "How long have I been unconscious?"

Marguerite glanced at the digital displays against the bulkhead. "Seventeen hours, a little more."

"The pod?"

"It's in the cargo bay, still in *Hecate*'s arms," she said. Then she touched a button and the table raised up behind my head slightly. Marguerite picked up a plastic bowl from the tray, sat on the edge of the table, and spooned up something from a bowl. "Now eat this."

It must have been broth of some sort, although it was bland and so tasteless that I couldn't tell what it was supposed to be. But it was very pleasant having her spoon-feed me. Very pleasant indeed.

"Where's Fuchs?" I asked.

"The captain's on the bridge, plotting our ascent back up to orbit so we can rendezvous with *Truax*."

"We'll have to go through the clouds again. The bugs . . ." I didn't finish the sentence. I didn't have to.

"He's trying to estimate the amount of damage they did on the way in," Marguerite explained as she ladled another spoonful of soup for me, "so he can work out our best rate of ascent to minimize their effect."

I swallowed, then nodded. "Once we're in orbit we'll be all right, then."

Marguerite nodded back. "The bugs can't survive in vacuum." Then she added, "I hope."

I must have looked startled, because she laughed and said, "Only joking. I've tested them in a vacuum jar. Their cells burst just the way ours would if we didn't wear spacesuits."

"Good." We started talking about the creatures that I'd run into down on the surface. Was it a single organism with many tentacle-like arms, or several different creatures?

"Whatever it was, it's dead now. It went down to hell when the fissure opened up."

Marguerite shook her head slightly. "Not entirely. There was a fragment of one arm stuck on *Hecate*'s back when you returned. It must have been torn off when—"

I gasped. "A piece of the monster?"

"Less than a meter long," she answered, nodding. "Its outer shell is a form of silicone, quite strong yet flexible. And heat-resistant."

"Silicone," I muttered. Yes, that made sense. Then I asked her, "What about its innards? What could possibly stay alive at such high temperatures?"

Marguerite said, "I'm working on that. It seems to be made of sulfur compounds, very complex, molecules no one's ever seen before; a totally new kind of chemistry."

"You'll get a double Nobel," I said. "First the bacteria and now this."

She smiled down at me.

"Too bad it got killed," I said, although inwardly I still felt glad that it had fallen into the white-hot fissure.

"There must be more than one of them. Nature doesn't make merely one single copy of a species."

"On Earth," I countered. "This thing might be one single organism. Maybe it's spread itself all across the planet."

Her eyes widened.

"That's going to make the surface even more dangerous than we thought," I added.

"Unless the whole surface erupts the way Professor Greenbaum expects it to."

"That'd be a pity," I heard myself say. "It would kill everything, wouldn't it?"

Marguerite hesitated, then answered, "I wonder."

"Based on sulfur compounds, you said."

"It's the first form of life we've found that isn't dependent on water."

"Life's much more varied than we thought."

"And much tougher."

I shuddered. "Tell me about it. It came close to killing me."

"The main body must be deep underground, and it sends those arms up to the surface to feed, like shoots of a tree."

"Feed on what?"

She shrugged. "Organic material raining down from the clouds?" she guessed.

"Is there any organic material falling out of the clouds?"

Marguerite shook her head. "None that I can find. If the bugs in the clouds sink toward the surface when they die, they must be totally decomposed by the heat long before they reach the ground."

"Then what do those things on the ground eat?" I asked again.

"I haven't the foggiest notion," she admitted. "That's why we've got to come back and study them more closely."

The idea of returning startled me for a moment, but then I understood that we had to. Someone had to. We have an entire new world to explore here on Venus. A whole new form of biology.

"What are you smiling about?" Marguerite asked.

I hadn't realized I was smiling. "My brother Alex," I said. "We wouldn't have discovered any of this if he hadn't come to Venus."

Marguerite's face took on a somber expression. "Yes, I suppose that's true."

"That's his legacy," I said, more to myself than her. "His gift to us all."

Marguerite left after a while and I drifted into sleep. I know that I dreamed, something about Alex and my fa—Martin Humphries, that is; but when I awoke the memory of it faded from my conscious grasp like a tantalizing will-o'-the-wisp. The more I tried to remember the dream, the flimsier its images became, until the whole thing disappeared like a mist evaporated by the morning sun.

I saw that all the IV drips had been disconnected, and I wondered how long I'd been asleep. I expected Marguerite to pop into the sick bay; she would probably be carrying a beeper that sounded off when the sensors monitoring me told her I had awakened. But I lay there for a good quarter of an hour all by myself; she didn't show up. Probably working on the arm *Hecate* had carried back from the surface.

Nettled by her neglect, I pulled myself up to a sitting position. My head throbbed a little, but that was probably from the pounding I'd taken when *Hecate* had gone into its spinning nosedive. I was totally naked beneath the thin sheet and I could see no clothes anywhere in the cramped confines of the sick bay.

That made some sense, I thought. The coveralls I'd worn in *Hecate* beneath the protective suit must have been rank with sweat.

I swung my legs off the table and stood up warily, keeping one hand on the edge of the table. Not bad. A bit wobbly, but otherwise all right. I wrapped the sheet around my middle and proceeded with as much dignity as I could toward my bunk in the crew's quarters.

Nodon and several others of the crew were sitting around the common table when I got there. They leaped to their feet as I padded in, newfound respect shining in their eyes.

I accepted their plaudits as graciously as I could while

clutching the sheet to my waist with one hand, thinking to myself that being a hero of sorts is rather pleasant. Then I went to my bunk and slid the privacy screen shut.

Six sets of coveralls and underwear were laid out neatly on the bunk, freshly laundered. They had even put out matching sets of slipper socks. A show of appreciation for my retrieving the escape pod? Or had Fuchs simply ordered them to do it?

I dressed, and Nodon insisted on escorting me to the bridge. Amarjagal was in the command chair. Fuchs was in his quarters, I was told. But when I went down the short stretch of passageway to his door, Marguerite was already heading toward me.

"We should inspect the pod," she said, her face somber.

I drew in a breath. "Yes, you're right."

"Are you up to it?"

"Of course," I lied. Every muscle and joint in my body still ached. My head felt as if it weighed eleven tons. My hands were stiff with the glossy artificial skin she had grafted onto them; the stuff made my hands feel like I was wearing a pair of gloves that were just a half size too small.

But I wanted to get to the pod. My heart was trip-hammering. Whatever was left of Alex must be in that big metal sphere, I knew. My brother. No, he wasn't my brother. Not biologically. But he'd been my big brother all my life and I couldn't think of him in any other way. What would I find in the pod? What would be left of the Alex who'd loved and protected me for as long as I could remember?

As we clambered down the ladder toward the cargo bay, Marguerite said, "We'll have to put on spacesuits. He's pumped out all the air in the bay."

Surprised, I snapped, "Why?"

"Vacuum's clean," she replied. "He wanted as low a level of contamination as possible."

"Where is he, anyway?" I demanded. "Why isn't Fuchs here? Doesn't he care what's inside the pod?"

She hesitated a heartbeat before replying, "He's in his quarters plotting our trajectory back into orbit. I told you that before."

"Still? How long does it take to plot a trajectory? The computer does all the work."

Marguerite answered simply, "He's working out the trajectory and he said he doesn't want to be disturbed."

We got to the cargo bay level. There was a locker with four spacesuits alongside the bay's personnel hatch.

As we began to pull on the suits, Marguerite said, "Your flight in *Hecate* took a lot out of him, you know."

Aha! I thought. Aloud, I said to Marguerite, "So, he's resting, then."

Again that little hesitation. Then she said quietly, "Yes, he's resting."

We checked each other's suits once we had buttoned up inside them, going down the checklist programmed into the computers built into the suit wrists. It seemed a bit odd, speaking through the radio to someone standing only a meter away, but the bubble helmets muffled our voices so much we would have had to shout to make ourselves heard.

Once we went through the airlock and into the cargo bay I saw what a battering poor old *Hecate* had endured. She sat lopsidedly on the deck, one landing skid and its support struts crumpled beneath her hull. The hull itself was scratched and dented, long gouges of metal torn away. I walked slowly around the ship, staring at the damage. The diving plane on her left side was simply gone, nothing there but an ugly gash where it should have been. That entire side was badly banged in; that must have been where she'd slammed against the boulder.

I reached out and patted her poor old pitted flank with a gloved hand. The ship had kept me alive, but she would never fly again.

"You're treating it as if it's alive." Marguerite's voice came through my earphones, sounding surprised.

"You're damned right," I said, startling myself at how strong a bond I felt with this broken heap of metal.

In the cargo bay's bright lighting I could see Marguerite's face through the fishbowl helmet. She was smiling at me.

"She'll find a good home back on Earth," Marguerite said. "I'm sure the Smithsonian will want her for one of their museums."

I hadn't thought of that. The idea pleased me. *Hecate* had served well; she deserved a dignified resting place.

My walk around the battered little ship ended at the escape pod, still clutched in *Hecate*'s mechanical arms. The sphere looked like some relic from a bygone century, heavy and crusted with handgrips, a singular circular hatch, a cluster of rocket tubes here, a mini-forest of stubby antennas there. It was more than twice my height in diameter, solid and thick. No portholes anywhere that I could see.

Marguerite pointed to a boxlike metal contraption off by the far bulkhead. "We'll have to get the portable airlock set onto the pod's hatch," she said.

Obviously she had been thinking out this job, step by step, while I had been wrapped up in the emotional turmoil of wondering what to expect once we looked inside.

So we rolled up the portable airlock. The pod's hatch was too low to the deck for the airlock to connect against it.

"We'll have to move it," Marguerite said.

She went to the power cables stored against the cargo bay bulkhead while I climbed back into *Hecate*'s cockpit. It seemed somehow roomier than before, even though the spacesuit I was wearing must have been almost as bulky as the heat-protection suit I'd been in.

The control panel's plastic had not melted, as I thought it had. That must have been due to blurry eyesight and more than a little panic.

"Power's connected," Marguerite reported as the control panel lit up before my eyes. Gingerly I maneuvered the manipulator arms until the pod's hatch was lined up with the portable airlock. Then I shut down *Hecate*'s systems, but not before I gave her control panel a gentle pat and whispered, "Good girl."

I was getting positively maudlin, I thought. But it felt appropriate. It even felt good.

Once I climbed out of *Hecate,* Marguerite and I connected the airlock to the hatch, then tested the seals to make certain that the air inside the pod would not escape into the cargo bay.

"I think we're ready to open the hatch," she said at last.

I nodded inside my helmet, my insides quivering.

Handing me a small case of sensors, Marguerite said, "These are to analyze the air inside the pod. I'll bring the other sensors with me."

"You know how to handle them," I said. "Why don't you bring them?"

"You should go first," she said.

Yes, I thought. She's right. Alex was my brother. It's my place to go in there first.

Nodding again, I ducked into the coffin-sized airlock. I found myself licking my lips nervously. I saw that the indicator light was red; the airlock was already in vacuum, so that when I opened the pod's hatch, no contaminating atmosphere would mix with the air inside.

I had to open the hatch manually, since we did not want to power up the pod's internal systems. We didn't even know if the systems would come on-line, after more than three years of baking on the surface of Venus. The manual control was stiff, but the servomotors on my gloves and the arms of my suit multiplied my muscular strength by a factor of five or more. Slowly, grudgingly, the little wheel turned as I grunted and strained with both hands.

The hatch cracked open. Inside my spacesuit I couldn't feel the puff of air that must have sighed out into the airlock. We'll pump it back into the pod afterward, I told myself. There wasn't room in the airlock to pull the hatch open all the way, but it swung back enough for me to get into the pod.

Picking up the sensor case, I lifted one booted foot and stepped over the sill of the circular hatch. It was very dark inside, of course. I switched on my helmet lamp and saw two bodies sprawled on the metal deck.

No, not bodies, I immediately told myself. Spacesuits. Fully sealed spacesuits. The two people, whoever they were, had had enough time to get into their suits before the final disaster struck them.

Both suits looked strangely crumpled, shriveled, as if the bodies inside them had melted away. More than three years in the roasting heat of Venus, I thought. The monomolecular fabric of the suits looked oddly gray, discolored. I understood why. They had been baking in the scorching heat of Venus for more than three years. It's a wonder that the fabric didn't burn up entirely, I thought.

Their suits may have been filled with an Earth-normal mix of oxygen and nitrogen at first, but that searing heat would break down any organic molecule and force who knows what kind of hellish chemistry inside the suits. It would turn the suits into slow-cooking ovens.

God! The enormity of their death agonies struck me like a hammer between my eyes. Baking to death, literally cooked inside their own suits. How long did it take? Did they undergo hours or days of that torture or, once they realized what they faced, did they cut off their airflow and asphyxiate themselves?

There were tears in my eyes as I bent over awkwardly in my own suit to examine the names stenciled onto the suits' torsos: L. BOGDASHKY, said the one closest to me. I had to step over it to read the other name: A. HUMPHRIES.

It was Alex. Or what was left of him.

Fighting back an almost overpowering feeling of dread, I peered into the tinted visor of Alex's helmet, more than half expecting to see a skull leering at me. Nothing. The helmet looked empty. I pushed my own fishbowl right up against the visor so my lamp could shine into Alex's helmet. There was nothing inside to be seen.

"Is that him?" Marguerite asked, in a hushed voice.

Startled, I turned to see her standing behind me.

I said, "It was him. It was."

THE CYCLE OF DEATH

There is a powerful difference between knowing something intellectually, up in the front of your brain, and seeing the truth of it with your own eyes. I had known Alex was dead for more than three years, yet when I finally saw that shriveled, seared spacesuit, saw his name stenciled on its chest, saw that his helmet was empty, I knew finally and utterly that Alex was dead.

"I'm sorry, Van," Marguerite said gently. "For what it's worth, I know what it's like."

I nodded inside my helmet. She had lost her mother. I'd lost the man who'd been a brother to me all my life.

But there was no time to mourn him.

"We've got to get inside the suits and see if there's any organic material still remaining," Marguerite said. To her, this was not a personal loss, not a tragedy like her mother's death. This was a problem in biology, a chance to learn something new, an opportunity for adding to the human race's store of knowledge.

"When bodies are cremated in high-temperature furnaces," she told me, "there are always bits of bone and teeth in the ashes."

"Even when they've been burned for more than three years?" I asked.

"We won't know until we've opened the suits and looked," she said firmly.

It would be best to open the suits in vacuum, she said. That would keep the level of contamination down as low as possible.

So, keeping my sorrow to myself, I started to help Marguerite pump the air out of the pod, to turn it into an airless biology laboratory. It actually helped, having something to do, a goal to work toward. In a way, it eased the pain of Alex's death for me. A little.

But we had hardly begun the work when our helmet earphones blared out, "DUCHAMP AND HUMPHRIES, REPORT TO THE CAPTAIN'S QUARTERS IMMEDIATELY."

We were both outside the pod, on the floor of the cargo bay. I glanced at Marguerite, who had turned to look up at the loudspeakers even before the echoes of Fuchs's demanding voice died away.

"Let's seal the pod first," I said.

"He said 'immediately.'"

"Immediately—after we seal the pod," I insisted. "I don't want to take the slightest risk of contamination."

She agreed, reluctantly, I thought. Then we left the airless cargo bay, peeled off the spacesuits, and jogged up to the captain's quarters.

I was shocked by his appearance. His face was gray, pallid, his right eye nearly closed. He looked tired, weak, as he sat behind his desk. His bed, which had always been made with military precision, was a wrinkled mess, covers thrown back, pillows sagging. I noticed that his dog-eared copy of *Paradise Lost* was open in front of him.

He looked up from it as Marguerite and I took chairs before the desk.

"How's it going with the bodies?" he asked, in a low, weary voice.

It seemed obvious to me that he'd had another stroke, perhaps more than one. I glanced at Marguerite; she did not seem surprised at his condition as she told him what we were planning to do.

"Look for remains, eh?" Fuchs muttered. "Present an urn with his ashes to his father? Is that what you want to do?"

Marguerite flinched as if he'd slapped her. "No. But if the prize hinges on finding Alexander Humphries' physical remains—"

"An empty spacesuit with his name on it won't do; yes, I see your point." Fuchs turned his gaze to me. "It would be just like Martin Humphries to renege on a technicality like that."

I saw pain in his eyes. They were rimmed with red, sleepless. In my mind's eye I saw that molten chasm splitting open down on Venus's surface.

But before I could say anything, Fuchs straightened himself in his chair and announced, "We're climbing into the clouds. In another eleven hours we'll be entering the top cloud deck, the one with your bugs in 'em."

Marguerite said, "They're not *my* bugs."

He gave her a sardonic smile. "You discovered them. You named them. You'll get a Nobel Prize for them . . . if they don't chew us to pieces on our way up."

"Is that a real danger?" I asked.

He shook his head, just the barest movement. "Not if we go through at maximum ascent rate. We'll drop all remaining ballast and climb through that layer as fast as we can."

"Good," I said.

He glared at me. "I'm so pleased that you approve," he said, with something of his old sarcastic fire.

"We should rendezvous with *Truax*," I said. "My medical supplies—"

"I'll put you off on *Truax* all right," Fuchs said. "But that escape pod and your brother's remains stay here, on *Lucifer*, all the way back to Earth."

Nodding, I replied, "Understood."

"I'm going to need you on the bridge, Mr.—" He stopped, made a face that might have been a grin or a grimace, it was hard to tell which. "—Mr. Fuchs."

I felt my cheeks flush, but I managed to say, "Yes, Captain."

He stared at me for a long, silent moment, then turned back to Marguerite. "Can you carry on with your biological studies by yourself for a day or so?"

"If I must," she said, almost in a whisper.

"It's only until we establish orbit," Fuchs said. "Then you can have him back until he's ready to transfer to *Truax*."

I said, "Perhaps I could stay here on *Lucifer* and have *Truax* ferry my medical supplies to me. That way I could continue to assist Marguerite."

Fuchs arched his left brow at me. "Perhaps," he conceded.

"I'll suspend the bio work until we're in orbit," Marguerite said.

"Why?" he asked.

"To attend to you," she answered.

"I'm all right."

"You're dying and we both know it."

"Dying?" I gasped.

Fuchs gave a snorting laugh and gestured toward me. "Now he knows it, too."

Marguerite said, "He's had at least two minor strokes while you were down on the surface. I'm doing all I can for him, but if he doesn't rest he'll—"

"I'll rest when we reach orbit," he said. "Now get to your duties: Van, to the bridge; Marguerite, back to the cargo bay and that pod. It's my ticket to ten billion dollars."

We both stood up, but Marguerite said, "I'm going to the sick bay and you should come with me."

"Later. Once we're in orbit."

"Your strokes are getting worse each time!" she railed at him. "Don't you understand that? It's only a matter of time before you have a fatal one! Why won't you let me help you? I can bring your blood pressure down, put you on blood thinners. . . ." She ran out of words, and I saw tears brimming in her eyes.

Fuchs struggled to his feet, or tried to. He got halfway up, then sank back into his chair again. "Later," he repeated. "Not now." And he waved us toward the door.

Outside in the passageway I whispered to her, "Nobody dies of strokes anymore!"

"Not if they have proper medical care," Marguerite agreed. "But I don't have the experience or the facilities or even the proper medical supplies to take care of him. And he's too stubborn even to let me do what little I can for him."

"He's got to run the ship, I suppose."

She shot me a furious glance. "That Amarjagal woman can run the ship! But he doesn't trust her to get us through the bugs. He doesn't trust *anyone!*"

Before I could think of what it meant, I said, "He'll trust me."

"You?"

"I'll take over as captain," I heard myself say, as if I believed it. "You get him down to the sick bay and do what you can for him."

She stared at me disbelievingly. "You can't . . ." But she didn't finish the sentence because I was already stepping back to the captain's door and rapping on it.

Without waiting for him to answer, I slid the door back and strode into his quarters. "Captain, I—"

I stopped dead in my tracks. He was still in his chair, but bent facedown over the desk. Unconscious. Or dead.

BACK IN THE CLOUDS

I helped Marguerite lug Fuchs's comatose body down to the sick bay. She had been tearful when she'd been arguing with him, but now she was dry-eyed and all business.

"You'd better get to the bridge," she told me, once we had him lying on the table.

"Right," I said.

But Fuchs opened one eye slightly and pawed at the sleeve of my coveralls. "Tell . . . Amar . . ." His voice was terribly slurred, his face twisted into a grisly rictus of pain.

"Don't worry," I said, grasping his shoulder. "I'll take care of everything."

"The bugs . . . sharp angle . . . of ascent."

I nodded as reassuringly as I could. "I know. I'll get the job done."

"You did . . . okay . . . down on . . . surface."

I forced a smile. Praise from him was vanishingly rare. "Thanks." Then on impulse I added, "Father."

He tried to smile back but he couldn't. He mumbled

something, but his voice was too slurred for me to understand what he said.

For an awkward moment I simply stood there, my hand
on his shoulder. Then his eyes closed and the medical monitors that Marguerite was setting up began wailing shrilly.

"Get out of my way," she hissed urgently.

I beat a retreat to the bridge.

Amarjagal was still in the command chair, looking tired
herself.

"When's the next watch due on duty?" I asked.

Her grasp of the English language was minimal. I asked
her again, slower and louder. Her eyes barely flicked to the
digital clock on the display panel. "Forty-two minutes."

"And when do we enter the top cloud deck?"

Again she had to translate my words in her head before
she could answer, "One hour and one half."

I went to the comm console and, leaning over the shoulder of the crewman sitting there, punched up the translation
program. He glared up at me but said nothing.

"Amarjagal," I said, thinking as I spoke, "I will relieve
you for one hour. Take a break and then get back here
before we enter the last cloud deck."

My words were repeated to her in her own language by
the computer's synthesized voice. Then she asked a question.

"What right do you have to give orders?" the synthesized
voice said, without inflection.

"I'm taking command of the ship," I said, looking
straight at her.

She blinked, then blinked again when the computer
translated my words. "But where is the captain?"

"The captain's in sick bay," I said. "I'm speaking for
him. You'll have the helm when we enter the clouds again,
under my command."

Amarjagal stared at me for a long wordless moment,
digesting the computer's words, her stoic face and dark
eyes revealing nothing.

"You are not the captain," she said at last.

"I am the captain's son," I said. "And I will act for hir while he's in sick bay. Is that understood?"

I hadn't the faintest idea of how she'd react. She simpl: stared at me, apparently digesting what I had just said thinking it over, trying to figure out how she should react te this new situation. She had been loyal to Fuchs whe Bahadur mutinied. If she accepted my command now, thought, the rest of the crew would follow her lead. If she wouldn't, then we'd have chaos—or worse, another mutiny

At last she said in English, "Yes, sir." And she got up from the command chair.

I tried not to let the relief I felt show in my face, but my insides were quivering madly. For the first time in my life, I took the seat of authority. Deep in the back of my mind that self-critical voice was warning me that I was going to screw everything up. But I remembered that I had indeed gone down to the surface and recovered Alex's remains. I was not a helpless, inexperienced, spoiled kid anymore.

Or so I hoped.

The two other crew members on the bridge eyed me warily but said nothing. Not that I could have understood them if they did speak. They watched Amarjagal leave the bridge, then turned back to their consoles in stony silence.

I called up the ship's planned flight profile. As I suspected, Fuchs had set *Lucifer* for the steepest possible ascent through the bug-laden clouds to get us past the danger as quickly as possible. *Lucifer* was essentially a dirigible, an airship that floated through Venus's thick atmosphere propelled by small engines whose main task was to maintain headway against any currents of wind the ship encountered. We could not force our way up through the final cloud deck; we had to climb, venting the gas in our envelope until it was down to vacuum so it could rise to the top of the atmosphere.

We had a set of rocket engines, but they were to be used only after we cleared the topmost cloud deck, to push us on up into orbit. I checked the figures in the computer's flight program. If we fired those rockets too soon we would not establish an orbit around Venus, we would merely fling *Lucifer* into a long ballistic trajectory that would arc back into the clouds halfway around the planet. Once in orbit, though, there was a nuclear propulsion module waiting to power our flight back to Earth. Fuchs had dropped it off in a parking orbit on the way into Venus's clouds.

So above all else, I had to resist the urge to light off the rockets. Fire them too soon, and we would doom ourselves to stay in Venus's atmosphere until the bugs chewed through the hull or the heat got us or our food ran out. A life sentence in hell. And not a long one, at that.

I was worried about those bugs. They had destroyed both Alex's ship and mine. Although Fuchs had bragged about how *Lucifer*'s overdesign had gotten him through the bugs without crippling damage, I wondered how much more of the bugs' attack the ship could take.

Was there anything else I could do? Coat the hull with something the bugs wouldn't or couldn't eat? I hadn't the faintest idea of what that might be, and even if I knew there wasn't much that we could do in less than ninety minutes.

How much damage had *Lucifer* sustained on the way in? I riffled through the captain's files and then the computer's maintenance and safety programs, finding nothing. Either Fuchs didn't get a chance to check the damage or the data were stored somewhere else in the files.

I wanted to ask the crewman running the communications system, but he didn't understand English. I called up the translation program and tried to make him understand what I needed. He stared hard at me, frowning with concentration, then turned back to his keyboard. A stream of data began pouring across the main display screen. Perhaps it was the data I sought, perhaps it was something else entirely. Either way, I couldn't understand a bit of it.

Amarjagal came back to the bridge and I got out of the command chair. Using the language program, I asked her about data on damage to the ship.

"We did check for damage," the computer's voice translated. "Hull integrity was not breached."

"But how much damage was done?" I demanded, feeling frustrated at this laborious process of translating from one language to the other. Time was ticking away. I thought that I should bring Nodon up to the bridge to translate for me.

"Not enough to breach the hull," came her answer.

I went from frustration to exasperation. "Is there any way to assess how much more damage we can take before the hull is breached?"

Amarjagal puzzled over that for what seemed like half an hour, then replied simply, "No."

So we were about to climb into that bug-infested cloud deck, more than fifteen kilometers thick from bottom to top, without the faintest idea of how much damage the hull had sustained during the first trip through or how much more damage we could take before the hull cracked open.

Holding back my anger and frustration, I said to Amarjagal—to the computer, really—"Rig the ship for the steepest ascent possible."

"Understood," she said back to me.

I left the bridge in a black fury. We were heading blindly into danger, without any idea of how to protect ourselves. But halfway down to the sick bay another thought struck me: What difference does it make? I almost laughed aloud at the realization. We're going back into the bugs and there's not a damned thing we can do about it. We're simply going to have to get through them as quickly as we can, and let the chips fall where they may.

Deep in my gut I was still totally dissatisfied with the situation. But up in my brain I adopted a fatalist's pose: Whatever happens, happens. If you can't do anything about it, that's it.

Yet something inside me refused to accept the situation. Something was gnawing at me the way the bugs would soon be chewing on our hull. There must be *something* we can do! But what?

Fuchs was unconscious when I reached the sick bay, and

Marguerite was staring at the monitors along the bulkhead as if she thought that if she looked at them long enough, hard enough, they would show her what she wanted to see. The monitors weren't whining any danger signals, at least, although I realized that might be because Marguerite had turned the alarms off.

"How is he?' I asked.

She jerked back, startled. She'd been studying the monitors so hard she hadn't noticed me.

"I've got him stabilized, I think. But he's sinking. It's slow, but he's losing it. Brain function isn't returning, despite the hormone injections."

"You're doing everything you can," I said, trying to soothe her.

But Marguerite shook her head. "He needs more! If I could talk to one of the medical centers on Earth—"

"Why not?" I said. "We can establish a comm link through *Truax*."

"He gave orders forbidding any contact, remember?"

I pushed past her and banged the comm unit on the bulkhead. "Amarjagal, I want a comm link with *Truax* immediately! Medical emergency."

It took a few moments, but she replied, "Yes, sir."

Turning back to Marguerite, I grinned. "Rank hath its privileges. And powers."

She didn't bother to say thank you. She immediately started telling *Truax*'s communication tech what she needed. At least they both spoke English and there was no translation problem between them.

I headed back for the bridge as the ship's intercom blared, "RIG FOR STEEP ASCENT. STORE ALL LOOSE ARTICLES SECURELY. ALL HATCHES WILL SHUT IN THIRTY SECONDS."

On impulse, I went past the bridge and sprinted along the passageway to the observation center, up in the nose. Through the thick windows I saw the underside of the cloud deck coming up fast. Then the ship began angling upward steeply. I almost toppled over; I had to grab one of the sensor packs Marguerite and I had installed to keep my balance.

It was going to be a wild ride, I thought, as I made my way cautiously back to the bridge, like stepping down a steep gangplank.

Nodon was at the comm console when I got to the bridge, Amarjagal in the command chair. She started to get up, but I waved her back.

"You have the con, Amarjagal," I said as I took the chair beside her. "You can handle this much better than I could."

If my words pleased her, once the computer translated them, she gave no indication.

Nodon said to me, "Sir, the captain of *Truax* is sending many questions. Some of them are addressed to you personally, sir."

I hesitated, then replied, "Tell *Truax* we'll talk with them after we establish orbit. For now, I want only the medical channel to remain open."

"Yes, sir," said Nodon.

So I belted myself into the chair beside Amarjagal as *Lucifer* angled steeply into the last layer of clouds between us and the relative safety of space. It's strange, I thought: I had always considered space to be a dangerous environment, a vacuum drenched with hard radiation and peppered with meteoroids that could puncture a ship's hull like high-powered bullets. But after our stay on Venus, the cold empty calm of space looked like heaven itself to me.

The topmost cloud deck is the thickest of Venus's three, and we seemed to be approaching it at a crawl. I watched the main screen's display of our planned ascent trajectory, a long curving line through an expanse of gray that represented the clouds. The blinking cursor that marked our position seemed to barely move toward the underside of the cloud deck. The bugs were going to have plenty of time to gnaw on our hull. I remembered what they did to Bahadur and his cohorts in the escape pod.

There had to be *something* more that we could do to get through the clouds. Thoughts whirled through my mind, flashing like kaleidoscope images. Bahadur. The escape pod. Our rocket engines. The acceleration that rocket thrust produces.

On impulse, I popped the tiny display screen up from the arm of my chair and called up the rocket propulsion program. How much extra rocket propellant were we carrying? Could we use the rockets to push us through the clouds and still have enough left to establish orbit once we were clear of the cloud deck?

No, I saw. The margins were too thin. It would be too much of a risk.

"Approaching dayside," the navigation technician called out, in English.

Amarjagal nodded wordlessly. Then she turned to me. "We will face the superrotation winds again," she warned.

"Understood," I said, imitating the clipped professional talk of the crew.

I turned my attention back to the display screen and called up alternative trajectories. Maybe . . . no, nothing. All the programs had us lighting up the rockets only after we had cleared the bug-laden cloud deck.

On a hunch, I checked the rocket engines' specs. They could run for five times longer than the brief burst Fuchs had programmed. I asked the computer to show a trajectory that minimized thrust and maximized burn time. Once the numbers appeared on my screen, I asked for a correlation with our ascent trajectory.

Yes! If we lit the rockets now, as we entered the clouds, they would push us through the cloud deck in twelve minutes and still produce enough thrust to establish us in orbit. Barely.

To me, getting through those waiting bugs in twelve minutes was infinitely better than spending twelve hours in the clouds.

"Amarjagal," I called to her, "look at this." And I put the new trajectory on her main screen.

She frowned at the display, brows knitted, the corners of her mouth turned down. But she grasped what I was showing her, that I could clearly see. After a few moments she turned to me and said, "It does not leave us any reserve for orbital maneuvering."

"Oh," I said, feeling crushed. We'd have to be able to maneuver once we got into orbit, to make rendezvous with the rocket engines that would take us back to Earth.

Amarjagal's frown softened. "The nuclear module has maneuvering jets."

I blinked at her. "We could get it to maneuver to us?"

She nodded. "If necessary."

"Then let's do it!" I said.

"This is not the trajectory your father planned," she pointed out.

"I know," I said. "But I'm in charge now."

For a long moment she said nothing, merely staring at me with those expressionless dark eyes. Then she nodded and said the best two words I'd ever heard.

"Yes, sir."

We were already in the clouds before she finished making the changes to the guidance and propulsion programs. I imagined I could hear the bugs chewing on our hull.

Amarjagal spoke into her lip mike in her own language, and the computer's flat voice boomed through the ship: "PREPARE FOR TWO-GEE THRUST IN ONE MINUTE."

I gripped the armrests of my chair, expecting to be flattened into it as we lit off the rockets. But it wasn't anywhere near as dramatic as I'd envisioned. The ship shuddered, trembled under the sudden acceleration, but except for the muffled roar of power, lighting off our rockets' engines was something of an anticlimax, really.

Until I glanced over at the screen that showed our progress. We were sailing through the clouds beautifully, that cursor rising through the gray region like a rocket-propelled cork popping up to the surface of the sea.

I grinned at Amarjagal and she actually smiled at me.

At last the cursor showed that we had cleared the cloud deck. No alarms ringing. The trajectory plot showed we were on course for rendezvous with the rocket pack. We

ad made it through the bug-infested clouds. I exhaled a
uge sigh of relief.

"I'd like to see the forward view," I said to Amarjagal.

She nodded her understanding and said a brief word to
Nodon. The main screen showed the dark expanse of infin-
ty, speckled with stars. I smiled gratefully.

"Rear view, please," I said.

Now I could see Venus again, those swirling cloud tops
brilliant with sunlight. We're safe, I said silently to the goddess. We've come through the worst you can throw at us.

That's when the superrotation wind gripped us. The ship
lurched like a prizefighter who'd just taken a punch to the
jaw. But I laughed aloud. Go ahead, I said to Venus, blow us
a farewell kiss.

BEYOND DEATH

I stayed on the bridge while Amarjagal fought us through
the superrotation winds, the ship bucking and shuddering
like a thing alive. I could see on the trajectory display that
we were being pushed off course, but there was nothing
we could do about it except hope that once we reached
orbit, the nuke module waiting to propel us back to Earth
would be close enough to make rendezvous with us.

The fact that we were accelerating at two gees, rather
than passively floating like a dirigible, actually helped.
Lucifer climbed past the superrotation winds in record
time. The jouncing and bouncing died away, but the ship
still rattled under the thrust of her rockets.

All of a sudden the engines cut off. One instant we were
shaking like a racing car on a rough track with the muted
rumble of the rockets in our ears. Half a blink later the
noise had snapped off and everything was as smooth as polished glass.

We were in orbit. In zero gravity. My arms floated up off
the arm rests and my stomach crawled up into my throat.

Amarjagal was speaking to the technicians on the bridge in their own language. It was crucial that we make rendezvous with the nuclear module; otherwise we'd be stuck in Venus's orbit.

But there was something even more important for me to do. Unstrapping from my chair, I flung myself toward the hatch. I had to find a lavatory *now,* or throw up all over the bridge.

The nearest toilet was in Fuchs's quarters. Even in my state of misery I hesitated a moment before barging in. But only a moment. I was really sick, and I knew he was down in the sick bay with Marguerite. I spent a miserable half hour upchucking into the plastic bowl. Every time I thought I was finished, it took only a slight movement of my head to bring on the nausea all over again.

But then I heard the intercom report, "RENDEZVOUS ESTABLISHED. BEGINNING SPIN-UP TO ONE GEE."

I staggered over to Fuchs's bed and almost instantly fell asleep.

When I awoke, everything seemed normal. All my internal organs were in their proper places and I could turn my head without making the world swim about me.

I sat up cautiously. I lifted one of the captain's pillows and let it drop to the floor. It fell normally.

I laughed. Amarjagal must have successfully rendezvoused with the nuclear module and now we were spinning at the end of the connecting tether, creating an artificial gravity inside *Lucifer.* Artificial or not, it felt wonderful.

I got out of bed and went down to the crew's quarters, where I showered and dressed in fresh coveralls. Feeling rested and relaxed, knowing that we would soon be getting my medical supplies from *Truax* and then heading back to Earth, I strolled down to the sick bay.

One look at Marguerite's face erased the smile from my face.

"He's dead," she told me.

Fuchs lay on the narrow table, his eyes closed, his face gray and lifeless. The monitors were silent, their screens dark.

"When?" I asked. "How long ago?"

She glanced at the digital clock. "Five—six minutes. I just finished disconnecting the monitors."

I stared down at his lifeless body. My true father. I had barely had the chance to know him and now he was gone.

"If we'd been on Earth," Marguerite said, her voice full of self-reproach, "if we'd had some *real* medical doctors instead of me . . ."

"Don't blame yourself," I said.

"He could have been saved," she insisted. "I know he could have been saved. Or even preserved, frozen, until they could repair the damage to his brain."

Cryonics, she meant. Freeze the body immediately after clinical death in the hope of correcting whatever caused its death and eventually reviving the patient. It had been done on Earth. Even at Selene, on the Moon, people had used cryonics to survive their own death.

A wild idea popped into my mind. "Freeze him, then. And quickly!"

Marguerite scowled at me. "We don't have the facilities, Van. It's got to be done—"

"We have the biggest, coldest freezer of them all, right outside the airlocks," I said.

Her mouth dropped open. "Put him outside?"

"Why not? What's going to harm him out there?"

"Radiation," she answered. "Meteoroids."

"Put him in a spacesuit, then. That'll give him some protection."

"No, it would take too long. He's got to be frozen quickly."

"One of the escape pods, then," I said. "Open its hatch to vacuum. It'll cool down to cryogenic temperature in minutes."

I could see the wheels turning inside her head. "Do you think . . . ?"

"We're wasting time," I said. "Come on."

It was an eerie sort of funeral procession, Marguerite and I carrying Fuchs's body down the passageway and ladders, through an airlock, and into one of the escape pods. We were as tender with him as we could be, a strange sort of treatment for a man who had spent so much of his life seething with hate, burning for revenge. But I knew the devils that drove him, I had glimpsed the fury and agony they had caused, and I felt nothing but regret for the life of frustrated rage he had led, a man of enormous strength and enormous capabilities whose life had been wasted utterly. My father. My true father.

We put him down on the narrow decking between empty seats inside the second of our three escape pods. It occurred to me that we ought to say some words of ritual, but neither Marguerite nor I knew any. Death was rare, back on Earth, and although Fuchs might be clinically dead, we hoped there would be a chance to revive him.

"I remember something," Marguerite said as we stood looking down at him, both of us puffing from the exertion of carrying him.

"What?"

"I remember it from a video I saw, about old-time sailing ships. Something about, 'in sure and certain hope of resurrection . . .' Something like that."

I felt suddenly irritated. "Come on," I snapped. "Let's get out of here and open the outer hatch so he can freeze down."

So we started our two-month journey back to Earth with a dead man lying in one of the ship's escape pods, its outer hatch open to the cryogenic cold and vacuum of space.

It was exactly a week after we broke orbit around Venus and started home that Marguerite told me about Alex's remains.

I'd had a long meeting with the captain of the *Truax*, answering as many of his questions as I deemed proper.

Then we'd transferred my medical supplies to *Lucifer* and our two ships started Earthward on their separate trajectories.

I'd appropriated Fuchs's quarters. I was hesitant about moving into the captain's compartment, at first, but it seemed like the logical thing to do. If I were to keep the respect of Amarjagal and the rest of the crew, I could hardly remain in my old bunk in the crew's quarters. I wanted them to know that I was in charge, even if I let Amarjagal run the bridge most of the time. So I moved into the captain's cabin.

There wasn't much ship's business for me to attend to. The crew was happy to be alive and heading home; they were already spending the huge bonuses Fuchs had promised them, in their imaginations. In a few cases, more than imagination was involved. I allowed them to communicate with Earth, and I think some of them spent so freely over the electronic links that they'd actually be in debt by the time we landed.

I was busy talking with Mickey Cochrane and flocks of other scientists, showing them the data and video we had collected on Venus. Perhaps "talking with" is the wrong phrase. Even light waves needed more than nine minutes to travel the distance between *Lucifer* and Earth. We could not have conversations; one side talked and the other side listened. Then we reversed positions.

I was surprised that Professor Greenbaum didn't get involved, until Mickey told me that he had died.

"Died?" I gasped with surprise. "How?" I could understand people getting killed in accidents, or dying because they didn't get proper medical treatment in time, like Fuchs. But Greenbaum must have been in the center of a great university. What on earth could have killed him?

Mickey couldn't hear my blurted question, of course. She simply went on, "The official cause of death was renal failure. But it was really just old age. He never took rejuvenation therapy and his internal organs simply wore out."

How could a man allow himself to die when he didn't
have to? I simply could not understand the man's way of
thinking. Life is so precious . . .

"He died a happy man, though," Mickey added, with a
smile. "Your telemetry data about the volcanic eruptions
convinced him that he was right, and Venus is starting an
upheaval phase."

I wondered if she thought so, too. When it came my turn
to talk, I asked her. Nearly twenty minutes later her reply
reached my screen.

"We'll see," she said, noncommittally.

It was shortly after that "conversation" with Mickey that
Marguerite came to my compartment, looking very serious,
very somber.

"What is it?" I asked, gesturing her to a seat in front of
the desk. I'd been reading one of Fuchs's crumbling old
books, something about gold mining in the Yukon nearly
two centuries ago.

"Your brother," she said, sitting tensely on the front few
centimeters of the chair.

My heart clenched in my chest. "Is there anything left of
Alex? Anything at all?"

"There was a fine, powdery residue inside his spacesuit,"
Marguerite said.

"Ashes."

"Yes. Ashes."

It all flashed before my eyes again: Alex trapped inside
the escape pod, broiling alive on the merciless surface of
Venus. How long did it take? Did he open his visor and let
death come quickly?

As if she could read my thoughts, Marguerite said, "His
suit was intact. Apparently he remained in it until the heat
overcame him."

I sagged back in the swivel chair.

"He . . ." Her voice faltered, then she swallowed hard
and resumed, "he left a message for you."

"A message?" Every nerve in me jangled.

Marguerite reached into her coverall pocket, took out a slim data chip, and reached across the desk to hand it to me. I saw that it had "Van" scrawled across it.

"It was in a thigh pouch of his suit. I presume it's a message," she said. "I haven't run it."

I held the chip in the palm of my outstretched hand. This is all that's left of Alex, a voice in my mind told me.

Marguerite got to her feet. "You'll want to look at it in private," she said.

"Yes," I mumbled. It was only when she reached the door that I thought to add, "Thank you."

She nodded once, then left, gently closing the door behind her.

How long I sat there staring at the chip, I don't know. I think I was afraid to run it, afraid to see my brother dying. I knew that he wasn't really my brother, not genetically, but there was no other way that I could think of Alex. He'd been my big brother all my life, and now I realized that he was thinking of me in the last agonized moments of his life.

Had he known that his father was not my father? Unlikely, I thought. Martin Humphries would never tell anyone, not even his much-loved son, that he'd been cuckolded by his most hated enemy.

With enormous reluctance, I clicked the chip into the desktop computer. Strangely, I noticed that my hand was steady. My insides weren't jumpy, either, not anymore. I felt glacially cold, almost numb, the only emotion I felt a consuming desire to learn what Alex wanted me to know in his last moments of life.

The computer screen lit up and there was Alex, his face barely discernable behind the visor of his helmet. The picture was weak, grainy. He was inside the escape pod, sitting in front of its communications console in his sealed spacesuit.

"I don't know if this will ever get to you, little brother," he said. "I'm afraid I've made a mess of this mission."

The audio quality was poor, but it was Alex's voice, a

voice I thought I'd never hear again. Tears sprang to my eyes. I pawed at them as he continued speaking.

"Van, there's something in the topmost cloud deck of Venus that's eroded *Phosphoros*'s gas envelope so badly that we've sunk down to the surface. I've tried to contact Earth, but it looks as if whatever it is that's destroyed us knocked out the communications antennas, too."

I caught myself nodding, as if he could see me.

"I don't know if this chip will ever get to you. I imagine the only way it could would be for someone to come down to the surface of Venus and find the wreckage, and I doubt that anyone would be foolhardy enough to try that for a long, long time."

Not unless they were offered a ten-billion-dollar prize, I thought.

"Van, the night before I left I told you that I wanted to help the Greens by bringing back imagery of a world where greenhouse warming has run amok. Well, that's been a bust, too. A total fiasco."

A burst of electronic snow nearly blotted out the picture on the screen, but Alex's voice continued, scratchy and weak.

"There's no relationship between what's happened here on Venus and what's happening on Earth. Just no relationship at all. The two planets might have started out with the same conditions, but Venus lost almost all its water very early. Where Earth built up oceans, Venus was so hot that almost all its water boiled off into space right away, billions of years ago."

He was speaking rapidly now, as if afraid that he wouldn't be able to tell me everything he wanted me to know.

"There's no way to compare Earth's greenhouse warming with conditions here on Venus. No way. The Greens are going to be very disappointed; they won't be able to use Venus as an example of what will happen on Earth if we don't stop our greenhouse warming."

He coughed suddenly. The picture cleared slightly, and I peered as hard as I could, trying to make out his face behind the visor.

"The pod's systems are breaking down," Alex said, his voice almost calm. Not quite, but he wasn't the least bit panicky. I imagine he realized there was nothing at all that could be done to save him.

"Getting really hot now . . . really . . . broiling." The screen went blank for an instant, then a faint, grainy picture came on again.

No! I screamed silently. *Don't go away, Alex! Don't die! Talk to me. Tell me—*

"Failed," Alex said, sounding sadder than I had ever known him to be. "I've failed . . ."

His voice faded out. I waited for more, but the audio gave me nothing except a background hiss. Then the picture winked out completely.

I sat staring at the blank screen, listening to the hiss of the speakers. Then even that sound stopped. I could hear nothing but the background hum of the computer itself.

Alex's final thoughts were about failure. With his last breath he believed that he had failed, Venus had defeated him, his bright hopes for helping the Greens to reverse the greenhouse warming of Earth had died on the hellish surface of Venus, along with his crew, along with himself. My brilliant, handsome, charming, laughing big brother died thinking of himself as a failure.

And thinking of me. He hadn't addressed his last message to his father. Or to the Greens. He wanted to speak to me! He wanted to confess to me his final thoughts, his last realizations.

I looked up from the dead screen, leaned my head back against the padded chair, and saw in my mind the times Alex and I had shared. They seemed so pitifully few, a handful of moments in our two lives.

I resolved to do better.

A NEW LIFE

called Marguerite to my compartment. She slid the door
back less than a minute later, and I realized she must have
been in her own quarters, next to mine. Then I glanced at
the desktop clock. It was past midnight, more than five
hours since she'd handed me Alex's chip. I'd been sitting
at the desk for more than five hours.

"I woke you," I said.

She almost smiled. "No, I don't dress that quickly."

She still wore the coveralls she'd been wearing earlier.

"You couldn't sleep?" I asked.

"I was working," Marguerite said, taking one of the
chairs in front of the desk. "Thinking, really."

"About what?"

"Your brother."

"Oh."

"He must have loved you very much."

"I loved him, too," I said. "I think he's the only person in
the solar system I've ever loved."

"So we've both lost the ones we loved the most," Marguerite said, her voice low.

"Your mother," I remembered.

She nodded once, tight-lipped, holding on to her emotions.

I stared at Marguerite. How like her mother she looked, yet she was a very different personality.

"Marguerite, how much . . . material is there in my brother's remains?"

She blinked at me, puzzled.

"Enough to get a good sampling of his DNA?" I asked.

"For cloning?" she asked back.

"For cloning," I said.

She looked away from me for a moment, then returned her gaze to meet mine. "It won't work, Van. I've already checked that. The heat was too much, too long a time. It dissociated all the polypeptides, all the long-chain molecules. The nucleic acids, everything . . . they were all broken apart by the heat."

My heart sank.

"There's nothing we can do," Marguerite said.

"He thought he was a failure," I told her. "My brother died thinking he'd accomplished nothing."

"I don't understand."

So I explained to her about the Greens and Alex's hope of using Venus to convince the people of Earth that they had to take drastic steps to avoid a disaster on Earth from global warming.

Once I finished, Marguerite said, "Yes, the Greens will be dismayed, all right. Crushed. They were counting on making Venus a visible example. They wanted people to think of the greenhouse warming every time they looked up and saw Venus in the sky."

I shook my head. "That's not going to work. The scientists like Mickey and the others will have to tell them the truth, that Venus's greenhouse and ours have nothing to do with each other."

"Your father will be very pleased."

I looked up sharply at her.

"He and his kind will trumpet the news, won't they? He even sacrificed his son to learn that Venus has nothing to tell us."

"But that's the good news," I heard myself say. Whisper, almost.

"Good news for your father," Marguerite countered.

"No," I said, my voice louder, stronger, as I realized the truth of it. "No, it's *bad* news for my father and good news for the rest of us."

She leaned forward slightly in her chair. "What do you mean?"

"The greenhouse warming on Earth has no relationship to the runaway greenhouse on Venus!" I said, almost jubilant.

"And that's good news?"

I jumped up from my chair and came around the desk. "Of course it's good news! It means that what's happening on Earth isn't the inexorable workings of nature, as it was on Venus. It's man-made!"

"But the scientists—"

I grasped Marguerite by the wrists and pulled her out of her chair. "The scientists have been telling us for nearly half a century that human actions are causing the global warming. We've been pouring greenhouse gases into the atmosphere by the gigaton."

"But the industrialists have claimed the warming is part of a natural climate cycle," Marguerite said, almost bemused at my sudden enthusiasm.

"Right. But now we have the imagery of Venus, where nature has produced a *real* greenhouse . . . and we can show that it's nothing like what's happening on Earth!" I was so excited I wanted to dance across the cabin with her.

Marguerite shook her head, though. "I don't see how that helps the Greens."

I laughed. "Let my father and his friends trumpet the news that Venus and Earth are two completely different cases. Let them tell the world that Venus's greenhouse has no relationship to what's happening on Earth."

"And how does that help the Greens?"

"Because we'll come back and say, 'Yes! You're right Venus is a natural disaster. . . . Earth is a *man-made* disaster. And what humans do, they can undo!'"

Marguerite's eyes flashed with understanding. She broke into a wide, warm smile. "If human actions are causing the greenhouse, then human actions can fix it."

"Right!" And I wrapped my arms around her and kissed her soundly. She didn't object. She kissed me just as hard in fact.

But then she pulled back slightly and said, "Do you realize what you're getting yourself into?"

"I think so. I'm going to be an even bigger disappointment to my fa—to Martin Humphries. He'll go ballistic Maybe he'll even attain escape velocity."

"You're going to become the spokesman for the Greens," she said, quite seriously.

"I guess I am."

"That's a heavy responsibility, Van."

I shrugged and nodded, without letting her out of my arms.

"Some of the Greens' leaders won't trust you. Other will be jealous of you. There's a lot of politics inside the movement, let me tell you. A lot of knives in the dark."

I realized what she was telling me. "I'll need someone to guide me, to protect me."

"Yes, you will."

"My father's people will be after my scalp, too. They can play very rough."

She looked directly into my eyes. "Are you certain you want to take on all this?"

I didn't hesitate for a nanosecond. "Yes," I said. Then I added, "If you'll come with me."

"Me?"

"To be my guide, my protectress."

An odd expression came over her beautiful face. The corners of her lips curled up slightly, as if she wanted to smile, but her eyes were dead serious.

"The mother of my children," I added.

Her jaw fell open.

"I'm a very wealthy man," I said, still holding her about
e waist. "I don't have any really bad habits. I'm in rea-
nably good health, as long as I get my medication."

"And?" she prompted.

"And I love you," I said. It wasn't exactly true, and we
oth knew it. Neither one of us knew what love really was,
ut we'd been through so much together, there was no one
n Earth—no one in the solar system, actually—whom I
as closer to.

"Love is a big word," Marguerite whispered. But she
nuggled closer in my arms and rested her head on my
houlder.

"We'll learn all about it," I whispered back. "Starting
ow."

wasn't prepared for the enormous interest the news media
howered upon me. As soon as we established orbit around
ne Moon I was deluged with requests for interviews, docu-
ramas, biographies. They wanted me to appear on global
et shows, to star in an adventure series! I was a celebrity,
sked to sit next to media stars and politicians and make
ppearances everywhere.

Politely but firmly I turned them all down, giving the
news media nothing except the highlights of our expedi-
ion—which was dramatic enough to keep viewers all
hrough the Earth-Moon system riveted to their screens
night after night for a week.

I granted interviews, of course, but very selectively. In
each interview I stressed the idea that Venus's greenhouse
was completely different from Earth's, that the Earth's
warming was largely the result of human actions, and that
humans could stop the greenhouse if they were willing to
make the necessary changes. The Greens at first were furious; I received loud demands to "recant" my heretical (to
hem) views. I even got threats. But as my message began

to sink in, some of the Green leaders started to realize th
what I was saying could be beneficial to them, very helpf
to their political stance. I still got threats from angere
fanatics, but the leadership began to use my interviews a
ammunition in their campaigns.

Meanwhile I handed all our data over to Micke
Cochrane, who flew up to *Lucifer* while we were still i
lunar orbit, quarantined until the medical inspectors dete
mined that we were not bringing alien diseases back hom
with us.

Of course we were carrying samples of the Venusian aer
obacteria and the fragment of the feeding arm from th
creature on the surface, which enormously complicated ou
quarantine period. Mickey and her fellow scientists wer
overcome with joy at the samples and all the data abou
Venus that we had brought back with us. I was offered a
honorary membership in the International Academy of Sci
ence. Marguerite received a full membership, and hints tha
a special Nobel Prize would eventually be awarded to her.

One of my chores while we waited in parking orbit wa
to contact Gwyneth, who was still living in the flat i
Barcelona.

She looked as exotic and beautiful as ever. Even on th
wall screen of my compartment aboard *Lucifer,* her tawn
eyes and rich, full lips made my pulse throb faster.

But after a few moments of chat, I told her, "I'm deedin;
the flat to you, Gwyneth. It will be yours, free and clear."

She didn't look surprised. She accepted it as if she'c
expected as much.

"This is good-bye, then," she said. It wasn't a question.

"I'm afraid so," I said, surprised that I didn't feel any
pain. Oh, perhaps a little twinge, but none of the pangs o
separation that I thought I'd suffer.

She nodded slightly. "I thought as much. I've been
watching your interviews on the news. You've changed.
Van. You're not the same person anymore."

"I don't see how I could be," I said, thinking of all tha
I'd been through.

"You're going to see your father soon?" It was her part-
g shot, with just enough of a barb in it to tell me that she
s far from pleased at my ending our relationship.

"I'm going to see . . . him just as soon as they lift quaran-
e on my ship," I said.

She smiled slightly. "To claim your ten bill."

"Yes, that," I replied. "And a few other things."

SELENE CITY

t took two weeks for the assorted medics and biologists to agree that *Lucifer* and her crew posed no threat to the human population of Earth and Moon.

Once they finally cleared us, I sent Marguerite to my house on Majorca, telling her, "I've got to see Martin Humphries before I go home."

"Can't you do this by videophone?" Marguerite asked. "Or you can set up a virtual reality meeting."

"No," I said. "This has to be face-to-face, him and me. On his turf."

So I went down to Selene City.

I was ushered into the sitting room of his residential suite in the Hotel Luna, and told, "Mr. Humphries will be with you shortly, sir."

I walked across thick carpeting to the room's actual window. Aboveground buildings were rare on the Moon; windows even rarer. I stared out at the rich glowing crescent of Earth hanging in the darkness outside. There was a stubby black telescope by the window, mounted on a slim tripod. I squinted through the eyepiece, searching for Connecticut, where the family home had been.

The sprawling house was in jeopardy from the swelling Connecticut River; as sea levels rose the entire valley was slowly being drowned by the encroaching waters of Long Island Sound. I swung the 'scope toward Majorca, but it was off on the limb of the globe, barely discernable. The Majorca house was safe enough, up on its hilltop, but the seawall protecting Palma was already crumbling, threatening the city.

It had taken more than a century for global warming to begin causing such disasters. It would take more than a century to correct them, I knew. We had long decades of toil and struggle ahead of us, but I was certain that we had the knowledge and the tools to eventually succeed.

"So there you are, stargazing."

I straightened up and turned at the sound of his sarcastic voice.

"Hello," I said, "Mr. Humphries."

He didn't look a bit different from the last time I'd seen him in the flesh, at his hundredth-birthday bash. Tall, straight carriage, slim. Dark, form-hugging suit with slightly padded shoulders. And those hard, cold eyes.

"Mr. Humphries?" If he was taken aback by the formality of my address to him, he hid it well. He crossed the room and sat on the upholstered sofa beneath an electronic reproduction of some garish neoclassical painting, Delacroix, I think: horse-mounted bedouins in swirling robes racing across the desert with long rifles in their hands.

"You're not my father," I said flatly.

He didn't blink. "Fuchs told you that?"

"DNA scans proved it."

He let out a breath. "So now you know."

"I know why you had my mother murdered," I said.

That popped his eyes wide. "She died of a drug overdose! She did it herself. It was suicide, not murder."

"Was it?"

"I loved her, for Christ's sake! Why do you think I

hounded Fuchs until he gave her up? I loved her, she was the only woman I ever loved, damn her to hell and back!"

"Very loving words," I sneered.

He jumped to his feet, face red, hands jittering agitatedly. "I wanted her to love me, but she never did. She wouldn't let me touch her! And then she went and had a baby—*his* baby!"

"Me."

"You."

"That's why you've hated me all these years," I said.

He gave a short, barking laugh. "Hated you? No, that's too active a word. I loathed you, you miserable little Runt. Every time I saw you I saw the two of them laughing at me. Every day of your life was another reminder that she couldn't stand my guts, that she loved that bastard Fuchs, not me."

"So that's why you set up this Venus mission, to get me to kill myself."

He seemed startled by the thought. "Kill you? Hah! Who cared about you? Who the fuck would've thought that you, the weakling, the cowardly pitiful Runt, would take up my challenge? Nobody in his right mind would've expected that. You surprised the hell out of me, let me tell you."

"Then why . . .?" All of a sudden I saw the truth.

Martin Humphries nodded, understanding the dawning light in my eyes. "It was to kill Fuchs, of course. He was way out in the Belt, where his fellow rock rats protected him. Besides, I promised your mother that I wouldn't go after him, and despite what you think I kept my promises to her. Despite everything, I let the sonofabitch live."

"Until you got the idea for the Venus prize. It was a trap, all along."

"Once Alex was killed I couldn't hold back anymore. I wanted that bastard Fuchs *dead*! So I dangled ten billion dollars' worth of bait and, sure enough, he came after it."

"And so did I."

Something of his old smirking expression crept back across his face. "That was a bonus. I never expected you, of all people, would take the challenge. But I figured, what the hell, Venus will kill both of you. Father and son."

"But I survived."

He shrugged. "I got what I was after. Fuchs is dead. Damned good and dead."

"Maybe not," I said.

He stared at me.

"We froze his body. Marguerite Duchamp is bringing together the world's top cryonics people to see if he can be revived."

Martin Humphries staggered back a few steps, his face ashy white, and plopped down gracelessly on the sofa.

"You son of a bitch," he whispered, pronouncing each word distinctly. "You fucking traitorous son of a bitch."

I suppose I should have enjoyed the look of utter shock and confusion on him, but I felt no sense of victory, no joy of triumph. Only a kind of disgust that he could hate a man—two men, actually—so deeply.

"I've come here to ask you a question," I said, feeling cold and implacable inside. "One question."

His eyes narrowed.

"Did you have Alex's ship sabotaged? Are the rumors true?"

"No!" he snapped, fists clenching. "Alex was my son, my flesh and blood! Not like you. He was part of *me!* How could I harm him?"

I believed him. I felt the steely hatred gripping my heart fade a little. I realized that I wanted to believe him, despite everything. I did not want to go through my life thinking that he had murdered Alex.

"All right, then," I said quietly. "Then it's over."

"Is it?" Looking up at me, he said, "You think I'm going to let you get your hands on my ten billion now? After what you've done?"

"I already have my hands on it," I said. "I contacted your lawyers as soon as we established lunar orbit. The money's still in escrow. All that's needed is my signature."

"And mine!" he snapped.

"You'll sign."

"Like hell I will!"

"If you don't, the news media get the whole story. You, Fuchs, my mother, me—the entire story. They'll love it."

"You . . . you . . ." He ran out of words.

Heading for the ornate desk in the far corner of the room, I said, "I'll be going Earthside as soon as I leave here. I've got to start organizing the next expedition to Venus."

"The next . . . ?"

"That's right. We've learned how to survive even on the planet's surface. Now we're going back to begin the *real* exploration."

Martin Humphries shook his head, whether in wonder or sorrow or disbelief I neither knew nor cared.

"You'll be able to sign the escrow papers electronically," I told him. "Your lawyers have already agreed to that. You won't have to leave Selene."

"Get out of my sight!" he snarled.

"Nothing could please me more," I said. "But I want to leave you something, something you've bought and paid for."

He glared at me as I slipped a data diskette into his desktop computer.

"Here's Venus," I said.

All the room's walls, even the windows, were smart screens. Suddenly they all showed the glowering red-hot surface of Venus, the views that little *Hecate*'s cameras had recorded. I punched out all the overhead lights; Martin Humphries sat, sagging and defeated, as the sullen red anger of Venus enveloped him. I could almost feel the heat as I stood by the desk.

Walking slowly to the door, I watched as the wall screens showed the wreckage of *Phosphoros* scattered across those baking rocks, with those strange feeding arms stretched over it. Martin Humphries sat transfixed, actual perspiration breaking out on his forehead.

I grasped the door handle and waited. The ground opened up, a white-hot fury of lava swallowing the wreck-

ge, burning, destroying, melting everything it touched
with its incandescent rage.

I left Martin Humphries sitting there, staring into the
blinding fury of Venus.

I left him in hell.

As I headed toward the rocket port and the shuttle that
would take me back to Majorca, back to Marguerite, I wondered if Alex had left samples of his sperm before he ven-
tured off on his space missions. It would have been the
prudent thing to do, if he'd intended to someday marry and
have children. A protection against the radiation levels that
could be encountered in space during a solar storm. Alex
was a prudent man; I felt certain that he had sperm samples
tucked away safely, perhaps in the Connecticut house.

I wondered how Marguerite would feel when I asked her
to carry his cloned zygote. Would she do that for me? It was
a lot to ask, I knew. We'd have children of our own, of
course, but first I wanted to bring Alex back.

I wondered how it would feel to be his big brother.